SCARLET RIBBONS

Also by Emma Blair

SCARLET RIBBONS

Emma Blair

BANTAM BOOKS
TORONTO · NEW YORK · LONDON · SYDNEY · AUCKLAND

SCARLET RIBBONS
A BANTAM BOOK: 0 553 40298 6

Originally published in Great Britain by Bantam Press, a division of Transworld Publishers Ltd.

PRINTING HISTORY
Bantam Press edition published 1991
Bantam edition published 1992
Bantam edition reprinted 1992
Bantam edition reprinted 1994

This book is set in 10/11 pt Plantin by Photoprint, Torquay, Devon

Bantam Books are published by Transworld Publishers Ltd, 61–63 Uxbridge Road, Ealing, London W5 5SA, in Australia by Transworld Publishers (Australia) Pty Ltd, 15–25 Helles Avenue, Moorebank, NSW 2170, and in New Zealand by Transworld Publishers (NZ) Ltd, 3 William Pickering Drive, Albany, Auckland.

Printed and bound in Great Britain by Cox & Wyman Ltd, Reading, Berks.

SCARLET RIBBONS

Chapter One

Sadie Smith was four years old and what she wanted more than anything else in the world was to be like other children. It was something she often cried about.

Right now she was sitting on an easy chair by the fireplace watching her mother make breakfast. Louise's face was lined with worry, and drawn from lack of sleep. In the kitchen's cavity bed Ken Smith lay gasping and wheezing, desperately fighting to draw air into his badly dust-coated lungs, that had weakened through years spent down the pit.

Suddenly Ken gave a particularly long drawn-out wheeze that rattled at the back of his throat like a couple of old tin cans. Louise, eyes filled with love and concern, paused in what she was doing to glance over at him.

'I'm starving, Ma,' Ian complained, plonking himself down at the table. But that was nothing new, she'd realized years ago that her son had 'hollow' legs.

'Won't be long,' Louise replied, and continued buttering the toast.

Morag appeared from the other room pulling up her knickers and yawning. The Smiths had seven children; Sadie was the youngest and Morag next to her, while young Ken, the oldest, was thirteen, and was already out of school and working.

'Your father had another attack last night so don't make too much noise,' Louise said.

Morag's eyes glanced over at her father. She would usually have run over and kissed him except she hated it when he was like this. It scared her.

7

Ken groaned, strange shapes dancing and weaving in front of him. He was aware he was partially delirious.

Louise swept a wisp of hair away from her face. God, she was tired. It had been a terrible night, Ken's latest attack which had gripped him shortly after they'd gone to bed had been worse than usual.

This would mean another few weeks off work, she thought grimly, perhaps even a month. It was taking him longer and longer to get over these attacks and during that time there was no money coming in other than the pittance young Ken earned and what the Union gave them.

She sighed inwardly. It was hard enough making ends meet at the best of times, but when Ken was off work the whole thing became a nightmare.

The kettle began to sing.

'Can I make the tea, Ma?' Lena asked, appearing in the kitchen doorway. Lena had bright ginger hair, the only one with such distinctive colouring. According to Ken she got it from his Great-Aunt Isa who'd been a cat fanatic and died when he was a little boy.

'Thank you, lass,' Louise replied. Then, as an afterthought, she said: 'Don't be too generous with the caddy. Your Da's had another attack.'

Lena knew only too well what that meant, short rations all round. Consequently she only put half the usual number of teaspoons into the pot. She would just let it steep longer and hope to bring it up to strength that way.

'How are you this morning?' Bill asked Sadie, hauling down a jersey that had seen better days. Sadie was the only one who slept in the kitchen with their parents, her brothers and sisters sharing a pair of double beds in the other room.

Sadie nodded, smiling at Bill. He was her favourite brother because he spent a lot of time with her. The others did too, but Bill was special.

He yawned and stretched himself. 'School!' he complained, and pulled a face.

8

Sadie laughed. She would have loved to have gone to school, but knew she never would. School was for children who could walk, which she couldn't, because she'd been born with a degenerated hip which meant she could only crawl and flop around the place. There would never be school for her.

Tom and young Ken came into the room, completing the family. 'Da bad again?' young Ken queried softly, studying his father in bed.

'Another attack,' Louise confirmed, placing buttered toast on the table. There wasn't any jam or marmalade. Those treats, when available, were reserved strictly for Sundays.

Young Ken went over to his father and stared at his sweat-beaded face. 'Not so well again, Da?' he said in a cheerful tone.

Ken swallowed and then tried to reply. His words emerged as a mumbled hiss.

'I'm going straight to the doctor after I've got you lot packed off out the door,' Louise said to young Ken whom, because of his age, she felt she could talk to more or less like an adult.

Young Ken nodded. 'Not to worry, Da, you'll soon be on your feet again and back down the pit.' It was a great relief to him that he'd managed to find a job in a factory. The work was hard, the conditions appalling, but at least he was above ground and breathing relatively clean air, unlike his da.

'Come on then,' said Bill and Tom, lifting Sadie up. Between them they carried her over to the table and sat her on one of the hard wooden chairs surrounding it.

Louise wondered if Ken could manage a cup of tea. He hadn't drunk the water she'd attempted to give him during the night.

'Ken?' she whispered, laying a hand on his stubbly cheek.

9

His answer was a wheeze that seemed to come from the very depths of his being. His fever hot eyes, she realized, weren't staring at her, but out into their own distant world.

Louise bit her lower lip. A month before he returned to work? It could even be longer. If only she could take on a part-time job, but how could she with Sadie to look after?

She glanced over at her youngest child. How serious the wee thing looked, but how could she blame the lass for that?

While the others tucked into tea and toast, she took a clean towel from a cupboard and wiped Ken's face. She needn't have bothered, his face was heavily beaded again within seconds.

She'd leave the washing-up till later, she decided. The quicker she got to the doctor the better.

'Aren't you having anything to eat, Ma?' Lena asked.

Ian was immediately alert, this could possibly mean another slice for him.

Louise shook her head. 'I've no appetite whatsoever. A swallow of tea will do me.'

Ian's hand leapt out to grab one of the remaining slices of toast which was swiftly transferred to his plate.

'Gannet,' Tom admonished.

Ian grinned. They could call him what they liked, he didn't care. He was determined to be a chef when he grew up. It must be sheer heaven to be continually surrounded by food. His mouth watered at the prospect.

'What about you, Sadie, would you like another slice?' Bill queried.

'No, thank you.'

'Are you sure now?' he persisted.

'I will if she . . .' Ian started to say, his mouth full. He hastily shut up when Ken shot him a warning look. In the end Morag got the other slice going begging.

Young Ken left the house first, giving Louise a peck on the cheek and his father a word of encouragement before clattering down the stairs.

Louise kissed her five children as they left for school. The school building was fairly close, so they didn't have much of a walk.

'Will you be all right, love?' she asked Ken when they were finally alone. When he didn't reply she decided to ask Mrs Crerar next door to pop in and keep an eye on him. She wouldn't be away for long.

'Right then,' she said to Sadie, as she picked her up. 'You're not getting any lighter, that's for certain,' she teased.

'I'm only thin,' Sadie answered in a tone that brought a lump to Louise's throat.

'Of course you are, darling. I was only joking.'

Sadie crooked an arm round her mother's neck knowing that made it easier for Louise to carry her. 'I've never seen Da sweat during an attack before,' she said.

'Neither have I, and that's what's worrying me.'

'Louise!' The voice was a cracked whisper.

She hurried over to find Ken back in this world rather than wherever it was he'd been. His eyes were still anguished while his chest continued to heave.

'I'm going for the doctor,' she explained.

'Can't . . .' He sucked in a deep breath. 'Can't afford . . .'

'Bugger that, we'll just have to. I've never seen you so bad. And you're sweating as if you've got the flu.'

'Feel awful,' he gasped.

And you look it, she thought. 'Is there anything I can get you before I go?'

The strange shapes were back again, dancing, weaving shapes that were extraordinary colours. They were totally mesmerizing.

He wheezed again before managing a reply. 'Nothing.'

'I'm away then.'

'Goodbye, Da,' Sadie said from her mother's arms.

Ken glanced at her, tried to smile, but broke out coughing instead, and then thumped the bed impotently with his clenched left fist.

Downstairs, having spoken with Mrs Crerar *en route*, Louise went into the back court where the pram was kept chained to a railing. She sat Sadie in the pram and covered her lower half with a small blanket.

Sadie held on to the sides as Louise bumped the pram through the close out into the street. Usually her mother chatted with her, but not today; today Louise's lips remained tightly shut as they headed very fast for the doctor's surgery.

Sadie watched enviously as the children, all under school age, played peever on the pavement. It was the local game known elsewhere as hopscotch.

A girl bent and expertly slid a stone along the ground into the chalked-out box she was aiming for. Then she straightened up and hopped forward.

What was it like to hop? Sadie wondered. Or to walk, run or dance? She gazed down wistfully at her own legs, one that was totally useless and the other that had only a little strength, and she felt heartily sorry for herself.

She would never be able to walk, would always be different, always a cripple. *A cripple*! Every time she heard that word it was as if a red hot dagger had been plunged into her heart.

The girl playing peever cried out joyously at completing some particularly complicated manoeuvre and leapt high into the air. On landing she whirled round, arms out-stretched.

Sadie dropped her head, unable to look any longer. She hoped her mother would hurry up. She wanted to be taken away from there.

It didn't matter where, just away.

* * *

'You were certainly right to call me in, this is different from his previous attacks,' Dr McLeod declared, staring at Ken.

'He's never sweated before, or gone away in his mind,' Louise clasped her hands. 'It seems to me to be more than the dust.'

It was certainly more than that, McLeod thought. But what? 'I'll wash my hands before examining him.'

McLeod washed his hands with soap, then carefully dried them on the clean towel Louise gave him. Every so often, clearly deep in thought, he glanced across at Ken.

'Now then,' McLeod said as he unbuttoned Ken's pyjama top. His forehead creased into a speculative frown as he stared at Ken's heaving chest.

'Hmmh!' he muttered, and then pulled the bedclothes back to expose Ken's entire right side. He felt first Ken's buttock, then leg, while Louise and Sadie gazed anxiously on.

'He's lost quite a bit of weight since I saw him last,' McLeod said slowly.

'Has he?' Louise looked again at Ken. 'I suppose he has. I can't say I'd noticed.'

'You sometimes don't when it's gradual.'

'I have,' Ken agreed.

'Any idea how much?'

'Enough for me to have to tighten my belt by a couple of notches.'

'You never mentioned,' Louise admonished him sharply, betraying her anxiety.

Ken opened his mouth to answer, but what emerged was a ghastly, wracking wheeze. His fist pounded the bed as he fought for breath.

'Jesus!' he gasped at last.

'Don't talk for now,' McLeod instructed, perching beside him. He listened to Ken's heaving chest with his stethoscope. McLeod gave Ken a thorough examination, during which his brows were furrowed in concentration.

Finally McLeod sat up straight and sighed. Going over to his bag he rolled up his stethoscope and replaced it, then took out a small bottle and removed its cap.

'I want a sample of your sputum for tests, Ken,' he said, going back to the bed.

'Sputum?' Ken queried.

'Spit, man. Your spit.'

'Oh!' Ken exclaimed, and attempted to lever himself into a sitting position, which he finally managed with McLeod's assistance.

When McLeod had enough of Ken's sputum, Louise helped him lie down again, and tucked in his bed-clothes.

'It is more than the dust, isn't it?' Louise said to McLeod after she'd finished fussing over Ken.

'It seems so,' McLeod replied.

'I thought . . . well, it crossed my mind that it might be the flu?' Louise went on nervously.

McLeod gave her a sideways glance. He was already fairly certain what was wrong with Ken Smith, the blood flecks in Ken's sputum corroborating his theory, but he wouldn't commit himself until he'd had the sputum tested.

'It isn't that,' he told her.

'Then what?'

'Anything I said now would just be a guess,' he prevaricated. 'However I'm sure the results of the tests will provide the answer.'

She nodded, suddenly feeling far older than her thirty-two years. It was the tiredness doing that to her, she told herself, wiping away a lock of hair that had fallen across her face.

McLeod placed a cardboard box containing two pills on the table, then clicked his bag shut. 'Give those to Ken directly I've gone. They're the usual sedative.'

Louise nodded. She knew these pills well because the

doctor always gave them to Ken when he was undergoing an attack.

'How long do you think till he's up and about again?' she asked.

'I really can't say until I've had the results back,' McLeod demurred.

That was the answer Louise had expected, but had felt compelled to ask the question anyway. 'I understand,' she murmured.

'Now if you don't mind I'd like to wash my hands again.'

'Certainly.'

When he'd done that McLeod took his leave, saying he'd be in touch just as soon as he had any news.

The pills worked as they always did. Within a little while Ken's breathing was more or less back to normal and his chest had stopped heaving.

Shortly after the children returned from school the dancing, weaving shapes reappeared. Thereafter Ken sweated so much Louise had to change the bed linen twice before joining him in bed later that night.

Sadie eased herself off the chair and on to the linoleumed floor. She then began to crawl purposefully, dragging her legs behind her.

'What do you want, Sadie?' Mrs Logie from the top landing asked. This was the first time she'd baby-sat for them. Usually Mrs Crerar or Mrs Matchett would have kept an eye on them, but they were both out that evening at an Eastern Star meeting.

'My dolly,' Sadie replied.

'I'll get it for you,' Mrs Logie declared, jumping to her feet.

Sadie stopped and twisted round so that she could look at Mrs Logie. 'I'll get it myself.'

'It's no trouble, lamb, honest.'

'I said I'll get it myself,' Sadie persisted, stubborn determination in her voice.

Mrs Logie stopped in her tracks, confused. 'It isn't a bother for me.'

Bill glanced up from where he was playing soldiers with Tom. 'Sadie prefers to do things for herself. That's her way,' he explained.

'She gets about fine. She's just slow that's all,' Morag added.

'I see,' Mrs Logie said, nodding.

Sadie resumed crawling, a painful business but one she was well used to by now. Her doll was in the other room where she'd left it several days previously. It would have been far simpler to have asked one of the others to get it for her, but as Bill had said, that wasn't her way.

Mrs Logie watched Sadie vanish out of the kitchen door, and, silently, thanked God that all her three had been born perfect. How she felt for the lass. What a dreadful prospect to go through life like that.

You had to admire her though, Mrs Logie thought as Sadie came sliding back into the room holding her doll. Oh aye, you had to do that.

Mrs Logie glanced at the clock above the range. It would be a while yet before Louise Smith was home from the doctor's. She decided to put the kettle on.

'Come in, Louise! Sit down,' Dr McLeod said, rising from behind his desk.

'I received your card and here I am,' Louise replied nervously.

'I thought it best if I spoke to you here rather than at the house,' he told her, ushering her to a chair.

'You've had the results of Ken's tests then?'

He sat again in his own chair and stared her straight in the eye. 'I have. And it isn't good news, I'm afraid.'

She found herself holding her breath waiting for him to go on.

'There is a complication that has been causing the deliriousness, but now it's been identified I can soon clear it up. No, it's the other thing that's important.'

He paused, then continued gravely. 'I'm sorry to have to tell you that over and above his pneumoconiosis, Ken has contracted pulmonary tuberculosis. Consumption, as you probably know it.'

'Consumption!' she gasped, the breath rushing out of her.

'I'm afraid so.'

Consumption! Her mind reeled at the thought. 'There must be a mistake . . .'

'There's no mistake, Louise,' McLeod cut in gently.

She swallowed, and swallowed again. She didn't know what she'd expected, but not this. Consumption on top of the dust, it just wasn't fair! She felt her eyes mist over, tears only a blink away.

'Would you like a glass of water?' McLeod asked.

She shook her head.

'His job at the pit,' she mumbled, desperately trying to put her thoughts in order.

'That's all over for Ken now. He'll never work again.'

Never work again! Those words made her physically cringe. If Ken was never to work again what was to happen to them and to their babies!

'I think it best you know the plain facts, Louise. The dust would have killed Ken in the long run, now that he's also got pulmonary tuberculosis the time factor has been severely shortened.'

The tears coursed down her face despite her efforts to keep them at bay. 'How . . . how long?'

'That's difficult to say, Louise. Six months, a year at the outside.'

She shook her head in disbelief. Of course she'd known that Ken would eventually die of the dust, but somehow that had been far off, well into the future. Now they had so little time left together, a year at the outside McLeod said.

'This has all happened so sudden, so quickly. Why you saw him not all that long ago and there wasn't a sign then?'

McLeod noted the faint accusation in Louise's voice, and sighed. 'I don't actually see Ken very often, Louise, for the simple reason it isn't easy for you to stump up my fee. But what you say is true, I didn't notice any signs of TB last time I saw him. They were undoubtedly there, but indistinguishable from the symptoms of his pneumoconiosis. It's only now that the TB has moved into a more advanced state that the manifested symptoms are displaying different characteristics.'

Louise wasn't quite certain she understood that, but was sure it was right. Remembering she had a hanky in her coat pocket she dug it out and wiped her face.

McLeod watched her in silence, slightly irritated that she might think he'd been remiss in any way. There again, he reminded himself, he shouldn't forget how shattered she must feel at the bombshell he'd just dropped. That mollified him a little.

'Is there nothing can be done?' Louise asked.

'There are local authority sanatoria, but the waiting-lists are horrendously long. Tuberculosis has become almost endemic in recent years. A bed could easily be found if you went private of course, but . . .' He spread his hands knowing that was out of the question for the Smiths.

'Should I tell him?' Louise queried in a hoarse whisper.

'You must do what you think is right. Personally I always believe it best to tell the patient. In my experience the vast majority of them prefer to know.'

'Then I'll tell him tonight.'

'If you'd like I'll come round and do it.'

'No,' she replied. 'It's best it comes from me.'

'It is infectious, you know,' McLeod said softly.

She put a hand to her mouth and worried the flesh of her palm. All she could think about was the children. She didn't matter, but they did. They had their whole lives ahead of them.

'I wouldn't recommend you shared the same bed any more,' McLeod added.

Not share the same bed as her Ken, not sleep by his side. Not have that familiar body next to hers – sound advice it may be, but that was something she was going to have to consider long and hard.

Opening her handbag Louise fumbled around for her purse, but she was stopped by McLeod.

'We'll forget about that this time,' he said. 'Considering the circumstances.'

'I can pay, Doctor,' she replied, her fierce Scottish working-class pride welling within her.

'I know you can, Louise. But on this occasion it isn't necessary.'

'Thank you, Doctor,' she husked, rising.

Ever the gentleman McLeod walked her to the door where he shook her hand as he said goodbye.

When she was gone he thoroughly washed his own hands before seeing the next patient.

Outside it had started to rain. Louise halted under a gas lamp to tie her scarf round her head. Her hands were shaking so much that it took her three attempts before she succeeded.

Consumption, a year at the outside, never work again, those words whizzed round in her brain.

She couldn't imagine life without Ken. It was simply inconceivable to her. And now . . . within such a short space of time . . .

She cried from the back of her throat like a stricken animal, fresh tears scalding her eyes. And the children, what about the children?

She walked homewards, but saw nothing. Once she stumbled and nearly pitched headlong, but hardly registered the fact.

When she came to she was standing on the bank of the canal staring into the black, still water. There, in the depths, myriad scenes from the past floated by. Her marriage to Ken, the birth of young Ken. The day trip by bus to Largs where they'd eaten fish and chips and ice-cream and had a wonderful time.

The birth of Tom, of Lena. The night Ken had got roaring drunk at a stag party and she'd almost locked him out of the house. Another night they'd both stayed up nursing Ian who'd developed croup. She'd told Ken to go to bed as he had his work in the morning, but he'd insisted on staying up nonetheless.

And the terrible, terrible day when he'd been diagnosed as having the dust, the scourge and fear of all miners. He'd tried in vain to get another job, but jobs were at a premium and there just hadn't been anything available. He'd eventually been offered something on the surface, but the wage difference was such that he'd elected to stay underground.

'Oh Ken, my bonny man,' she whispered, anger and resentment boiling up in her.

It had stopped raining she suddenly realized, and then wondered what the time was. She'd been out far longer than she'd intended. Those at home would be getting worried about her.

She took a deep breath, then another. She must be composed when she got back, she told herself.

God give her strength, she thought. Then, bitterly, if there was such a thing as God. And if there was he was a cruel God to make people suffer as he did.

A few minutes later she passed a courting couple kissing in the shadows which brought a wry smile to her face. She and Ken had done exactly the same when courting, kissing and cuddling in all manner of places.

And now within a year that same Ken would be dead. She gagged, thinking she was going to be sick, but she wasn't.

When she reached her landing she paused to wipe her face before going inside.

'That's the last one off,' Louise announced quietly, returning from the other room. Sadie was long since asleep on the made-up sofa that doubled as her bed.

Ken, propped up by pillows, coughed into a large handkerchief. They'd agreed to wait until they were alone before Louise told him what the doctor had said.

'Would you like a cup of tea?' she asked.

'Not for me thanks. But you go ahead.'

She wouldn't she decided. Making for only one would be a waste. And from now on, they'd have to watch every farthing even more so than they had in the past.

'I won't either,' she replied.

Crossing to the cavity bed she perched herself on its edge. She then clasped his right hand between her own.

'Well?' he asked.

'It's consumption, Ken. You've got consumption,' she heard a distant voice say, a voice she recognized as her own. She hadn't been aware of either opening her mouth or speaking.

Shock contorted his features. He hadn't thought, never dreamt . . .

'Pulmonary tuberculosis McLeod called it.' She could feel the tears bubbling up and fought to keep them back.

'There's no . . .'

She shook her head. 'There's no mistake, Ken. The tests were quite definite. The doctor said the only reason he didn't pick it up sooner was because of the dust. The symptoms of that were hiding the earlier symptoms of the other, if I understood him correctly.'

Ken sank back into the pillows, his face having gone white and waxen. His mother had died of consumption, a plump jolly woman who'd been reduced to less than five stones at the time of her passing

'Stupid of me. How stupid of me,' he said.

'What is?'

'I should have guessed. I don't know what I thought it was, but never that. Not consumption.'

'It isn't fair,' she said, squeezing his hand.

He barked out a hard laugh. 'What made you think life ever was?'

'But that on top of the dust.'

His eyes fastened on to hers, eyes filled with fear and a lot more she couldn't interpret. 'How long does McLeod give me?'

'Six months. A year at the outside.'

He smiled cynically. 'Six months to a year. Nothing at all. It'll be a case of here today, gone tomorrow.'

'Don't, Ken!' she protested.

'It seems . . . it seems no time whatever since I was young Ken's age. And now . . . six months to a year.'

'McLeod said there wasn't any hope of you getting into any of the local sanatoria, according to him the waiting-lists are horrendously long.'

'And what about the pit?'

'Your working days are over, Ken. That's all finished.'

'So I just lie here till the end, eh?'

She couldn't hold back the tears any longer. Throwing herself forward she buried her face in his chest.

Ken gazed down at Louise, thinking how much he loved her. It wasn't a love he declared very often, men of his background considered it a soft and cissy thing to do. But he did now, because it was important for them both.

'You do know I love you, don't you, Louise?'

She glanced up at him, her face awash. 'Of course I do. Just as you know I love you.'

He nodded. 'We might have been unlucky in some ways, but we've been lucky in others.'

'Yes,' she agreed.

'You and the children are everything to me. Everything in the whole wide world.'

'Oh Ken!' she exclaimed, voice riven with despair.

He was about to answer that when he was seized with such a severe bout of coughing that his entire body shook. When it finally subsided, he was left gasping, the breath rattling in his throat as he inhaled.

'What are we going to do?' she asked when he had recovered slightly.

He weakly shook his head. 'I've no idea.'

'A few weeks on young Ken's wages and what the Union gives us is one thing, but over the long term . . .?' She trailed off, and once more took his hand in hers.

'Perhaps . . .'

'What?' she queried when he failed to go on.

'We have to think of the children other than ourselves. We have to put their welfare first.'

She nodded her agreement, wondering what he was driving at.

'My sister Joyce might take one in. They've got four of their own, but Bobby is a good and Christian man. I'm sure he'll want to help.'

Louise's heart plummeted within her. 'You mean break up the family?' The thought had also occurred to her, but she had swiftly banished it from her mind.

'Is there any other solution?' he whispered in a quavering voice.

Break up the family! she repeated mentally. No, that was too much. She couldn't lose her babies as well as Ken.

'Then there's your brother John. He might help out.'

'Liz is a bitch! Sour as vinegar. I'd never let her get her mitts on any of my children.'

'She isn't as bad as that,' Ken countered, but without much conviction. He didn't like his sister-in-law any more than Louise did. Beggars couldn't be choosers, he reminded himself.

'And what about Sadie?' Louise husked, her eyes straying to her youngest daughter. 'We could never expect anyone to take her. Not the way she is.'

23

'Jesus!' Ken felt utterly defeated. To talk like this of giving their own flesh and blood away. It was an even greater agony than the knowledge he was soon to die.

'I feel so impotent,' he said tightly.

At that, Louise laughed through her tears.

'What's the joke?' he queried, frowning.

'The joke is, my darling husband, whatever else you may be, you're certainly not impotent.'

She paused, then explained, tears glistening in her eyes. 'I'm pregnant again.'

He stared at her aghast.

'Another child, just what we need,' she said.

'Another child?' he echoed.

This just about capped it all. And then he wondered if he'd still be around when their new baby was born, or would Louise already be a widow?

It was a goal to aim for Ken told himself, something positive to focus on.

Suddenly he was exhausted, shattered beyond belief. Not that he would sleep well after this conversation. There was an awful lot to think about.

'Come to bed,' he whispered.

Louise remembered what McLeod had recommended, which made her hesitate. It was something she should discuss with Ken.

'I need you here beside me,' he added.

That was it, blow McLeod's recommendation. Ken needed her, that was all that counted.

'I'll just wash my face first,' she said, gazing down at him. The love between them was so strong she felt it almost had a physical presence.

'A fine old mess, eh girl?' he said, attempting a smile.

Bending, she kissed him on the lips, put her arms round him and held him tight. 'A fine old mess,' she agreed.

As she washed her face, he broke into a wheezing fit, and was still wheezing when she crawled over to him at her place on the inside of the bed.

24

Dawn was breaking over the rooftops before a mind-tortured Ken finally drifted off to sleep.

'Is that all?' Ian queried as Louise placed his dinner before him. It was the midday dinner, and the main meal of the day, but it only consisted of one and a half large spoonfuls of mince and a single slice of dry bread.

'That's all,' Louise confirmed.

'But it's not enough. I'm starving!' Ian wailed.

'I know it's not enough. But it'll have to do.'

'Shut up you. No one else is complaining,' young Ken said threateningly.

'I will not shut up. My stomach thinks my throat's been cut,' Ian retorted. His hunger enabled him to stand up to his big brother.

'You can have mine,' Lena offered.

Ian's eyes gleamed. 'Thank you very much. Just pass it over here.'

'You'll do no such thing, Lena!' Louise declared hotly. 'You'll eat what you've been given and that's an end of it.'

'Can I have a drink, please?' Sadie asked. When her father had been working she would have been given tea, now she was given water.

'Where's yours, Ma?' young Ken queried suspiciously.

'Oh, I'll have mine later when you're all out of the house.'

Young Ken looked over at the pot standing by the side of the range and wondered if there was any mince left. Guessing what was on his mind Louise put the lid on the pot and shoved it out of the way. Her action told young Ken he was right, she hadn't saved any for herself.

Ken, propped up in bed, interpreted Louise's action the same way as his eldest son had. It made him feel sick to think he'd eaten when his wife hadn't. He'd speak to her when next they were alone. If anyone should go without it was him.

25

He quickly reached for a handkerchief as he felt phlegm surge into his mouth. He spat it into the hanky and then viewed the mess with revulsion.

'The foreman called our section together this morning,' young Ken said.

'Uh-huh?'

Young Ken took a deep breath. 'According to him there's the possibility that the factory will be going on short-time.'

Ken swore under his breath.

'Short-time?' Louise repeated, another blow.

'The orders haven't been so good of late so short-time will possibly be the result.'

'When will you know for certain?'

'If and when it happens.'

Louise turned away so that her eldest son couldn't see the expression on her face. Short-time would mean even less money coming into the house, and they could hardly get by as it was.

If he did go on short-time she'd try the Parish again. They had turned down her first request for assistance because young Ken was working and the Union was helping them. Surely, for pity's sake, the Parish would now relent and given them something? Or if not, perhaps the Union would give them more than it was at present.

'I'm sorry, Ma,' young Ken said behind her.

'You've nothing to be sorry for. It's not your fault.'

Young Ken hung his head. It might not be his fault, but he felt guilty nonetheless. He might only be thirteen, but in many ways he was already a man. Conditions and his environment had seen to that.

'Well, *I'm* still hungry,' Ian said.

Louise couldn't help herself. Striding swiftly to the table she slapped Ian so hard she knocked him right off his chair.

'Enough!' she shrieked at him, threatening to slap him again. Then, with a great sigh, 'Enough.'

26

'Serves you right,' Tom said to Ian who glared back at him.

'If I was old enough, I'd run away,' Ian muttered, rubbing a bright red cheek.

Joyce, Louise thought. She would speak to Ken's sister as soon as possible.

'I'm sorry, Ma. It was an accident,' Tom said.

Louise gazed in dismay at the seat of his trousers where his underpants now gaped out of a large, jagged hole.

'How did it happen?' she asked.

He muttered something which she couldn't make out.

'Speak up!' she told him.

He bit his lip, then said sheepishly, 'Climbing spiked railings. My trousers got caught as I jumped off.'

'That's no accident, you shouldn't be climbing railings or any other bloody thing in the first place!' she exploded venomously.

Alarmed by her tone Tom shrank away.

God, she was coming apart at the seams, she thought, running a hand over her face.

'I'm sorry, Ma, honest. I won't do any more climbing I promise,' Tom said.

'I'll try and patch that hole tonight, there's no money for new trousers.' Nor were there any hand-me-downs she could give him. She wondered briefly if she could cut down Ken's sole pair of trousers to fit Tom, then dismissed that as being out of the question. Trousers, she thought swallowing hard, Ken would never wear again.

She looked into Tom's face seeing how pale and wan he'd become. And there were dark smudges under his eyes just as there were under hers.

'Come here,' she commanded, and hugged him.

'Can I go out and play now, Ma?'

'Aye, away you go. But put your raincoat on to cover your backside,' she replied, playfully cuffing his ear.

'And me?' Bill asked.

27

'Aye, all of you away out and play. The fresh air will do you good.'

With delighted whoops the children, with the exception of Sadie, scampered from the house.

'I miss Ian,' Sadie said wistfully, wishing she could have gone with the others. It was now a fortnight since Ian had gone to live with his Auntie Joyce and Uncle Bobby.

'I do too, pet. Very much so.'

Louise glanced over at Ken to find him studying her intently. She knew what he was thinking.

'I'll go and see John and Liz tonight,' she said.

He nodded. 'Which one? Have you decided?'

'No, not yet. I suppose it depends upon whether they have a preference for a boy or girl.'

In the event it was Morag's lot to go to live with John and Liz. None of the other children envied her, they didn't like Liz either.

Louise, despite the two cardigans she was wearing, sat shivering in front of the unlit range. It was freezing cold in the house, and outside compacted ice and snow lay hard upon the streets and pavements.

She stared longingly at the half-bucket of coal and small pile of sticks lying beside the range. She would dearly have loved to use the fuel to light the range, but needed to keep it till later when she would cook. Tea was their principal meal now, dinner reduced to a single slice of bread and dripping.

There was a butterfly movement inside her belly reminding her of the baby she was expecting. Poor wee mite to come into this, she thought disconsolately.

Reaching up she touched her hair. How lifeless and dry it was, just like herself. She thought of Ken who'd deteriorated drastically in the last few weeks. He'd lost so much weight he was skeletal. But there again, she remembered grimly, they'd all lost weight. It was inevitable on the little they had to eat.

She winced as hunger pangs gripped her stomach, and wondered what effect all this was having on the baby. She wouldn't be at all surprised if the child was born dead. In fact it was probably best if it was.

Black despair rose up to engulf her and made her contort her face into a terrible grimace.

Watching from the bed Ken saw her expression, but couldn't bear to look at it. He turned his head and stared desperately at the bed's inside wall.

Sadie woke to the sound of quiet sobbing. Louise, illuminated by moonlight lancing through the windows, was sitting by the range, slumped forward with her head in her hands.

Pulling back the bedclothes Sadie wriggled from the sofa to the floor and crawled over to her mother.

'What's wrong, Ma?' she asked when she reached Louise.

Her mother blinked back tears to gaze down at Sadie. 'What are you doing out of bed?'

'You woke me.'

Judas Iscariot, that was who she felt like, Louise decided, only in her case there wouldn't be thirty pieces of silver. Reaching down she grasped hold of Sadie and lifted her on to her lap.

'I couldn't sleep, I've got a lot on my mind. So I thought I'd get up,' Louise explained.

'Are you crying because of Da?'

'Yes,' Louise replied, which was only partly true.

'Bill says he's going to die. Is that so?'

'And who told him that?'

'A boy at his school says that everyone who gets consumption dies.'

'Oh lamb!' Louise whispered, and clasped Sadie tightly to her bosom.

'I don't want him to die,' Sadie choked.

'Neither do I, neither do I.'

'Will he, Ma?'

Neither she nor Ken had fully explained the situation to the children. Young Ken knew what was what, and so too did Tom, they thought, though he'd never said anything. But as far as the younger children were concerned their father was merely having an extended illness.

Louise took a deep breath. 'How would you like to be able to walk at long last?' she smiled.

Sadie's mouth fell open, all thoughts of her father driven from her mind.

'I wasn't going to tell you till the morning, but I'll do so now,' Louise went on. 'Tomorrow you and I are going on a long tramcar ride. In fact two tramcar rides. We're going to a place called Babies Castle where you're going to stay for a while so that a nice doctor can operate on your hip. Now what do you say to that?'

Sadie, mouth still open, was completely lost for words.

'Pleased?'

Sadie nodded.

'It means we won't see you for a time, but that can't be helped.'

Able to walk, to be like other children. Not be a cripple any more. To be *normal*! Sadie swallowed. 'We go tomorrow?'

'Early. To Babies Castle.'

'Babies Castle,' Sadie repeated, thinking how lovely that sounded.

'You're going to enjoy it there, I promise you. And you'll get lots and lots of scrumptious things to eat.'

'And the doctor will fix my hip?'

'He will, darling. What's wrong with you can be put right providing you have the money to pay for the operation.'

'And you now have the money?' Sadie queried quizzically.

Louise's smile thinned. 'Not exactly. But I have made another arrangement which will take care of that side of the matter.'

30

Babies Castle, what a wonderful name, Sadie thought. She couldn't wait to get there. And lots of delicious things to eat! Her mouth watered at the thought.

'Will there be ice-cream?' she asked.

Louise gave a low laugh. 'I don't know about that. But there might be.'

Ice-cream! Sadie adored ice-cream. Particularly if it was served with jelly.

'When I can walk I'll be able to go to school with the others,' Sadie said.

'That's right, darling.'

Excitement was mounting inside Sadie, like a runaway snowball rolling downhill, getting bigger and bigger with every passing second.

'Oh Ma!' she exclaimed, thrilled to bits.

'But now I think you'd better get back to bed before your fingers and toes turn to icicles. And I want you to be nice and fresh for the morning so that you make a good impression.'

'Will you tuck me in again?'

'Of course I will.'

Louise hoisted Sadie up against her shoulder, then rose and carried her to the sofa.

When Sadie was well tucked up she kissed her on the forehead.

'I've never been on a tram,' Sadie said.

'I know, darling.'

'And now tomorrow I'm going on two.'

'It'll be fun.'

'And we're going far?'

'Miles and miles.'

'I've never been miles and miles,' Sadie said.

'Well, you will tomorrow. With Babies Castle at the end of it.'

'Babies Castle,' Sadie repeated yet again, the name having assumed something of a magical ring about it. In her mind's eye she saw a huge medieval type castle with creamy skinned, golden-haired babies hanging out of every window, shouting her name in welcome.

'Now night night, sleep tight . . .'

'Don't let the bugs bite,' Sadie finished off for her mother.

Louise gave Sadie another kiss before returning to her own bed.

Sadie didn't need a second calling next morning. She was up and dressed in half her usual time.

'I'm having my hip operated on after which I'll be able to walk,' she announced to young Ken when he entered the kitchen.

'Is that so, wee one?' he replied slowly, glancing over at his mother.

'At a place called Babies Castle.'

Louise bit her lip.

'And where's that?' young Ken enquired.

'Miles and miles away, isn't it, Ma?'

'Yes,' Louise husked.

'I've to stay there till I've had the operation. And while I am there I'll get lots and lots to eat,' Sadie burbled on.

'What's all this?' Lena asked, coming into the kitchen.

Sadie repeated what she'd told young Ken.

'That's marvellous,' Lena enthused, hugging her little sister.

'And when are you going to this Babies whatsit?' young Ken queried.

'Today. This morning,' Sadie replied.

'A bit out the blue, isn't it?' young Ken said pointedly to his ashen-faced mother.

'We kept it as a surprise,' Louise answered, refusing to look young Ken straight in the eye.

'Wait till you hear Sadie's news,' Lena said to Bill and Tom who'd now put in an appearance.

They were as delighted as Lena had been. 'You'll soon be playing football with me,' Bill joked to Sadie.

'I'll play as well. You just wait and see if I don't,' she replied earnestly, which raised a laugh.

They all settled down for breakfast which consisted of water and a single slice of dry bread.

They all kissed Sadie as they left, a wistful young Ken waiting till last. He added a hug and squeeze to his kiss. 'You look after yourself now,' he said, a catch in his voice.

'I'll be fine. Won't I, Ma?'

Louise didn't reply.

Young Ken fled from the house, the outside door slamming shut behind him.

Louise went to the sink, bent over it and sighed deeply. Put a face on, she told herself, for the child's sake.

'When are we off, Ma?' Sadie asked eagerly.

'In a minute.'

Ken was sitting up in bed staring hard at his youngest. His eyes were moist, his expression one of complete wretchedness.

Louise put on her coat, then helped Sadie into hers. 'Mrs Crerar will be popping in from time to time,' she said to Ken.

'Right then!' she exclaimed, hefting Sadie into her arms. 'You'll want to give your da a big kiss.'

Sadie kissed Ken on the cheek, and laughed because his stubble prickled.

'Goodbye, lass,' he whispered in a strained, cracked voice.

'Next time I see you I'll be walking,' she replied.

'Aye, that's right.'

'Walking and running.'

'Running like the wind,' Louise said, forcing herself to smile.

'We're away then, Ken.'

'Enjoy the tram,' he said to Sadie.

'I will, Da. Have no fear of that.'

33

Louise walked briskly from the kitchen, and out of the house.

'I'm going on a tram,' Sadie yelled to Mrs Murphy, a neighbour they passed mopping her close.

Mrs Murphy paused to wave her mop at Sadie. 'Good for you, hen!'

Sadie talked non-stop all the way to the tramstop, but if asked Louise wouldn't have been able to repeat a word of what she'd said.

'It's here! It's here!' Sadie exclaimed as their tram clanked into view.

They went inside and Sadie sat at a window seat. She peered out as the tram drove away, her eyes large and round with excitement.

Louise studied her daughter who was rapt by the passing scene. She'd have to comb her hair before they arrived, she thought. The wind had blown it into a right tangle.

With every passing stop Louise's heart grew heavier and heavier.

They alighted from the first tram in front of a draper's shop which gave Louise an idea. She'd wanted to give Sadie a parting gift anyway, what had now sprung to mind would be the very dab.

'We're going in here for a minute,' she informed Sadie.

A bell tinkled as Louise opened the shop door, and a pleasant-faced, middle-aged man looked up from behind the counter and smiled at them.

Louise sat Sadie on the counter. 'I'd like two lengths of ribbons please for my daughter's hair,' she said.

'Certainly, madam.'

As the assistant moved away Louise produced an old comb from a pocket with which she attacked Sadie's hair.

'There,' she declared when the hair was untangled again.

The assistant returned to lay a selection of colours before them. All the colours of the rainbow it seemed to Sadie.

'What colour would madam prefer?' the assistant enquired.

Louise was about to name one when she suddenly thought Sadie should choose. The ribbons were for her anyway.

'You decide,' she told Sadie.

Sadie looked from roll to roll, taking her time, thoroughly enjoying herself. Finally she made her mind up.

'That one,' she stated, pointing.

'Scarlet,' smiled the assistant. 'An excellent choice in my opinion, miss. It will contrast beautifully with your dark hair.'

Sadie giggled, thinking the man spoke funnily. She watched as he unravelled about three feet of ribbon and then picked up a large pair of scissors.

'What length would you like the ribbons, madam?' he asked Louise.

'About that,' she replied, using extended fingers to indicate a length.

The assistant nodded and snipped as instructed.

'Do you wish them in a bag?' he queried.

'No, she'll wear them,' Louise answered.

Louise then paid for the ribbons, only able to afford this extravagance because her brother John had stopped by the house one night recently to slip her a ten-shilling note and, with a wink, asked her not to mention the fact to Liz.

John might be in work, but his wages were poor and every week was a struggle to get through. But as John had put it to his sister, it was only money after all and at the moment, she needed that ten shillings more than he.

'How's that?' Louise queried, flicking down the tails of the two bows she tied at the back of Sadie's hair.

Sadie half turned so that she could see the effect in the mirror on the wall behind the counter.

'They're lovely,' she acknowledged.

'And set off your hair a treat, just as I said scarlet would,' the assistant beamed.

'I feel like a princess going off to a castle,' Sadie told him, the castle she had in mind being Babies Castle.

Louise had her out of the shop before Sadie could elaborate further.

'There we are, that's it,' Louise declared, pointing at a large sandstone building situated within its own grounds.

'Doesn't look like a castle,' Sadie said, disappointed.

'But it's nice all the same though, isn't it? And you can always pretend that it is a castle.'

Sadie visibly brightened. She could easily pretend as she had a vivid imagination developed by hours of playing by herself while her brothers and sisters were at school.

'And just look at those lovely gardens. They must be really beautiful in the summer,' Louise went on.

'I'll be home long before then though,' Sadie said.

Louise smiled at her daughter, but didn't reply. 'Shall we go in then?' she suggested instead.

A young woman dressed in uniform answered their ring. Ushering them into a small waiting-room she said that matron would see them shortly. And in the meantime, would Louise care for a cup of tea? Louise tried not to appear too eager when she replied that she would.

Delight of delights! The tea arrived with several cream biscuits on the saucer. Louise couldn't remember the last time she'd had a cream biscuit.

They weren't kept long, and soon they were shown into a brightly lit office where Matron was sitting at a desk on which were piled a number of ordered papers and stacked ledgers. Matron immediately rose and came forward to meet them.

'So this is Sadie,' Matron smiled at her. 'Your mummy wrote me a marvellous letter telling me all about you.'

Sadie dropped her head, feeling shy.

Matron's gaze swept over Sadie, taking everything in. Skin and bone, she thought, as was the mother. But a 'good' working-class family nonetheless. You could tell.

'Have you had tea?' Matron asked Louise.

'Yes, thank you.'

'As I'm about to have some myself would you like another cup?'

'Please.' She hoped there would be some more cream biscuits.

'And what about you, Sadie? Have you had anything?'

'No,' Sadie replied in a small voice.

'Then how about a glass of milk?'

Sadie nodded.

Matron left the office for a few moments, then briskly returned.

'So, just what have you told Sadie?' she asked Louise.

'That she's come here to have her hip fixed,' Louise answered tightly.

Matron stared hard at Louise. 'I see.'

Crossing to her desk she sat again, and pulled out a form from a drawer. 'Please sit down. Sadie must be heavy.'

Louise placed Sadie on a chair in front of the desk, then drew another alongside.

'I'll need full details you'll appreciate,' Matron said, unscrewing the top from a fountain pen.

'Of course.'

While the two women talked, Sadie gazed about her, somewhat awed by her surroundings. There was a lovely rug on the floor and several colourful pictures on the walls. One picture was of a country scene that looked positively idyllic to Sadie used to the grime and general squalor of her home.

The tea and milk arrived, but no cream biscuits this time Louise quickly noted, brought in by another woman in the same uniform as before.

'Miss Tupper is one of our housemothers, and will be directly responsible for looking after you, Sadie,' Matron explained.

Miss Tupper was in her late twenties, Louise judged, and had a kind face dominated by sparkling blue eyes.

Louise and Miss Tupper shook hands, then Miss Tupper squatted beside Sadie. 'And how are you, little lady?' she asked.

'Fine, thank you,' Sadie replied, all shy again.

'You and I will be seeing a great deal of one another from now on.'

'Will you be doing my operation?'

Miss Tupper laughed. 'No, a doctor will be doing that.'

'Today?'

'I shouldn't think so. But I imagine he'll want to examine you later on this week. They have to do that you know, examine you before they operate.'

'Will it hurt?'

'You mean the operation? It might be uncomfortable for a while afterwards, but you won't feel anything during the actual operation. They'll put you fast asleep for that.'

She had a good way with children, Louise noted. An easy, natural way that had already won Sadie over. Some of the fear and anxiety she felt disappeared, but not all of it. Trepidation still beat within her breast.

Miss Tupper returned to the tray and handed round the tea, after which she gave Sadie her milk.

'It's very nice,' Sadie declared politely, having tasted it.

'You know something,' Miss Tupper said, squatting again.

'What?'

'You and I are going to get along like a house on fire. I just know it.'

Sadie's face broke into a broad smile at these words spoken with such sincerity.

'Now the remainder of these questions,' Matron said to Louise.

'Do you wish me to go, Matron?' Miss Tupper asked, coming once more to her feet.

'No, wait here. The formalities are almost over.'

She was doing the right thing, Louise assured herself. This was in Sadie's best interests, she mustn't forget that.

'Now then,' said Matron shortly afterwards. Leaning across she deposited the form in front of Louise. 'All that remains is for you to sign between the two crosses I've marked, Mrs Smith, and that will transfer Sadie into our custody.'

Reluctantly Louise laid her cup and saucer aside, and picked up the form intending to glance over it. Only she found it impossible, her eyes having suddenly misted over to such an extent that she couldn't read.

'Your signature, Mrs Smith,' Matron said softly and sympathetically.

Louise swallowed, laid the form back on the desk. Then she signed, using Matron's own fountain pen.

'Don't cry, Ma. I'll soon be home again,' Sadie said, putting a hand on her mother's arm.

Louise had a lump in her throat that seemed the size of a golf ball. She didn't trust herself to speak in case she completely broke down.

Realizing the situation Matron dropped the form into the drawer it had come from, then she came round to the front of her desk. 'If you'll just take Sadie off, Miss Tupper, I'll attend to Mrs Smith,' she said.

Louise pulled Sadie into her arms, and hugged her tight. 'God bless you, lass. God bless and keep you,' she blurted out, voice raw with emotion.

Matron gestured to Miss Tupper to prise Sadie away from Louise.

'Come with me, Sadie, and I'll show you your bed and where you're going to be. And perhaps you'd like a nice hot bath and I could help you wash your hair if you want?' Miss Tupper said, grasping hold of Sadie.

Louise felt herself coming apart inside. This was a hundred times worse than Morag and Ian. A thousand times even!

Miss Tupper finally managed to detach Sadie from the distraught Louise, and immediately headed for the office door. She and Matron knew from experience that these things were best done quickly.

'Goodbye, Ma!' Sadie called out cheerily at the door, which swiftly shut behind them.

Seconds later a great cry rent the air, as if some animal had just been mortally wounded.

'That wasn't Ma, was it?' Sadie asked in sudden fright.

'No, of course not,' Miss Tupper smiled reassuringly. 'It was probably just somebody playing silly beggars.'

'Now,' she went on, changing the subject. 'I want you to tell me all about yourself, Sadie.'

Sadie did, and soon the terrible anguished cry was forgotten, exactly as Miss Tupper had intended.

'She can get dressed again,' Dr Weismann announced on completing his examination. Miss Tupper immediately hurried over to Sadie while he wrote up his notes.

When he'd finished, he put them aside and smiled at Sadie. 'Do you think you're going to enjoy doing exercises?' he asked.

She couldn't see what that had to do with his examination. 'Why, doctor?'

'Because you're going to have to do plenty of them after the operation to build up those leg muscles of yours. It'll take a while, mind, and a lot of hard work on your part, but we'll get there.'

Elation flooded through Sadie. She didn't care how many exercises she had to do just as long as she could walk. She gazed into Miss Tupper's eyes which stared triumphantly back into her own.

'When will you operate, Doctor?' Miss Tupper asked Weismann, buttoning up the collar of Sadie's dress.

'Not right away. We need to build her up first, put some weight on her. So I suggest double helpings of everything from now on.'

'Even ice-cream?' Sadie demanded.

A small smile twisted the corners of his mouth upwards. '*Particularly* ice-cream. There's nothing better for building up wee lassies than ice-cream. I'll make sure that's specifically mentioned in my report to Matron.'

Sadie was in seventh heaven. Then her spirits dropped remembering the brothers and sisters she'd left at home. If only she could have sent some of the lashings of food she got here back to them. How little they had to eat, and how much she now had. Every meal was a feast as far as she was concerned.

'I'll see you again in a month's time and we'll review the situation then,' Weismann said, tickling Sadie under the chin.

'Double ice-cream on the doctor's orders,' Sadie beamed at Miss Tupper.

'Starting this very afternoon,' Miss Tupper replied.

'Who are you?' the big girl demanded. There were four of them who'd just come bursting into the room where Sadie was on the floor playing with a doll's house and the family that went with it. It was now a week since she'd come to Babies Castle.

'I'm Sadie.'

'Sadie what?' the same girl demanded, her tone sneering and unpleasant.

'Sadie Smith. What's yours?'

'Never you mind.'

The girl swaggered further into the room to stand staring down at Sadie. 'New, are you?'

Sadie nodded.

'Thought so. Haven't seen you before. And stand up when I'm talking to you.'

'I can't. That's why I'm here. To have an operation so that I will be able to stand, and walk and run.'

The other three girls crowded round the one who'd been doing the speaking.

'Many of the children who come here have operations,' one of the three explained to Sadie.

'The Home specializes in that,' another added.

The use of the word in that context confused Sadie. Home was where she lived with her family.

'My ma's coming for me after my operation to take me back to our home,' she said.

The first speaker laughed nastily. 'Oh no she's not!' the girl declared in a sing-song manner, the same way those words are delivered in a pantomime. She then wagged a finger at Sadie.

'Don't, Gloria,' the fourth girl implored.

'Och, you be quiet, Marlene.'

Marlene shut up, clearly intimidated by Gloria who now returned her attention to Sadie.

'You won't be going home again, Sadie, none of us who land here ever do. I mean, don't you understand where you are?'

It was some sort of joke, Sadie told herself. Just like the jokes Bill used to play on her, only his were never cruel.

'I'm in Babies Castle,' she replied falteringly.

Gloria laughed, a laugh both shrill and scathing. She was thoroughly enjoying this. 'That's only a nickname, what people outside call it. But it's really a Dr Barnardo's Home.'

Sadie was now both bewildered and frightened. 'Dr Barnardo?' she queried. She'd never heard of him. Dr Weismann who'd examined her and Dr McLeod who visited the house. But never Dr Barnardo.

'She really doesn't know,' Gloria said to her three companions, and sniggered.

'This is a Home for bastards, unwanted children and the like,' the taller of the two girls informed Sadie.

Unwanted children! That rocked Sadie to the very core of her being.

'There are many Barnardo's Homes in Scotland and England,' said the other unnamed girl. 'Isn't that so, Jamesina?'

Jamesina nodded. 'Aye, that's right, Beth. Quite a number, I believe.'

The joke had gone far enough, Sadie decided, her lower lip trembling. 'Stop teasing me,' she said to Gloria.

Gloria bent over Sadie, her eyes sparking wickedness. 'We're not teasing you, it's all true. For whatever reason, you've been abandoned here by your family, none of whom you'll ever see again.'

Sadie burst into tears.

'You're rotten,' Marlene said quietly to Gloria, who rounded on her.

'Any more of that and you'll leave our group,' Gloria hissed.

From Marlene's expression it was obvious that was something she didn't want. 'I'm sorry,' she mumbled.

'You're too soft. It's a fault. What is it?'

'It's a fault,' Marlene repeated.

'I'm not an unwanted child,' Sadie blubbered.

'If not, then why are you here?' Gloria jibed. 'Or are you one of the others, a bastard?'

'I don't know what that is,' Sadie confessed.

'Is your father married to your mother?' Jamesina queried.

Sadie nodded.

'Certain about that?'

Sadie nodded again.

'Then you're not a bastard.'

'I'm a bastard,' Beth confessed proudly.

43

'Through and through,' Gloria said, which raised a laugh amongst her companions.

'My ma is coming back for me. She promised,' Sadie persisted.

'She was lying,' Gloria smirked.

'No, she wasn't. My ma doesn't lie!'

'Well, she did this time. You've been given the old heave-ho. Institutionalized. Got rid of. Given the elbow.'

Sadie gazed up at Gloria, loathing this big girl with the orangey red hair. 'It's you who's lying,' she accused.

'Oh no, I'm not!' Gloria replied in the same pantomime manner as before.

'Oh no, she's not!' Jamesina echoed, raising another laugh.

Marlene looked on Sadie with pity, but said nothing. It was far better to have Gloria as a friend than an enemy.

'What's going on here?' Miss Tupper demanded, having appeared silently at the door.

'Nothing, miss,' Beth answered quickly, twisting to face the housemother.

'We're just leaving, miss,' Gloria said. And with that the four girls marched smartly from the room, passing Miss Tupper who stepped into the room to let them by.

Miss Tupper then went over and squatted beside Sadie, who was obviously sorely distressed.

'What happened, lamb?' she asked.

Sadie repeated what she'd been told.

'I see,' Matron sighed when Miss Tupper had finished.

'That Gloria Connell's a bad lot,' Miss Tupper added softly through clenched teeth.

Matron couldn't have agreed more. She would deal with Gloria and her cohorts in the severest way. It only confirmed that it was time for Gloria to leave them and move on. The girl had always been more trouble than she was worth.

'Where's Sadie now?' Matron queried.

'Sitting outside.'

'Then you'd better bring her in.'

Sadie's eyes were pink and puffed when Miss Tupper brought her into Matron's office. Her crying had now stopped, only to be replaced by sniffling.

'Do you wish me to stay?' Miss Tupper asked after she'd sat Sadie on a chair facing Matron.

'I think you should.'

Miss Tupper stood beside Sadie, resting a hand protectively on the wee girl's shoulder.

'You are *not* an unwanted child,' Matron started off. 'Your mummy and daddy loved you very much indeed. And that explains why in the end your mummy brought you here.'

'But she is coming back for me?' Sadie queried hopefully.

Matron shook her head. 'I'm afraid not. And that's something, however hard, you're going to have to accept.'

'But she said . . .'

'She simply couldn't bring herself to tell you the truth. That's often the case. Your mummy knows if she had told you the truth she wouldn't have been able to leave you behind.'

Sadie crumpled in on herself. Never to see Ma or Da again! Or Bill or . . . Fresh tears sprang into her eyes and rolled down her cheeks.

Sadie dabbed at her face while her thin body shook all over. She was so stunned she could hardly think.

'Why?' she asked.

'Why were you brought here?' Matron queried.

Sadie nodded.

'What do you know about your father's illness?'

'That he has the dust and now consumption, which made him stay in bed all day.'

'That all?'

'Yes, Matron.'

Just as she'd suspected, Matron thought. 'Well,' she said, taking a deep breath. 'The reason you're here and your brother Ian and sister Morag have gone to live with relatives is . . .'

When she'd concluded that explanation Matron went on to tell Sadie about Dr Barnardo, what a good man he'd been, whose chief aim in life had been to help poor and deserving children like herself.

Miss Tupper found Sadie lying curled underneath a table, thumb in mouth, staring blankly at the wall.

'Sadie?'

Sadie didn't reply, or acknowledge Miss Tupper's presence.

'Sadie, this can't go on. Dear sweet thing, you've got to snap out of it.'

Sadie continued to ignore her.

'I know it's difficult, but you've got to come to terms with the situation. I'll help you all I can if only you'll let me.'

Sadie stared at the wall, seeing only memory pictures of her and Bill playing together. Bill had found some cards and taught her snap. The pair of them had roared with laughter as they banged the cards down on top of one another.

'Would you like to go into the garden? It's lovely out.'

Mine! Sadie could hear herself cry. It's mine! And then there she was, gathering a large pile of cards towards her while Bill pulled a disappointed face.

And Da, on one of his good days, giving them all a kiss before going off to the pit and coalface. And Ian, always hungry.

'Sadie, will you answer me?'

Sadie closed her eyes, and curled up tighter. The memories continued to roll past.

Sadie woke up to find her mouth gummy, with an unpleasant taste in it.

Where was she? And why did she feel so strange? Then it all came back to her. She'd been for her operation.

Dr Weismann's smiling face swam into view. 'How do you feel?' he asked.

She tried to answer, but all that came out was a hoarse croak.

'Nurse, some water please.'

Sadie's head was gently lifted, and a porcelain spout slipped between her lips. The water was warm, but that didn't matter. It was such a relief it was wet.

'That's enough for the moment,' the nurse said, removing the spout.

'Better?' Weismann queried, still smiling.

'Yes, thank you,' she husked.

'So how do you feel?'

'Funny.'

'But not sick?'

'No.'

He nodded; that pleased him.

'Can I have some more water?'

'Not yet. You can have a little more later. Too much at this stage isn't good for you.'

Dr Weismann turned to the nurse and said, 'We will start the exercises fairly soon. The operation should be a complete success. I'm one hundred per cent certain Sadie will walk normally in time.'

Tears blossomed in Sadie's eyes. But these tears were totally different to the others she'd shed since arriving at Babies Castle.

For these were tears of joy.

Chapter Two

Sadie was in class, being taught by stern Miss Donald, when Tich Thompson came in to inform Miss Donald that Sadie and Janet Bone were to go to Matron's office straight away. Matron wanted to speak to them.

'What's it all about?' Sadie asked Tich out in the corridor.

He shrugged. 'Search me. I was just told to get you, that's all.'

Sadie looked at Janet, the pair of them best friends. 'What do you think?'

'We haven't done anything, have we?'

'Not that I know of.'

Janet furrowed her brow. 'I can't think of anything either.'

'You two better stop jawing and get along. You know how Matron hates to be kept waiting.'

Tich left them, having another errand to perform. Side by side Sadie and Janet hurried towards Matron's office.

It was 1927, and Sadie, now eight years old, had been at Babies Castle for four years. Those years had been marvellous ones for her, filled with happiness, well being and contentment. Babies Castle had become a second home, Miss Tupper, whom she idolized, a second mother.

Sadie had grown considerably during this time, and filled out thanks to the plentiful food she received. As for her operation, that had proved the complete success Dr Weismann had predicted, and she could now walk and run just as well as any of the other children.

'It's jam roly-poly for lunch,' Janet said.

'How do you know that?'

'I was in the kitchens earlier and saw it being made.'

Sadie adored jam roly-poly, it was probably her favourite pudding.

'Come in!' Matron called out when Sadie knocked on her door.

Inside Sadie and Janet found Margaret Swanson already waiting; Margaret a girl of their age. When Marion Kirkbride and Aly Paterson, also the same age, arrived, Sadie guessed what this was all about. A glance at Janet's suddenly fearful expression told her that Janet had realized too.

Mikey Sullivan and Pat Black were the next to put in an appearance, followed closely by Barbara McGurk.

When the last of those summoned stood before her, Matron laid down the pen she'd been writing with, and looked at them.

'As you all know this is a Home for babies and very young children, and I'm afraid you have all now reached the point where it is time for you to move on.'

She'd been right, Sadie thought, though it was several months before that yearly event was due to take place.

Matron now explained. 'Normally I would have kept you all here a bit longer, but because we've recently had a larger intake than usual, I'm sorry but I'm going to have to move you on earlier.'

This was the moment Sadie had been dreading, leaving Babies Castle for a Home that catered for older children. How she was going to miss Babies Castle, and Miss Tupper. It was simply her bad luck that she was having to leave these few months prematurely.

Every single child in the room looked morose and dejected, as each of them would have elected to stay if that option had been available.

Tony Woods stuck up his hand. 'When Matron?'

'This Monday. You'll be departing after breakfast.'

Sadie stuck up her hand. 'Are we girls all going to the same Home, Matron?' It would be awful if she was parted from Janet.

'Yes, Sadie,' Matron replied, much to Sadie's relief. 'All the girls are going to the same Home, which is in Ayrshire. The boys will be going to one in Midlothian.'

'No more rotten lassies around from here on in,' Aly Paterson muttered quietly.

Carrie Hedderwick standing beside him stuck her nose in the air on hearing that.

Aly grinned, he loved upsetting the girls and quite contrary to what he'd said he would miss them dreadfully. He didn't at all fancy the idea of an all-boys Home.

Monday, Sadie thought miserably. Three days away. The time would pass in a flash.

Matron went on. 'Suitcases will be provided for every child who will do his or her packing on Sunday evening.'

She paused, then said softly, 'The staff and myself wish you all the luck in the world, and hope you'll be a credit to us here. I have every confidence in you all. Now, any more questions?'

There weren't, so she dismissed the group. They filed despondently from her office.

'Monday,' Sadie said to Janet out in the corridor.

'At least we'll be together. That's something.'

'And we must try and get beds alongside one another.'

'Aye,' Janet agreed.

They fell into step, returning to Miss Donald's class.

'Are you scared?' Janet asked.

'Honest injun?'

'Honest injun.'

'I'm petrified.'

Janet laughed. 'Me too. I'm shaking in my shoes at the thought.'

'We knew it was coming, mind. We've known that for a long time.'

'That doesn't make it any easier when it does though. At least, it hasn't for me.'

'Me neither,' Sadie admitted.

There was jam roly-poly for lunch, but Sadie only picked at hers. She couldn't help but wonder if there would be jam roly-poly where they were going.

'All aboard then!' Matron called out, having been round each and every child now leaving to say a personal goodbye.

'I know you'll be a good girl and not let us down,' Miss Tupper said to Sadie.

'I'm going to miss you,' Sadie muttered.

'And I'm going to miss you.'

'Perhaps I'll see you again sometime?' Sadie said hopefully.

'Perhaps. Who knows?' Miss Tupper was trying to keep her tone light and cheerful, but finding it extremely difficult. She'd become more attached to Sadie than any other child she'd had to care for. A special bond had developed between them.

If only she'd been married she'd have adopted Sadie, she thought, not for the first time. But she wasn't, nor was there any likelihood in the foreseeable future.

Sadie fell into Miss Tupper's embrace, feeling she was losing a mother for the second time in her short life.

'Now, don't cry or you'll get me started and that wouldn't please Matron at all,' Miss Tupper whispered.

'I won't cry. I'm a big girl now,' Sadie replied.

'That's right,' Miss Tupper said, stroking Sadie's hair.

'Come along girls!' Matron called out, gesticulating towards the single decker's door.

Miss Tupper bent and pecked Sadie on the cheek. 'On you get then.'

Sadie turned quickly away and ran to the bus, her suitcase already packed into the boot.

Up the metalled stairs she went, and down the aisle to where Janet was keeping a seat for her.

'It'll take hours to get to Ayrshire according to the driver,' Janet informed her.

Sadie spotted Mikey Sullivan and waved to him. The boys were going on a different bus that would be leaving soon after theirs. Mikey waved back.

A cluster of tiny tots stood at a window staring solemnly down, a housemother behind them. One day it would be their turn to say farewell to Babies Castle.

'Come on!' grumbled Fiona Salmon who was sitting across the aisle from Sadie and Janet. She was anxious to be off.

Sadie waved at Miss Tupper who smiled weakly at her before returning the wave.

'I'm proud of you,' Miss Tupper mouthed to Sadie, who indicated she didn't understand by shaking her head.

'Never mind,' Miss Tupper muttered to herself, and waved to Barbara McGurk who was another girl she'd been close to, though nowhere near as close as Sadie. When all the departing girls were safely aboard Matron closed the door and signalled the driver that he could go. She then stepped back and clasped her hands in front of her.

'Good old Matron,' Janet said.

Sadie wouldn't have argued with that. Matron couldn't have been better. She wondered what their new matron would be like – not a dragon, Sadie hoped.

The driver tooted his horn as the bus moved off. Everyone, with the exception of Matron, waved frantically, while Matron just stood there with a sad, woeful expression on her face. She was losing a good bunch, both boys and girls, some of the best to have passed through her hands.

'That's that then,' said Sadie when Babies Castle was finally lost to view. Sinking back into her seat she let out a great sigh.

For the first few minutes the atmosphere inside the bus was light-hearted and jolly. Then gradually gloom descended as they all began to ponder what lay ahead of them and all they had left behind.

'That's your destination, girls!' the driver announced over his shoulder in a loud voice.

The building was about twice the size of the one they'd come from, Gothic and slightly sinister in appearance. Sadie didn't like the look of it at all.

'Big, isn't it,' Janet muttered.

Sadie nodded.

'And doesn't appear very friendly either.'

'Not very,' Sadie agreed, wishing with all her heart she was back at Babies Castle with Miss Tupper.

Janet reached out and took hold of Sadie's hand. She squeezed it, then continued holding it for comfort.

'Be there in about five minutes,' the driver said, again over his shoulder.

It was completely silent inside the bus, no excited chatter whatever, as the single decker drew up outside the Home's main entrance. Even after the bus had come to a halt, no one made a move.

'It looks like a place where the bogeyman might live,' someone said, a comment which fell on stony ears.

A figure in the familiar uniform appeared and marched to the bus door. When she reached it the driver was standing there waiting for her.

'Everyone present and correct?' the woman demanded.

'Yes, miss.'

'Then open the boot so the girls can get their luggage.'

'Yes, miss.'

The driver hurried to the rear of the bus while the woman stared up at a row of apprehensive faces gazing back at her. She crooked a finger, and waggled it several times. Her meaning was clear, the girls were to get out.

'My name is Miss Mulgrew. You will collect your cases and follow me. Understand?'

'Yes, miss,' they all chorused in reply.

Sadie glanced at the notice above the main entrance. Doctor Barnardo's Home it proclaimed. Exactly the same sign had been above the entrance at Babies Castle, but she hadn't been able to read it when her mother had first taken her there.

Sadie and Janet collected their cases, then waited till the others joined them. When they were all ready, Miss Mulgrew led them into the building.

It was dim inside, with shadows everywhere. The wooden floor they tramped over gleamed like a new pin. Their shoes squeaked on the polish.

'This place gives me the creeps,' Janet whispered to Sadie, who nodded.

They were escorted down a long corridor containing many shadowy nooks and crannies, till they reached a staircase. They then climbed three flights of creaky stairs to another corridor, this one narrow and wood lined.

They passed several girls *en route*, all of whom seemed cheerful enough which surely meant the Home wasn't that bad.

'Your dormitory, girls,' Miss Mulgrew said, throwing open a door.

There were two rows of beds, each bed having a locker and small table beside it. All of them had been stripped and neatly folded fresh linen had been piled at the bottom of each bed.

'This room is quite free so you can pick whichever beds you fancy,' Miss Mulgrew informed them.

She then went on. 'I'm going to leave you now and will return in half an hour by which time I'll expect you to have unpacked *and* made up your beds. All right?'

'Right, miss!' they all chorused.

'When I come back I'll take you on a tour of the building and grounds, showing you where things are and we'll end up in the refectory where you'll have lunch with the second sitting. We have two sittings for every meal, which I'll explain further to you later.

'After lunch you will meet Mr Lewis who is head of this institution.'

Sadie held up her hand.

'Yes . . . what's your name?'

'Sadie Smith, miss. Does that mean Mr Lewis is above the matron?'

Miss Mulgrew's face cracked into a smile. 'An intelligent question. The matron is Mrs Forbes, who you will also meet later. And yes, Matron is responsible to Mr Lewis.'

'Please, miss?'

'What's your name?'

'Pat Black, miss. Please, miss, where's the toilet? I'm bursting.'

They all laughed at that, the first sign of levity since coming in sight of the Home.

Miss Mulgrew grinned. 'Out of here and directly on the left,' she replied.

'May I . . . ?'

'Yes, of course.'

Pat rushed from the dormitory and somehow that small incident, and Miss Mulgrew's relaxed reaction to it, took the edge off their fear and apprehension.

'Half an hour now, don't forget,' Miss Mulgrew reminded them, and with that left them to their own devices.

Sadie had already eyed up the beds and decided which one she wanted. Running over to it she threw her suitcase on to it. 'Bags I have this bed!' she shouted.

'And I want this one!' Janet declared, throwing her suitcase on to the next bed up from Sadie's.

A wild scramble then ensued until everyone had laid claim to a bed, with a few left over.

'Hard as iron,' Janet moaned, bouncing on her mattress.

Sadie felt hers which was the same. They'd had lovely soft comfortable mattresses at Babies Castle.

'I suppose we'll get used to them,' she muttered philosophically.

'I suppose so,' Janet echoed.

Sadie sat on her bed and gazed around the room. The walls and ceiling were painted a dull shade of green, the woodwork brown. The floor was wooden and highly polished and the curtains hanging at the four windows were green.

'We'd better get cracking,' Janet said. 'Half an hour isn't that long.'

'Bed or unpacking first?'

'Bed?'

'Bed!' Sadie agreed.

When her bed was made up, Sadie set about putting her few things away. She smiled when she came to her most precious possession, the pair of scarlet ribbons her mother had bought her the day she'd taken her to Babies Castle.

It upset Sadie that she couldn't remember what her mother or the rest of her family looked like. Over the years their faces had faded from her memory till they'd eventually disappeared altogether.

What had become of them all? she wondered. Where were they now? She could vaguely recall certain events and her father's coughing. But no faces – where the faces should have been was now blank.

Very carefully she rewrapped the ribbons in the tissue paper Miss Tupper had once given her, and placed them at the back of the shelf situated at the top of her locker.

They were all ready and waiting when Miss Mulgrew returned, which pleased the housemother. They'd got off to a good start.

'Right girls, follow me in a line of twos,' she said.

When the line was formed, with Sadie and Janet side by side, they set off.

Mr Lewis beamed at the new arrivals over the rim of his gold-framed spectacles. He was a short, fat man who positively exuded charm and *bonhomie*. His nickname among the staff, which he knew nothing about, was 'the cherub'.

'Welcome girls, welcome!' he declared in a lightish voice.

'Say good day, Mr Lewis,' Miss Mulgrew instructed.

'Good day, Mr Lewis,' the girls parrotted together.

'And a good day to you too.'

They were in a small, square shaped hall which boasted a magnificent stone fireplace. Above the fireplace hung a painting of Dr Barnardo that had been executed shortly before the doctor's death in 1905.

'I hope, sincerely hope, you enjoy your stay with us here,' Mr Lewis went on. 'A stay destined to be a short one.'

Sadie glanced at Janet. What was this?

Mr Lewis clasped his hands behind his back, raised himself up on to his toes, then dropped down again. 'A short one,' he repeated, and paused once more.

'And do you know why?'

The question was purely rhetorical, he didn't expect an answer. 'Because you girls are extremely lucky, indeed fortunate, in having been selected for a wonderful opportunity.'

'You girl,' he said, pointing at Sandra Ralston, 'selected for what?'

'A wonderful opportunity, sir.'

'Correct. Quite correct, young lady. A wonderful opportunity.'

He went up and down on his toes again. 'And that opportunity is you are being sent abroad to begin a brand new life.'

'Abroad!' someone gasped.

'Abroad,' he repeated.

Sadie was stunned, as were most of the others present. They'd had no inkling whatever that this was in the wind.

'The Dominions need new blood, fresh blood, to help them expand already blossoming populations. And we at Dr Barnardo's have been assisting in supplying that new, fresh and, above all, *British* blood.'

Mr Lewis went on, his voice crackling with enthusiasm. 'You will be going to young countries abounding with potential, countries that can offer you far, far more than the mother country.

'Why!' he cried out, 'From now on, the world is literally your oyster. Isn't that so, Miss Mulgrew?'

'Quite so, Mr Lewis,' she confirmed.

He beamed at her, then brought his gaze back to the girls standing before them. 'How lucky you all are. I envy you, you know what? I envy you!'

Young countries abounding with potential, those words revolved round in Sadie's mind. What did that mean? She couldn't conceive of leaving Scotland, the thought had never crossed her mind. And now she'd been told she was going abroad to the Dominions.

'It's not only Barnardo's that is sending children, so too are many other institutions and charities throughout the length and breadth of Great Britain. Large parties are being sent to Canada, Rhodesia, Australia and New Zealand, these last two countries are at completely opposite ends of the globe, the furthest flung representatives of our commonwealth and empire. Isn't that exciting?'

Sadie didn't find it exciting at all – not only abroad, but to the *completely opposite end of the globe*! It seemed very frightening to her.

'And best of all, girls, the choice of where you go is entirely in your hands. You choose the country, the rest is up to us.'

He paused to glance from face to face. He couldn't remember how many times he'd made this speech, but every time he did he enjoyed it even more than before.

A hand crept up.

'Yes, that girl?' he said, pointing.

'Please, sir, what do we do when we get there?'

'Ah! I was just coming to that. You go and live with families where you will be treated as one of their own. In exchange for a little work, of course, for which you'll be paid. Oh yes! You will be earning wages from the day you start.

'What sort of families I hear you wonder? Families who are mainly to do with the land. Farmers and the like. You will be joining farming families through whom you will lead a thoroughly pleasant and healthy life in rural surroundings.'

Another hand went up. 'Yes?' he queried.

'Please, sir, when do we go?'

'That depends entirely upon which country you choose. But whichever, soon lassie, soon. A matter of several months at the most.'

He laughed at their expressions which delighted him.

'Now what I want you all to do is sleep on this, and then inform Miss Mulgrew first thing in the morning as to your choice of country. Miss Mulgrew will then pass that information on to me and I will set the necessary wheels in motion. Any further questions?'

'Please, sir,' piped up Margaret Swanson, raising a hand.

'Yes?'

'What if you don't want to go?'

That was the question Sadie had wanted to ask, now Margaret had done it for her.

'Of course you do! You'd be foolish not to. And you're not that, are you? You certainly don't look it.'

Margaret grinned sheepishly.

'Wonderful opportunities aren't to be missed, but grasped with alacrity.'

He pointed at Janet. 'What's alacrity, girl?'

'Quickly, sir.'

'Excellent. Quite correct. *Quickly!*'

'But what if I still don't want to go, sir?' Margaret persisted.

He smiled at her. 'I'm afraid you've no option, girl. We have decided you're going and so you will. But' – he paused dramatically – 'to a far better life, I promise you!'

Margaret appeared uncertain, but didn't speak further.

'Canada, Rhodesia, Australia and New Zealand,' Lewis repeated, eyes gleaming behind his gold-framed spectacles. 'A *wonderful* opportunity!'

Sadie was in bed and the lights had just been switched off. Throughout the dorm girls began whispering among themselves.

'Sadie?'

She turned to face Janet. 'What?'

'Have you decided yet?'

'Yes. I'm choosing Canada.'

'Why there?'

'Because it's closest. And therefore easiest to get back from.'

'I was considering Rhodesia. It's such a lovely name.'

'Fine if you like snakes.' Sadie had read that somewhere.

'Snakes!' Janet exclaimed in sudden alarm. 'Are there snakes there?'

'Millions of them. Rhodesia is in Africa and Africa is full of snakes. There are snakes in Canada, too, mind, but nowhere near as many.'

Snakes, Janet thought, and shuddered. She loathed creepy crawlies of any kind.

'Sadie, where are you going to go?' Fiona Salmon asked, who was sleeping on the other side of Sadie.

'Canada.'

'Me too. I can't wait to get there.'

'I'm choosing Australia,' Carrie Hedderwick quietly called out in the darkness.

'Same here,' said Pat Black. 'It'll be an awful long boat journey though.'

'Six weeks. I asked Miss Mulgrew about that earlier,' Marion Kirkbride stated.

'Six weeks!' Pat exclaimed in awe.

'Longer if you hit really bad weather,' Marion added.

'And longer if you're going to New Zealand,' said Sandra Ralston.

'Is that your choice?' Sadie queried.

'I don't know. I'm still undecided.'

'Well, you'll have to make up your mind by morning,' Pat warned her.

Sandra sighed. 'I think I'll choose New Zealand. Or maybe Rhodesia.'

'They've got millions of snakes in Rhodesia,' Janet informed her.

She was dead beat, Sadie thought, yet understandably wide awake. What a day it had been, first of all leaving Babies Castle, then arriving at this new Home to be more or less greeted with the bombshell that they would shortly be going abroad.

And after the meeting with Mr Lewis there had been school lessons followed by preparing food for the next day. Then there had been prayers and a bible reading. After which it had been time for bed. Like Babies Castle the routine didn't allow for a lot of free time in which to be idle.

'We'll be on the move again so soon it was hardly worthwhile unpacking,' Barbara McGurk complained.

'Where do you fancy?' Agnes asked her.

'I don't much care. Any of them will suit me.'

'Do they have wolves in Canada?' Janet asked Sadie.

'I believe so.'

'I don't much like the idea of those either.'

'They aren't as slimy as snakes,' Sadie replied.

'That's true,' Janet said.

'Snakes are horrible.'

Janet nodded. She couldn't have agreed more.

'Wolves don't scare me half as much.'

Janet wasn't sure she agreed with that.

The whispering continued for quite some while until eventually, one by one, the girls fell asleep.

That night Sadie dreamt of her family, only where their heads should have been were those of snakes and wolves.

In the morning, directly after breakfast, they told Miss Mulgrew what they had decided and she jotted it down in a notebook.

'I belong to Glasgow, dear old Glasgow town, there's nothing the matter with Glasgow except it's going round and round . . .'

Sadie was enjoying the singing coming from the next compartment along the train, it contained half a dozen kilted soldiers on the first stage of rejoining their regiment in Gibraltar. Chrissie MacLean, one of their party, and a brazen hussy, had spoken to them.

'I'm so excited my goosepimples have goosepimples,' Janet said quietly to Sadie who grinned at her.

She was a bit that way herself, Sadie thought. Her initial reserve about going to Canada had long since vanished, only to be replaced by mounting enthusiasm as the date of departure drew closer. Now the actual day had finally arrived, and that evening would find them well on their way.

Twenty-three girls from the Home were off to Canada, and of those five were from the Babies Castle contingent.

They were travelling down to Greenock under the supervision of Mrs Moffat, a representative of the Irene Dunbar Agency which had made all the arrangements. None of the girls as yet had any idea who they would eventually be staying with, but Sadie and Janet had requested that they stay with the same family, or failing that, with two families who lived close by.

'What an adventure, eh?' Janet breathed to Sadie.

'It certainly is.'

'Not that the Home was bad, in fact I got to rather like it in the end.'

Sadie had come to like it as well, because it transpired that the Home was a great improvement on what they had initially imagined. The building itself had remained slightly sinister, but they'd got used to that until eventually it hadn't bothered them in the least.

The compartment door slid open. 'All right?' Mrs Moffat demanded.

'Yes, thank you.'

'Good.' Mrs Moffat glanced in the direction the singing was coming from, and frowned. Trust her to join a train with drunken soldiers travelling on it. Not that they'd been any trouble, she reminded herself, but you could never be too sure.

'You know where I am if you need me,' she said and with that slid the door closed and left them to themselves.

'Look!' Jean Hay squealed, pointing out of the window.

The Firth of Clyde had suddenly come into view, its blue water glinting in the winter sunshine. A solitary single-sailed fishing boat could be seen beating down the Firth.

'Isn't that bonny,' Jean Hay murmured appreciatively, staring out of the window.

'It's beautiful,' Janet stated, going one step further.

It was, Sadie thought, and very soon, she and the others would be sailing down that same strip of water. Her pulse raced with excitement.

'She'll be coming round the mountains when she comes, she'll be coming round the mountains when she comes . . .' the soldiers sang, their voices even louder and more raucous than before.

'I wonder what the food will be like on board?' Agnes Aitken said to no one in particular.

'Hopefully yummy,' grinned Elspeth Cochrane who was thin as a reed, yet ate twice as much as any of the other girls. At the Home Mrs Forbes had several times had her checked for worms, but luckily the tests all proved negative. She was simply a huge eater who never seemed to put on any weight.

They stayed in sight of the Firth after that, as it gradually widened and wound its way seaward.

'Greenock! It has to be,' Jean Hay declared, indicating a town that had appeared further along the coast.

'I should think that's right,' Sadie nodded.

'And I can see big ships,' Jean went on.

The girls all crowded round the window, wanting to miss nothing.

Sadie spotted the ships Jean was referring to. One could be seen plainly, the others just stacks and sections of super-structures sticking above buildings.

'I wonder which of those is ours?' Agnes Aitken breathed.

Sadie hoped it wasn't the ship that they could see. Even at that distance she could make out that it was covered in rust.

They stayed at the window for a few minutes longer, then decided they'd better get their things down off the overhead racks where they'd been put at the outset of their journey.

They climbed on to the seats where the taller girls helped those who couldn't reach that high. Sadie got her new coat down first, then her suitcase. She, like all the others, had been given new clothes before leaving the Home: a heavy coat, a navy blue cardigan, two dresses, underwear, a stout pair of shoes, thick socks and a knitted woollen hat.

Mrs Moffat slid back the door. 'When I give the word you'll all follow me on to the platform where you'll then wait till I see what arrangements have been made.'

'Yes, Mrs Moffat,' they replied.

'And no malarkey mind, this is a serious business.'

'No malarkey, Mrs Moffat,' Janet replied, tongue firmly in cheek.

Mrs Moffat stared hard at Janet, then swept away. The girls immediately burst out laughing.

'No malarkey, Mrs Moffat,' Fiona Salmon mimicked, taking off Janet.

A kiltie stopped at the door which had been left open. His face was flushed, his eyes unnaturally bright. It was obvious he'd been drinking.

'Everything all right, lassies?' he demanded in a friendly tone.

'Fine, thank you,' Agnes Aitken replied.

'Are you off to Canada with the other lassie?'

'That's right,' Agnes confirmed.

He raised a fist with its thumb extended upwards. 'Good on you. All the best for you and that.'

'And to you!' Agnes smiled.

He disappeared off in the direction Mrs Moffat had taken.

Agnes giggled. 'He was nice, don't you think?'

'I can see some more ships,' Jean declared excitedly from the window where she was standing, holding her case.

They came into the station and the train juddered to a halt.

'We're here,' Fiona said unnecessarily.

Sadie's stomach was heaving with excitement as she lined up behind Agnes, Janet behind her.

'Watch it!' she protested sharply when the line lurched forward to send her staggering.

'Sorry,' Jean called out. 'I just got carried away.'

The kiltie who'd talked to them charged back past their compartment to be greeted by his pals with an expletive that made Sadie lower her gaze in embarrassment.

A furious Mrs Moffat, who'd clearly also heard the word, appeared at their compartment door. 'Right girls, follow me,' she said through thinned lips, and led them on to the platform where the rest of the party was already waiting.

'Stay here till I return. Grace Western, you're in charge.' And with that Mrs Moffat strode purposefully off, glaring at the soldiers when she passed them. Grace had been put in charge because at fifteen she was the oldest girl in the party.

A few minutes later, Mrs Moffat had made her enquiries and was back. 'A short walk that's all,' she informed them.

As she spoke a pair of porters came up with trolleys on which she instructed them to stack their cases.

'The *SS Polynesian*,' she told the porter closest her, who nodded.

'*SS Polynesian*,' Janet whispered to Sadie. It was the first time they'd heard the name of their ship.

'Sounds nice.'

Janet thought so too. '*SS Polynesian*,' she repeated.

Sadie glanced up at some gulls crying and wheeling overhead. The smell of the sea was strong in her nostrils when they moved off.

Sadie would have called it more than a short walk, but eventually they arrived at a quayside where the ship was berthed. Sadie was relieved to see it wasn't the rusty tub she'd spied from the train.

The ship had two gangways running down to the quay, up the nearest of which a cartful of luggage was being drawn by several seamen. Passengers were leaning on railings at various levels looking down curiously.

'In here,' Mrs Moffat said, ushering them towards a wooden building. Once inside she asked the porters to stand with them while she went off to make further enquiries.

It didn't take long for the formalities to be gone through, then they were making for the for'rad gangway, the gangway reserved for passengers. The aft one was for luggage and crew.

SS Polynesian was emblazoned in large white letters on the ship's prow. Sadie wondered what the SS stood for. She'd have to find out.

A woman standing on deck waved at Mrs Moffat who returned the wave. Mrs Moffat then herded the girls up the gangway, shooing them as though they were a herd of geese.

A thrill ran through Sadie as she stepped on to the metal deck, moving along the deck to make room for the others coming behind.

'Everything hunky dory?' the woman who'd waved at Mrs Moffat demanded, shaking her by the hand.

'Yes, thank you, Sybil. No problems at all.'

'Good! Good!' Sybil enthused.

'Girls!' Mrs Moffat said, indicating them to gather round. 'This is where I leave you. From here on you are under the auspices of Mrs Pringle, one of three adults who will be accompanying you and the other children to Canada.'

Mrs Pringle smiled warmly at them.

'All that remains for me to say,' Mrs Moffat went on, 'is good luck to each one of you.'

'Thank you, miss,' some of them replied.

Mrs Moffat handed over their documents to Mrs Pringle who stuffed them into the Gladstone bag she was carrying. Mrs Pringle then kissed Mrs Moffat on the cheek.

'Goodbye, girls!' Mrs Moffat cried gaily, and went off back down the gangway.

'When do we set sail, please?' Fiona Salmon asked Mrs Pringle.

'In just over an hour. Yours is one of the last parties to arrive.' She took a deep breath. 'Now I

67

think it best I get you down below and into your cabins.'

A terribly elegant lady dressed in the most gorgeous fur coat and matching hat strolled by. Sadie gaped at her. The woman might have popped straight out of a glossy magazine.

'Look at her!' Janet whispered.

'I am. Isn't she something?'

'Something else,' Janet agreed.

Both girls were thinking the same thing. That some day, somehow, they would love to look just like that.

'Come along!' Mrs Pringle commanded, and made for an open hatchway which she ducked through.

The smell inside the ship was most distinctive. Sadie couldn't even have begun to describe it, except to say that it had an oily undertone to it.

'What about our suitcases?' an anxious Beth Coburn demanded of Mrs Pringle.

'Not to worry. They'll be taken direct to the cabins,' Mrs Pringle replied.

Sadie gazed about her, fascinated by the strangeness of her surroundings. She overheard a steward in conversation with a passenger, and was entranced by his cockney accent.

A sign fixed to the bulkhead informed them they were on Green Deck. A flight of stairs took them to the deck below where the Purser's office was located.

Off in the distance Sadie spotted another group of girls dressed identically to themselves and then she saw a gang of boys in what was obviously the male version of their new clothes.

'Make sure we get in together,' Janet said to Sadie, who nodded.

They made their way to a lower deck where the distinctive ship smell was stronger than ever.

'Don't straggle now!' Mrs Pringle called back along the line, which immediately closed up.

What a big ship it was, Sadie thought, as they descended yet again.

A door was suddenly wrenched open and a middle-aged man thrust his head out. He glanced left and right as if looking for someone. 'Damn!' he muttered, and slammed the door shut again.

Sadie laughed, because his expression had been extremely comical.

A steward brushed past carrying a silver tray on which were some tea things. He smiled at the girls before hurrying on his way.

'Not again!' Fiona exclaimed when they were taken to an even lower level.

'We're going to end up in the bilges at this rate,' Isa McIntosh said to Kate Dyer.

'What are bilges?' Sadie queried, overhearing them.

'The very bottom of the ship,' Isa informed her.

Mrs Pringle held up a hand to stop the procession. 'The first eight girls in this cabin,' she said, and opened a door.

Sadie and Janet were among the second eight who claimed the cabin after that. Excitedly they piled inside and took possession of their bunks.

Sadie was on the bunk above Janet whom she now peered down at. 'No portholes,' she complained.

'We're below the waterline, idiot,' Kate Dyer said scathingly. 'If there were portholes all you would see would be the fish.'

Of course they were below the waterline, she should have realized that, Sadie told herself. She just hadn't been thinking.

'I wonder where the toilets are?' Janet mused.

'Why, do you want to go?' Sadie asked her.

Janet shook her head. 'I was simply wondering, that's all.'

The door opened and Mrs Pringle entered. 'Everything all right here?' she asked.

'Yes, Mrs Pringle,' they all replied.

'I'm in Cabin 46 with Miss Devitt should you need me. You'll meet Miss Devitt and Mr Barr later, they are the other supervisory adults. Now I want you to remain here until your luggage arrives which you can then unpack and put away. Any questions?'

There weren't any.

'Who's the oldest here?'

'I am,' Isa McIntosh said. Newly turned fourteen, she was six months older than her pal Kate.

'Then I'm putting you in charge of this cabin. What's your name?'

'Isa McIntosh, Miss.'

'You other girls will do as Isa says. Is that clear?'

'Yes, miss!'

'You can rely on me to keep order, miss,' Isa growled, a joke as the other girls well knew. You couldn't have found a sweeter, kinder lass than Isa.

'There's no need to go over the top,' a slightly alarmed Mrs Pringle warned her.

Isa's face broke into a smile. 'Don't worry, miss. We'll all get on like a house on fire in here, I promise you.'

'Hmmh!' murmured Mrs Pringle. 'Let's hope you do.'

'Mrs Pringle!' a voice called out in the corridor, causing Mrs Pringle to leave the cabin abruptly.

'Listen!' exclaimed Sadie a few moments later.

'I can hear it too. What is it?' said Minnie Jones who'd literally cocked an ear.

'The ship's engines?' Jean Hay suggested.

'I think you're right. What else could it be?' Isa nodded.

The sound was a far off rumbling that gave the impression of having tremendous power about it. Sadie placed a palm against the steel bulkhead to find it was vibrating slightly.

It wasn't a very large cabin for eight of them, Sadie thought, they were going to be awfully cramped. The one thing she was going to find strange was not having any windows to look out of – it was going to be like living inside a metal box.

Kate opened the door because she heard a commotion outside. She discovered several seamen distributing their luggage from trolleys similar to the ones the porters ashore had used.

Sadie retrieved her suitcase and took it into the cabin where she began unpacking as Mrs Pringle had instructed.

'Can we go and explore?' Sadie asked Isa when she and Janet had finished this task.

Isa frowned. 'I don't know.'

'Mrs Pringle said we were to stay here until our luggage arrived and then unpack. She didn't mention anything else.'

'Tell you what,' proposed Isa. 'I'll nip along to her cabin and ask her. What was that number again?'

'Cabin 46,' Elspeth Cochrane reminded Isa. 'And I'd like to go exploring too.'

Isa vanished out of the door to return a few minutes later. 'There's no reply and she isn't in any of the other cabins belonging to our party. Nobody knows where she or the other two adults are.'

'So can we go?' Sadie persisted.

Isa thought further on the matter. 'No more than twenty minutes then. Is that a promise?'

'A promise,' Sadie assured her.

Sadie and Janet went off in one direction, Elspeth and Jean in another, 'We mustn't get lost,' Sadie said.

They hadn't gone far when they were stirred by a delicious smell of cooking food. A little further on they came to the galley where a number of tall-hatted chefs were toiling over the evening meal, lunch having already been served.

'Hoi!' a steward shouted at them when they'd gone up a number of decks.

Sadie and Janet turned to face him.

71

'You can't go along there. Can't you read?' He pointed to a sign which stated 'First Class Only'.

'Sorry,' Sadie apologized. 'We didn't see it.'

The steward grunted and hurried away.

Sadie and Janet stared into a lounge abounding with club armchairs and deep cushioned sofas. Ferns grew out of tubs while in one corner stood a small palm tree. A man wearing a Panama hat was chatting to the elegant lady who'd so impressed them earlier.

'Might have guessed she was first class,' Janet muttered.

'Probably absolutely rolling in it,' Sadie speculated, but completely without malice.

'Or her husband is,' Janet giggled.

Sadie contemplated what it must be like having a rich husband, where money was no object. She sighed at the thought.

'Come on, we'd better get back or we'll be late,' Sadie said.

'Aw! Just when I was beginning to enjoy myself.'

'I gave a promise and I'm not going to break it.'

Janet pulled a face, knowing Sadie was right. They both had one last lingering look at the elegant lady, then retraced their steps.

A flushed Mrs Pringle breezed into the cabin. 'I'm taking all those who want to come up on deck to watch the ship get under way,' she announced.

Sadie whooped and leapt from her bunk to the floor. All eight of them went, joining the others already outside in the corridor.

As they made their way upwards they merged with other parties of boys and girls, one group led by a woman Sadie correctly guessed to be Miss Devitt and later a group of lads led by Mr Barr.

Miss Devitt was younger than Mrs Pringle, but plain, whereas Mrs Pringle was really rather pretty. Mr Barr had a dashing, cavalry officer air about him. He spoke with a posh accent and sported a neat little moustache.

Sadie noticed there were an assortment of outfits being worn by the boys and girls. She assumed that all the children were from other institutions and charities.

Somewhere a female laughed stridently, which was followed shortly by the pop of a champagne bottle.

Outside the winter sun was streaming down making everything look bright and jolly. A band was playing on the quayside while aft a great many streamers had been thrown from ship to shore, linking the two.

As Sadie watched the second gangway was pulled free, and then trundled away.

The band broke into 'Scotland the Brave', and then a woman began sobbing, stifling her sobs with a scrap of hanky she held to her face. A man standing beside her, presumably her husband, put a comforting arm round her shoulders.

A loud cheer went up as the first rope left its capstan to splash into the water. As the third rope went there was a hoot from the ship's funnel.

Janet took Sadie's hand in her own. 'I've gone shivery all over,' she confided. Sadie knew exactly what she meant. She felt the same herself.

Some boys cheered, yelled, and waved their flat caps in the air. One unfortunate let go of his which went sailing away to land among the band.

The last rope had gone now, the *Polynesian*'s propellers churning up white foam at the rear of the ship. There was another hoot from the funnel, this somehow more urgent than the previous one.

Excitement gripped Sadie. She squeezed Janet's hand and Janet squeezed back.

'We're on the move,' Minnie Jones said beside them.

Sadie gazed down at the widening band of water between the ship and quayside. They were most definitely on the

73

move. The band was belting out 'Will ye no' come back again . . .'

The woman with the scrap of hanky collapsed into her husband's arms. He murmured soothing words in her ear as he gently, and with great tenderness, stroked her hair.

'Goodbye, Scotland! Goodbye!' Beth Coburn shouted, dancing up and down.

Everywhere people were waving frantically, both aboard ship and on the quayside.

'I'll write as soon as I can!' a man cried out, somehow making himself heard above the din.

As the *Polynesian* moved out into deeper water, the girls watched as the figures on the quayside shrank till they were no bigger than toy soldiers.

A number of the passengers started to disperse. Others remained rooted to the spot, eyes glued to the shore and the sprawl of Greenock.

'I want everyone to return to their cabins as I shall be bringing Miss Devitt and Mr Barr round to meet you all,' Mrs Pringle smiled.

Sadie and her companions joined those going below.

The food on the ship was simply gorgeous, Sadie thought, as she left the dining-room where they'd had their first meal. Food at the Home and at Babies Castle before that had been good, but this was in a different class altogether.

She stopped by a porthole, waiting for Janet who'd gone off to the ladies. They had planned to go on a longer and more comprehensive exploratory trip than their last one.

It appeared they were to be allowed a considerable amount of freedom, Sadie thought. Mrs Pringle and her colleagues weren't turning out to be the keepers they might have been.

It was pitch black outside, she noted, peering through the porthole. And there were lights in the far distance, that twinkled like fireflies.

74

It suddenly dawned on her that these lights were the last she'd see of Scotland, certainly for a long time to come.

Her eyes misted over and a large lump blocked her throat. She hadn't been all that affected when they'd left Greenock earlier, but it seemed to catch up with her now.

'Scotland,' she whispered. First her family had been taken away from her, now the land of her birth, a land which she regarded, as nearly all Scots do, as a physical extension of herself. And now this extension of herself was disappearing over the horizon.

Grief rose in her, and self-pity. She didn't want to go to Canada, she wanted to stay in Scotland where her heart, family and roots were.

She choked as the words from 'Scotland the Brave' echoed in her brain. Land of my heart forever, Scotland the Brave!

It wasn't fair, she thought. It just wasn't fair!

'How do you feel now?' Sadie asked Janet, whose reply was a dreadful groan.

'That bad, eh?'

'Worse,' Janet mumbled.

'I'm dying,' Kate Dyer said from her bunk where she was lying with the bedclothes pulled right up over her head.

Minnie Jones, also seasick, moaned as the ship rolled particularly violently. Then she moaned again when the stern of the ship, having reared high out of the water, smacked back down again.

The gale had started sometime during the previous night, but the girls had only noticed it once they woke up. They'd all tried to get up, but the rolling and pitching had soon sent Janet, Kate, Isa and Minnie diving back into their bunks. All had been provided with receptacles, courtesy of their steward, in which to be sick. Minnie had already used hers.

'There was hardly anyone in the dining-room. Mrs Pringle got there, but had to hurry away again shortly afterwards. Mr Barr is also ill,' Sadie said to Janet who couldn't have cared less. All she was concerned about was herself.

Sadie grabbed the side of her bunk as the *Polynesian* rolled once more, her feet nearly sliding away from under her. She had every sympathy for her cabin mates, and was only too thankful she was unaffected. In fact, she was actually enjoying the rough weather, though she didn't dare admit it to the others. She found it exhilarating.

'Is there anything I can do?' she asked, her question directed to all the seasick girls.

'Stop the ship doing this,' Minnie murmured.

Minnie's face was a pale shade of green, Sadie noted. Janet's was a dirty white, as were Kate's and Isa's.

'You know I can't do that,' she grinned at Minnie. 'How about a drink of water?'

'Noooo,' Minnie groaned, praying with all her soul that this would soon cease. She'd have given anything, pledged anything, made any promise, if only the rolling would stop.

'I'll leave you to it then,' Sadie said, wanting to be away from the cabin which stank of vomit. 'Ta ra!' she added, trying not to sound too cheerful.

The only reply she got was Kate throwing up yet again into her bowl.

Out in the corridor Sadie wondered what she should do. Try the various lounges she thought, there were bound to be games going on there.

She hadn't gone far when she met Fiona Salmon staggering in her direction.

'The weather's getting worse. I'm going to have to go to bed,' Fiona said in a shaky voice.

'You too?'

'I feel really foul.'

'Did you have any breakfast?'

Fiona shook her head. 'I managed a cup of tea, but that was it. And I think that'll be coming up before long.'

Fiona wiped away beads of sweat that had gathered on her forehead. Her skin was cold and clammy.

'Do you want me to help you back to the cabin?' Sadie offered.

'I'll be all right, thanks.'

Sadie watched Fiona stumble away, and then continued on her way. She was only too delighted that she hadn't as yet been affected.

The first lounge she went into contained a group of the boys and girls, some of whom were playing ludo, others snakes and ladders.

A door flew open and the wind howled in. 'Come and see the whales!' a young lad shouted excitedly.

Whales! Sadie didn't want to miss them. She ran to the door and went out on to the deck where she clung to a metal railing.

She spotted the whales right away. Three of them were swimming on the surface about five hundred yards off-ship. What majestic and awe-inspiring creatures they were, she thought. Suddenly, the largest of the whales spouted which caused exclamations of delight among those watching.

'Just like a roller coaster,' a Canadian man commented as the *Polynesian* rolled violently again. He then turned his attention on Sadie.

'You OK, hon?' he asked her, as she clutched the railing with both hands.

'Yes, thank you,' she nodded.

The man frowned, thinking these kids shouldn't be out on deck in such weather. It would be only too easy for one of them to go overboard.

A sailor obviously felt the same way for he was shooing the children back into the lounge.

'They're diving!' a boy cried, pointing out to sea.

The middle whale sank out of sight, its huge flukes waggling in the air before following the massive body down into the deep. The other two did likewise, before vanishing underwater.

A sigh of disappointment went up from the onlookers who'd thoroughly enjoyed this unscheduled treat.

Sadie didn't know why, but she glanced over at the boy who'd shouted that the whales were diving. He was about her own age, perhaps a little older. He had a strong, slightly cheeky face topped by spiky hair. His shoulders were broad and powerful, his body chunky.

He, sensing he was being stared at, rounded on Sadie and for the space of a few seconds, their eyes locked. Then she looked away.

'Come on, miss, inside. It's dangerous for you out here,' the sailor said, as he reached Sadie.

She gasped as spume broke over the side of the deck drenching them both.

'See what I mean,' the sailor muttered, and grasping Sadie by the arm led her to the door she'd come through.

Back in the lounge, she wiped the water from her face and smoothed down her partially wet hair.

'Did you see the whales?' a girl in a Barnardo's outfit demanded.

'I did.'

The girl screwed up her face in disappointment. 'I missed them.'

She would go to the nearest toilet and tidy herself up, Sadie decided. Then she remembered the boy and realized he hadn't come back into the lounge. She looked out on the deck, but he had gone.

The toilet, she thought, and headed off in that direction.

By the time she'd finished drying off, she'd completely forgotten the boy who'd momentarily caught her attention.

It was a horrible day, the sky steel grey, the weather bitter cold. Sadie and Janet, who were standing on deck, were glad of the heavy coats they'd been given. Neither had ever experienced cold like this before.

They gazed at Halifax Docks which they were slowly steaming towards. It wouldn't be long now till they landed on Canadian soil.

'Let's keep our fingers crossed that we are going to be with the same family,' Janet said to Sadie, taking her by the hand. They still didn't know their ultimate destination or the name of the people taking them in. Mrs Pringle had told them that information would be forthcoming on their arrival in Halifax.

Sadie took a deep breath, and wished she hadn't. The air was so cold it made her chest ache.

Somewhere a horn blew, a sad melancholy sound that came wafting over the bluey grey water.

'The Canadian flag,' said Janet, indicating a small motor craft passing relatively close by, the flag fluttering proudly from its stern.

The docks came gradually nearer, its wharves and buildings becoming larger and more distinguishable. Ships and boats were everywhere, of all shapes and sizes. There was a tanker, beside it a medium-sized cargo vessel and to one side a passenger liner twice the size of their own.

'Snow!' Sadie exclaimed, glancing up into a sky suddenly filled with swirling flakes.

The fall of snow got heavier until at last the laughing girls, who were adoring it, were driven inside. Still giggling, they shook their coats and hats before going down to the cabin where they'd been instructed to wait prior to disembarkation.

'Here she is now!' said an impatient Elspeth Cochrane standing by their open cabin door. She was referring to Mrs Pringle.

Sadie glanced meaningfully at Janet. This was it.

When the girls were all collected in the corridor Mrs Pringle led them upwards to Green Deck, their point of disembarkation.

Arriving on deck the girls found the *SS Polynesian*, or the Rolling Polly as some wag had nicknamed her, securely moored with covered gangways in place.

'Keep together now, girls!' Mrs Pringle shouted, heading for another far bigger group of girls milling about further down the deck. Mr Barr came running back up the nearest gangway having just delivered a contingent of boys ashore.

'I'll take this lot down now,' he called to Mrs Pringle, who nodded her agreement.

Sadie streamed down the gangway with the rest of them, emerging on to a bustling area where the first thing she saw was a sign saying 'Pier 21'.

A wind had sprung up that tore at them, and was so forceful it would have blown over more than one of the smaller girls if they hadn't been so densely packed together.

They went into a very long, open-ended, passageway along which the wind howled and screamed like a demented banshee. The same icy wind cut through their coats as though they were made of nothing more substantial than thin cotton.

Sadie shivered, and slapped her free hand against her side. Thank goodness for the woollen gloves she was wearing, without them her hands would have been frozen solid.

The passageway was endless, but eventually they reached a drab, high-ceilinged hall.

They were taken over to where the boys were standing round a man they didn't recognize. Then Mr Barr was off again, back to the ship.

The new man was late middle-aged and wore a Homburg. He was carrying a cardboard folder while at his feet lay a battered, much used, canvas bag.

About a yard away from him was a flat cart piled high with brown paper bags.

Mr Barr returned sooner than they'd expected, having met Mrs Pringle and Miss Devitt with the remainder of the girls halfway back to the ship. These girls now mingled in with those already waiting.

Mr Barr held up a hand for attention, which he got immediately. 'Boys and girls,' he said, 'this is Mr Schroeder of our organization who will now speak to you. Mr Schroeder!'

'Thank you, Mr Barr,' Schroeder smiled. He paused before addressing the children. 'Welcome to Nova Scotia, and Canada. I am now going to read out your names in alphabetical order. When your name is called, come up to me and I will give you a button on which will be typed your name, the name of the family you are going to, the town or village where they live, and a group number.

'You will then take one of these sacks,' he pointed to the cart on which the paper bags were piled, 'after which you will form yourselves into your pre-arranged groups.

'Group one forming there,' he indicated a spot on his right, 'group two there,' he jabbed a finger at a spot behind him, 'and group three there.' He pointed to a spot on his left. 'Is that clear?'

'Yes, sir,' many young voices replied.

He nodded. 'OK. I'll start then.'

He opened his folder, extracted a sheaf of papers and then took out a pen.

'Adams, John!' he called out.

A thin, gawky lad emerged from the press of boys and crossed to Schroeder. The next to be summoned was Agnes Aitken.

'That's me,' said Janet when her turn came shortly after that. Going to Schroeder she was presented with her button, which informed her she was in group three and bound for a place by the name of Clarke City, Quebec.

Being an S it was ages before Sadie's name was called. She smiled thinly when it was.

Schroeder ticked her name off the list, then handed her her button with the instruction to pin it on after she'd read

81

it. She was destined for Peterawa, Ontario. Her group, number two.

Her heart sank on reading the latter. How could she and Janet be with the same family, or even close to one another, if they were in different groups.

'Please, sir . . .'

'Move along, Miss Smith, please,' he said curtly.

'But, sir . . .'

'I said move along.' This time his tone was terse and clipped.

Sadie joined group two where she was stared at by a horrified Janet.

Sadie shook her head, then shrugged her shoulders. She would try and speak with Schroeder when he'd come to the end of his list.

The final name was that of Yuill, Eric. He was group two, same as Sadie.

Mr Barr, Mrs Pringle and Miss Devitt clustered round Mr Schroeder and a quiet conversation ensued. Something made Miss Devitt laugh and Mr Barr smile with amusement.

'Sadie?' whispered Janet, tugging at her arm.

Sadie turned to her friend who'd sneaked over from group three.

'I'm going to Clarke City, Quebec. What about you?'

'Petewa . . . or whatever! Ontario,' Sadie replied, stumbling over the unfamiliar name.

Janet's already long face fell even further.

'I'll speak to Mr Schroeder in a moment. Perhaps there's been a mix-up or he can rearrange things,' Sadie declared hopefully.

Janet laid her brown paper bag down beside Sadie's. She'd already established that the bags contained food and drink.

Schroeder glanced at his watch and frowned. Time was getting on. He had another quick word with his colleagues, then switched his attention back to the children.

The three groups fell quiet when he gestured for silence. 'Let me now explain the significance of these groups. Groups one and two will head shortly by train for Ontario, group one travelling straight through to Toronto where they will be met by another member of our organization. Group two will accompany them as far as Montreal where they will transfer to another train that will take them north. That group will be dropped off individually and in pairs along the way. Group three will be coming with me, as they have been placed in Nova Scotia, New Brunswick and lower Quebec.'

He paused, then went on. 'Buses are waiting outside to take groups one and two to the station, so could they now please collect up their bits and pieces and follow Mr Barr, Mrs Pringle and Miss Devitt. That is all.'

'Now, talk to him now,' Janet urged Sadie, pushing her forward.

Sadie strode purposefully over to Mr Schroeder. 'Please, sir, can I speak to you?'

He frowned down at her.

'Sadie Smith, sir. I tried to speak earlier.'

'Is something wrong, Smith?' he queried.

'My friend and I, sir, Janet Bone that is, we'd asked to be with the same family, or at least close to one another. But she's to go to Quebec while I'm for Ontario. Please sir, can you help?'

His severe expression softened a little. 'I don't know what you were told in Scotland, or what promises were made. What I do know is I can't alter what has already been settled. I'm sorry.'

'You can't, sir?' Sadie echoed, her voice betraying her bitter disappointment.

He shook his head. 'You'll just have to say goodbye to your friend, I'm afraid.'

'Come along groups one and two!' Mr Barr commanded in a loud voice.

Sadie and Janet looked at one another, each feeling absolutely wretched at being parted. They'd been best pals a long time.

'Goodbye then,' Janet husked.

'Goodbye.'

'I hope everything goes well for you.'

'And you.'

'I was sure . . . I was certain . . .' Janet trailed off.

'Good luck.'

'And you.'

They fell into one another's arms to clutch each other tightly. Nor were they the only ones, other friends were also saying emotional farewells.

Sadie tore herself away from Janet, picked up her brown paper bag and suitcase, and hurried after those from groups one and two already on the move. A disconsolate Janet rejoined her group.

'Minnie's gone with group three,' Elspeth Cochrane said, falling in alongside Sadie.

'Oh?'

'And Jean Hay.'

Sadie sniffed, willing herself not to cry. She was going to miss Janet dreadfully.

'Where are you going?' she asked Elspeth.

'Clayton in Ontario.'

'Is that group two?'

'Yes.'

'Then you'll be changing trains with me in Montreal.'

The two buses waiting for them were sleek, silver-coloured single deckers, the roofs of which were already several inches thick with snow. Sadie and Elspeth climbed aboard the second one where they sat side by side.

Throughout the ocean crossing Sadie had been eagerly looking forward to arriving in Canada, but it hadn't turned out as she'd expected. She felt thoroughly miserable, dejected and somehow very alone.

Miss Devitt got on their bus, Mr Barr and Mrs Pringle the lead one. And soon they were off, *en route* to the station.

'I wonder how long we'll be on the train for?' Elspeth mused.

'No idea. But it must be a pretty long journey if they've given us this amount to eat and drink.'

Elspeth nodded, that made sense. The contents of the paper bags were substantial.

Sadie gazed out at the passing scene, familiar in some ways, yet totally alien in others. What big cars they had, and so many of them!

She removed the button she'd pinned to her coat lapel; it was a cardboard circle about four inches in diameter that had plain paper pasted to its front, and stared at the name of the people she would be staying with.

Trikhardt, what a strange name she thought. 'Trikhardt!' she muttered aloud.

'Eh?'

'Trikhardt, the name of the people I'm going to stay with.'

'Oh!'

'What about you?'

'Osborn.'

That sounded far more normal, Sadie thought. What sort of name was Trikhardt? It certainly wasn't Scots!

Elspeth opened her paper bag and peered into it. 'I think I'll have a sandwich to be getting on with.'

'But it isn't that long since we ate!'

'I know but . . .' Elspeth pulled a face. 'I get hungry quickly again.'

'Well, I wouldn't if I were you,' Sadie advised. 'As I've already said, we must be in for a pretty long train journey. Eat now and you could regret it later.'

'I suppose you're right,' Elspeth sighed, scrunching closed the top of her paper bag, removing temptation from sight.

The snow had almost stopped, Sadie noted. There was a lot of slush on the streets, and patches of ice round the kerbs.

The coaches drew to a halt in front of the railway station and they all got out. They then followed the adults into the station itself where they were taken to a waiting-room. Miss Devitt stayed with them while Mr Barr and Mrs Pringle went off.

'Shall we sit together on the train as well?' Elspeth asked Sadie.

'If you like'

Fiona Salmon came over. 'Are you group one or two?' she enquired.

'Two,' Sadie and Elspeth both answered.

'I'm one.'

A tannoy blared out, the female voice sounding as though she was speaking from inside a tin drum. The party of children were given a considerable amount of quizzical stares from passers-by. A couple of lads started larking about, and had to be told off by Miss Devitt.

Canadians certainly dressed differently to the British, Sadie thought. The men's lumber-jackets looked fun, as did the flattish, material hats with ear flaps they wore. She wouldn't have minded one of the latter at all.

She wondered how Janet was getting on, and just where her friend was at that moment. Was she also going by train? Couldn't be, Sadie decided, or surely they would all have come to the station together. There again, perhaps Halifax had more than one station? She was lost in her thoughts when Mr Barr and Mrs Pringle returned to announce they would now be boarding their train.

Like the buses, the train was different in design to its British counterpart. Its engine was absolutely massive, and reminded Sadie of the whales she'd seen.

Mr Barr paused to help one of the smaller girls who was having some kind of trouble, leaving Mrs Pringle to carve a way down the platform to their carriages, Miss Devitt bringing up the rear.

'Here we are!' Mrs Pringle cried gaily, stopping beside an open door.

Two black men in uniform appeared from inside the train to assist the children with their luggage. The carriages were very well laid out, with plush seats which Sadie and Elspeth sank into when they sat down.

'I like it!' Elspeth exclaimed in delight, and laughed.

Sadie liked it, too, this was luxury indeed. She closed her eyes, but quickly opened them again when Elspeth began bouncing up and down, which of course she copied.

'Everything all right, missy?' another uniformed black enquired as he passed by.

'Yes, thank you,' Sadie replied, thinking what shiny white teeth he had. Before the station she'd only ever seen black folk in magazines and on the rare occasions she'd gone to the pictures.

Elspeth giggled when the black man moved away, blacks were a new experience for her also.

Mrs Pringle bustled past, then Miss Devitt was there addressing them. 'We shall be saying goodbye to you here, children. Mr Barr, Mrs Pringle and myself will be returning on the *Polynesian* when she leaves.'

'You mean you're not staying on the train with us?' Sadie queried.

'That's correct. But you're not to worry. Everything has been taken care of and you will be well looked after.'

And with that Miss Devitt moved away to repeat what she'd said to Sadie and Elspeth. Further down the carriage Mr Barr was giving a version of the same speech to some boys.

'I didn't realize they wouldn't be accompanying us on the train,' Elspeth said.

'Me neither.'

Elspeth worried a nail.

'I don't suppose it matters all that much anyway,' Sadie said. 'We're all used to looking after ourselves.'

'Anyone brought up in a Home, irregardless of how good the Home is, has to be,' Elspeth agreed.

Which prompted Sadie to think of darling Miss Tupper whom she'd also lost. Her life to date seemed to consist of losing people. Her family, Miss Tupper and now Janet.

'I am going to have something to eat, whether I regret it later or not.' Elspeth lifted her paper bag on to her lap and delved into it.

'Hmmh!' she murmured in ecstasy, having bitten into a sandwich.

'What kind is it?' Sadie asked.

'Don't know. Some sort of fish.'

Sadie gazed at the sandwich Elspeth was holding. The filling was pinkish, salmon? Salmon was pink. 'Can I have a taste?'

'Sure.'

Sadie had a nibble. 'It's not salmon,' she pronounced.

'You've had salmon?'

'Once. It had a lovely flavour I'll never forget.'

'It's tuna, missy,' said the same black man as before, having suddenly reappeared beside them.

He giggled, which startled both Sadie and Elspeth. They were used to girls giggling, but a man doing it – it was extraordinary, and made them giggle even more.

'Tuna. You take Lincoln's word on that. You is eating tuna fish.'

'You're called Lincoln?' Sadie queried.

'I am, missy. Lincoln Washington Ulysses T. Harrison at your service.'

Sadie raised an eyebrow, talk about a mouthful! 'Pleased to meet you, Lincoln.'

'And a's pleased to meet you, miss.' He peered at her button. 'You is one of those getting off at Montreal?'

'That's right.'

'And you,' he added, peering at Elspeth's button.

'Me too,' she told him.

He beamed at them. 'Montreal is one real nice city. I been there many times. You staying in Montreal, missy?'

Sadie shook her head. 'I'm going to . . .' She consulted her button. 'Peterawa.'

'Peterawa,' he repeated. 'Never heard of that.'

'And I'm going to Clayton,' Elspeth chipped in, her sandwich momentarily forgotten.

'Never heard of that, neither. But here, I gotta move along. I got chores to do before we leave.' He gave them a broad wink. 'But I'll come back later and see how you doin'. OK?'

'OK,' Sadie smiled.

'We'll be all right if the people we're going to are as nice as him,' Elspeth commented after Lincoln had gone.

Sadie couldn't have agreed more.

It was ages before the train left, but at long last it did, pulling away from the platform where Mr Barr, Mrs Pringle and Miss Devitt stood waving, with some of the children waving back.

Once out of the station they saw that it had started to snow again.

'Montreal! Montreal!' Lincoln cried, making his way down the carriage.

'How are you two kids?' he asked, stopping beside Sadie and Elspeth whom he'd talked to several times during the journey from Halifax.

'Fine, thank you,' Elspeth replied.

'This is where I lose you, eh?'

Sadie nodded.

Lincoln stared at them sadly. He'd gleaned their story earlier when he'd given them some chocolate bars he'd just 'happened to come by' as he'd put it. He'd thought then, how awful it must be to be torn away from your native land at such a tender age and even worse, to be sent to live with strangers.

He bent over them, and whispered, 'Here, get your-selves something during your stopover in Montreal.' And with that he slipped them both a folded piece of paper.

Sadie gazed at the paper in amazement, then opened it up, and smoothed it flat. 'A dollar note!' she exclaimed.

He put a finger to his lips. 'Sshhh! It's a dollar, OK, but not a note. We says a bill over here.'

'A dollar bill,' Sadie nodded. 'Thank you.'

He straightened up and beamed down at them, his white teeth and the whites of his eyes gleaming out of his black face. 'The pleasure is all mine, ladies, I assure you.'

Sadie brought a hand to her mouth to cover her amusement and slight embarrassment. It was the first time she'd ever been called a lady.

'Goodbye then,' Lincoln went on, and shook hands with Sadie. When he'd completed that he shook Elspeth's hand. 'I sure hope you kids have all de luck dere is.'

'Thank you,' Elspeth smiled.

Throughout the carriage other farewells were being made as the group divided itself between those getting off and those continuing to Toronto.

Fiona Salmon came up and hugged them both, followed by Beth Coburn as she, too, was heading for Toronto.

Lincoln helped Sadie and Elspeth from the train, blowing them a kiss when they were safely on the platform with their luggage. He gave them a final wave, then disappeared back inside.

'Gather round me! Gather round me all the children from the Irene Dunbar Agency!' a female station official called out. Sadie and Elspeth joined those already milling round the woman.

The woman consulted the list that had been wired ahead to her, and counted their heads. When the one tallied with the other she instructed those now in her care to follow her.

They were still on the platform when the train moved off again. Sadie saw Fiona's face pressed to the window as their carriage went by. She would have waved but her hands were full with her suitcase and brown paper bag.

They trudged the length of the platform, then across a concourse till they arrived at a waiting-room where they were told by the female, who hadn't introduced herself, to wait. Their connecting train wouldn't be leaving for another hour and a quarter.

Everyone congregated round a large open fire, grateful for its heat as it had been freezing outside.

'Shall we go and spend our dollars?' Elspeth whispered to Sadie after the female had left them saying she'd return shortly.

'Do you think it's all right?'

Elspeth shrugged. 'Why not? She didn't say we had to stay in here.'

True enough, she hadn't, Sadie thought. 'Let's then.'

Out again on the concourse they both shivered. 'Canada certainly is cold,' Elspeth complained.

They wandered about till eventually they stopped in front of a hot dog stand. Elspeth gazed up at the painted picture of a hot dog drenched in tomato ketchup.

'I'm having one of these,' she declared.

Sadie decided she would also, so they gave the man their order and dollar bills.

'Ketchup or mustard?' the man queried, having filled a bun.

'Ketchup, please,' Elspeth quickly replied.

She sighed as she tasted hers. 'It's delicious.'

'And you, kid?'

'Same for me,' Sadie replied.

She had to agree with Elspeth, the hot dog was delicious. She hoped all Canadian food was going to be as tasty.

They spent the remainder of their dollars in a candy shop, then returned to the waiting-room where they were relieved to find they hadn't been missed.

'It's true I tell you!' Grace Western was saying to Isa McIntosh.

'You actually saw them kissing?'

Grace made the sign of the cross over her left breast. 'I swear to God I did. Mr Barr and Mrs Pringle. You should have seen the clinch, I wouldn't have been at all surprised if steam had come out their ears.'

Those listening laughed.

'Do you think they might become . . .' Agnes Aitken paused to gulp, '*lovers*?'

'I should think it's quite possible,' Grace replied airily.

Mr Barr and Mrs Pringle, kissing and lovers! Sadie could hardly believe what she was hearing. She, of course, knew what was meant by being lovers, she'd learnt all about that sort of thing ages ago.

'Wow!' Agnes exclaimed, eyes wide.

'Where did you see them kissing?' Josephine Martin asked Grace.

'Late one night I got out of bed and went to the lav. I heard something round the corner where the lav was, had a quick look and there they were. It might have been Romeo and Juliet except for their ages.'

'Is there a Mr Pringle?' Agnes queried.

Grace shrugged. 'No idea. Does anyone?'

No one had.

'I suppose she could be a widow or divorced,' Isa speculated.

'Or there again,' said a girl Sadie vaguely knew as Margie, 'maybe she's not. Maybe there's a Mr Pringle waiting at home while she's dallying with Mr Barr.'

Someone sniggered, followed by several people laughing.

Sadie glanced over to where some of the boys were variously squatting and kneeling on the floor playing marbles. Elspeth stripped the wrapper from a Tootsie Roll she'd bought, and began chewing on that.

'When I grow up I shall meet my Prince Charming,' Agnes Aitken suddenly declared, her eyes adopting a faraway look.

The person who'd sniggered before did so again, the sound unmistakably coming from the same source.

'He'll be handsome and rich and everything a Prince Charming should be,' Agnes went on.

'I don't care if mine's handsome just as long as he's *rich*,' Isa McIntosh said, which earned her a large laugh and a few mutterings of agreement.

'I wonder who we'll marry?' Elspeth said to Sadie.

'I wonder?' Sadie mused. 'I only ask that he's nice, that's all.'

'And madly in love with you, eh?'

Blond or dark haired, Sadie further wondered? Or perhaps he would have red hair. No, she decided. He wouldn't have that. She didn't particularly like red hair.

They were still chatting away nineteen to the dozen when the female station official arrived back to tell them they could now board their train, and if they would collect up their things she would lead them to it.

'Here we go again,' Sadie said, gathering her paper bag into her arms and then lifting up her suitcase.

'I could do with another of those hot dogs,' Elspeth said hungrily when they passed the stall.

They'd certainly been appetizing, Sadie thought. She could easily have eaten another herself.

Sadie and Elspeth sat together again on this train, along with Agnes who'd elected to join them. And luckily it wasn't long before the train got underway.

The new conductor was also black, though nowhere near as friendly as Lincoln. He gave them a lecture about behaving themselves, and promised to warn them in good time when their stop was coming up.

They'd been travelling for less than half an hour when they halted and lost their first child, a boy by the name of Lesley Graham.

Sadie explored the bottom of her paper bag to see what was left. The pickle was about the size of a sausage

93

and green in colour which Sadie didn't think looked too appetizing.

'If you don't want it I'll have it' Elspeth said hopefully.

Sadie passed the pickle over and delved again. This time she came up with a little tub marked *Jello*. What on earth was that?

'Same as our jelly, as in jelly and custard,' Elspeth informed her, munching on the pickle.

Sadie ate it with the small wooden spoon she'd been provided with, and decided that she was going to enjoy Canadian food.

Agnes Aitken was the next to leave them, then a pair of boys.

'Clayton! Who's for Clayton?' the conductor sang out.

Sadie and Elspeth's eyes met, Elspeth's filled with sudden fear and apprehension.

'Me!' Elspeth answered.

'Ten minutes, you got ten minutes to get ready,' the conductor told her.

'Ten minutes,' she nodded.

Sadie glanced out of the window, wincing at the weather. Sleet was lashing down, while as far as she could see looked like God forsaken wilderness. What sort of place was this? she asked herself. It appeared forbidding in the extreme and completely inhospitable.

'Will you walk me to the door?' Elspeth asked Sadie.

'Of course.'

Elspeth bit her lip. She'd have given anything for Sadie to be getting off with her.

Elspeth sat rigidly still, suitcase at her feet, waiting for the conductor to reappear – which he did all too quickly.

'Bye!'

'Good luck, Elspeth!'

'Bye, Els!'

The farewells and good wishes rang out as Elspeth, with Sadie in attendance, made her way up the carriage to the nearest door.

The train started to slow down, then drew into a platform where it stopped. Almost directly opposite the door were a man and woman dressed in rough working clothes sitting on a horse-drawn wagon. Elspeth knew instinctively that they'd come for her.

Sadie squeezed her arm, then kissed her lightly on the cheek. 'On you go,' she urged.

Elspeth stepped down on to the platform where she stood, waiting to be approached.

Sadie closed the door, and seconds later the train moved off again. As it did the man jumped from the wagon and began walking over to Elspeth. He hadn't quite reached her when they were both lost to Sadie's view.

She returned to her seat where three of them, herself, Elspeth and Agnes, had started out from Montreal.

Now only she was left.

Sadie woke to find her shoulder being gently shaken by the conductor. 'What time is it?' she mumbled, her mouth dry and tacky.

'Almost two o'clock. Your stop's next.'

Sadie yawned, still half asleep. Glancing about her she saw that the carriage had emptied further. Isa McIntosh had already left, as had Grace Western.

'Ten minutes,' the conductor said, and moved off.

Sadie rose to her feet and got herself ready. She remembered how anxious Elspeth had been at this point, and found herself feeling exactly the same way. She'd come to the end of a long journey.

Somebody was snoring, and Sadie grinned to see it was the girl named Margie. She was lying on the seat with her mouth wide open, her Adam's apple bobbing up and down every time she snored.

She folded her empty paper bag and laid it to one side to be collected by the cleaners. Then she sat and waited.

The conductor reappeared and beckoned to her. Picking up her suitcase she followed him to the carriage door where a boy was already standing with case in hand.

His face was familiar, she thought, frowning. Then she recognized him. He was the boy on the ship who'd shouted that the whales were diving. He had momentarily caught her attention, but she hadn't been aware of him since.

'Hello,' he said, pleasantly enough, though warily. 'I'm Robbie.'

'And I'm Sadie.'

'You're getting off here, too?' he said.

She nodded. 'Pete . . .' She hastily consulted her button. 'Peterawa.'

'That's it,' he agreed.

'I'm going to a family called Trikhardt.'

His eyebrows shot up in surprise. 'So am I, Trikhardt.'

Sadie peered at his button and saw that the family name printed there was the same.

The train slowed down, and the conductor who'd been attending to some business at the other side of the carriage rejoined them.

'Robbie what?' Sadie asked.

'Hendry. And you?'

'Smith.'

An awkwardness sprang up between them. She gazed down at her feet, he up at the roof.

Sadie's thoughts were racing. This boy, Robbie, and she were going to the same family. That meant they were to be pitched together like brother and sister.

She glanced quickly up at him, then dropped her gaze again to her feet. He seemed all right and his strong, slightly cheeky face wasn't unappealing.

She wondered what he thought of her? She couldn't sense any of the antagonism girls sometimes felt from boys who were uneasy in their company.

Would they get on? She certainly hoped so. Sadie then decided to do her best to ensure that they would. After

96

all, it was far better to have a friend and ally rather than an enemy.

Robbie, for his part, was feeling shy in the company of this good-looking lassie he was going to be staying with. He remembered her staring at him that day on the boat, and how she'd glanced away when he'd stared back. He'd thought her pretty then. But there again, he'd thought lots of them pretty. There had been some fairly attractive lassies in the party.

The train came to a sudden halt, they'd arrived.

'Excuse me,' the conductor said, and opened the door. He hopped on to the platform, and then helped the two of them down.

The three of them found themselves apparently alone on the platform. 'Hello?' the conductor called out. Then again, 'Hello!'

Sadie shivered as she gazed about her. The only lighting on the platform originated from the train, except for a solitary lamp hanging from what appeared to be a small building further along the platform.

'Hello!' the conductor cried out yet again, this time very loudly.

There was no answer. The only sound to be heard was the train hissing.

'You're supposed to be met. Everyone else was,' the conductor said to Sadie and Robbie. Perplexed, he tapped the platform with his foot.

'Goddamn!' he exclaimed under his breath.

The conductor glanced at his watch, then at the stationary train. 'Someone's supposed to be here to meet you,' he repeated.

The hissing sound intensified, then abruptly ceased. With a clearing of his throat the conductor made a decision.

'Listen, I can't keep this train here any longer. We have a schedule to meet. Whoever's going to meet you is obviously late, so what I suggest is you go along to that waiting-room,' he pointed at the building with the lamp hanging outside, 'and remain there until they show. OK?'

Sadie, didn't see that they had any choice.

'OK?' the conductor repeated.

'OK,' Robbie told him.

The conductor grunted, then leapt back aboard the train. 'You'll be all right. No worry. Your party will be along in no time.' And with that the conductor slammed the door shut.

Sadie and Robbie, carrying their suitcases, started trudging towards the waiting-room. Halfway there the train started up again and began to slide past them.

'I hope the Trikhardts hurry up and get here,' Sadie said. It was bitterly cold, and her cheeks were already stinging.

The last carriage rattled by, and they were immediately encased by blackness, as the solitary lamp was now the sole source of light.

'I don't like this,' Sadie complained as they continued along the platform.

Robbie didn't either, but had no intention of saying so. He wasn't going to admit that he was scared in front of a lassie.

At last they reached the waiting-room, and Robbie tried the door handle. The door creaked open.

It was stygian inside, and musty smelling. Robbie removed the lamp that was hanging outside and holding it before him, stepped inside.

'Not exactly the friendliest of waiting-rooms, is it?' Sadie commented, which provoked a wry smile from Robbie.

The door creaked again as Sadie closed it behind them. She then turned back to face Robbie who was standing in the middle of the room with the lamp held above his head.

A pot-bellied stove dominated the room, with several wooden benches arranged in front of it. On one side was an ancient rocking-chair, while an equally ancient leather armchair stood several feet away from that.

'Another lamp,' said Sadie, pointing to a wall where a second lamp hung from a metal arm similar to that outside.

'Should we light it?' Robbie wondered out loud.

Sadie stamped her feet, then banged her hands together. It wasn't so cold inside the waiting-room, but cold enough. 'No reason why not,' she replied. 'Presumably it's there to be used.'

Robbie crossed to the lamp and discovered it contained fuel. 'I need a match or piece of paper,' he said.

'Try the stove,' she suggested.

He thought that a good idea, and sure enough found a box of matches on top of a pile of wood beside the stove. Within seconds the second lamp was lit.

Robbie sank into the leather armchair and sighed. 'Imagine coming all this way to be left standing on a railway platform in the middle of the night.'

'The Trikhardts must have been delayed.'

'Must have,' Robbie agreed.

Sadie sat on the rocking-chair, and smiled to herself as it rocked gently back and forth. 'This is fun,' she said.

'I've had a thought.'

'What's that?'

'There aren't any initials with the surname on either your button or mine. Maybe it's not the same family, but different families with the same name. Brothers or cousins perhaps?'

Sadie stopped rocking. Robbie could be right, in which case they wouldn't be staying in the same house. She was disappointed by that.

'On the other hand, I could be wrong,' he added.

She hoped he was. And, unknown to her, he was hoping the same. He saw her as she saw him, a potential friend and ally. Not that that wouldn't be possible if they were living relatively close to each other, but it wouldn't be the same as if they'd been under one roof.

'Which Home were you with?' Sadie asked, having noted he wasn't wearing the Barnardo's issue.

Robbie reluctantly talked about himself for a short while. He was an orphan who'd been handed into an independent charity that had taken care of him until sending him to Canada. He had no knowledge whatever of who or what his own family had been.

'And what about you?' he demanded.

Sadie told him her story, the little of it she knew. They both fell silent when she'd finished.

'Life can be hard,' Robbie said eventually, having been deep in introspection. It certainly could, Sadie thought, and shivered for the umpteenth time.

Robbie jumped from his chair and walked over to a side window that looked down the far side of the platform. There was nothing to be seen except darkness.

'How long do you think we've been here now?' he queried.

'I couldn't say.'

He removed a glove and stuck his fingers into his mouth. 'If they don't hurry up we'll be frozen stiff when they do get here.'

'Imagine . . .' Sadie started, and then trailed off.

'Imagine what?'

'I might have come off the train on my own. Or you on your own. That would have been a lot worse.'

Especially being a lassie, he thought, and younger than him.

'Can you see anything?' she asked.

'Not a thing.'

'What about the other window?'

'Same here. Nothing at all.'

Sadie wrapped her arms round her chest, and held herself tight. 'I enjoyed the whales, didn't you?'

He smiled. 'They were grand. The best part of the whole voyage. I never dreamt I'd ever see whales.'

'You never got seasick then?'

'Not a twinge of it,' he replied, shaking his head. 'Some of my pals were throwing up all over the place. But not me.'

'Same with mine, including me best pal Janet who's gone to Quebec. We asked if we could be placed with the same family, or at least live near one another. We didn't want to be parted. But they sent her off to Clarke City, Quebec instead, and me here.'

Robbie regarded Sadie steadily. 'You mean you wanted her to be standing where I am now?'

Sadie didn't reply to that.

'Well, I'm sorry, but it had nothing to do with me.'

'I know that.'

'Just so you do!' he said aggressively.

Oh dear! she thought. She'd upset him which was the last thing she'd meant to do. 'I was only explaining. Nothing more.'

He muttered.

'Janet and I were best pals for a long time. It was awful being parted from her.'

His face softened a little. 'I understand. There's no need to go on further.'

'Did you have friends from the same Home on the boat?' she enquired.

'There were six of us, all good lads. I was with some of them a long time too.'

She nodded her sympathy. 'It's rotten losing friends, isn't it? Particularly people in our situation, brought up in Homes and that.'

'Rotten,' he agreed softly.

He returned to the first window and peered out again. 'Where *are* they?' he exclaimed.

Sadie had begun to feel cold inside now which worried her. It worried Robbie too when she told him.

'Stand up and flap your arms about. That may help,' he suggested.

She did, and stamped her feet for good measure.

Then Robbie had another thought. Going to the stove he opened it and was delighted to discover it was made up, ready for lighting.

'If they're not here soon I'm putting this on,' he said.

'Perhaps they've had an accident and that's what's holding them up?'

'Could be,' he replied.

'I hope no one's been hurt.'

If there had been an accident and if someone had been hurt we could be here for hours, he thought with a sinking heart.

Robbie gazed again out of the window, and this time he did see something – faces and events from his memory.

'You've gone all quiet,' Sadie said after a while.

'Sorry, I was thinking.'

'How long would you say it is now?'

'Long enough to put that stove on.'

His pronouncement instantly cheered Sadie. 'I'll help,' she cried, coming to her feet.

'There shouldn't be much to do. A single match hopefully.'

Sadie exhaled in ecstasy as heat began radiating from the stove.

'Terrific, eh?'

'Terrific,' she wholeheartedly agreed.

Once the fire had really caught, and the logs had collapsed downwards, Robbie added more from the pile. While he was doing that Sadie pulled the wooden benches out of the way and dragged the rocking-chair close to the stove.

'Now we've lit this they'll probably turn up any minute,' she said, rocking backwards and forwards as warmth washed over her.

'Probably,' Robbie agreed, pushing the leather armchair level with the rocker.

'You know what?'

'What?'

'I could really do with a nice cup of tea.'

'Hmmh!' he murmured. 'Same here.'

'And a bite to eat. Have you finished everything that was in your paper bag?'

He nodded.

'Me too.'

'We'll both just have to wait till breakfast then.'

Sadie opened the front of her coat. She was now baking on the front, but was still cold behind.

'Our first night in Canada,' Robbie mused.

'Stranded in a deserted railway station waiting-room,' Sadie said.

'Who would have thought,' Robbie said.

The heat following the cold and the events of the day now took effect on Sadie. Her eyelids began to droop.

Realizing what was happening she snapped them open again. 'Mustn't drop off,' she mumbled.

'Why not?'

'The Trikhardts will come and . . .' She yawned.

'Don't you worry about that, Sadie. If you're tired go to sleep. I'll look after you till they get here.'

Look after her, she thought that sounded lovely.

He went on. 'If they have had an accident it could be ages before they turn up.'

True enough, she told herself. 'I did get some sleep on the train.'

'And now you need some more. Off you go, I'll be here.'

She gave him a warm smile, pleased that she'd fallen in with Robbie Hendry. Whatever happened they were going to be good friends, she was certain of that.

Later, Robbie put more logs on the stove. Then, whacked as Sadie was, he too fell fast asleep.

* * *

Sadie awoke with a start. Where was she? What was she doing here? Where was . . .?

It all came flooding back. Their arrival in Halifax, being parted from Janet, the train journey, Robbie, the waiting-room, the Trikhardts not turning up.

Rising to her feet she hastily rebuttoned her coat. A quick inspection of the stove showed it to be smouldering inside, but not producing any worthwhile heat.

She considered putting some logs on, and decided against it. It was morning out, the light shining through the windows harsh and very bright.

'Robbie?' She touched him on the shoulder. 'Robbie?'

'Uh?'

'It's morning, Robbie. Time to wake up.'

His eyes opened to regard her quizzically, then he too remembered where they were and what had happened.

'The Trikhardts couldn't have come,' he said, pulling himself out of the leather armchair where he'd spent the night.

'Seems not.'

He went to the nearest window and looked out. 'I'd say it's still very early. Not long after dawn.'

'So what do we do now?'

'Hoof it, I suppose. What else can we do? Peterawa can't be that far away.'

'The sooner we get started then the better,' Sadie said, reaching for her suitcase.

'I'll carry that for you if you like.'

She considered his offer. The suitcase wasn't that heavy, and it would be nice if . . . 'I'll carry it myself, thank you,' she decided.

'All right.'

He opened the waiting-room door and stepped out on to the platform. There he paused to stare out over the surrounding countryside.

There was no mistaking that it was farmland, currently under winter's iron grip. Off to the right was a stand of conifers, with more trees on a hill beyond that.

'The gate's there,' said Sadie pointing, having joined him.

The gate was set in a picket fence which ran the length of the platform. The fence was white and recently painted. Shame that they hadn't painted the waiting-room at the same time, Sadie thought, inside and out.

'Let's get moving then,' Robbie said. He opened the gate to let her through, then followed her.

'Listen!' exclaimed Robbie.

She heard a rushing sound, coming from far off. 'Train,' Sadie declared. 'That's a train.'

They gazed back along the track, and sure enough the train could be seen in the distance.

'If it stops here someone might come along to meet it and give us a lift into Peterawa,' Robbie said.

'We'll wait then. Shouldn't be more than a few minutes at the rate that train's going.'

Robbie looked along the road they'd found themselves on, but there wasn't a sign of anyone or anything.

The train raced past like a silver bullet, to go speeding off in the opposite direction.

'So much for that idea,' Robbie grinned ruefully.

'It might have stopped here. How were you to know?'

Picking up their suitcases again, they continued walking, the ground underfoot rock hard.

'I suppose this will take us into Peterawa,' Robbie said.

'It wouldn't make sense for it not to. It is the road to the station, after all.'

A long screen of firs masked their view. The trees were tall, the light filtering through their branches dappled and dancing. Beneath the trees themselves it was dark and forbidding.

'Who's afraid of the big bad wolf! The big bad wolf! The big bad wolf!' Robbie sang.

Sadie laughed. 'Don't try and scare me. I'm much more frightened of snakes than wolves.'

Robbie grinned at her. 'I wouldn't like to run into either.'

Sadie gazed about her. Robbie was right. It was the perfect setting for Little Red Riding Hood. She wouldn't have been at all surprised to see a girl dressed in a red cloak flitting from tree to tree, or a wolf with slavering fangs hurrying after her.

As they left the trees, they followed the road round a bend, and there ahead of them, not more than half a mile off, was Peterawa.

'I didn't think it could be that far away,' Robbie said.

It wasn't all that large, Sadie thought, not having known what to expect. And she wondered how many people lived there.

'I suppose a lot of folk will live on farms round about,' Robbie said, having spotted a two-storey farmhouse from whose chimney a stream of smoke was spiralling heavenwards.

'I suppose so,' Sadie agreed.

They came to an intersection and crossed over that, continuing in to town. A few minutes later a car passed them, and the driver didn't even give them a second glance.

'He might have offered us a lift,' Robbie grumbled.

Soon they were in Peterawa itself, and were speculating what they should do next.

'I knew it was early,' Robbie said, for there was hardly anybody about.

They stopped in front of a building which claimed to be Klein's Drugstore.

'What's a drugstore?' Sadie asked.

'From the things in its window it looks like some sort of chemist. Anyway, it's shut same as the other shops.'

As though to prove him wrong its double doors banged open and a man came striding out on to the porch.

The man called out, smiling, when he spotted them. He glanced down at the suitcases they were carrying, then up again at their faces. 'You kids new in town, or just passing through?'

'We came off the train last night. But unfortunately the family who were supposed to meet us never showed up,' Robbie explained.

'You mean you spent all night at the station?' the man said in surprise.

'We did. But it wasn't too bad after we lit the stove.'

The man pursed his lips, and whistled. 'Well, I'll be damned! You English?'

'Scots,' Sadie chipped in. 'We're both Scottish.'

'Quite a few Scotties round these parts,' the man smiled. 'And this family who were supposed to meet you, wouldn't be the Trikhardts by any chance?'

Robbie nodded.

'Yeah. I heard they had some British kids coming out here. So you're they.'

'We are,' Sadie confirmed.

'And you spent all night in the railway station! Well, if that ain't something.'

'There was nothing else we could do,' Robbie said.

'Oh, I agree, kid. I agree. And now you want to get in touch with Julius and Anna, I take it?'

Robbie and Sadie both frowned.

'The Trikhardts,' the man explained. 'Julius and Anna Trikhardt.'

'Oh yes!' Robbie answered quickly. 'That's why we came into town. So we could contact them.'

'I'll tell you what, youngsters. You come in here and I'll telephone them for you. How's that?'

'That would be marvellous!' Robbie exclaimed.

'Well, come on in then, and meet Mrs Klein. I'm Mr Klein by the way. You can call me Herb, everyone does.'

Robbie and Sadie mounted the few steps that took them on to the porch. 'Pleased to meet you, Herb,' Robbie said, extending a hand.

Herb shook hands with Robbie, then Sadie, after which he ushered them inside.

'Maw! Where are you, Maw!' Herb shouted.

Mrs Klein came bustling out from the rear of the store to be introduced by her husband and told the children's story.

'Lucky for you there was a stove, otherwise you could have froze to death,' Mrs Klein commented, her tone and expression ones of concern and sympathy.

'I'll call the Trikhardts,' Herb said, and went behind a counter where he picked up a telephone.

Sadie glanced about her, intrigued by what she saw. Stools stood in front of the counter, while the wall behind it was covered in signs either advertising a product or else stating its price. Coke, malts, fries, cherry lemonade, peppermint ice-cream, frozen custard, drink-a-plenty, root beer . . . The list went on and on.

Over on the other side of the store was the pharmacy where prescriptions were dealt with. Various shelved stands stood in between, selling all manner of things, at the end of each a carousel of paperback books.

Overhead were two large electrical fans, and another smaller upright fan on the counter in front of a cardboard sign advertising Clarke Bars.

'That's right, Julius, the kids are right here with me now,' Herb said into the phone.

'It's always been my dream to go to England. Maybe some day,' Mrs Klein said to Sadie.

'We're Scots from Scotland. We're not English,' Sadie pointed out.

'Of course! You Scotties are always touchy about that.'

Sadie didn't think she liked being called a Scotty. They were dogs, not people.

'OK, Julius,' Herb said shortly after that, and hung up. He stared at Sadie and Robbie over the counter.

'Julius is busy at the moment, but he will be along directly. In the meantime you're to hang on here.'

'You kids must be starving,' Mrs Klein said.

'We are a bit peckish,' Sadie admitted.

'How about a nice cup of coffee to warm you while Maw rustles up some breakfast?'

'That would be lovely,' she replied.

'Yes, please!' Robbie said with enthusiasm.

'OK then, hop on these stools and coffee will be right up.'

Sadie sat on the nearest stool, Robbie beside her. Two heavy cups and saucers were placed on the counter, and piping hot coffee poured into them.

'Help yourselves to cream and sugar,' Mr Klein told them, these items already on the counter. The cream contained in small, foil sachets both amused and delighted Sadie.

'And how about a Danish to tide you over till breakfast?' Mr Klein proposed.

Sadie had no idea what a Danish was, and shyly admitted so. Mr Klein laughed, and told her she would soon find out.

'There,' he said, plonking a plate before her on which sat a sticky pastry.

It looked gorgeous, Sadie thought, biting her lower lip in anticipation. 'Thank you.'

Robbie bit into his and rolled his eyes.

It was delicious, Sadie thought, wiping a streak of jam from the side of her mouth. Imagine eating sticky pastry at this time of the morning! Canadians had some funny habits.

The coffee was strong and slightly bitter even though

she'd put sugar in. It was quite unlike British coffee, a different taste entirely.

A woman entered the drugstore. 'Hi, Herb!' she called out.

'Hi, Mary-Jo. These here kids,' he gestured at Sadie and Robbie, 'are the British ones the Trikhardts are expecting.'

A sad expression came over the woman's face, then vanished abruptly when she smiled. 'Welcome to Peterawa.'

'Thank you,' Sadie and Robbie replied together.

The woman glanced at Herb, then back at the children. 'I hope you get on OK out at the Trikhardts. You'll certainly earn your keep, and that's for sure.'

Sadie didn't quite know what to make of that.

'Now, how can I help you, Mary-Jo?' Herb enquired.

As Mary-Jo left, she gave them a cheery wave.

'People here seem very friendly,' Sadie said to Herb.

'Oh, most of them are. With a few exceptions. But then there are always those, eh?'

When they'd finished, Herb asked if they'd care for some more coffee, and both said they would.

'How long do you think before Mr Trikhardt gets here?' Sadie queried.

'Hard to say. He said directly which, knowing Julius, could be anything. Ten minutes, an hour, later on this afternoon. Julius is a farmer, and farmers don't think of time the way we townies do.'

'And what sort of man is Mr Trikhardt?' Robbie asked.

Herb's expression went blank. 'OK,' he replied slowly. 'Julius minds his own business and expects others to do the same. His wife, Anna, and he are the silent types, both quiet, homely bodies.'

Mrs Klein, now wearing an apron, reappeared. 'Come and get it! It's on the table.'

Sadie and Robbie slid from their stools and followed Mrs Klein into the rear of the store where the kitchen was located.

'Sit down now!' Mrs Klein instructed.

Sadie saw that only two places had been laid. 'Aren't you eating?' she queried.

'Paw and I ate earlier, so don't you go worrying about us.'

'What are they?' Sadie whispered to Robbie, staring at a plate heaped with golden brown rectangles that were covered in square indentations.

'Don't know,' he whispered back, shaking his head.

Mrs Klein loomed over them. 'What's up? Never seen waffles before?'

'No,' Sadie replied.

'Then I'll show you how you eat them.'

Mrs Klein speared a waffle with a fork, then shook it off on to Sadie's plate. Lifting an earthenware jug she poured some of its contents over the waffle.

'That's maple syrup,' she explained.

Sadie cut a section of waffle, and put it into her mouth. The syrup was amazingly sweet, but not sickly so.

'Do you like it?' Mrs Klein demanded.

'Oh, yes,' Sadie enthused.

'Thought you would. Most kids do.'

Robbie tried a piece of his, and his eyes lit up with pleasure. 'We didn't get anything like this in our Home,' he said to Sadie.

'Nor at Barnardo's. Though, in fairness, their food was good. But they didn't have anything to compare with this.'

Sadie managed three waffles, Robbie five and when they finally laid down their knives and forks both pronounced themselves full.

'I'll help you wash up,' Sadie said politely, rising from the table.

'That's kind of you. But hardly necessary.'

'I'll help all the same.'

Robbie volunteered as well, but there were hardly enough dishes for three of them, Mrs Klein laughed.

When that was done she escorted the children out to the front where they were to wait for Mr Trikhardt.

Hours passed, and many people came and went. Sadie and Robbie were introduced to every one of them. It was just before noon when a short, thickset man with greying hair entered the store to stand staring at Sadie and Robbie. Sadie instinctively knew who he was.

'Hi, Julius!' Herb said with a smile.

Julius grunted, and continued to stare at the children with hard, yet somehow dead, eyes. 'You weren't due to arrive till tonight,' he stated in a flat voice.

Sadie and Robbie got off their stools to stand before him. Sadie judged him to be in his late forties.

Robbie sensed an underlying danger. 'I'm sorry, Mr Trikhardt. It had nothing to do with us. They put us on a train and then told us when to get off again. We had no say in the matter.'

Julius grunted a second time. 'Name, boy?'

'Robbie Hendry, sir.'

He turned slowly on Sadie. 'And you?'

'Sadie Smith, sir.'

He eyed Sadie up and down, then Robbie, the way he might animals he was considering buying.

'Would you like some coffee?' Herb asked.

Julius shook his head. 'Too many chores to do back on the farm. Ain't got time for idle coffee drinking.'

'They stayed the night in the waiting-room out at the railway station. How about that, eh?' Herb said to Julius.

'We lit the stove,' Robbie added.

'We didn't expect you till tonight. Mistake somewhere along the line,' Julius said. He poked a thick, stubby finger at their suitcases. 'If those are yours bring them out to the car.'

Julius turned to Herb. 'I'm beholden for what you've done. Thank you.'

'Thanks ain't necessary, Julius. It was a pleasure. They're sure two fine kids.'

'We'll see about that,' Julius replied, and stalked from the store with Sadie and Robbie hurrying after him.

'Goodbye! Thank you!' Sadie and Robbie shouted from the double doors.

'You're welcome, kids. Any time!' Herb answered.

The old car was parked outside the drugstore, and smelt inside of stale human sweat and animal odour. They loaded their suitcases into the boot, then got underway. 'Is it far to the farm?' Robbie asked.

'A little over four miles.'

Robbie gazed at Julius's hands which were rough, work-worn and calloused in the extreme. The man himself reminded him of an old oak tree that had stood in the grounds of the Home.

'We had a fairly rough crossing on the ship,' Robbie said, attempting to make conversation.

'That so?'

'And we saw whales. Didn't we, Robbie?'

'We did,' Robbie confirmed.

'I lost a calf this morning. I was dealing with the beast when Herb called about you,' Julius said, his tone accusatory.

'I'm sorry to hear that,' Robbie replied.

Julius's brows furrowed in anger. 'Yeah. Damn good calf that too. Might not have lost it if Herb hadn't called when he did.'

Robbie didn't realize it, but he'd shrunk away from Julius.

Julius went on. 'We got a letter, said you were coming tonight. We would have met you then.'

'Must have been a mix-up. But it wasn't our fault,' Robbie husked.

Julius glared at him. 'No, I suppose not. But now I'm beholden to Herb Klein. Don't like being beholden to no one. They always wants more back than they gave. Leastways, that's my experience.'

Neither Sadie nor Robbie answered that.

The car rattled as it hit a pothole, then there was a bone-jarring thump when it hit a larger one.

'Goddamn son-of-a-bitching road!' Julius snarled, hands tightening on the wheel till his knuckles shone white.

'Can I ask a question?' Sadie piped up from the back seat.

Julius glanced at her in the rear-view mirror. 'Go ahead.'

'What kind of name is Trikhardt?'

Their eyes met in the mirror, and a sudden chill of fear lanced through Sadie. Had she said the wrong thing?

'Dutch,' Julius growled. 'I'm of Dutch descent, as is Anna my wife.'

Sadie tore her gaze away from those eyes and stared out at the passing countryside. Her heart was hammering, and she'd gone weak at the knees. Julius scared her.

They fell silent until they pulled up outside the Trikhardt's farmhouse.

The house was double storied with a shingle roof and shabby in appearance. It gave Sadie the impression of being uncared for.

'Bring your bags inside,' Julius said, and strode off into the house.

Sadie and Robbie exchanged glances, but neither made any comment. Both were wondering what Anna Trikhardt was like.

The interior was gloomy, the faded wallpaper torn in places. The linoleum on the floor was as faded as the wallpaper.

Julius appeared. 'Leave your bags there and come through to the kitchen.'

They followed him into the kitchen where Anna Trikhardt was waiting for them.

Anna was taller than her husband, and painfully thin. She had no figure at all. Her face was gaunt and pinched, her skin sallow, cheeks concave. Her eyes were black and beady, and there was a large mole with hairs sprouting from it on her chin. Her hair was dark and pulled back into a pony-tail.

'Sadie and Robbie,' Julius said.

'Pleased to meet you,' Robbie smiled, and extended a hand, which Anna ignored.

'We lost a calf today,' she said.

'I told them,' Julius informed her.

She nodded. 'A good calf too.'

'It wasn't our fault the train came in last night and not tonight,' Sadie stated.

Anna murmured, her beady eyes boring into Sadie.

'Well, I have to get on with the chores,' Julius said.

'You two go with him. We'd better start as we mean to go on. You work before you eat. Is that understood?'

'Yes,' replied Robbie, while Sadie nodded.

'We don't want no freeloaders here. You earn your keep same as we do. I won't have any idle hands in this house.'

How ugly she was, Sadie thought, and immediately ticked herself off for being unkind.

'You got some old clothes?' Julius asked.

'Yes,' said Robbie. 'At least I have.'

'Me too,' Sadie confirmed.

'Then you'd better change. Anna will take you up and show you where your rooms are. When you're ready come to me in the stables.'

They retrieved their suitcases, then Anna led them upstairs. Sadie's room transpired to have a sloping roof which rather tickled her fancy. There was a window in the slope which gave her a view out over the farm.

The furnishings were sparse. A single bed, wooden wardrobe, rickety chair and a washstand with a bowl and jug on it. The bowl and jug were decorated with an extremely pretty floral design, she noted.

She hurriedly changed, but had to put her good coat back on as that was the only one she had. She had two changes of clothing, an old set and the new one.

Sadie and Robbie emerged from their rooms simultaneously. 'What's yours like?' he whispered.

'Could be worse. And yours?'

He wrinkled his nose. 'Same.'

They went downstairs again where they found Anna waiting for them. 'You wearing that coat out to the stables?' she demanded of Sadie.

'It's all I've got.'

Anna flung open a cupboard and took a raggedy coat off a hook. 'Try this for size. Can't recall where it came from, but it's small.'

The sleeves hung down below her hands when Sadie put it on.

'That's easily solved,' Anna declared, and rolled the sleeves up.

'You'll do,' Anna pronounced when that was done. She then turned her attention to Robbie.

'I got just the thing for you. Was left by an employee some years back. He was tiny, but a real good worker despite that.'

The lumber-jacket was dirty on the outside, but thick and warm nonetheless.

'You'll soon grow into it,' Anna said to Robbie as she steered them both towards the door.

'Where are the stables?' Robbie asked.

'Off to the left. You can't miss them. They got horses inside.' And having said that Anna laughed thinking it a very fine joke.

Outside they soon found the stables and Julius. The stables contained two Shire horses, Trixie and Dixie, Julius informed them.

'Some of the farmers hereabouts have switched to tractors, but I prefer the Shires,' Julius said. 'Anyway, can't afford no tractor, so I ain't really got no choice.'

They were beautiful animals, Sadie thought. She stroked Trixie's nose, not in the least afraid.

'I'm mucking out, understand that?'

Robbie shook his head.

Julius explained the term, then said they could continue with the job while he got on with something else. He threw Robbie his pitchfork, and found another for Sadie.

'Don't be all day about it either,' he warned before leaving them.

The children found it hard work, and soon both were sweating. It fell to Robbie to take the dirty straw away as Sadie wasn't strong enough to push the wheelbarrow.

When they'd completed that job to Julius's satisfaction he took them into the barn where he instructed them to pitch down fresh straw to spread in the stables, and fresh hay for the horses' feed. And when they'd finished that the pigs' troughs needed filling.

When the pigs' troughs had been attended to they were given another task and yet more after that until nightfall.

Sadie wouldn't have believed such a storm possible. It was something straight out of a nightmare.

She lay in bed watching it through the window in the sloping roof. The thunder crashes were incredible, causing her to wince and press herself further and further down into the bed.

But worst of all was the lightning, jagged tears that split the night sky, momentarily illuminating the dark room as if a light had been switched on.

And through it all, rain lashed down, and the wind howled, making the house creak and groan in protest.

Anna had told them earlier that it was an electric storm and that they were common in these parts at this time of year.

Sadie gave an involuntary gasp as the loudest clash of thunder yet boomed overhead, followed by a mesmeric series of flickering lightning flashes.

There was only one thing for it. Closing her eyes she pulled the bedclothes up over her head. How she wished

Janet was there, the pair of them could have snuggled up together for comfort.

What sort of family had Janet gone to? she wondered. Were they working Janet as hard as the Trikhardts were working her? It had been non-stop since their arrival earlier that day. Their only break had been for supper, after which it had been more graft, this time inside the house.

She ached all over, and knew that would be even worse in the morning. Her hands were covered in extremely sore blisters.

Robbie had blisters too. They had soaked their hands in salt water before coming to bed, advice given them by an unsympathetic Anna.

Things could only get better, Sadie assured herself. She and Robbie would soon settle in.

Thinking of him made her smile. Thank goodness for Robbie. It would have been far worse if he hadn't been there. He'd become her friend, her pal in place of Janet.

Then she smiled again. She could have snuggled up with Janet, but not with Robbie. That was something they couldn't do together.

She wondered if he was asleep yet, or lying awake listening to the storm. Rain rattled on the window like a thousand peas from a peashooter. Outside the storm continued to rage.

Chapter Three

'Now pay attention to the route,' Anna told Sadie and Robbie. 'For this is the only time you'll be driven there.'

'Is it far?' Sadie asked.

'A fair stretch of the legs, that's all. Won't be no problem for you. Now get into the car.'

Sadie clambered into the rear, Robbie climbed in front with Anna. It was Monday morning and they were going to school. Both children were excited, and apprehensive, at the prospect.

'There's a big grade school in Peterawa, but the country school I'm taking you to is closer and just as good,' Anna said.

Sadie didn't know what grade school was, it was a new expression to her. So she asked Anna to explain it.

'You go from first grade which is one step up from kindergarten, to eighth in grade school, then you leave and go to high school. It's a bit different in the local country school where there's only one class-room, but the principle is the same.'

Sadie spotted a small plane overhead and thought how marvellous it must be to fly. She would have loved to have been up there with the pilot and was convinced that she wouldn't have been at all scared.

'Stop day-dreaming and watch where we're going!' Anna snapped, glaring at Sadie's reflection in the rear-view mirror.

'Sorry,' Sadie mumbled, and brought herself back down to earth.

'You got it now?' Anna asked as they halted in front of a brick building.

119

'I've got it,' Robbie answered.

'You won't have no trouble getting home?'

'No,' Robbie replied confidently.

'OK then, let's go in and get you introduced.'

The class was already settled, the pupils hard at work. Some were reading, others writing, a small group were sitting together in a corner.

'Good-day to you, Mr Paterson.'

'And good-day to you, Mrs Trikhardt,' the teacher replied, laying aside the chalk he'd been using.

'I've come that little bit later as you said.'

'Fine,' he nodded. 'And these are my two new pupils.'

'Sadie Smith and Robbie Hendry.'

'How do you do, children?'

'Pleased to meet you, sir,' Sadie answered shyly.

'Pleased to meet you, Mr Paterson,' Robbie echoed.

He nodded his approval of their politeness. 'And how old are you, Sadie?'

She told him.

'And you, Robbie?'

Robbie did likewise.

'And all the way from Bonny Scotland, eh? My father came from Scotland. A little place called Tomintoul in the Highlands. Ever heard of it?'

Sadie shook her head, as did Robbie.

'Well, that's hardly surprising. As I said, it is small.'

Sadie had already taken a liking to Mr Paterson. The fact that his father had been Scots made matters even better.

'I'll leave them with you then,' Anna said, anxious to get back to the farm. 'They've each got a lunch pail as you instructed.' The lunch pails referred to were old ones that had been knocking around the farm for years.

'Excellent. Thank you for bringing them in, Anna. I'm sure we will get on handsomely.'

He turned to the class. 'Stand, children!'

The class did as ordered.

'Say goodbye, Mrs Trikhardt.'

'Goodbye, Mrs Trikhardt!'

That done Mr Paterson escorted Anna to the door. He was smiling broadly when he returned.

'Sit class!' he ordered, and they did, resuming whatever they'd been doing before.

'Now I have several things to find out about you,' he said to Sadie and Robbie. 'But, first of all, I must enter you in the register.'

Mr Paterson sat behind his desk, extracted a green coloured ledger-type book from a drawer, and placed it in front of him.

'Is Robbie short for Robert?' he asked.

'Yes, sir.'

'And do you have any middle names?'

'No, sir.'

When asked Sadie informed him that she had no middle names either.

'No complications or fripperies, eh?' he smiled.

Robbie glanced at Sadie, he'd also taken a shine to Mr Paterson. They'd fallen on their feet here.

'Now,' said Mr Paterson, 'I shall take you to your desks and in a few minutes give you what's called an IQ test. Do you know what that is?'

'IQ stands for intelligence quotient. It means an intelligence test, sir,' Robbie replied.

Mr Paterson raised an eyebrow. 'Correct. And when you've completed that I have some other tests for you. All fairly simple and straightforward, nothing to worry about. OK?'

Sadie and Robbie both nodded.

Intelligence quotient, Mr Paterson thought. No one else in the class could have told him that.

Sadie and Robbie had eaten their lunches at their desks, and were now out in the yard for the remainder of the break.

They were talking to one another when two boys approached them. Robbie glanced at them and alarm bells immediately went off inside his head.

'Hi!' said the taller. 'I'm Grant and this is Mark. We're the Miller brothers.'

They didn't look like brothers, Sadie thought. Grant had sandy hair, a pasty freckled complexion and red-rimmed watery eyes. His left eye was also marred by a nasty sty. He was tall and broad shouldered whereas Mark was small and skinny.

Mark was smiling, but it was a weasly, ingratiating smile. In repose his mouth had a sly quality about it. His hair was dark, his eyes a peculiar shade of blue. He fidgeted and jerked the whole time reminding Sadie of a bird.

'Hello,' a wary Robbie responded.

'We thought we'd come over as a sort of welcoming committee. It's good to have some new kids in the school. Ain't that so, Mark?'

'Sure is,' his brother agreed.

'So why is it you've come to live with the Trikhardts?' Grant asked.

Robbie considered not explaining, but realized their story would get out sooner or later anyway. 'We were in institutions in Scotland and sent over here for a better life.'

'No kidding!' Grant exclaimed. 'Institutions, eh, Mark?'

'Well, well,' declared Mark, shaking his head.

'You mean like orphanages?' Grant further probed.

'We had orphans in our Home. I was one of them,' Robbie replied.

'And what about you? Are you an orphan also?' Mark enquired of Sadie.

Sadie felt shame creeping over her, and wished the Miller boys would go away. 'No,' she replied quietly. 'In my case it was because my family were so poor.'

'Tut, tut!' said Mark, and shook his head again.

'An orphan,' Grant repeated, staring at Robbie.

'Do you live near us?' Sadie asked, trying to change the subject.

'You mean near the Trikhardts? Yeah, not far away,' Grant answered.

'With our folks,' Mark sniggered.

'You got funny accents,' Grant smiled at Robbie.

'Yours sound odd to us.'

'Yeah, I suppose so. But yours are real funny. I can see we're going to get a lot of laughs out of you.'

'Lot of laughs,' Mark repeated.

This habit of repeating what each other said was beginning to irritate Sadie. Again she wished they'd go away.

Mark turned towards her. 'I think you're cute.'

'Thank you.'

'Pretty hair.' And having said that, he reached out, attempting to stroke it.

Sadie drew away, not wanting him to touch her.

'S'OK,' he said. 'I wouldn't harm you. Would I, Grant?'

'Naw. He's just being friendly. We both are.'

'Yeah, friendly,' Mark repeated.

Robbie decided he didn't like the Millers, not one little bit. There was something about them that rang totally false.

'Do you play baseball?' Mark asked Robbie, who shook his head. 'Then we'll have to teach you. Won't we, Grant?'

'I'd enjoy that.'

'He's very physical,' Mark smiled.

'Very,' Grant agreed.

'Show Sadie your muscles.'

Grant flexed an arm.

'Strong as an ox,' Mark said.

Grant flexed the other arm.

Pathetic, Sadie thought.

'What do you think?' Grant asked her.

'I've seen bigger,' she lied.

'From Robbie here?' Mark queried. 'Come on, Robbie, show us your muscles.'

'No, thank you.'

'But I insist. We insist.'

'I said no.'

'Won't take that for an answer. Come on, be a sport, not a party pooper. Show us your muscles. It's all in good fun.'

'Come on!' Grant further urged.

'I said no, and I mean it,' Robbie declared softly, but firmly.

'The guy's a party pooper,' Mark said to Grant.

'Yeah, a weiner.'

Sadie wondered what a weiner was.

'Last chance,' Mark said, sticking his face close to Robbie's.

Robbie recoiled, and saw laughter and mockery in the blue eyes, eyes that disturbed him.

Robbie was about to reply when the bell was rung announcing the end of the break.

'Aw!' said Mark, pretending disappointment. 'Pity.'

'Pity,' Grant agreed.

'Anyway, welcome to school,' Mark smiled at Sadie and Robbie.

'Yeah, welcome,' Grant repeated.

'Let's go in,' Robbie said to Sadie.

They entered the school flanked on either side by the Miller brothers.

'You found your way back then OK,' Anna stated as Sadie and Robbie strolled into the kitchen, having just returned from their first day at school.

'It wasn't difficult,' Robbie said.

Anna picked up a large wooden bowl and began beating its contents with a wooden spoon. She was baking. 'You'd better get changed quick and get outside. There are still a mountain of chores to be done.'

No enquiry as to how they'd got on at school, Şadie noted, but that didn't really surprise her. She was beginning to know the Trikhardts.

'You can start with the cows,' Anna went on. 'They need milking.'

'Right,' said Robbie.

'We all have to pull our weight round here,' Anna added unnecessarily.

Robbie raced Sadie upstairs, and won easily. Ten minutes later they started on the chores.

Sadie's bedroom door flew open. 'Rise and shine, it's four a.m.!' Anna announced.

Sadie groaned. She just couldn't get used to this terribly early rise. As far as she was concerned four a.m. was still the middle of the night.

Anna lit Sadie's oil-lamp, then flitted away.

'Rise and shine, it's four a.m.!' Sadie heard Anna say loudly through in Robbie's room.

Sadie tossed the bedclothes aside and swung her feet on to the floor, shivering from the cold that immediately assailed her.

She dressed swiftly, then went over to the jug and bowl where she had to break a thin film of ice before she could wash her face. As she dried herself she noted that her hands had already turned blue. She hurried down to the kitchen where it was warm and first breakfast would shortly be served.

First breakfast, which they had when they got up, consisted of coffee and toast. Second breakfast was served when the initial round of chores was over, and that was more coffee plus lashings of bacon and eggs. It was one of Julius's favourite sayings that he liked a 'humungous' breakfast, in other words extremely large.

When Sadie stepped outside after the first breakfast the cold was so fierce it took her breath away.

'Jeez!' Julius muttered, clapping his hands together.

Sadie thought of the lovely warm bed she'd left and wished with all her heart she was back in it. Reality was the pig trough, and feeding the chickens after that.

The walk to school seemed interminable. When she and Robbie finally arrived every piece of exposed flesh was completely numb.

Mr Paterson completed marking Robbie's IQ test and stared at the results in astonishment. He glanced up at Robbie, beavering away at his desk, and then down again at the paper before him.

Slowly he went through it again, checking that he hadn't marked it incorrectly. According to this he had a boy of exceptional ability on his hands, by far and away the brightest pupil ever to attend the school. Excitement flared in Paterson. This was the sort of pupil every teacher dreamt of teaching – an academic high-flyer.

He began to hum, the hum of a truly happy man.

'Play catch with us, Robbie?' Grant said, he and Mark joining Robbie and Walt, a boy who sat next to Robbie.

'No, thank you,' Robbie replied.

Mark had a baseball which he tossed in the air, and caught again. 'Here!' he said, and passed the ball to Grant.

'Aw, come on!' Grant cajoled.

Robbie shook his head.

'Too cissy for catch?' Mark sniggered.

Robbie didn't reply to that.

Walt fingered his spectacles nervously, the Miller brothers had never asked him to play. They weren't interested in him.

Grant threw the ball over Robbie's head to Mark, who deftly caught it as he danced round Robbie and Walt.

'Excuse me,' said Walt. 'Speak to you later, Robbie.'

Robbie watched Walt walk away, then focused his attention on the Millers. Both were grinning like Cheshire cats.

'Come on, play catch with us?' Mark urged.

'We want you to,' said Grant.

'Very much so.'

'We like you.'

'You're a great kid,' declared Mark, throwing the ball to one side of Robbie where Grant was ready to receive it.

'A great kid,' Grant repeated, and threw the ball back, this time round the other side of Robbie.

A frown creased Sadie's face when she saw what was going on. She was with Polly, a girl she'd become reasonably friendly with.

'The Miller boys are most peculiar, don't you think?' she said to Polly.

Polly glanced over at them. 'They're fun. A good laugh.'

'You like them then?'

'Sure. Don't you?'

Sadie shook her head. 'There's something about them. I . . . I just don't know.'

'They're popular at school.'

That surprised Sadie. She'd have to talk it over with Robbie on the way home.

The cat screeched when Robbie accidentally trod on its tail, giving him a fright and causing him to drop the milk churn he was carrying. Milk splashed everywhere and the churn was more than half empty before Robbie could right it again.

'You stupid son-of-a-bitch!' Julius snarled, and lashed out with a meaty paw to send Robbie flying.

Blood spurted from Robbie's nose which had taken part of the blow.

'That milk's money to me. Understand, boy? Money!'

Robbie nodded. 'I'm sorry. It was an accident.'

'Saying sorry don't bring back the milk.' And with that Julius picked up the churn and stalked out of the milking shed.

Sadie had watched all this wide eyed. She now ran to Robbie, and knelt beside him.

'He shouldn't have done that,' she said, wondering how she was going to stop the bleeding.

'He hit me with his full force,' Robbie stated.

'I saw.'

'I thought he'd knocked my head clean off. It's still going round.'

'Is your nose sore?'

'Yup.'

'Put your head forward and keep your head in that position.'

It took a few minutes, but eventually the bleeding stopped. Then Sadie proceeded to clean up Robbie's face using a cloth she'd found on the other side of the shed.

He winced when she dabbed his cheek.

'Painful?'

Robbie gingerly touched the spot with the tips of his fingers, and grimaced. 'He might just have cracked the bone.'

'I hope not.'

'So do I,' Robbie muttered.

Sadie glared at the door through which Julius had gone. There was no excuse for what he'd done, none at all.

'We'd better get back to work before he returns or that will be another fault,' Robbie said, rising to his feet.

Sadie left the cloth, now covered with blood, in a prominent place to remind Julius of what he'd done.

'We're going to play Cowboys and Indians. Want to join in?' Mark asked.

They just wouldn't leave him alone, Robbie thought. They were obsessed about getting him to play with them. Perhaps he should, it would make life easier. But there again, why should he? He loathed the Miller brothers, finding them both quite appalling. Besides, if he did agree to play, that would be seen by them as a victory, a victory he had no intention of conceding.

He shook his head.

'We'll be the Cowboys and you can be the Indian chief,' Grant proposed.

'And you can capture us and even pretend to burn us at the stake,' Mark added.

He wouldn't have minded burning them at the stake, Robbie thought. Only there would have been no pretence about it.

'I'm not interested,' he replied.

Anger, and other emotions crowded on to Mark's face. His lips thinned, and twisted viciously. 'You think you're too good to play with us, don't you?' he spat out.

'Stuck up prick,' Grant said, catching Mark's new mood.

Robbie glanced from one to the other. These two really were awful. Nasty through and through.

He started to walk away, but Mark darted in front of him blocking his way. 'You *will* play with us,' Mark hissed.

'No, I won't,' Robbie replied quietly.

'We want you to, and you will,' Mark persisted.

'I told you I'm not interested. Now leave it at that.' Robbie tried to get past, but was blocked.

'Are we going to play Cowboys and Indians or not?' Philip Schmidt demanded, having come over to where Robbie and the Millers were. With him were another dozen boys.

'He won't join in. Thinks he's a cut above us,' Mark said spitefully, jabbing a finger at Robbie.

'That's not true. I simply don't want to play,' Robbie replied.

'Well, leave him if he doesn't want to,' Philip advised.

'What a jerk,' Grant said, meaning Robbie.

'You mean jerk off,' Mark added quickly and laughed at his own joke.

Robbie stared at them stony faced, feeling acutely embarrassed. Then he realized he wasn't embarrassed for himself, but for Mark and Grant. They were a couple of fools who didn't understand it. He might find them loathsome, but he also pitied them.

'Jerk off,' Grant repeated and made obscene hand-pumping gestures in Robbie's direction.

'Robbie Hendry's a jerk off! Robbie Hendry's a jerk off!' Mark intoned and copied his brother's gestures.

Robbie eyed them contemptuously, aware that a number of girls were now present. Some of whom were laughing.

Mark bent over and waggled his bottom at Robbie, grinning spitefully. Robbie fought back the almost over-whelming temptation to kick him.

Now it was Grant's turn to copy Mark. He bent over and waggled his bottom.

Pathetic, Robbie thought. Truly pathetic.

'Go on, show us your ass!' Craig Grode called out.

'I would do if it wasn't so cold,' Mark replied, which got a loud, all-round laugh.

Mark straightened, and resumed making the obscene gestures at Robbie. And Grant did likewise.

'What about this game? It's going to be too late soon!' Philip Schmidt complained.

Mark suddenly galloped off as though on a horse, and Grant followed suit. The other boys went after them, and within moments the game was in progress.

Sadie came over to Robbie, her expression sympathetic. 'Don't let them get to you.'

'Don't worry, they won't.'

'God, they're such babies!'

Robbie couldn't have agreed more.

'They just never leave you alone.'

Robbie shook his head. 'I don't know what it is, but they're obsessed with me.'

'Maybe they're jealous.'

'What?'

'Perhaps they think you really are better than them.'

'How could I be that?'

'You're nice for a start. Whereas they're the complete opposite. And you have a very strong personality. Maybe they envy you that.'

'Or are trying to dominate me.'

'Possibly.'

It simply seemed to them both that there was no reasonable answer.

Mr Paterson finished marking Robbie's latest test paper, and felt like purring. Not a single error. The boy had positively waltzed through the paper.

He glanced up at Robbie who was busy writing. The boy certainly had a flair for mathematics. He had a remarkable ability to grasp a theoretical explanation. Once Robbie had been taught the theory, he not only understood it, but was able to discuss its finer points.

Geometry and trigonometry would prove easy for Robbie, he had no doubts about that, but he wouldn't teach Robbie those subjects. They would be taught in high school. But what satisfaction it would have given him.

Robbie became aware that he was being stared at. He looked up and sure enough, there was Mr Paterson gazing at him, a huge smile plastered all over Paterson's face. The smile widened even further, a smile Robbie knew was directed straight at him. He smiled back, then got on again with his assignment.

Sweat coursed down Sadie's body as she pitched hay for the stock. Beside her Robbie was doing the same.

'Not long now till supper. I'm starving,' she said.

'Me too.'

'There's pumpkin pie and cream for afters.'

'At least we can't complain that they starve us,' Robbie said. There was never a shortage of good, wholesome food.

'If they did we wouldn't be able to graft as hard as we do,' Sadie commented wryly.

He nodded, acknowledging her wisdom.

Sadie paused to wipe her steaming forehead, and take a breather. 'I was watching you in school today,' she said. 'You really enjoy the work there, don't you?'

He stopped and smiled at her. 'Yes, I love it. I get a tremendous sense of achievement out of it.'

'I wish I could say the same,' Sadie replied, pulling a face. 'But I'm just a thickie, not clever like you.'

'You're not thick!' he protested.

'Well, if not that, then very average. You, on the other hand, have brains coming out of your ears.'

He laughed at that expression, finding it delightfully daft.

'You are terribly clever though, aren't you?'

He thought about that, then said slowly. 'It's just not difficult for me, you see. Everything seems so obvious. I get fascinated by facts and figures, and find both incredibly exciting. They belong to a world other than the real one, a magic world I wish I could be in all the time.'

'Oh, Robbie!' she whispered, staring at him in admiration.

'I don't think of school work as work,' he went on. 'Work is this sort of thing, pitching hay. What happens at school is sheer pleasure, something I could happily do from morning to night.'

She didn't know what possessed her, but going to him she pecked him on the lips. 'I think you're a smasher, Robbie Hendry.'

He blushed furiously, as it was the first time he'd ever been kissed. 'You're not so bad yourself,' he husked in reply.

'You're going to go places in this life, I predict it,' she told him.

'We'll see.'

'You will. With your intelligence there's nothing you can't do.'

A faraway look came into his eyes. 'It would be lovely if it were true and it would almost make up for . . .' He stopped and bit his lip.

'Make up for what?' Sadie queried quietly.

'Being an orphan and being brought up in an institution,' he replied just as quietly.

'And having to come and live in a place like this?'

He smiled thinly. 'Yes.'

'I know exactly what you mean,' she stated.

There was a shared moment between them, an empathy of past grief and experience, of loss, and loneliness, a lack of love in the family sense, and of profound hurt.

Then the moment was gone as they hurriedly returned to pitching hay, having heard Julius enter the barn.

Sadie and Robbie sat side by side in the back of the car as they made their way to church and Sunday school. The Trikhardts occasionally went to church, but Sadie and Robbie had to attend Sunday school every week, as it was a stipulation of the Irene Dunbar Agency's contract with the Trikhardts. Most Sundays the children had to walk there and back, but that Sunday, because the Trikhardts were going to church, they had the luxury of a car ride.

Julius rolled down his window and flicked the butt of the cigarette he'd been smoking away. Then he spat, a great gobbet that went flying away in the breeze.

Sadie wrinkled her nose in disgust. Julius had some dreadfully uncouth habits, some of which literally made her feel ill.

'Got a lot to do when we get home,' Julius growled.

Sadie sighed inwardly. It might be Sunday, but that didn't mean a day off. Once they got back she'd be at it till bedtime.

They parked close by the church and got out. Julius looked stiff and starchy in his Sunday best, Anna entirely in black as though bound for a funeral.

'We'll meet back here afterwards. And that's straight afterwards, no hanging about,' Julius told the children.

They both nodded, Sadie thinking he should have saved his breath. She and Robbie knew the drill by heart.

Julius extended a crooked arm which Anna hooked hers round. The pair of them adopted pious, sanctimonious expressions as they headed for the church where folk were streaming in through the open doors.

A nasty surprise awaited Sadie and Robbie when they arrived at Sunday school. Two new members had presented themselves that day.

Mark and Grant Miller.

Sadie, having been woken by Anna, crawled out of bed at the usual ghastly hour. And, after dressing and washing, she hurried downstairs for first breakfast.

'Snow blizzard out,' Julius said, slurping his coffee.

Sadie was joined by Robbie, who'd overheard what Julius had said, and together they peered out of the window.

Snow had fallen since their arrival in Peterawa, but nothing like this. Sadie gazed at it in awe. 'How beautiful,' she murmured.

Julius snorted. 'Beautiful, my ass! It's a goddamn pain, that's what it is. A goddamn pain!'

'There will be no school for you two today,' Anna announced, placing more toast on the table.

Sadie and Robbie turned to look at her, Robbie in dismay.

'You'd never get there,' Anna explained.

Sadie glanced at Robbie in sympathy, knowing how much he loved school.

'What about tomorrow?' Robbie asked.

Anna shrugged. 'Who knows? Maybe, maybe not.'

'You won't be idle. I've got plenty for you to do round the farm,' Julius said.

Sadie hadn't doubted otherwise. There was always plenty to do round the farm. The work was never finished, because when you reached the end it was time to start all over again.

Julius belched, and scratched his chest. 'The pair of you better hurry up and eat. The morning's wasting.'

Sadie and Robbie bolted through their coffee and toast.

'But the roads are clear now, the ploughs were out yesterday,' Robbie said to Julius.

Julius glanced up at Robbie, and considered the situation. 'I need you here again today. You can go back tomorrow.'

'But . . .'

'Don't argue with me, boy!' Julius roared, and half rose from his chair.

Robbie clamped his mouth shut, knowing it was useless to discuss it further.

'I got a mess of logs to move which will need Trixie and Dixie. Then I gotta split the logs for firewood. You and Sadie can help with that.'

'I could use her for housework,' Anna said to him.

'Then you can have her for the morning, and I'll have her for the rest of the day. OK?'

Anna nodded, thinking she'd ensure Sadie worked twice as hard to make up for the time she'd be with Julius.

The class gasped, while Robbie blushed. 'An A-plus,' Mr Paterson repeated, 'the first I have ever awarded.'

Robbie glanced down at the paper he'd been handed, wishing the floor would open up and swallow him. He was squirming inside with embarrassment at being so 'spotted out' as the local children called it. He wished he could return to his seat, but Mr Paterson had told him to stand where he was, which was to one side of the teacher's desk, facing the class.

Mr Paterson went on. 'I want you all to know that we have an extremely bright student among us. A student with a remarkable brain for whom I have great hopes. Great hopes indeed!'

Sadie beamed at Robbie, and couldn't have been more pleased for him. Her beam faded when she caught sight of Mark Miller glaring at Robbie, sheer malevolent hatred pouring from his eyes.

'I think Robbie's A-plus deserves a round of applause, don't you, children?' And with that Mr Paterson led the clapping.

Only two people didn't join in the applause, Mark and Grant Miller.

There would be more trouble on the way for Robbie, Sadie thought.

Sadie and Robbie were bent against an ice-cold wind blowing directly in their faces. They were on their way home from school.

There was the sound of a car behind them, then a brand new American Chevrolet went by with the grinning Miller boys peering out of the rear window.

'The father might have stopped and offered us a lift,' Sadie grumbled.

Robbie glanced at her in surprise. 'You mean you would have accepted? I certainly wouldn't. I want nothing whatever to do with that family.'

'You're right,' Sadie agreed. 'I don't know why I said that.'

'I wonder why they came this way? They don't normally,' Robbie mused.

'Could be going into Peterawa for some reason or other.'

'Could be.'

They walked a little way in silence, then Sadie said 'Polly mentioned recently that Mr Miller is one of the biggest farmers in these parts. According to her he's a very rich and powerful man.'

'Really? I didn't know that.'

'Very rich and powerful she said. Lots of influence.'

'Well, he's certainly got a lovely car,' Robbie commented, thinking of the Chevy that had passed them.

He then changed the subject. He didn't want to talk about the Millers, he found even talking about them distasteful.

'What's wrong?' Robbie asked, coming up to Sadie in the school yard. He'd noticed from where he'd been standing that she seemed distressed.

'Nothing.'

He frowned. 'Then why are there tear stains on your cheeks?'

She dabbed at her cheeks, trying to wipe the stains away. 'You're imagining things.'

'No, I'm not. What's going on, Sadie?'

She shook her head. 'Nothing. I swear.'

'Don't fib to me. I'm Robbie don't forget.'

She smiled at him. 'All right then. I'm just feeling a bit upset. But there's no reason for it.'

'There must be a reason!' he exclaimed. 'You don't feel upset for no reason.'

'Well, I do. So there!' she flared.

'OK, OK, keep your hair on!'

Her mouth twisted into a bitter smile at that remark.

'Is there anything I can do?'

'No.'

'You're sure?'

'I'm positive.'

'Right then. But I'm staying with you till the bell.'

Taking out her handkerchief she wet it with her tongue, then proceeded to wash away the tear stains. She felt a lot better after that.

Robbie glanced across the class-room and there was Mark staring at him, those peculiar blue eyes twinkling with amusement, his sly mouth smiling broadly. Mark obviously found something funny, though if it was to do with him Robbie couldn't think what.

Robbie brought his attention back to Mr Paterson writing on the blackboard. It was probably just some plan of Mark's to make him worried, he decided, and put Mark firmly out of his mind.

The spitball hit Robbie on the neck causing him to sharply inhale and jerk in his seat. He knew it was a spitball when he saw the tightly folded piece of paper, which had been propelled by an elastic band, lying at his feet.

'And Jesus said . . .' droned on sanctimonious Mr Morrison who was addressing Sunday school.

Another spitball hit him, this time on the back of the neck. It stung like fury.

Robbie knew who had fired them. He looked back over his shoulder to where the Miller boys were sitting, the pair of them with the most angelic, innocent, expressions on their faces.

'Face the front, boy!' Mr Morrison snapped, pointing at Robbie.

Robbie did as he was ordered, knowing that it was only a matter of time before another spitball hit him.

He was hit by seven altogether before the end of Sunday school.

Robbie managed to get outside before the Miller boys, and waited for them. They both grinned insolently when they spotted him.

'Don't do it again, ever,' Robbie said to them.

'Is he talking to us, Grant?'

'I believe he is, Mark.'

'Mr high and mighty actually bothering to talk to us. Well, well!'

'Well, well,' Grant repeated.

'And what can we do for you?' Mark asked, assuming the innocent expression he'd adopted inside Sunday school.

'You heard what I said. Don't do that again, ever.'

'Do what? I've no idea what he's on about, have you, Grant?'

Grant shook his head. 'No idea at all.'

'Spitballs,' Robbie stated.

'That mean anything to you, Grant?'

'Not a thing, Mark. What about you?'

'Same here. Not a thing.'

'Are you accusing us of something?' Grant asked mildly.

'I know it was you two,' Robbie replied.

'Then you're mistaken,' Grant said.

'No, I'm not.'

'I don't take kindly to being falsely accused,' Grant said.

'It doesn't bother me whether you take kindly to it or not. Because I know it was either you, your brother or both of you,' Robbie said without a flinch.

'Come on,' said Sadie who'd appeared at Robbie's side, and was tugging at his coat.

'Spitballs! Spitballs! We know nothing of spitballs!' Mark sang, dancing on the spot.

He's a lunatic, Robbie thought, a shilling short in the pound. Out of the corner of his eye, Mark spied Mr Morrison and Mrs Cronkshaw, another Sunday school teacher.

'Please don't hit me! Please don't hit me! It's all a mistake!' Mark cried out, falling to his knees where he cowered with his hands held before his face.

Robbie stared at him in astonishment.

'Please! Please don't hit me, Robbie!' Mark screeched, and grovelled on the ground before Robbie.

Morrison came charging over. 'What's going on here?' he demanded.

Mark jumped to his feet again. 'It's all right, sir, nothing to worry about. Robbie just got the wrong idea, that's all. I'm sure he wouldn't have hit me. I'm far smaller than him after all.'

Morrison rounded on Robbie. 'Were you going to hit him, boy?'

'No, sir.'

'Liar,' Grant muttered, just loud enough for Morrison to hear.

'I'll have no fighting in or outside Sunday school. Do you understand that, Hendry?'

'Perfectly, sir.'

Morrison turned to Mark and Grant. 'You two run along, and I'll see this ruffian doesn't follow.'

Ruffian! Robbie thought, outraged.

'Thank you, sir. Thank you,' Mark said. And he and Grant ran off.

Morrison tapped Robbie on the shoulder. 'Make sure there's no repetition of this disgraceful incident, or it will be the worse for you. I promise you that.'

Robbie watched Morrison stride away. 'You wouldn't believe it, would you?'

'Those two are dangerous. You must be careful,' Sadie warned him.

'Liars through and through,' Robbie said.

And bullies too, she thought, but didn't say so out loud.

Sadie woke to find that she had a headache and that her forehead was unusually hot. As she got dressed, she coughed, which made her wince in pain.

'I think maybe I should stay in bed today,' she said to Anna on reaching the kitchen.

Anna frowned. 'Why?'

Sadie coughed, then explained about the other symptoms.

'Looks healthy enough to me,' said Julius, spreading a thick layer of peanut butter on a slice of toast.

Robbie felt Sadie's forehead. 'She's certainly got a temperature.'

Anna felt the forehead then. 'This ain't hot! Well, hardly at all. As for the cough, why I gets those all the time. If you stay home, young lady, you work. I told you your first day here, we all pull our weight round this farm.'

'But she's ill,' Robbie protested.

'She's up and dressed, ain't she? So she can't be that bad,' Anna argued.

'I'll be fine,' Sadie assured Robbie.

'But you should be . . .'

'Enough,' Anna said to him. 'Sadie either goes to school, or works round the farm. It is entirely up to her.'

Sadie elected to go to school thinking that would be easier on her than chores.

Outside the cold made her headache worse, while the pain in her chest became a tight iron band.

A worried and concerned Robbie listened to her cough incessantly during their walk to school.

It was mid-morning break and Robbie was looking for Sadie to see how she was feeling. He'd been kept behind by Mr Paterson while the other children escaped to the yard as the teacher had wanted to discuss a minor matter with him.

Where was she? Robbie wondered. He couldn't find her anywhere.

'Do you know where Sadie is?' he said to Polly, who shook her head. Pat Armstrong didn't know either. But when he asked Beth-Anne Schuster she said she thought she'd seen her heading towards the toilets which were round the other side of the school.

There was no sign of Sadie there either, but he hung on for a few moments thinking she could still be inside.

He heard the cry of pain, and recognized the voice immediately. He hurried behind the toilets where he came up short.

Grant Miller was pulling hard on Sadie's hair while Mark had her arm twisted up behind her back, as he giggled girlishly.

Rage enveloped Robbie, and the next thing he knew he was flying at the Millers.

Grant spotted him first, and released Sadie's hair. He flailed at Robbie, and missed. Robbie hit him as hard as he could in the face, then repeated the blow. Grant squealed like a stuck pig as blood spurted from his nose to spatter his face and front.

Robbie whirled on Mark who was about to make a bolt for it, and threw himself at the smaller boy. The two of them went crashing to the ground where Mark writhed pleading for mercy.

There was no mercy in Robbie, not for these two after what he'd just witnessed. His clenched fist pummelled into Mark.

Grant grabbed hold of him, and tried to pull him off Mark. Robbie backhanded Grant who then punched him on the back of the head.

Mark somehow succeeded in throwing him off, and Robbie went rolling away. A furious, gibbering Mark jumped to his feet and began kicking Robbie, trying to reach Robbie's crotch but failing miserably.

Sadie, nursing her arm, bumped Mark, sending him flying. As Mark careered past, Robbie knocked Grant's leg out from under him bringing Grant tumbling to the ground.

Robbie grabbed hold of Grant's red splashed front and hit his nose again which caused fresh blood to fountain. Then Mark had clasped him by the neck and tried to throttle him.

He flipped Mark over his shoulder, then dealt with Grant who'd sunk his teeth into his leg. A blow to the side of the head soon dislodged Grant who'd gone puce with fright and anger.

Robbie bounced to his feet and threw a massive punch at Grant. Grant's eyes rolled heavenward as he flopped over to lie still.

Robbie grasped hold of a sobbing Mark, again pleading for mercy and promising he'd do anything if only Robbie would let him go. The anger drained away as quickly as it engulfed Robbie. He pushed Mark away from him and he scuttled off on all fours like some terrified animal.

Robbie, chest heaving, turned to Sadie. 'This isn't the first time either, is it? Now I know why you'd been crying the other day.'

'I didn't tell you because I didn't want this to happen,' she replied.

'The rotten bastards,' he said, his tone indicating utter contempt.

She went over to him and took his hand. 'It's over. They'll leave me alone from now on.'

'I'm sorry,' he whispered.

'It's not your fault they're as mean as they are, or that they're obsessed by you.'

'But they were getting at me through you,' he replied, sick at the thought.

'I don't approve of violence. But having said that you were wonderful,' she smiled.

'I couldn't let them get away with what they were doing to you. They asked for all they got.'

And deserved it, she thought, looking at Grant sitting on the ground shaking his head. There was no sign of Mark. He'd deserted his brother, just like the rat he was.

'How's your headache and the pain in your chest?' Robbie asked.

She squeezed his hand. 'Better than they were, thank you.'

For them to do what they'd been doing to her was wicked enough, Robbie thought, but to do it when she was clearly unwell was outrageous.

He only wished he'd given them a bigger hiding.

Mr Paterson surveyed the three boys and single girl in front of him. He was shocked at the state of the Miller brothers while Robbie appeared to have come through the fight relatively unscathed.

Grant's face and front were covered in rapidly drying blood, his left eye blackened and closing fast. Mark had abrasions and weals all down one side of his face, and he, too, a black eye. One ear was swollen to three times its normal size.

'What a sight,' Mr Paterson commented.

'He attacked us,' Mark said.

'That's not true,' Sadie told the teacher. 'They were torturing me when Robbie intervened.'

'Torturing!' Mr Paterson exclaimed, raising an eyebrow.

'Pulling my hair and twisting my arm.'

Mark shook his head. 'She's making that up because she's a friend of his, and doing it to protect him. He's been giving Grant and me a hard time ever since he arrived.'

'Why should Robbie do that?' Mr Paterson queried.

'I've no idea. We've done everything to try and be friends with him, often inviting him to play with us. But he never accepts, all he ever does is make fun of us, calling us rude names. Isn't that right, Grant?'

'Every word of it,' Grant nodded.

'It's quite the other way round. They're the ones who've been harassing me,' Robbie protested.

'You're lying, the pair of you are,' Mark said hotly.

'Attacked us for no reason. I'd swear to that on our family bible,' Grant added.

Mr Paterson stared at all four. Although he'd never had any trouble with the Millers he'd long suspected there was more to them than met the eye. And he just couldn't believe that Robbie would behave as they claimed. 'Were there any witnesses other than yourselves?'

'No one,' Sadie said.

'So it's Mark and Grant's word against yours and Robbie's?'

When he didn't get a reply to that, he went on, 'Rather than punish all four and make a mistake, I'm not going to punish any of you. And if you Millers were to blame I judge you've already been punished enough.'

Mark glared venomously at Robbie.

'Now, Grant,' Mr Paterson continued, 'go to the faucet and try and clean up a bit. You other three take your seats.'

Mark was seething inside. He'd get Hendry for this. He'd make him pay. And then it came to him just how he could achieve his end. Witness! He could provide one of those, and a genuine one at that.

Sadie and Robbie were feeding the chickens and gathering eggs when a grim-faced Anna appeared to summon them to the house. Julius wished to speak with them. Their suspicions were confirmed when they saw the new American Chevrolet parked outside the front door. They both knew then it meant trouble.

Mr Miller was a tallish man with the same sandy hair and watery red-rimmed eyes as Grant. Mark, Sadie presumed, must take after their mother.

'Erwin here says you attacked his boys,' Julius said to Robbie.

'That's not so.'

Robbie repeated more or less what he'd told Paterson, as did Sadie. Mr Miller looked disbelievingly on.

'I know my kids,' Miller said when Robbie and Sadie had finished. 'Those two are lying through their teeth.'

'We're not!' Robbie retorted.

Until then Mark had remained silent but he now chose to play his ace. 'Tell Mr Trikhardt about Mr Morrison, Paw.'

'Morrison at the Sunday school saw Hendry threatening my Mark. According to Morrison Mark was on the ground pleading not to be hit.'

Julius swung his gaze on to Robbie. 'That's true?'

'Mark had been shooting spitballs at me and when I told him to stop it he suddenly dropped to the ground and did all this acting about me supposedly going to hit him.'

'That's right,' Sadie corroborated.

Miller sneered at Robbie and Sadie, then said softly to Julius, 'If you believe that story you're a fool. And I've never considered you that.'

Julius nodded. 'Leave it to me, Erwin. I'll deal with them.'

'No, I want you to deal with them right here and now. And I want my boys to see justice done.'

A smirk crept on to Mark's aching face. Oh, how he was going to enjoy this!

'Justice was done in the school yard for what they did to Sadie, and for what they've been doing to me,' Robbie protested.

'Quiet boy. We've had enough of your lies,' Julius said, starting to remove the thick leather belt from round his trousers.

It was so unfair! Sadie inwardly raged. She and Robbie were the innocent parties in all this. Mark and Grant were the villains, particularly where Robbie was concerned.

'Come here,' Julius said quietly to Robbie.

Robbie didn't budge, even though he knew the inevitable would happen. It was awful enough to be leathered, but in front of the Millers!

'I said come here,' Julius repeated.

A defiant Robbie still didn't budge.

Julius moved swiftly to grab Robbie by the collar. He then threw him across the kitchen table, so that Robbie was half on and half dangling, and began in with the belt.

The belt whistled through the air to land with a resounding crack. He wouldn't cry or make any sound at all, Robbie told himself. He wouldn't give the Millers that satisfaction. He would take whatever was to come silently.

The belt whistled again and again, and every time it landed Mark's and Grant's smiles got bigger.

Sadie didn't count how many times the belt landed, but it seemed to go on for ever. Then finally it was over and Julius released Robbie who staggered away from the table like a drunken man.

'Satisfied?' Julius asked Miller.

'Now the girl. She was in on this.'

Fear clutched at Sadie's insides. Fear that made her go cold all over and shiver with apprehension.

Julius strode to her, grasped her by the wrist, dragged her to the table and pushed her into the same position that Robbie had been in.

'She's not well,' a white-faced Robbie gasped, swaying where he stood.

Julius registered the point, and softened his blows. Sadie couldn't be as stoic as Robbie, she screamed when the belt cracked against her backside.

Through a haze of pain and tears she saw the Miller boys' gloating faces staring at her.

She averted her head as the belt whistled down yet again.

Sadie woke up, having been sent to bed without any supper directly after her punishment. Gingerly she touched her bottom which was still incredibly painful. She wondered how Robbie was who'd received far more strokes than she had.

She groaned as she slid her legs off the bed, and then gradually levered herself up on to her feet. She'd been sleeping on her front with her bottom exposed to the air.

She groaned again when she tried to walk, the muscles of her bottom and thighs protesting with every movement.

She lit her lamp, then squirmed into a dressing-gown. Then she staggered across the landing and tapped on Robbie's door.

'Who is it?' he called out.

'Sadie. Can I come in?'

'Wait a mo'.' There was a short pause, then he said, 'You can come in now.'

He too was in bed, under the clothes and lying on his side. He'd been reading by lamplight.

'How are you?' she asked, noting how drawn and haggard he looked.

'I'll live. What about you?'

'The same. Though don't ask me to sit down.'

He grinned at that. 'I'm sorry you got involved.'

'None of it was your fault, Robbie. That lies entirely with the Miller boys. But don't worry, they'll get their come-uppance.'

'How?' he queried.

'I originally stayed at a Home called Babies Castle where there was a Miss Tupper who was like a second mother to me. Well, Miss Tupper used to say that you always, eventually, get back what you give out. By doing what they did, the Miller brothers are actually harming themselves far more than they've harmed us.'

'It doesn't feel like that at the moment,' Robbie commented ruefully.

'I know what you mean. But I believe Miss Tupper was talking in the long term rather than the short. According

148

to her if you are good and kind then that's what is dealt out to you, but if you are nasty and wicked then that's measured out to you in return.'

Robbie thought about that. 'I don't think I agree with your Miss Tupper.'

'Why?'

'What have you and I ever done to deserve the lives we've landed?'

It was a fair point, Sadie told herself. 'But we're still young, with everything hopefully before us. Agreed, we've had a difficult start, but who knows what lies ahead?'

'I know what lies ahead.'

'What?'

'A mountain of chores.'

She smiled. 'You're thinking in the short term, and negatively. Always think positively according to Miss Tupper.'

'I'll tell you something, and I don't know whether it's negative or not, but I hate them. Mark and Grant Miller, and the Trikhardts. If they all ended up roasting in hell tonight I wouldn't be in the least bit sorry. Not in the least.'

Sadie stared sadly at her friend, knowing only too well why he felt this way.

'One day, when I'm old enough, I'm going to run away from here. You just wait and see if I don't,' he added.

Sadie wouldn't have minded running away herself. Staying with the Trikhardts was hateful. They were never shown an ounce of love or affection, it was all just work and more work. There were occasions when she felt like a slave rather than a free person.

Robbie moved under the bed clothes, and winced. He knew that both of them would have black and blue backsides in the morning.

'How are you feeling apart from the sore bottom?' he asked.

'The headache and chest pain has gone and I haven't coughed since waking. So I suppose the answer is a lot better, thank you. And thank you for saying what you did just before I got belted. It would have been even worse for me if you hadn't.'

'I suppose we'd better get some sleep, don't forget there's still that early rise in the morning. And you can bet we'll be expected to do just as much as usual, if not more.'

'They're certainly demanding taskmasters. There's no argument about that,' Sadie agreed.

'I don't know what I'd do without you here,' Robbie stated frankly.

'Nor me you.'

'We are good pals?'

'The best.'

'Even closer than you and Janet?' he teased.

'You're a boy so it's different. Let's just say I lost one best pal and gained another.'

'I'll settle for that.'

'Goodnight then.'

'Goodnight, Sadie.'

Back in her own bedroom, despite the chill, she lay on her front again and pulled up her nightie at the back to let the air get at her throbbing bottom.

When she eventually fell asleep she dreamt of Robbie.

'You've just got to forget school for a while. It's a busy time round here now, what with planting and the like. I need you on the farm, the pair of you.'

'Are you talking about days?' a dismayed Robbie asked.

'I'm talking about as long as I need you here on a full-time basis.'

Robbie's heart sank. Was that weeks? Months? He was aware that Julius could keep him off school with impunity, he'd already discussed that with Mr Paterson. The only thing Julius was obliged to do was ensure the pair of them attend Sunday school. If Julius failed to do that he would have been breaking the terms of their contracts.

Robbie glanced at Sadie who was biting her lip, she as dismayed as he.

'Now that's an end to the matter,' Julius said bad temperedly, and stalked away.

Robbie glanced again at Sadie who shrugged. 'There's nothing we can do about it,' she said.

'That's the problem.'

Anna strode into the room. 'Are you two idling again? There are a pile of things to be done.'

Robbie and Sadie got on with the chores.

'Look!' Sadie said to Robbie, pointing. They were in one of the fields sowing wheat. When they were finished Julius would come along with either Trixie or Dixie and rake in the seed.

The dog was a collie and clearly a young puppy from the way it was behaving. It bounded here and there with enormous vitality, then pursued a rabbit with great vigour until losing the animal down a hole.

'It would be lovely to have a dog like that,' Robbie commented, eyes shining at the thought.

Sadie agreed. 'Far better than Buster.' Buster was the Trikhardts' dog, and a more disagreeable dog you'd have gone a long way to find. He was best left alone, which was precisely what Sadie and Robbie did. Julius fed and watered him, no one else, not even Anna.

'I'd teach it tricks,' Robbie said.

'Could you do that? I mean, would you know how?'

'I've never done it before, but I don't see why I couldn't. Patience and kindness would be the main things.'

'What sort of tricks?'

'All sorts. Fetching sticks, standing on its hind legs. I don't know!'

Sadie laughed with sheer delight, and closed her eyes, enjoying the gentle wind that was caressing her cheeks. She breathed in the smells of freshly turned earth, apple blossom from close-by, the distinctive odour from the small creek that meandered not far from where they were standing, and all manner of things growing.

'I can't wait for the summer,' she said.

'It gets very hot here, you know.'

'The hotter the better. I hope the sun blazes down day after day.'

'A change from Scotland, eh?'

She thought of the Scottish weather, and laughed again.

'Do you miss Scotland?' he asked.

She considered that. 'I don't know if I miss it, but I do think about it a lot.'

'Me too. And *I* miss it.'

'Even though you didn't leave a family behind?'

'Yes,' he said.

'I also often think about my family,' Sadie went on. 'I wonder about them, what they're doing and where they are. And I also wonder if they ever think about me.'

'Surely they do.'

She shrugged her shoulders. 'Who knows! I'd certainly like to think so.'

Robbie glanced up as a flight of geese in triangular formation flew overhead. How graceful, he thought, and watched them wing their way into the distance. There was no doubt about it, Canada might be a harsh land in winter, but with that fast fading there could be no denying its natural beauty, much of which could now be seen and appreciated.

He looked at Sadie and thought how pretty she was. No, beautiful, he corrected himself. He adored her dark lustrous hair which cascaded down over her shoulders, hair that glistened and gleamed with health.

Sadie caught him staring at her. 'What is it?' she asked.

He blushed and glanced away. 'Nothing.'

What an odd expression, she thought.

They resumed sowing, and as they scattered the seed Sadie sang songs from the old country.

'Having a good time?' Robbie asked, sitting beside Sadie on a bale of straw.

'A whale of a time.'

'It is great fun.'

'The Millers?'

'Not coming. They weren't invited.'

That was excellent news, Sadie thought, now they could both relax properly. This was the first barn dance which the Trikhardts had brought them to.

The caller was in full flow, instructing the dancers what moves to make next, while behind him the four fiddlers fiddled with gusto.

The dance was being held at the Robsons, close neighbours of the Trikhardts, and over a hundred people were present. It was a colourful spectacle, the majority of men dressed in jeans and plaid shirts, the women in all hues of the spectrum.

'Do you fancy getting up for the next one?' Robbie asked shyly.

'Me!'

'Why not? Children are allowed to dance. I've seen plenty up.'

'OK,' she smiled.

When the time came he took her by the hand and led her on to the floor where, within minutes, they were right in the swing of things, and looking as though they'd been barn dancing all their lives.

When they came off the floor Sadie was panting, her forehead covered in perspiration. 'Certainly takes it out of you,' she commented.

'You can say that again.'

When they reached the bale of straw they'd previously been sitting on, he realized he was still holding her hand, and reluctantly let it go.

'Hello Robbie, how are you?'

Robbie jumped to his feet when he saw who the speaker was. 'Fine sir, thank you very much.'

'And you, Sadie?'

She, too, came to her feet. 'I'm fine also, Mr Paterson.'

He stared at Robbie sadly. 'I'd hoped to see you back at school when we restarted after the summer recess, but was disappointed.'

Robbie glanced at the floor. 'I would have loved to come back, sir, but I wasn't allowed.'

'What a shame, and what a waste,' Mr Paterson breathed.

'Both of us would have loved to come back,' Sadie said.

Paterson glanced over to where his wife was deep in conversation, then returned his attention to them. His brow furrowed in thought. 'I take it the Trikhardts are here? I haven't noticed them, but then my wife and I have just arrived.'

'Yes, they're here,' Robbie confirmed.

Paterson stroked his chin. Then came to a decision. 'I don't normally interfere, but in your case, Robbie, I'll make an exception if you want me to. Would you like me to speak to Mr Trikhardt on your behalf?'

Robbie's face lit up. 'You mean speak to him about me going back to school?'

'That's right. He might change his mind if I point out certain things to him.'

'Oh, please do!' Robbie urged.

'What exactly is the position? What has he said to you on the subject?'

'For various reasons he kept us off for a few days here, and a few days there. But when planting time came round he announced he needed us on a full-time basis. We haven't been allowed back since.'

'I see,' Mr Paterson mused.

'Robbie desperately wants to attend,' Sadie said.

Paterson smiled. 'Then let's find Mr Trikhardt and have that word, eh?'

'He's drinking at the bar,' Sadie said.

'Then let's go.'

Robbie and Sadie eagerly went with Paterson to the makeshift bar, where beer, cider and hard liquor were being sold. Julius was in the company of some cronies, his flushed face and slightly glassy eyes betraying the fact he'd already taken a fair amount on board.

'Good evening, Mr Trikhardt, I wonder if I could speak to you in private?' Mr Paterson requested.

Julius took in the presence of Robbie and Sadie. 'Sure! How can I help you?'

They moved a little way off to where they wouldn't be overheard. 'It's about Robbie,' Mr Paterson said.

'Oh, yeah?'

'I wanted to explain to you that he's an extremely bright child. Quite exceptional in fact. By far and away the most clever student I've ever had at our little school.'

'That so!'

'He has enormous potential, if he's allowed to continue his studies, that is. He's certainly top-stream university material with, I predict, a brilliant career after that.'

'I see,' Julius murmured, and took a swallow from the paper cup containing rye whisky he was holding.

'It would be a tragedy for him if he were to miss out on school, a terrible tragedy.'

'That so!' Julius repeated, staring at Robbie. 'Bright, eh?'

'Yes, and a joy to teach. He absorbs everything as if he were a piece of blotting paper. Just soaks it up, particularly in the field of mathematics. He has the makings of a first-rate mathematician.'

'Mathematician!' Julius mused. 'Ain't got much call for one of those round the farm.'

Paterson smiled thinly, realizing Julius might be joking, but was also deadly serious. 'I suppose you haven't.'

'What I need is a strong back and two willing hands. That the boy has.'

'He also has a fine brain, Mr Trikhardt.'

'Yeah, I noticed that already. He's real good at organizing things. For a kid his age, that is. He's got initiative. I admire that. Because it's useful, saves time. And time is money, after all.'

Paterson took a deep breath. 'Mr Trikhardt, I'm asking on Robbie's behalf that you release him through the day again so that he can once more attend school.'

Julius had another sip of rye, then snorted. 'You do understand they're both contracted to me for a monthly wage.'

'I do.'

'And that there's nothing nowhere, contract or otherwise, says I got to send them to school.'

'I understand that also.'

'I need help round the farm,' Julius went on. 'Before school and afterwards just wasn't enough. That was putting too great a workload on me and my wife. Nor can I afford to pay them and take on another hand. And I certainly can't send them home to Scotland. So they're landed with me till they're old enough, just as I'm landed with them. And that's the position.'

'Surely some sort of compromise . . .' Paterson trailed off when Julius shook his head.

'Nope. No compromise. I need them all the time round the farm, and that's that.'

'But Robbie is capable of so much!'

'May be, but I didn't contract for no intellectual. I contracted help for Anna and me, and that's how it's going to be,' Julius replied stubbornly, and had another swig of rye.

Paterson could see he was up against a brick wall. Julius's mind was set, and there would be no changing it. 'I'm sorry,' he said to a crestfallen Robbie.

Robbie gave him a bitter, strained smile. 'Thank you for trying anyway, sir.'

'Excuse me,' Julius said to Paterson, and rejoined his cronies.

'You did your best, sir,' Robbie mumbled.

'Which just wasn't good enough, I'm afraid.'

Sadie grasped Robbie by the arm, and squeezed it in sympathy. 'How about another dance?' she suggested.

'I think I'd like to go outside for a little while.'

'Do you want me to come with you?'

'No, I'd rather you didn't. I'd prefer to be on my own.'

She watched him walk disconsolately away, his shoulders slumped, body bowed.

Life could be a bitch at times, Paterson thought. And this was one of them. He could have wept for the lad.

'You've got a letter,' Julius said, throwing it in front of Sadie.

'For me!' she gasped in astonishment, staring at it.

'Your name's on the front.'

She glanced at Robbie, then back at the letter. *Who* could be writing to her!

Sadie Smith, Peterawa, Ontario it stated on the cream-coloured envelope. She didn't recognize the handwriting.

'Look at the frank and see where it's from,' Robbie suggested.

The frank was smudged, but decipherable. 'Clarke City, Quebec!' Sadie squealed in delight. The letter was from Janet.

Eagerly she ripped open the envelope and read the five double-page contents, devouring each and every word.

Robbie knew well enough who lived in Clarke City. As he sat watching Sadie read he experienced a new emotion, that of jealousy. Janet, Sadie's best pal before him, had

157

gone out of Sadie's life, now that link was re-established. He no longer had her all to himself, and that knowledge, however irrational, upset him.

You're being silly, he told himself. But jealousy continued to gnaw at his insides. He realized then just how much Sadie had come to mean to him: in terms of human relationships, simply everything.

'How is she?' he enquired when Sadie reached the end of the letter.

He forced himself to listen patiently as Sadie gave him Janet's news.

Robbie grunted with exertion as he heaved a box of stores into the car's boot. He manoeuvred it into the position he wanted, then bent to pick up another box.

It was Saturday afternoon and he and Julius had come into town with a long list of items that Anna wanted, and with another list written by Julius himself. Shopping done, Julius had left Robbie to load up the car while he went off to the tavern where he'd spend at least an hour.

'Hi, Robbie!'

Robbie took off his cap to Mr Paterson. 'Hello, sir.' It was now mid-December, several months since the barn dance.

'You're growing. Whatever else, farm life certainly seems to agree with you.'

'Both Sadie and I have shot up since arriving here.'

'How is she?'

'Grand, sir. Never better.'

'And where's Mr Trikhardt?'

'Gone to Niko's, sir.' That was the name of the tavern Julius frequented.

Paterson nodded. A farmer visiting the tavern on a Saturday afternoon was reasonable enough, and regular practice for many of the farmers thereabouts.

'Well, nice speaking to you, Robbie,' Mr Paterson said, and started to move off.

'Sir!'

Paterson stopped, and turned again to Robbie.

'Sir, I've just had a thought. Do you think I could borrow some school books from you? That way I could do a bit of work at home.'

'Of course! I'd be only too happy to lend you whatever you'd like.'

Robbie's face shone with excitement. How he itched to get back into school work. Why hadn't he thought of this before?

'Tell you what,' said Mr Paterson. 'How would you like it if I set you out a schedule? And I could correct and comment on what you do.'

Robbie looked uncertain. 'Unless you come out to the house regularly, sir, I don't see how we could manage that. I'm always there, on the farm that is, with the exception of Saturday afternoons when I come into town.'

'Then we can meet every Saturday afternoon. How about that?'

'Are you sure you wouldn't mind, sir?'

Paterson laughed. 'Mind is the last thing I'd do. It would give me great pleasure to meet up with you every Saturday afternoon, great pleasure indeed!'

Robbie felt like shouting for joy. 'If we could take up where I left off, sir.'

'Agreed. How much time per day do you think you can devote to this?'

'Now that Sadie and I are full time on the farm there's always an hour before bedtime during which we're allowed to do as we wish. So that would be seven hours a week, plus any other time I can squeeze in.'

Seven hours a week wasn't a lot, Paterson thought, but better than nothing. And someone of Robbie's capabilities would be able to cram far more into that than other, less gifted children.

'I'll be here this time next Saturday with books, paper, pencils and the schedule I'll have drawn up. How's that?'

Robbie beamed broadly at Paterson. 'Marvellous, sir. Absolutely marvellous! And could you do the same for Sadie? I know that's what she'd want.'

'Of course, a schedule for her as well.'

Mr Paterson ruffled Robbie's hair, then continued on his way. What a fortunate encounter that had been. He only prayed that Trikhardt allowed Robbie to study. You never knew with a man like that.

Julius switched on the radio, then plonked himself down in his favourite armchair. Picking up a can of beer, he opened it and took a gulp. He then belched loudly.

Anna was knitting, her wooden needles going twenty to the dozen. Knitting was her usual form of relaxation.

Robbie glanced at Sadie, and gave her an almost imperceptible nod. They left the room together to fetch their books that Mr Paterson had given Robbie in town that afternoon.

When they returned they laid their things out, and sat down.

'I'll help you with anything you don't understand,' he told her.

Anna was frowning. 'What are you kids up to?' she demanded.

'I've arranged with Mr Paterson that we'll do school work during the hour before bed,' Robbie explained.

Julius swivelled his gaze on to them. 'What's that?'

Robbie repeated himself.

'Who gave you permission to do school work in my time?'

'Chores are finished, everything's done for the day,' Robbie replied.

'That's for me to say,' Julius growled.

'Is there something you wish me to do?' Robbie asked softly.

Julius stared at Robbie, his expression one of irritation. 'I can soon find a chore if I want to.'

'I didn't think you'd mind us doing this in the evening,' Robbie stated politely. 'It keeps us busy and quiet after all.'

Julius grunted, that was true. 'I ain't turning off my radio, or not speaking because of you two.'

'That's fine by us. Isn't it, Sadie?'

She nodded, knowing Julius was like a volcano which would explode at any moment. Robbie had told her to let him do all the talking.

'What do you think?' Julius demanded of Anna.

'I can't see any harm.'

Julius couldn't either, which didn't necessarily mean he'd agree. He felt his authority was somehow being challenged.

'May I say something?' Robbie smiled.

'What?' Julius asked.

'It will make Sadie and I very happy to be allowed to do school work at this time, and it's well known that you get better overall work out of a happy person than an unhappy one.'

Julius glared at Robbie, then gradually the glare melted into a grudging smile. 'You're sure sassy, kid, and smart. Paterson was right about that.'

'Then we have your permission?' Robbie asked softly.

Julius wagged a finger at him. 'But only at this time of night when everything's done, OK?'

'We promise,' Robbie replied.

Julius felt he had to score at least one point, so he turned up the volume of his radio.

In the summer of 1931, when Sadie and Robbie had been with the Trikhardts for three years, Buster the dog died. After Julius had buried him, he declared he'd have to get himself another dog. After all, a farm needed a dog.

Sadie and Robbie discussed the matter between themselves, then waited till supper that evening before broaching what they had in mind.

'The Keenher's bitch had puppies a while ago. They should be ready now,' Robbie said.

Julius never glanced up from the meat loaf he was wolfing.

'She's a lovely bitch,' Robbie went on. 'What's her name again?'

'Purdey,' Sadie stated. They had arranged that she would act as his foil.

'It's a Great Dane,' Anna said, chewing on a cob of sweet corn dripping with butter. Although she had a hearty appetite and never stinted herself at table she never put on so much as an ounce.

'A Great Dane,' Robbie confirmed, nodding his agreement.

'They'll be giving the pups away? I mean they won't be charging for them?' Sadie said to Robbie.

'So I heard. Absolutely free.'

'Are the pups cross bred?' Sadie queried.

Robbie shook his head. 'No, the father is a Dane as well. Belongs to a friend of the Keenhers. A pedigree animal, I believe.'

'Should be first-class pups then,' Sadie mused.

'Should be,' Robbie agreed.

Julius paused and used the back of his hand to wipe tomato sauce from his face. 'A Great Dane's no use to me. Eat far too much for a start.'

'That's the surprising thing, they don't,' Robbie countered.

'Who told you that?'

'Mr Keenher himself, and he should know.'

Julius forked more meat loaf into his mouth. 'Would still be more than I gave Buster.'

At least they'd succeeded in getting him to discuss the matter, Robbie thought triumphantly. 'Not necessarily. You simply don't give them all that much.'

'And why's that?'

'For health reasons. It's to do with the size of their

frames in relation to their hearts. It's best to keep them sleek and trim, with ribs showing. If overweight they're prone to heart attacks.'

Robbie smiled. 'And they have marvellous dispositions. Think they're people.'

Julius looked at him disbelievingly. 'That's crap. How can a dog think it's a person?'

'They do apparently. They are usually very loving, but at the same time are excellent guard dogs.'

'And they're hounds,' Sadie chipped in, knowing Julius had a soft spot for hounds.

'You mean like a hunting hound?' he queried.

'That's right,' Robbie corroborated. 'They were bred for precisely that.'

Robbie glanced at Sadie, they'd caught his interest with that piece of information.

'A dog that would look good beside you when you went off hunting deer,' Robbie said. This was something Julius did in the season.

Julius sat back in his chair and pictured himself with a Great Dane, the pair of them striding through the woods together.

'Besides,' Robbie went on smoothly, 'someone like you should have a large dog. It's far more manly. Isn't that so, Sadie?'

'Far more,' Sadie agreed.

'Are they good ratters?' Anna asked. Buster had excelled at that.

'I'm sure they can be if it's required of them,' Robbie answered.

Julius thought of the German Shepherd Gene Robson had, a Dane would put that right in the shade.

'Very noble animals,' Robbie said.

Noble! Julius liked the idea of that as well. A hound, noble, a large dog that was far more manly. It got better and better.

'I'd prefer another mongrel. A Great Dane is far too

high falutin' for such as us,' Anna said, which was a mistake on her part.

Julius was instantly incensed. 'Why too high falutin' for us!' he retorted sharply. 'We're as good as any round here. We're certainly as good as the Keenhers, and it ain't too high falutin' for them.'

Robbie kicked Sadie under the table. They were winning. 'Wouldn't do any harm to look at the pups,' he suggested.

'No harm at all,' Julius snorted. 'We'll drive over there tomorrow.'

This time Sadie kicked Robbie. They'd achieved what they'd set out to do and realizing that they had, they dropped the subject, leaving it to simmer in Julius's mind.

Frank Keenher greeted them as they drove up and parked in front of his house. 'Hello there!' he called out as they emerged from the car. Sadie and Robbie had accompanied Julius, Anna electing to remain behind.

The two men shook hands. 'I've come about your pups, Frank. Thought I might have a look-see at them.'

'You're more than welcome,' Frank enthused. 'Come on inside. They're in the kitchen.'

'Are you thinking of having one?' Frank asked as he led them down a hallway.

'Don't know. Never had a Dane before.'

'Wonderful dogs, Julius. Can't speak too highly of them.'

'And your pups are free, I believe?' Julius probed.

'They're free OK. Could charge I suppose, but there again . . .' He trailed off and shrugged. 'Dane's always drop a large litter and I could hardly charge for some and then give the others away. The alternative to giving away those I couldn't find buyers for would be a sack and the river, and that I just couldn't do.'

'Where's the wife?' Julius enquired as they entered the kitchen.

'Out doing a bit of sketching. You know how she's crazy about her art.'

'She's a fine artist. I've always liked her stuff,' Julius replied.

Sadie was amazed to hear Julius say that. Through admitting an appreciation of art, he was showing a completely new side to his character and one she found very difficult to believe existed.

'Here are the proud mom and babes,' Frank said.

Purdey was lying on an old strip of carpet that was her bed gazing soulfully at the puppies moving about her. A pair were cuffing one another, one was chasing his tail, several others were asleep, another precariously walking along the length of Purdey's back

'Certainly a large litter,' Julius acknowledged. 'How many?'

'There were sixteen, but two are now gone.'

Julius whistled. 'Sixteen!'

Two of the puppies were a grey colour, the remainder a marvellous golden brown. One dashed out to run round Sadie's foot, then it darted off to play with a screwed up piece of newspaper.

'That little fella's just full of mischief,' Frank smiled. 'And simply oozes personality.'

Frank bent and picked up the puppy. 'Look at this. If that ain't endearing I don't know what is.' The puppy had cross eyes which gave it a quizzical, bemused look.

Sadie laughed, as did Robbie. 'He's cute,' Sadie said.

'Real cute, ain't you, boy,' Frank murmured, stroking the puppy's head.

'Can I hold him?' Sadie requested.

'Sure.'

Frank handed the puppy over, and Sadie stroked its head the way he'd been doing.

'Here's a gorgeous bitch,' Robbie said, scooping up one of the greys.

'No bitch. If I do take one it'll be a dog. Bitches are too much trouble,' Julius declared.

'I think this guy is terrific,' Robbie said, tickling the cross-eyed pup and making it squirm.

'He certainly has appeal,' Frank smiled.

Julius picked up a pup that was larger than the rest which promptly nipped him when he went to chuck it under the chin. 'Bastard!' he exclaimed, and threw it back on to the floor.

Frank frowned at that, but didn't comment on it. 'You after a puppy for the kids?' he asked innocently.

'For me, round the farm and to hunt with,' Julius replied.

'But Robbie and I will be taking care of him. Isn't that so?' Sadie said.

Julius grunted, and nodded his head.

That was all right then, Frank thought.

They looked at a few of the other pups, but kept returning to the cross-eyed one who'd stolen both Sadie's and Robbie's heart. During all this Sadie kept hold of him, refusing to put him back down.

'And they don't eat much?' Julius queried of Frank.

'Very economical to run,' Frank joked. 'Robbie here knows all about Danes, don't you, kid? You and I had a right old palaver about them once.'

'Can we have this one, please?' Sadie pleaded of Julius.

'Do these cross eyes make any difference?' he asked Frank, who shook his head.

'Not at all.'

'I've already got a name for him,' Sadie announced.

'What's that?' a surprised Frank asked.

'You said he was full of mischief and that's exactly what I'd call him. Mischief.'

'Yeah,' Julius nodded. 'I like that. Mischief!'

'So can we keep him, please?' Sadie repeated.

'As two are already gone I take it they're already weaned?' Julius queried of Frank.

'Yup.'

'Then we'll have Mischief.'

Sadie and Robbie couldn't have been more pleased. They both felt they'd found a new friend.

'Can you help me with this?' Sadie asked Robbie, the pair of them at the kitchen table doing their nightly school work.

'What's the problem?'

She told him, and he quickly explained what she'd failed to grasp. Before returning to what she was doing she smiled down at Mischief lying patiently on the floor between them. He was four months old now, and growing fast.

Julius, smoking by the stove, saw her smiling at the dog. 'He'll have to go outside soon. He's a working dog, don't forget, and a working dog's place is outside, not in the house. I don't want no house dog.'

'Danes don't thrive when they're left outside. They're people dogs,' Robbie explained patiently.

'Don't matter. He goes outside.'

Sadie glanced at Robbie, the last thing either wanted was for Mischief to be kennelled outside. Particularly in winter time when the temperature plummeted.

'I heard Klein's drugstore was broken into,' Robbie said.

'Who told you that?'

'Mr Paterson mentioned it when I spoke to him on Saturday.'

'Well, I didn't hear nothing about it.'

'Not much was taken, but there could have been.'

Anna laid down her knitting. 'If anyone ever broke in here Julius would shoot the son-of-a-bitch stone dead. Wouldn't you, Julius?'

'I sure would. I'd blast him right between the eyes.'

Robbie had no doubt Julius would do exactly that. 'Providing you could get to your gun of course. You could be murdered in your bed first.'

'Sheeett!' Julius swore. His guns were kept locked away in the basement.

'There's truth in what the boy says,' Anna declared slowly.

'Maybe I'll keep a gun in the bedroom from now on. Just to be on the safe side.'

'Such a gun could always be removed while you were asleep,' Robbie told him.

Julius grunted, and drew heavily on his cigarette.

'But no one would ever get as far as your bed if there was a guard dog in the house. The barking would wake you and give you plenty of time to get your gun,' Robbie went on.

Julius and Anna both thought about that.

'And you must have read in the newspapers how violence and burglary are on the increase of late. Not just in the big cities, but everywhere. As one article put it, things aren't as they used to be.'

'A dog outside would bark as well if intruders tried to break into the house,' Julius mused.

'But a dog who's outside can be got at, nobbled. That can't happen when the dog's inside the house,' Robbie skilfully countered.

'Murdered in our beds,' Anna said quietly, touching her throat. And shuddered.

'Butchered,' Robbie elaborated gruesomely. 'It does happen.'

'Times certainly are a'changing,' Julius said, grinding out his cigarette.

'There would be no butchering with Mischief on hand. Would there, boy?'

Mischief came to his feet and barked as though he understood.

'You'd give us all plenty of warning. We could count on you. Go to bed without worry knowing you were the best alarm system a family could have.'

Mischief, tail wagging furiously, barked again.

'The Kleins today, who knows whose house tomorrow,' Robbie said softly, nodding thoughtfully.

Sadie bent her head to hide her smile. Good old Robbie. He'd become quite an expert at manipulating the Trikhardts when he wanted to.

Mischief would continue to spend his nights in the house now, she was certain of that.

She could have hugged Robbie.

'Play dead!' Robbie commanded, and immediately Mischief fell to the ground where he rolled on to his back with his legs sticking up in the air.

Robbie laughed with pleasure. 'OK, up!'

Mischief sprang to his feet and wagged his tail.

'Good boy. Play dead again!'

Mischief repeated his performance, this time adding the refinements of closing his eyes and dropping his head to one side.

'Oh, you clever boy. You clever boy,' Robbie smiled, and bent to tickle Mischief's tummy.

Before he could do so a boot thudded into his backside sending him flying. He cried out in pain and surprise as he slid along the ground.

Mischief growled threateningly at Julius, then whimpered when he, too, was kicked.

'There's no need to take it out on the dog,' Robbie said, scrambling to his feet. The base of his spine was throbbing where Julius's boot had caught it.

'I pay you to work, not play with the goddamn dog,' Julius snarled.

'It was only for a moment or two.'

Julius glared at him. 'Don't lie your ass off to me. It takes time to teach a dog to do a trick like that, my time.'

'You get more work out of me than you'd get out of two grown men, so you can hardly complain.'

'You got a mouth, kid, that's going to be your undoing

169

someday.' And with that Julius stepped quickly forward and slapped Robbie.

When Robbie managed to focus again on Julius he saw three of him. The inside of his head was spinning round, unsettling his balance. He had to hold out his hands to stop himself falling over.

'Now get on with that fencing like you're supposed to be doing,' Julius instructed.

He turned his attention to Mischief whose tail was curled between his legs. 'Come here, boy. You'll go with me now.'

Mischief backed away.

'I said come here, boy,' Julius repeated crossly.

Mischief stayed where he was, not budging.

Julius advanced towards Mischief who immediately retreated. 'Goddamn mother-fucking dog!' Julius spat out, lunged at Mischief, and succeeded in catching him by the collar.

'I said you'll go with me and go you will,' he said, groping in the top pocket of his overalls.

Robbie watched helplessly as Julius produced a length of twine, and proceeded to tie one end to Mischief's collar. Mischief whined and tried to pull free while Julius was doing this, but Julius held the dog fast.

Julius wrapped the free end of the twine several times round a meaty hand. 'Now you get on with the fencing like I said. And I'll be back later to see just how much you've done,' he told Robbie.

When Julius attempted to drag Mischief off, the dog dug in its back legs, for which he was rewarded with another kick.

'Come on!' Julius yelled angrily, and yanked hard on the twine. This time Mischief went, though most reluctantly. As he trotted behind Julius he gazed mournfully back at Robbie.

Robbie was seething inside. God how he hated that man! And his wife. He hated them both, passionately.

Some day, some day when he was old and big enough . . . He'd go for the swine, he would.

He clenched his hands into fists, and sucked in a deep breath. His head was still spinning, but not as violently as it had. And his single vision was restored.

'Some day,' he muttered to himself, swinging a sledge-hammer to drive a post deep into the ground. 'Some bloody day.'

'He's useless, no good at all as a ratter,' Julius said.

Mischief's head drooped, then drooped even lower.

'We're overrun with rats since Buster died,' Julius went on. 'And what does this damn dog do? Nothing. Not a goddamn thing!'

'He's still young,' Sadie said.

'Buster was catching and killing rats at his age. We never lost no chickens when Buster was about.' The latter was refer-ring to the fact they'd lost two fowls to rats in the past week.

'He'll learn, you'll see,' Robbie said, patting Mischief's neck.

'You spoil that dog, that's his trouble,' Julius accused, his gaze going from Robbie to Sadie, then back again to Robbie.

Robbie decided not to argue, Julius was in an explosive mood. The slightest thing could cause an eruption.

'I could try and train him to catch rats if you'd like?' Robbie volunteered.

Julius sneered. 'Train! Killing rats should come natural, it shouldn't need no training.'

The trouble was that Mischief simply wasn't aggressive, Sadie thought. He was just a big soft nellie who wouldn't have hurt a fly. She and Robbie loved him for that, though both realized lack of aggression and the killing instinct were hardly assets for a farm dog.

Mischief's head drooped even lower still, his black jowls hanging like soggy pendulums. He was the picture of dejection.

'Buster didn't need no training,' Julius ploughed on. 'But then Buster was a good dog, not like this heap of shit.'

'That's unfair!' Sadie protested.

'What?'

Sadie shrank away from Julius. 'You're being unfair and unkind,' she stated bravely.

'What the hell has fairness or kindness got to do with it? What I'm saying is fact.'

Just then a rat broke from cover and went scurrying off towards the barn.

'Go get it, Mischief!' Robbie urged.

Mischief glanced up, and saw the rat. His ears rose, but he didn't move.

'Go on!' Robbie urged again, to no avail.

'I should get me a real dog,' Julius muttered, and stalked away.

Mischief sat on his bottom and crossed his forelegs in front of him, his expression one of profound, cross-eyed, comical sadness.

'Damn!' Robbie swore.

Sadie tumbled on to the grass where she lay laughing. They were having a marvellous few hours together while the Trikhardts were over at the Robsons.

Mischief jumped over her to go racing away, his feet thundering on the ground making him sound like a pony. He veered to one side, then jinked to the other. He vanished into tall grass, to suddenly reappear heading back towards them. He raced straight at the fallen Sadie as though he would run right into her, but at the last moment changed direction to brush past.

Robbie ran alongside Mischief, but could only keep up for a dozen feet or so. Then the dog was away, and furthering the distance between them with every passing second.

Sadie flattened a blackfly that landed on her cheek, then

did the same to another that landed on her leg. Blackfly were real pest at that time of year, but an annoyance she'd come to live with.

Mosquitoes were another evil, particularly if you went anywhere near the creek in the breeding season. Then the water surface and surrounding areas were alive with them.

She smiled to see that Mischief was now chasing Robbie who was running towards her. Mischief passed Robbie to end up in her arms licking her face.

Robbie came puffing up, and threw himself down beside Sadie where he lay on his back regaining his breath.

The three musketeers, Sadie thought. That's what we've become. One for all and all for one!

A revived Robbie grabbed Mischief by the neck and started wrestling the dog, the two of them rolling around on the ground.

'Come on, help me!' Robbie cried out to Sadie.

She did, and instantly the three of them became an intertwined muddle of bodies and limbs.

Mr Paterson ticked the final answer to the latest test he'd set for Robbie and sighed with gratification. It never ceased to amaze him how quickly Robbie learnt and how Robbie could apply that learning.

If Robbie shone in mathematics he'd also come to shine in all the sciences. Biology had been a snip for him, the same with chemistry. And now here he was being outstanding in physics!

Mr Paterson glanced again at one problem that Robbie had correctly solved, and shook his head in wonder. The lad was working with coulombs, joules and teslas as if he'd been doing so all his life. It was quite incredible.

As for Sadie, she was coming along nicely. She was intelligent, though nowhere near Robbie's level. She'd certainly have been university material if that had been open to her.

That it wasn't was a pity; in Robbie's case, a catastrophe.

Setting his anger aside he began writing out Robbie's and Sadie's schedules for the coming week.

Julius tossed his gun on to the kitchen table, and stood fuming. He'd just returned from hunting, the first time he'd taken Mischief with him.

'What's wrong?' Anna demanded.

'I've been made to look a fool, that's what's wrong. A goddamn fool!'

'How so?'

He pointed an accusing finger at Mischief who was lying on his bed. 'Because of him, that thing!'

Anna frowned as Julius strode over to the cupboard where the liquor was kept. He took out a bottle of Jack Daniels and poured himself a shot which he downed in one. He then poured himself another hefty tot. While he was doing this Anna waited patiently for the explanation she knew would now be forthcoming.

'The dog with the goofy eyes they called him, and laughed. At me as well as that stupid animal. At *me*!' Julius's tone was one of outrage. 'It was humiliating I can tell you. I've never been so humiliated.'

'Did the dog do OK though?'

'Yeah yeah, he wasn't that bad. For a dog new to hunting, that is.' Julius paused, then snarled. 'I can still hear those guys laughing. Real thigh-slapping laughter it was, too.'

He glared at Mischief. 'Goofy eyes!'

'I don't see why the guys should laugh at you.' Anna said.

'Because the mother fucker belongs to me, that's why! I just never thought . . . figured they'd react that way. It was all Ted Krumbeck's fault. He started it. Hey, what a goofy-looking dog! he said. And within seconds they were all howling and shrieking with laughter.'

Julius downed his second shot, and poured a third. He was squirming inside with embarrassment, nothing like this had ever happened to him before.

'Did you get a deer?' Anna asked.

'Naw. Not even the sight of one.'

Anna looked at Mischief who gazed balefully back at her. 'That dog was a mistake,' she pronounced.

'No good round a farm.'

'No good at all,' Julius agreed.

Anna didn't like her man being laughed at, she took it personally.

'They'll bring it up again in the tavern this Saturday afternoon, I just know it,' Julius said.

'Then don't go.'

'But I always go! If I don't turn up they'll know why and that'll make matters even worse.'

'A mistake,' Anna repeated.

Mischief cocked a leg over his head as though hiding himself.

Sadie would never forget that summer's day in 1932, the scar of it would remain in her memory for ever. She and Robbie were working out at the rear of the house when Mischief suddenly appeared lolloping towards them.

'Mischief!' Sadie cried in delight as the Dane first nuzzled her, then attempted to lick her face.

Robbie patted Mischief on the back, and was almost knocked over when Mischief nudged him hard with his bottom as a sign of affection.

'Good boy!' Sadie laughed, scratching Mischief under the chin.

Mischief's tail was now waggling furiously. A leg came up to rest on the squatting Sadie's shoulder, another sign of affection.

'I think he wants to play,' Robbie grinned.

Mischief looked at Robbie, and almost nodded his head in agreement.

'Is that it? Do you want to play?' Sadie said.

Mischief gave a huge yawn, and this time did manage to lick Sadie's face.

Robbie sat astride Mischief, careful not to put his full weight on him as that could damage the dog, and pretended to ride him cowboy style. Mischief, joining in the fun, removed his leg from Sadie's shoulder and began going round and round as though chasing his tail.

Sadie found this an extremely amusing sight and laughed loudly, a laugh that died in her throat when she saw a clearly livid Julius glaring at them.

When Robbie noticed Julius he promptly got off Mischief's back and stood upright.

'He ran away,' Julius said in a tight, crackling voice. 'The stupid no good mother-fucker ran away.'

Sadie bit her bottom lip.

Mischief's tail curled between his legs and he dropped his head in shame.

'I took him hunting and he ran away. Just took off in front of everyone!'

Mischief sank to the ground where he made a sort of mewing, crying noise.

'Just took off,' Julius repeated, features contorted with fury.

Robbie's thoughts raced as he tried to come up with something to defuse the situation. If matters continued as they were, Mischief was in for a hiding at least. Julius would tie him up, then use either his belt or a length of rope on him.

Mischief put both paws over his eyes and hid behind them.

Anna came out the back door, instantly aware that something was wrong. 'What's happened, hon?' she asked.

Julius pointed an accusing finger at Mischief. 'He ran off. We flushed a deer and the other dogs gave chase, except for this here thing which ran in the opposite direction. The totally opposite direction, would you believe!'

Anna's lips slowly thinned as she stared malevolently at Mischief.

'Ted Krumbeck positively hooted, as did the others. Billy Mitchell laughed so hard he almost choked. His cousin Jake had to pound him on the back.'

Julius's hands went white at the knuckles as he fiercely gripped the rifle he was carrying, a .303 that had been his since a boy.

Sadie glanced at Robbie, and bit her lip again. She, too, feared Mischief was in for a hiding.

'I ain't never looked so foolish. Never in all my born days. As they laughed I got redder and redder until I was as red as a sugar beet.' Julius shook all over at the memory.

'Enough is enough, he's got to go,' Anna said.

'No! Please!' Sadie exclaimed. She went over to Anna intending to plead with her, but Anna threw her aside.

'Yeah,' Julius muttered.

'The sooner the better,' Anna went on, hands on hips.

'Yeah,' Julius repeated in a soft, deadly tone.

Robbie's brain was whirling, but for once it let him down. He couldn't for the life of him think of a single thing to say in Mischief's defence. The dog, meanwhile, continued to make mewing, crying noises.

'He'll be better next time. He'll . . .' Sadie started to gabble.

'Shut up!' Julius hissed, his unyielding gaze fixed on the dog.

'Perhaps . . . Perhaps . . .' Robbie said, then trailed off not knowing what to say next.

Anna strode over to Mischief and lashed out with her foot, kicking the dog in the ribs. 'Useless animal,' she accused.

'He's not useless,' Sadie mumbled. 'He's lovely.'

'He's useless,' Anna spat at her.

Julius raised his gun into a firing position. 'Get away from there,' he instructed his wife.

Oh my God! Robbie thought in horror, realizing what Julius had in mind.

'No!' Sadie screamed, suddenly understanding also. She started forward, thinking to throw herself in front of Mischief to protect him, but before she'd taken more than a couple of steps Julius's gun boomed and blood fountained from between Mischief's paws.

'No! No!' Sadie wailed, falling on the dog which was jerking horribly.

A cruel smile curled Anna's lips upwards as she stared at the bloody scene. Julius had done the right thing in her opinion. The animal had deserved to be shot.

Sadie cradled Mischief's head in her lap, blood pouring from the gaping wound to stain first her hands, then her clothes. Miraculously, Mischief was still alive, though fading fast. One eye had disappeared, while the other fastened on her disconsolately.

Robbie knelt beside them and placed a hand on the still jerking dog. There were tears in all their eyes. When Robbie tried to speak he found he was so choked he was unable to do so.

Mischief whimpered, a sound that tore at Sadie's heart. He whimpered again, then suddenly went still while his head fell to one side. He was dead.

'Useless,' Anna smiled.

Sadie couldn't believe this had happened. That Mischief, the third musketeer, had gone. She shuddered, feeling sick.

'Poor dog,' Robbie croaked, finding his voice at last.

Sadie gazed at the Trikhardts through hot, blinding tears. She'd never loathed or hated them as much as she did then. How could Julius have killed Mischief, how could he?

Robbie stroked Mischief's flank, thinking how much he and Sadie were going to miss this dog they'd both loved so much. Anger and resentment bubbled within him, mingling with the revulsion he also felt.

'He won't run away on me no more,' Julius said with satisfaction.

'Or cause folks to laugh at you,' Anna added.

'Or that,' Julius agreed.

Abruptly, Julius turned on his heel and went inside.

'You two bury it,' Anna said, then followed her husband.

'Bastards,' Robbie mumbled through clenched teeth. 'Bastards!'

Sadie bowed her head, and openly wept.

'Sadie? You asleep?'

Sadie sat up. 'No,' she whispered into the darkness. It was that night and they'd both gone to bed about an hour previously. It was one of the few evenings that they hadn't done any school work, because neither had felt up to it.

Robbie sat down beside Sadie. 'I've made up my mind,' he whispered. 'I'm going to run away.'

'Oh, Robbie!'

'I can't take any more, not after today. Not after Mischief.' Robbie paused, then said slowly, 'If I'd had a knife in my hand this afternoon I'd have used it. I'd have killed him, I swear.'

'That's a terrible thing to say, Robbie,' she gently admonished.

'I know, but it's true. But I see it as one other reason why I must get away. I had thought to wait till I was sixteen, but at fifteen and a half I'm close enough to that.'

'Where will you go?'

Robbie shook his head. 'I don't know yet. Montreal perhaps, or Toronto. Certainly one of the cities.'

'And what will you do when you get there?'

'Find work.' He smiled ruefully. 'I'm used to hard work, after all. I doubt there's anything I'll come up with that will be worse than working round here.'

She caught his hand, and squeezed it. First Mischief,

now Robbie. What had dawned as such a golden day had degenerated into one of the blackest of her life.

She mustn't try to persuade Robbie to stay, she told herself. That would be selfish. She must think of him, what his best interests were and not take into account what effect this would have on her.

'It's going to be difficult. You're going to have to plan things carefully,' she warned him. 'God help you if you attempt to run away and get caught.'

Robbie thought grimly of that prospect, and tried to put it out of his mind. He simply couldn't be caught.

'What about money?' Sadie asked.

'I have what I've managed to save over the years. It's not a lot, but will get me on my way.'

'Wait a minute,' she said, and slipped out of bed.

He heard the scratch of a match being struck, and moments later Sadie'd lit her lamp which she turned down low. Holding it before her she padded over to the corner of the room where there was a loose floorboard that she'd discovered shortly after her arrival at the Trikhardts'. She set the lamp down, then tapped one end of the board which brought the other end up. She removed the board and reached into the recess that now lay open.

'What's this?' Robbie asked when she handed him the dusty handkerchief tied to secure its contents. It was a rhetorical question, the chinking sound from within the handkerchief had already told him what was inside.

'My savings,' she informed him. 'I want you to have them.'

'But I can't do that!' he protested, his voice rising above a whisper.

She put a finger to her lips, cautioning him to be quiet. 'Of course you can.'

'But this is all the money you've got.'

'Listen Robbie, right now you need this whereas I don't. I'm still only thirteen, it'll be another three years at least before I can consider running away, by which time I'll have more saved.'

He stared at the hanky, his heart swelling within him. 'You're ace, Sadie, simply ace,' he husked.

'You're pretty ace yourself.'

'I feel rotten at leaving you. Unless . . .'

She cut him off by shaking her head. 'I'm far too young yet. I'd only be a hindrance, a liability. No, you must go by yourself.'

She was right, and he knew it.

'You mustn't worry about me, I'll be all right,' she said.

'Are you sure?'

'Of course I am.'

He clutched the money to him. 'Thank you.'

They whispered together for a little longer, then Robbie tiptoed back to bed.

'Load up, I'm off to the tavern,' Julius said to Robbie, and immediately strode away.

Robbie's heart was hammering nineteen to the dozen. This was the day, this the hour. The train he'd selected, and which only ran once a month, was due in at the station in twenty-five minutes. If all went well, and the train wasn't late, then he'd be clear of Peterawa before Julius emerged from the tavern.

He didn't want to leave the groceries and other items lying on the sidewalk as that would only cause premature comment, so he loaded them into the car in double quick time. Then he set off at a very fast pace for the station.

He was carrying a small leather bag that he normally used on Saturdays for his and Sadie's school work which that day was jammed to bursting with the few spare clothes, and other bits and pieces he'd crammed into it.

He thought guiltily of Mr Paterson who'd been so good to him over the years. He'd considered telling the teacher what he was planning, then decided against it. Why take a risk, any risk? There was far too much at stake. Hopefully Mr Paterson would understand once he learnt that he'd absconded.

He came in sight of the station and slowed down, knowing he was on time. Please God, don't let the train be late, he prayed yet again. The service didn't exactly have a name for punctuality, though most of the bad hold-ups were in the winter on account of the weather.

Reaching the platform he glanced nervously about. There was a couple further down whom he didn't recognize. And a man he did, whose name escaped him.

The small ticket-office was open, but Robbie had no intention of using it. He would buy his ticket on the train.

He stared at the waiting-room, remembering the night he and Sadie had sheltered inside. That now seemed a lifetime ago.

How awful it was to be losing Sadie. The thought that he'd never see her again made him feel empty.

A horn wailed in the distance announcing the imminent arrival of the train. Robbie didn't know if it was early or late, for he didn't own a watch. All that mattered was that he was there to catch it.

He glanced behind him, half expecting Julius's car to be hurtling towards the station, an irate Julius inside. But there was no sign of either the car or Julius, who should still be in the tavern.

Minutes later the train drew alongside and a handful of people got off. Robbie turned his face away from one, Mr Cloos who managed the larger of the two banks in Peterawa.

He climbed aboard, and hurriedly found a seat. There, covered in sweat and goosepimples, he sat with his bag on his lap waiting for the train to leave.

The breath rushed out of him when the train started up again. He'd made it! He'd escaped! He began trembling all over from sheer relief.

Peterawa came into view as the train gathered speed.

'Goodbye, Sadie. Goodbye,' he whispered to himself, tiny tears appearing in his eyes.

Then Peterawa and Sadie were gone, and the future ahead. A future that would be entirely of his own making.

'Where the hell is Julius?' Anna complained for the umpteenth time, glancing at the kitchen clock. 'He should have been home hours ago.'

Sadie continued kneading dough. Mentally she had had two fingers crossed since her hurried farewell to Robbie, and his departure with Julius into town.

'I only hope he ain't drunk in that tavern,' Anna muttered, slicing a round of strawberry shortcake into portions. She and Julius adored strawberry shortcake.

Sadie stopped what she was doing when she heard the car. The moment of truth had finally arrived. 'He's here,' she said.

'And about time too,' Anna grumbled.

Sadie quickly towelled her hands. 'I'll only be a moment,' she said, and left the kitchen for a window overlooking the front of the house.

The car pulled up and Julius, clearly furious, got out, banging his door behind him. Sadie waited, but no one else appeared.

A soft smile lit up her lips. Robbie had been successful. He'd broken free of the hateful Trikhardts and the back-breaking graft of the farm.

Her happiness for him became clouded as a profound sadness settled on her. Robbie and Mischief, the other two musketeers, had blown away like morning mist.

Alone. That's what she was now. Totally and utterly alone.

Bowing her head, she wept.

Sadie dived into the cool, clear water, touched the bottom then shot to the surface again. The pool had been a favourite of hers and Robbie's and one they'd often used.

Of course when they'd used it together she hadn't swum naked as she was now.

It was the height of summer and the heat was intense. Stooking in the adjacent field had caused her to sweat profusely which was why she'd decided to take a quick break for a dip.

Treading water she wiped her hair away from her face, then turned over on to her back and swam slowly round and round while high overhead a fat yellow sun blazed in a baby blue sky.

When she'd had enough she made for the bank and hauled herself up on to it. As she hadn't brought a towel she'd have to dry in the sun, she thought, a pleasant prospect which she'd thoroughly enjoy.

She'd do her front first, she decided. Lying down she closed her eyes and let the heat wash over her.

She smiled as she listened to some flies buzzing, the flies concerto, she thought, and smiled even more.

'I realized you were a big girl, but not that big,' Julius's voice said.

Sadie sat up with a start to find him standing a few feet away staring down at her. She hadn't heard him approach.

Sadie snatched up her clothes and did her best to cover herself. 'Please go away,' she pleaded, coming to her feet.

But Julius had no intention of doing that, at least not yet. He moved position, and she did likewise, keeping her partially covered front facing him. Sadie's face was flaming, her embarrassment acute. Julius shouldn't have been anywhere near, he'd been stooking several fields away.

'I noted you weren't working so I came over to find out what you were up to. And here you are naked as the day you were born. Quite a sight. Yes, sirree! Quite a sight,' Julius said in a thick voice.

'Please go away,' she pleaded again, wishing she'd

never thought about going for a swim. Despite the heat she shivered all over.

Julius moved closer so she stepped backwards. He moved closer still and she back-pedalled further only to find herself up against a tree.

She shrank into herself when he stopped inches away, his eyes boring into hers. She grimaced at the smell of his rank breath which clogged her nostrils. The thought of Julius touching her revolted her.

He dropped his gaze to the swell of her breasts visible behind the clothes she was clutching to her.

Sadie would have given anything to be able to suddenly sprout wings and fly off. She watched mesmerized as he raised a gnarled hand.

'No!' she whispered. 'No!' She felt terrified as his hand came towards her. A cry choked in her throat when it came to rest on her bottom.

'Julius! What you doing?'

Julius's hand darted back at the speed of a striking rattlesnake. 'Look what I found. Swimming in my time!' he said, turning to smile at a stony-faced Anna.

'I want to get dressed,' Sadie quavered.

Anna ignored Sadie, continuing to concentrate on Julius. 'I brought your lunch,' she informed him, indicating to a small cloth-covered basket she was carrying. 'I was on my way to give it to you when I saw you walking over here.'

'Checking up on Sadie. And there she was having taken time off, my time, to go swimming.'

Anna went over to him and handed him the basket. 'You'd better go and let her get dressed as she's asking to.'

'Sure thing. OK, hon.' And with that he walked swiftly away.

As he disappeared Sadie slumped with relief. She dreaded to think what might have happened if Anna hadn't turned up. She found that her legs were shaking, while her stomach was screwed up in a knot.

'Get those clothes on and get back to work,' Anna said in a harsh, grating voice.

Sadie nodded.

Anna glared at Sadie, as though what had happened was Sadie's fault. Then she swung round and strode after her husband.

Sadie sagged against the tree feeling as though she might vomit. 'God,' she whispered. How awful that had been, horrendous in the extreme.

It was ages before her legs stopped shaking.

Chapter Four

It was the eeriest weather Sadie had ever known. The air was completely still and somehow lifeless. Not a bird could be seen. Not a cricket chirped.

The sky was various shades of dull grey, the cloud level high. The clouds themselves weren't moving, but static, as though glued in place.

Trixie snorted, and stamped his foot. Then he threw back his head and rolled his eyeballs.

'Easy boy, easy,' Sadie soothed.

That calmed him a little, and they resumed working the ground together.

It was now three years since Robbie had left, three years during which Sadie had grown into a fine young woman of sixteen. The Peterawa area had suffered one set back after another. Drought, crop failure and other misfortunes had caused widespread misery and, in some cases, bankruptcy. The Trikhardts continued to get by, but only through some radical cutbacks.

Sadie brought Trixie to a halt when she saw Anna hurrying towards her. She could see even at that distance that Anna was beside herself with worry.

'You're to take Trixie back to the stables at once,' Anna gasped on reaching Sadie. 'There's a twister on the way. Julius has just heard the news on the radio.'

'You mean a tornado?' Sadie queried. She'd heard about them, but this would be her first experience of one.

Anna nodded. 'A big one, too. And it's heading straight in this direction.'

A shiver of combined fear and apprehension ran down Sadie's spine. So this explained the weather and the lack of birds, she thought.

'Make tracks now,' Anna said, and rushed off with a multitude of things to settle before the twister reached them.

Nothing had been mentioned about the heavy equipment Trixie was trailing, so Sadie unshackled it and left it where it was. If that was the wrong thing to do she'd get the usual verbal abuse or physical cuff from Julius.

Halfway home Trixie took fright and reared up on his hind legs. They lost a few minutes while Sadie calmed him down again, then continued their journey to the stables.

Julius was flying about like a man demented. 'Get Trixie inside right away, and into his stall,' he ordered. Dixie was already in his, snorting and stamping restlessly about.

In the pig pen, a pig started to squeal setting them all off. Then the chickens began, adding to the din, with the rooster crowing louder and more aggressively than he usually did.

'How long?' Sadie asked Julius.

'Ain't seen nothing on the horizon yet, so can't say.'

When Sadie had dealt with Trixie she went outside again to discover that a wind had sprung up, which she quickly realized was strengthening with every passing second.

She shooed the protesting chickens and rooster into their house and shut them in. The pigs were more difficult, but eventually she got them under cover.

Suddenly she saw it, a grey swirling funnel shape coming directly towards them.

How mesmeric it was, Sadie thought, prickles of fear dancing over her skin, a moving finger of destruction.

'Julius has gone to try and round up the cattle. We're to get the sheep into the barn,' Anna said, appearing beside Sadie.

Sadie's reply was to point at the twister.

'Oh my God!' Anna exclaimed, and bit her lower lip.

Anna stared at the twister for a few seconds, then snapped out of her reverie. 'Jack. Jack!' she shouted, calling the mongrel who'd replaced Mischief. But Jack, cowering under one of the outbuildings, didn't respond to Anna's call.

'We'll have to get the sheep in without the damn dog,' Anna said angrily.

'Maybe he went to help with the cattle?'

'Naw. Julius went by himself. He said it was best for us to have Jack.'

There was a commotion in the stables, followed by the crack of splintering wood. 'That's Trixie or Dixie,' Sadie said.

Anna considered that for a brief second, then made a decision. 'You go to them, I'll try and handle the sheep on my own. I should at least be able to bring some in.' And with that she charged off.

Sadie found both horses rearing and plunging in their stalls. Before she could attempt to calm them, Dixie put a foot through his stall door, which was already partly smashed from a previous kick.

'There there, Dixie, there there,' Sadie said in as soothing a tone as she could muster. She then proceeded to speak non-stop to both horses trying to calm them down again. Normally she wouldn't have had much trouble, but these were unusual circumstances. The Shires were now well and truly terrified.

Finally Sadie gave up, this was beyond her. Perhaps Julius, when he returned, would have more success.

Outside again the wind whipped at her clothing, causing her dress to flap and billow. Neither Anna nor Julius were anywhere in sight. What should she do next, she wondered?

The twister was already a lot closer, bigger and more frightening. A mournful howling rent the air, as Jack gave voice.

A shingle came off the roof of the house to go spinning away, and was closely followed by another. And still the wind increased in force.

Anna appeared round the side of the house shepherding a handful of sheep, all she'd managed to round up. Sadie went to her aid, and between them they got the sheep into the barn where they stood cowering in a corner.

The wooden partition between the two horses was now all but demolished, Trixie and Dixie jostling alongside one another.

Sadie explained how she'd been unable to calm them, then said, 'I'm worried they're going to do themselves harm. They might well if they carry on as they are.'

A window broke, its glass shattering inwards and one of the splinters cut a sheep's face. Sadie went to the animal, but there was nothing she could do other than comfort it until all this was over.

'We'd best get down into the basement,' Anna said. 'That's the safest place.'

Sadie patted the sheep, and left. Before they could reach the barn doors they, too, flew open and the wind howled in.

Sadie and Anna tried to shut the doors again but found that, because of the strength of the wind, it was beyond them.

With a shriek Anna went tumbling over, to be carried by the wind for several yards before being able to scramble upright again.

The wind was ferocious now, and seemed to be gaining yet more force. They were almost at the house when Anna spotted Julius behind a dozen of their milkers.

'We'd better help him,' Anna shouted, and together they battled their way over to Julius and the cows.

Sadie stared at the twister in awe. It had grown beyond belief and now dominated the sky. It was evil, malevolent, she thought, and scared the pants off her.

She grabbed a stick to herd the cows with, and used it to poke them in the direction of the barn. They went in willingly where they milled around in confusion.

Julius swore when he saw how distressed Trixie and Dixie were, Dixie now foaming at the mouth.

Anna clutched at Julius's sleeve. 'We must get into the basement.'

He shrugged her off. 'I can't leave these two like this.'

'But you can't stay here!'

He stared grimly at his wife. 'If anything happens to those two horses we and the farm go under. We can't afford to replace them, and I certainly can't run the farm without them.'

Trixie lashed out and more wood was smashed. He then made a desperate attempt to climb over the ruined partition separating him from Dixie.

'Sheeett!' Julius exclaimed, and hurried to the horse which had got itself caught on the splintered wood.

Sadie went to the barn doors and peered out. The twister was huge now, and she could actually see things caught up in it. It suddenly dawned on her that this could be her last day on earth, a thought that made her heart sink.

One of the outbuildings, a rickety affair, crashed to the ground. Then bits of it were snatched up by the wind and hurled about indiscriminately.

A bicycle Sadie had never seen before went clattering by, and disappeared. Then a clothes line, complete with pegged-out washing, snaked through the air as though it was alive.

She turned back to Anna and Julius who were still arguing, but in the meantime had managed to get Trixie off the partition.

'Leave me alone, goddamnit!' Julius roared.

More glass smashed somewhere, followed by the crash of something heavy hitting the ground.

Anna left Julius, and scurried over to Sadie. 'He insists on staying with the horses, stupid son-of-a-bitch.'

They started for the house and it was a miracle they made it, the wind now being capable of lifting them off the ground. Sadie banged into the porch, then crawled up the steps on her hands and knees. She felt that at any moment the wind would whisk her away.

Yet more glass shattered, and somewhere far off was the sound of an explosion. They fought their way to the basement door, opened it, and plunged down the stairs.

Anna clicked on the lightswitch, but nothing happened. Obviously the cables were down.

Sadie knew where a flashlight was, and clicked that on instead.

'Gimme that,' said Anna, and snatched the flashlight from Sadie. She stumbled over to where certain spare supplies were kept, dug out a bottle of rye whisky, opened it and knocked it back feverishly.

'Dutch courage,' she said, and giggled hysterically. She then had another slug, after which she wiped her mouth with a sleeve.

'Have you lived through a twister before?' Sadie asked.

'Yeah. Once, years ago. It was nowhere as close as this baby though, and I can tell you that was bad enough.' Anna's eyes took on a faraway look, then she repeated very quietly, 'Yeah, and that was bad enough.'

They fell silent for a few minutes, waiting. Every so often Anna took a nervous drink from the bottle.

There was a tremendous crashing above them, followed by lots of little ones. The wind shrieked and howled, battering the basement door which bent inwards against the onslaught.

The noise became so great Sadie clamped her hands over her ears. Then the basement door gave way, ripped right off its hinges, and bounced down into the basement where it just missed smacking into Sadie's legs.

The wind that followed the door blew her off her feet, and pinned her against the nearest basement wall. There it tore at her, like a thousand busy fingers trying to tear off her clothes.

She forced herself round, but couldn't see Anna. The flashlight had gone out.

'Anna?'

There was no reply.

She shouted at the top of her voice. 'Anna?'

Again there was no reply.

A chair came hurtling down the stairs to smash to smithereens. Then a couple of squawking chickens flew down which told Sadie that the chicken house had gone.

Dust and grit crowded into her mouth making her choke and still the crashing continued above.

Time seemed to stretch on into eternity, with no let-up in either noise or wind.

Sadie became incredibly weary, exhaustion weighing heavily on her. Then the noise and wind receded, and there was only peace. Peace, and blackness.

Sadie became aware that her mouth was silted with dust and grit, and that one nostril was completely blocked.

Sitting up she coughed, then salivated which made her breathing easier.

She felt her hair, which was matted and thick with the same dirt and grit. It must look awful, she thought, climbing to her feet.

Sadie peered into the gloom. 'Anna?'

As before, there was no reply.

Sadie made her way over to where she'd last seen Anna, and almost tripped over the flashlight. Using that she looked round the entire basement, but of Anna there was no sign.

She was heading for the stairs when a clucking chicken popped into view and strutted about as though proud of itself. She then spotted another one busy preening itself.

Halfway up the stairs she realized with profound shock that she was staring at the sky. She emerged from the basement to total devastation. The roof was gone, and two sides of the house. One of the remaining sides was at an angle and would clearly collapse at any moment.

Smashed-up furniture and other household items lay everywhere. Crazily, a standard lamp remained upright, and she could only wonder how that hadn't been blown over and destroyed like everything else.

She recoiled in fright and horror when she came across a pig lying in a pool of blood. Its eyes were open, the top of its head caved in.

Behind a mound of debris the car was lying on its side. All its windows, including the windscreen, were smashed, the side facing skywards badly scratched and dented. The pungent smell of petroleum hung over it.

Lifting her eyes she gazed out across the surrounding fields and countryside. Everywhere crops were flattened, trees uprooted, hedges destroyed. She recognized the Robson's truck which lay not far away, its cab completely squashed.

'Anna!' she cried out, but there was still no response.

The barn, she thought. They would both have sheltered there. Only the barn had disappeared, marks in the ground the only reminder of where it had been.

She then found Trixie lying dead with a pitchfork protruding from his massive neck.

A sheep wandered into view, and moaned sorrowfully. It stood looking stupidly at Sadie for a few seconds, then wandered off again.

Shock was beginning to take hold of Sadie. She started to tremble, her mind became foggy and slow. She stared down at Trixie and remembered how hardworking he had been. But what about Dixie, and Julius?

'Anna!' she cried out yet again.

The sobbing was quiet, and contained. Sadie found Anna, behind what had been the roof of the house, sitting on the ground with Julius's head in her lap.

'He's dead,' Anna sobbed. 'He's dead.'

Sadie gazed at the dead farmer, and idly wondered how he'd died. There were no outward signs of injury.

As though reading Sadie's thoughts Anna said, 'There are two holes in his back. I don't know what made them, but they killed my Julie.'

Sadie wanted to laugh. Julie! She'd never heard Anna call Julius that before. It sounded so childish!

Anna began rocking back and forth, and as she did she softly sang a child's lullaby.

Sadie felt totally drained, like a floppy rag doll. She looked at the devastation surrounding her. What were they going to do? The house and barn were destroyed and Julius was dead. She just simply couldn't take it all in.

'Anna?'

Anna didn't answer, but continued to sing and rock back and forth.

Sadie spotted an armchair, which she struggled to set upright and then collapsed into. And there she sat, oblivious, as the hours ticked by.

The sound of a car gradually invaded her consciousness. She glanced up curiously as a man approached her. He was a young man in his early twenties, she judged.

'Excuse me, can you tell me the way to Peterawa? All the signs are down, and what with one thing and another I'm lost.'

What a good-looking young man, she thought, tall and slim, with something of a dashing air about him.

'Are you OK?' the young man enquired.

'Yeah, I guess,' she replied, coming to her feet.

He gazed about, and whistled. 'I was lucky, completely missed the twister. What a mess. I've passed several places just as bad as yours.'

He stared into her eyes, and frowned. For a moment something intangible seemed to pass between them, then was gone.

'Speaking of luck, you were certainly lucky to have come through it alive,' he added.

'We sheltered in the basement, Mrs Trikhardt and myself. Her husband stayed in the barn with the Shires, and got killed. The two of them are over there.' She waved vaguely in that direction.

'They're not your parents then?'

Sadie shook her head. 'I'm just the hired help, at three bucks a month. Slave labour you could call it.'

'I don't understand. *Three* dollars a month?'

'It's a long story, and one I'm sure you don't want to hear.'

He did, but this was hardly the time or the place. 'Mrs Trikhardt, did you say?'

'That's her. The biggest bitch there ever was.'

'Look,' he said, 'I've got some brandy in the car. Would you like a tot?'

'I don't know. I've never tasted brandy.'

'Wait here then.'

What a stunning car! Sadie thought, noticing it for the first time. She'd never seen anything like it in Peterawa.

The young man returned with a silver flask which was engraved with the initials EJF. He unscrewed the top and handed her the flask. 'Here.'

The brandy was cold and warm at the same time. It burnt its way down to her stomach and left her gasping. Then heat began to radiate through her, overcoming the coldness of her body.

'How's that?' he smiled.

Nice smile, she thought. It lit up his face, which she found attractive. His hair was dark with a reddish tinge. His eyebrows were dark and thick, like two shaggy caterpillars, his eyes brown and melting.

'A lot better,' she replied, returning the flask.

'I always carry this with me for emergencies,' he explained. 'Or' – the brown eyes twinkled, – 'if I just fancy a drop.'

There was a bit of the rogue in him, she thought, an appealing quality.

She put a hand to her hair, suddenly remembering how filthy it was. She must look a proper sight!

'And Mr Trikhardt is dead?' he queried softly.

'As mutton according to his wife.'

The young man nodded, noting her irreverence. There was no love lost between her and the Trikhardts he guessed correctly.

'Perhaps there's something I can do? Some way I can help?'

Sadie considered that. 'We'll go and ask.'

She led him to where Anna was still sitting, bowed over Julius's corpse.

The young man blanched when he saw Anna – he'd never seen such an ugly woman. The sheer ghastliness of the hairy mole on her chin fascinated him.

'Anna, this young man was passing by and has offered to help. Is there anything he can do?'

Anna looked up at the young man, her face clearly reflecting her anguish. Her sallow skin had become creased and crumpled, like old parchment.

'I'm sorry for your loss,' the young man said respectfully.

'He's dead. My Julie's dead,' Anna stated in a flat, emotionless voice.

Again Sadie experienced the urge to laugh. Julie! She thought it was hysterical.

'Perhaps I can give you a lift into Peterawa?' the young man suggested. 'You can't stay here.'

Anna stared at him as though he was speaking Chinese.

'The house has gone,' Sadie said.

Anna continued to stare unblinkingly at the young man, who now said, 'Or I could send someone out? The fire brigade, or the police, or . . .?' He trailed off, then added, 'Or whoever.'

'Two holes in his back,' Anna said. 'That's what killed my Julie. He stayed with the horses because we couldn't afford to lose them. But we did lose them, and me him.'

'I am sorry,' the young man repeated.

Anna tenderly stroked Julius's face. Tears appeared in her eyes and ran down her cheeks. 'He was a good man,' she said, 'the very best.'

To you maybe, Sadie thought bitterly. But certainly not to me. He'd been a relentless taskmaster who'd driven her as if she was a slave. As far as she was concerned the world was well rid of Julius Trikhardt.

The young man wished he'd never stopped, then he glanced at Sadie and was pleased he had. 'I have nothing to leave you, no provisions of any sort,' he said to Sadie. 'But I will see that some get sent out. I promise you that.'

She gave him a wan smile. 'Thank you.'

There was a hiatus between them, then he said, 'Well, I'd better be getting on my way. If you can just give me directions?'

She watched the young man walk to his car, and get inside. Should she wave? No, she decided. He was simply a stranger, after all.

The beautiful car moved off. Would he wave? She half expected he would, but he didn't. She watched his car till it was lost to sight, then returned to Anna and the dead Julius.

The car returned some while later. The young man saw that Sadie had constructed a make-shift tent out of some old sheets. She was in the tent, Anna still in the same position with Julius.

Sadie came out of the tent and smiled a greeting. She was pleased he'd come back.

'Half of Peterawa's been blown away, the other half is falling down. I couldn't find anyone to come out and help,' he explained.

God! Sadie thought. This was a nightmare.

'I brought food though, and beer. The water in Peterawa's been contaminated.'

'That's kind of you.'

'It's in the car. I'll get it.'

He went to the car boot and took out a cardboard box which he carried to the make-shift tent. 'It's not a lot, I'm afraid. But it's just chaos there.'

'Were many killed?'

'A number. And quite a few were badly hurt. Someone said that aid and troops are being rushed to the area, though no one has any idea when they arrive.'

Sadie nodded.

'How's Mrs Trikhardt?'

'The same.'

'I also brought a spade. Mr Trikhardt should be buried. It could be days otherwise.'

'I'll do that then. If she'll allow me.'

'I'll do it,' he said. He fetched the spade from the car, then together they approached Anna.

The young man explained what he wanted to do, and surprisingly encountered no resistance from Anna. He chose a site well away from the house, and started to dig.

Maybe she could somehow get to Clarke City and Janet, Sadie thought, except she now had no money. It would have disappeared with her bedroom when the twister struck.

The young man paused to glance over thoughtfully at Sadie. Then he resumed digging.

Anna roused herself to search out another old sheet to wrap Julius in. She began talking quietly to him as if he could hear her and might, at any point, reply.

When the hole was ready the young man threw down the spade, went over and had a word with Anna, then the three of them carried the corpse to its grave.

'I would say something but don't have a Bible,' the young man told Anna.

Anna suddenly fell to her knees and let out a great heart-rending wail. She threw her arms up towards heaven in a gesture of supplication, then bending over beat the ground with her fists.

'Fill it in,' Sadie said.

The young man did, the dirt spattering the sheet. Finally it was all over, and the perspiring young man wiped his forehead. Going over to his jacket he removed the silver flask from a pocket and had a swig. He offered it to Sadie, but she shook her head.

'Can I speak to you?' the young man asked her.

'Of course.'

He grasped her by the arm and they moved off a short distance. 'What are you going to do?'

'I've no idea,' she admitted. 'None at all.'

'You must have relatives?'

'In Scotland, where I come from. But I haven't seen them since I was a child.'

He stared at her, concerned and curious. 'Haven't you anyone?'

'A friend in Clarke City, Quebec. A girl who came over in the same party as me. And a chap who worked here with me, but ran away three years ago. He could be anywhere, Canada, Scotland . . .' She trailed off and shrugged.

'What about Mrs Trikhardt?'

'How do you mean?'

'What's your situation regarding her?'

'There was a contract, but how can I stay here? There isn't a farm any more, and she certainly won't be rebuilding, she hasn't any money.'

'What about insurance?'

Sadie considered that. 'I've no idea about that side of things. But knowing those two, and how desperate things have been of late, I doubt very much that they ever took any out. And even if they had, it would take ages to come through. No, I'm finished here.'

'You're in quite a pickle then.'

She gave a hollow laugh. 'That's putting it mildly.'

'I've had a thought . . .' He smiled. 'I come from up-country where my family own a substantial business, a saw and pulp mill. I live at home with my father Jack, brother Courcy and sister Erin. The thing is we're looking for a housemaid and it crossed my mind you might be interested?'

A job! Her thoughts raced at the prospect.

'I don't know how much you'd earn, but you can bet it's a fair wage. My father is a stickler for that sort of thing. It'll certainly be a lot more than three dollars a month!'

She should jump at this, she told herself. And yet . . . caution must prevail. She didn't know him from Adam, after all. But he was nice, and seemed kind. And there didn't seem to be anything 'odd' about him, she'd heard about men like that. He came over as being genuine, if she was any judge of character.

'Would that be live-in?' she queried.

'Your own room and all board. Plus a day and a half off per week.'

A day and a half per week! The luxury of that after the farm was the most tempting prospect.

'Why are you offering me this job?' she asked.

'We're looking for someone, you're in need of a position. And you strike me as an honest, hard-working girl, so why not?'

True enough, she thought, why not! 'OK,' she nodded. 'I accept.'

His face broke into a beaming smile. 'Great. We'll get started just as soon as you're ready.'

And I've told Anna, she thought with grim satisfaction.

'What!' Anna shrieked on hearing the news.

Sadie had already rooted round to see if she could find any of her possessions. A sweater and cap were all she'd come up with. 'So it's goodbye,' she said.

Anna was aghast. 'But you can't go, not just like that!

Think of all we've done for you. Where's your loyalty, for Christ's sake!'

'Loyalty!' Sadie exploded. 'To you! I don't owe you any loyalty. I don't owe you anything. For years you've exploited me, worked me to the bone. And you talk of loyalty!'

'We gave you a home, you ungrateful cow!'

'You gave me nothing. Anything I got from you was earned a hundred times over. You were vicious, and cruel, and I hope Julius is paying for his part of it right now in hell.'

Anna sprang at Sadie, and tried to claw her face and tear at Sadie's hair. She yelled bloody murder when an astonished young man dragged her off.

'Enough!' he commanded authoritatively.

'Don't talk to me you . . . you pirate!' she spat.

Although shaken by Anna's attack, Sadie couldn't wait to escape her clutches. As she turned on her heel to leave, Anna started to cry. 'Please don't leave me alone,' she pleaded. She clasped her hands in front of her, and begged. 'Please!'

Sadie felt sick, but she was determined, 'Let's go,' she said to the young man, and started for his car.

He fell into step beside her. 'That was nasty.'

She didn't reply, but quickened her pace.

Anna dropped her wheedling pretence. 'Bitch! Asshole, bitch!' she howled.

'There's a bitch round here all right, and it isn't me,' Sadie muttered.

She was pleasantly surprised when the young man opened the door for her. How lovely after what she'd been used to.

The young man climbed in beside her, and started the engine. He glanced at Anna who was screaming non-stop obscenities, then eased the car into motion.

Sadie didn't look back once.

* * *

They drove in silence for a while, then he said, 'My name's Edward Fitzgerald by the way. What's yours?'

'Sadie Smith.'

'Sadie Smith,' he repeated. 'I like that.'

'What does the J stand for?'

'What J?'

'Your flask is engraved EJF.'

He laughed. 'You are observant! It stands for John, my father's name. He was christened John, but is always called Jack. You'll like him, everyone does. He has enormous charm.'

You're fairly charming yourself, she thought. 'And what about your brother with the unusual name?'

'Courcy? He's a few years younger than me, and a bit wild. My sister Erin is seventeen, I'd imagine about your age?'

'I'm sixteen,' she confessed. 'Can I say something?'

'Go ahead.'

'I love your car. It's simply beautiful.'

He fondly patted the steering wheel. 'She's a super charged Cord with a V-8 engine, concealed headlamps and front-wheel drive. And I agree, she is a beauty.'

Sadie ran a hand along the leather interior, and wondered how much a Cord cost.

'Do you like cars?'

'Ones like this I do. By the by, what do I call you? And the other members of your family?'

'You call me Edward, and Father, Mr Fitzgerald. Erin will be Erin, but I can't speak for Courcy. He'll soon let you know how he wants you to address him, but it depends entirely upon what he thinks of you.'

Courcy sounded difficult, she thought. She'd have to watch him.

'Then there's Mrs Ritter, the housekeeper, who'll be your immediate superior. She's something of a tyrant, but nice really. I wouldn't recommend you call her anything other than Mrs Ritter.'

'I'll remember that. What other staff is there?'

'Miss Dobson the cook, another maid called Heather, the gardener Mr Labott, and Sam the chauffeur. We have a chauffeur because Father prefers to work in the car rather than drive.'

'It's a big household,' Sadie commented.

'And a big house.'

Sadie could hardly wait to see it. 'Is it far up-country?'

'A fair way. We're just outside Bald Rock Falls. Ever heard of it?'

She shook her head.

'It's OK, despite being very small. I enjoy it there. Wouldn't live anywhere else.'

'Why were you going to Peterawa? If that's not too rude, of course.'

'I had business there for the company. If it had only been the one call, I would have flown down, but I had a number of calls to make *en route*.'

Her eyes opened wide. 'You fly?'

'Yup, the company plane. It's a Gipsy Moth. I use it all the time.'

That impressed her. She'd always thought how wonderful it must be to fly.

'It's a great time-saver, takes me places far faster than other transport. It's particularly useful when I have to make lightning calls to a crew operating a considerable distance away from the mills.'

'How long have you been flying?' she probed, genuinely interested.

He thought about that. 'Four years now.'

'And can Courcy fly?'

'No,' he smiled. 'He says he prefers to keep his feet planted firmly on the ground.'

'What colour is your Moth painted?'

He laughed, thinking that a very feminine question. 'It's painted scarlet,' he replied.

Scarlet! The same colour as the ribbons her mother had given her, her most treasured possessions, which she'd just lost in the tornado, she thought morosely.

He sensed her change of mood. 'What is it?'

She told him then about the ribbons, how they'd been given to her and from there her life-history followed right up to when the tornado had struck.

He listened appalled, filled with compassion for this young lady he'd rescued from such an awful couple.

'Why are we stopping here?' Sadie asked as Edward swung the car off the road.

'It's a store. I'm going to buy you a few things.'

'But I've no money!' she protested.

'I said *I* was going to buy. I can't take you home looking as you do. It would hardly be fair on you.'

He was so thoughtful. 'I'll pay you back,' she promised.

'There's no need for that. Take it as a gift from one who has a great deal to one who's just lost everything.' He held up a silencing finger when she opened her mouth to argue. 'Not another word, I insist.'

How masterful he was, but not in the bullying way that Julius had been. 'Thank you,' she whispered in an appreciative voice.

The store sold everything from pegs to perfume. They had to wait to be served, and, in the interim, they browsed. Edward saw something that made him smile, he would buy those without Sadie's knowing.

'Can I help you, sir?' the assistant eventually enquired, while staring quizzically at Sadie.

Edward noted the stare and explained Sadie's appearance. 'This young lady's just survived the tornado that struck further south. I want to replace some of the things she's lost.'

'The twister!' the assistant exclaimed. 'The radio's been full of it. Thank God it didn't come up here.'

'It looked as though there had been a war, shambles and chaos everywhere.'

'And quite a few dead, I believe.'

Edward nodded. 'Fraid so. Now how about a pair of jeans to start with. And a couple of shirts.'

'And could I please have some shampoo?' Sadie requested.

'Of course.'

Edward completely rigged her out, the crowning glory being a buckskin jacket that was as soft as velvet. Sadie fell in love with it the moment she saw it, but protested that it was far too expensive.

'Would you deny me the pleasure of giving it to you?' Edward demanded, pretending to be hurt.

She relented. 'OK then.'

'Good. Wrap it up.'

They took the packages out to the car, then Edward asked her to wait inside while he popped back for something he'd forgotten. When he returned to the car he had a smug grin plastered all over his face.

'There's a motel up ahead. We'll stay the night there,' he said.

Alarm broke out in her. Had she been wrong about him? 'Is it too far to drive without stopping over?' she queried.

He shrugged. 'I could drive through, but why bother? I'm sure you could use a good night's sleep. I know I could.'

She sat, thin lipped, praying she hadn't misjudged him. She found it almost impossible to believe that she had. And yet . . . Memories of Julius's advances danced before her and anxiously she sank further into her seat. Could Edward really turn out to be as monstrous as Julius?

'Have you stayed at this motel before?' she asked, trying to disguise the fear from her voice.

'Yeah, a couple of times. It's OK. At least it was on the last occasion I was there.'

The motel proved to be only a few miles up the road. Edward parked in front of the office, and they both went in, in silence.

The person in charge was a stout woman with grossly fat legs encased in heavy stockings. 'Can I help you folks?' she smiled.

This was it, Sadie thought, clenching her hands, while her heart pounded.

'We need two single rooms for the night,' Edward stated.

'Next to one another?'

He shook his head. 'Not necessarily.'

Sadie heaved a sigh of relief. She hadn't misjudged him after all.

Edward signed the register and then they were handed their keys. Sadie had been given Room 6, Edward, Room 14.

'We'll drop your stuff off first, then say I pick you up in an hour and we go eat? There's a diner not far away.'

Sadie realized she was ravenous. After all it had been an extremely long and eventful day. 'Fine. Thank you,' she answered.

Sadie's room was pleasant enough with sky blue painted walls and a thick carpet underfoot. The first thing she did was run the bath.

She lay there wallowing thinking of Edward, and the job that lay ahead. Bald Rock Falls! It did sound very Canadian, even though she'd long since got used to Canadian place-names. What would Bald Rock Falls be like, she wondered? And, more importantly, the Fitzgerald family? If Edward was anything to go by they'd all be nice, and easy to get along with. The only problem, it seemed, would be Courcy, but she was sure she would soon come to terms with him.

A day and a half off every single week, she still couldn't believe it. She'd really fallen on her feet. If Edward hadn't happened along, God alone knows what she would have done.

Edward, what a lovely man he was. She felt warm inside as she thought about him, surprising after such a short acquaintance. In a peculiar way it seemed as though she'd known him for ages.

And what about the house she'd be working in, what would that be like? He'd said it was a big house, but how big? How many rooms? And what would her own room be like? It would inevitably be better than the one at the farm, they didn't come much more spartan than that. And what condition would the house be in? Not shabby and run down as the farmhouse had been, she thought, but well cared for, sparkling inside and out like a new pin.

Her thoughts turned to the Trikhardts, causing her to shudder. She wasn't in the least bit upset by Julius's death, it would have been hypocritical to pretend that she was. She visualized his dead face cradled in Anna's lap. What would become of Anna now? Truth was, she just didn't care. Didn't give a goddamn, as Julius would have said. And with that she put the horrible Trikhardts from her mind.

One thing she would miss, however, were the animals, Trixie and Dixie in particular. She and they had become good pals over the years especially after Robbie had run away. They were the closest thing she'd found to replacing him and his friendship.

How she missed Robbie. Hardly a day went by without her thinking about him, wondering where he was and what he was doing. How had he changed in the past three years? What did he look like now? He would have grown a lot, and started to shave. She giggled at the thought.

'Oh Robbie! Oh dear Robbie!' she whispered aloud. Losing him had been like losing her family all over again.

She sat up and slowly soaped herself, smiling as she thought about Edward's car. What a fantastic machine! She'd felt like a rich girl riding in it, a rich girl with the world at her feet. How wonderful it must be to be rich, she thought, to have anything you wanted.

She stopped. She was being ridiculous, letting her mind

208

run away with itself. She was going to the Fitzgeralds' house as an employee, a servant, *not* as an equal.

Sadie sighed, and with a start realized that time was slipping by and Edward would be coming for her shortly. She must be ready when he knocked. Or at least, *almost*.

Edward nodded his approval. 'The bath and hair wash have done wonders,' he said. He knew she'd had a bath because the smell of it filled the room.

She put on her new buckskin jacket, and twirled round. 'What do you think?'

'Terrific. I'll be honoured to take you to dinner.'

She ran her hands down the lapels of the jacket. 'I really can't thank you enough for this, and for everything.'

'Don't mention it. Now come on, I'm dying to sink my teeth into a T-bone.'

Outside it was a warm July night, the sky clear and studded with stars. A soft-scented breeze was blowing while crickets made music in nearby fields. It was the very stuff of romance, Sadie thought, climbing into the Cord.

'How different it is now to this morning,' Sadie commented. 'That was the strangest weather I've ever known.' She then went on to describe it to an attentive Edward.

'Must have been quite something when you were down in that basement,' he said.

'It was. The noise was unbelievable. I passed out after a while, then when I came round it was all over. It's incredible to think this is still the same day.'

The diner wasn't far away. They parked and went inside.

'Coffee to begin with?' Edward asked.

'Please.'

'I'll get those while you decide what you want.'

He went up to the counter and ordered the coffee, chatted briefly with the counter hand while it was being poured.

'I've ordered,' Edward announced as he sat down.

'What are you having, other than steak, that is?'

'French fries and a side salad, with a slice of blueberry pie and cream to follow.'

'I'll have exactly the same as you,' she smiled.

'Including the blueberry pie and cream?'

'Especially the blueberry pie and cream.'

He laughed, and went back to place her order. 'I bought you a gift in the store,' he said once he'd settled down opposite her.

'I know. You bought me many.'

He shook his head. 'Not those. I mean a *special* gift.'

Whatever could it be, she wondered? Intrigued, she waited, but he didn't elaborate, teasing her.

'Well, what is it?' she demanded eventually.

He reached into an inside pocket and brought out a small brown paper bag. 'Here,' he said, handing it to her.

She opened the bag and glanced inside. She then tipped the contents on to the table.

'A pair of scarlet ribbons!' she exclaimed in astonishment.

'I hope you don't think me presumptuous? It was just that I saw those in the store and, after hearing how you'd lost the originals, I thought you might like them. I know they won't replace the ones your mother gave you, but . . . well, there we are,' he ended lamely.

She laid them out side by side. They were longer than the others and hand stitched along the edges. She was so overcome she could have wept. 'Thank you,' she whispered, a choke in her voice.

He could see how touched she was, and knew he'd done the right thing.

'It wasn't presumptuous of you at all,' she whispered.

He watched her fold them up and carefully place them in a pocket. When she looked up, her eyes were glistening with tears of gratitude and happiness.

'You're not going to bawl on me, are you?' he asked thickly.

'No, I won't bawl,' she promised.

She wiped her eyes, then said, 'I told you all about me in the car, now I'd like to hear all about you.'

'It's boring.'

'Surely not!'

'Tedium unlimited.'

She realized she was being teased again. 'I really would,' she stated softly.

He shrugged. 'OK then.'

She listened, fascinated, thinking at one point what a completely different life he'd led to her. And while he spoke he made her laugh, because he had a lovely, and occasionally wicked, sense of humour.

The meal came to an end far too quickly, Sadie thought. She could have sat there listening to Edward talk all night.

'That's Clare, our house,' Edward said, pointing through the windscreen.

Sadie drew in a long breath. The house was huge, built out of a pinky brown stone topped by a double-peeked slate roof. The paintwork was white, and gleamed as though newly done. The front door was a Gothic arch.

'It's . . .' She shook her head, lost for words.

'It's called Clare after the county in Ireland where my great-grandfather, the founder of our Canadian dynasty, hailed from. It's more or less a replica of the squire's house in Kilcorfin, the village in which that same great-grandfather was born. He'd always admired the squire's house, therefore when he came to build his own, having made his fortune, he found an architect to design a replica, and so Clare came into being.'

'Is it a happy house? It certainly looks it.'

He glanced at her in surprise. 'Yes, it is. Most definitely.'

'If I was an artist I'd paint it,' she stated. 'It would make a beautiful painting.'

'My grandfather had the same idea. You'll find such a painting in the drawing-room.'

She shook her head again. 'There can't be anything else like it in the neighbourhood.'

'There isn't.'

'It's simply magnificent.' What a thrill it was going to be living here, Sadie thought. And what a contrast to the Trikhardts!

Edward parked the car in the garage. 'Let's go and see who's in, shall we?'

He took Sadie's canvas bag from the back seat, and together they headed for a nearby door.

'I've suddenly had a thought,' Edward said, nervously.

'What's that?'

'I hope they haven't taken anyone on in my absence.'

Sadie bit her lower lip, she fervently hoped so too. It would be awful to have come all this way to find the post already filled.

They found Mrs Ritter and Miss Dobson earnestly discussing menus in the kitchen. They both glanced in surprise at Sadie, then looked enquiringly at Edward.

'Home is the hunter back from the hill, and the sailor home from the sea,' he smiled.

Neither female replied. Both were clearly curious about Sadie.

'First things first, have you taken on that new house-maid yet?' he asked Mrs Ritter, who was responsible for the staff.

'No, I haven't,' Mrs Ritter replied, and again glanced at Sadie.

'Well, I've found someone who'll do admirably.'

There was a slight pause, then Mrs Ritter replied somewhat reprovingly, 'This is most irregular, Edward.'

'I quite agree. Normally I would never dream of interfering, but there is always the exception. And Sadie here is just that. Sadie Smith, late of Peterawa, our house-keeper, Mrs Ritter.'

'I'm pleased to meet you, Mrs Ritter,' Sadie said pleasantly.

Mrs Ritter, her expression stern but not unfriendly, looked Sadie up and down. 'How old are you, Sadie?'

'Sixteen.'

'Hmmh! You appear strong and healthy enough, are you?'

'I'm strong, and healthy, and well used to hard work,' Sadie replied respectfully, but completely without subservience.

Mrs Ritter stared hard at Sadie, weighing her up. Sadie, intending to establish herself in her own right, stared right back.

'What sort of hard work?' Mrs Ritter asked softly.

'Cleaning, cooking, baking, sewing, anything and everything to be done inside a house. I'm also knowledgeable about animals and can plough a straight furrow.'

'A straight furrow!' Miss Dobson exclaimed, and put a hand over her mouth.

Sadie smiled. 'I'm proud of that. It isn't easy, I can assure you.'

'Sadie worked on a farm,' Edward explained. 'But I'll tell you about that later. In the meanwhile, Sadie, this is Miss Dobson, our cook.'

'Pleased to meet you,' Sadie nodded.

'And you, Sadie.' Miss Dobson chuckled. 'A straight furrow! I like that.'

'So you're experienced in housework,' Mrs Ritter said.

'Yes, ma'am.'

'I see.' She didn't at all. Who was this girl, and why had Edward brought her for the job?

'When can she start?' Edward asked.

He was determined to have his own way on this, Mrs Ritter thought, best to let him have it then. Edward usually knew what he was doing. And if the girl proved to be unsuitable she'd take it up with him later.

'You start tomorrow morning, five thirty sharp. Is that too early for you?'

213

'I'm used to a four o'clock rise, ma'am. Five thirty will be a lie-in for me.'

'What about uniform?' Edward queried.

'She's about Mary-Anne's size, so the same ones should do. I'll take them up to her later.'

Edward nodded. 'Good. I'll leave Sadie with you then. I want to go up to the mills to speak with Father. I'll have that word with you when I return.'

He turned to Sadie and smiled. 'Good luck. I'll see you later, no doubt.'

'Thank you again, Edward, for everything.'

'Don't mention it.'

And with that he was gone, leaving Sadie alone with Mrs Ritter and Miss Dobson.

Mrs Ritter then explained to Sadie what her duties would be, and how much she'd be paid. Sadie was delighted with the sum, a fortune after the pittance she'd earned at the Trikhardts.

'Now you'd better go to your room and get settled in. I'll have you called when it's mealtime,' Mrs Ritter said.

'I'll take her. I'm going up that way anyway,' Miss Dobson volunteered.

Sadie picked up her canvas bag and followed Miss Dobson out of the kitchen.

'It's a beautiful house,' Sadie said as they mounted a flight of stairs.

'Very.'

'Have you been here long?'

Miss Dobson thought about that. 'Twelve . . . no, thirteen years now. They're a fine family to work for.'

'Who is Mary-Anne?' Sadie queried.

'She's the girl you're replacing.'

'And why did she leave?'

Miss Dobson gave Sadie a strange look, then said, 'I may as well tell you, you'll find out soon enough. She got herself in the club.'

Sadie was baffled. 'What club?'

214

Miss Dobson smiled when she saw that Sadie was serious. Ingenuous, she thought. 'It's a slang expression meaning to be pregnant,' she explained.

'Oh.'

'Who by?' Sadie then asked.

'A man,' Miss Dobson prevaricated. That was something she wasn't personally prepared to disclose. Let it come from someone else.

They entered a hallway where they came face to face with a small dumpy girl carrying some empty teacups plus a pile of newspapers.

'Heather, this is Sadie Smith who's taking over from Mary-Anne.'

'Thank goodness we've got a replacement at last. I'm run off my feet,' Heather grumbled. 'Hi!' she said to Sadie.

'Hi.'

'When do you start?'

'Tomorrow morning.'

Heather nodded her approval. The sooner the better as far as she was concerned. It was no fun doing two people's work, even if she was being given extra money. Mrs Ritter had been very fair about that.

'You and Heather have adjacent rooms,' Miss Dobson said.

Heather seemed pleasant enough, Sadie thought, and doubted she was going to have any trouble there. The pair of them should rub along fairly well together.

'I'd better get on. See you later then,' Heather said, and left them.

'Here we are,' Miss Dobson declared further down the hallway, opening the door into a room filled with streaming sunshine.

Sadie immediately loved the room which somehow welcomed her into it. It was attractively decorated and seemed very homely.

Radiators! Sadie noted excitedly. The room was centrally

heated. Oh, what a joy that was going to be throughout the winter.

'Your bathroom's here,' said Miss Dobson, indicating a door off to one side.

'You mean the room has its own bathroom?' Sadie gasped.

'Every bedroom in the house is *en suite*, ours included. It's one of the many reasons why the Fitzgeralds are such a marvellous family to work for.'

En suite bedroom for a housemaid! Sadie could hardly credit it.

She put her bag down, and went to look in the bathroom. It was all sheer perfection. 'I'll leave you to it then,' Miss Dobson said. 'There will be someone along for you when it's time to eat.'

'Where are you?' Sadie enquired.

'Further down the hallway and to the left. Mrs Ritter has the room further down to the right.'

When Miss Dobson had closed the door behind her, Sadie went and sat on her bed. It was divinely soft, so much so she couldn't wait to sleep in it. She gently bounced up and down several times, then crossed to the window and gazed out.

There was a magnificent view over a lawn, and a number of paddocks with horses in them. In the far distance were low lying hills.

She'd certainly fallen on her feet, she thought, filled with a warm glow of satisfaction. She was going to be extremely happy at Clare, of that she had no doubt.

Mrs Ritter was in the little room she used as an office drinking coffee and eating cherry cake when Edward returned to have the promised word.

'So who's the mystery then?' she asked.

Edward laughed. 'By that I take it you mean Sadie?'

Mrs Ritter nodded. She was bursting with curiosity, though trying not to let it show.

Coffee and cake were gradually forgotten as Sadie's tale unfolded.

Sadie was lying on top of her bed reading a magazine she'd found in one of the drawers when there was a knock on the door. 'Come in!' she called out, throwing down the magazine and climbing off the bed.

It was Heather. 'The family have had their dinner and are now asking to meet you,' she said.

'You mean the Fitzgeralds?'

Heather nodded. 'They're waiting for you in the drawing-room. I'm to take you down.'

'Right,' said Sadie, feeling just a little apprehensive. Then she remembered that the family included Edward which somehow made everything all right. As they walked downstairs her apprehension melted away.

'OK?' Heather asked when they reached the closed drawing-room door through which came the sound of voices.

'Yes,' Sadie affirmed.

Heather knocked, then opened the door and ushered Sadie in ahead of her.

Edward, brandy in hand, jumped to his feet. 'Sadie, come and meet my family!'

He went to her, and took her by the arm. 'Happy with your room?' he enquired

'It's fabulous. I couldn't be more pleased.'

'Good. Now say hello to Father first.'

Jack Fitzgerald rose as they approached him. He was an older version of Edward, Sadie thought. Tall, and still handsome, though no longer slim. He had the same dashing air as Edward.

'So you're Sadie,' he said, smiling kindly. She took to him right away.

'Yes, Mr Fitzgerald.'

'You forgot to mention she was so pretty,' he rebuked his elder son.

'I thought I'd let you find that out for yourself.'

Jack gave a low laugh. 'Pretty as a picture. And Scots I'm told.'

'Yes, sir.'

'That makes us all Celts together, we being Irish through and through.'

'Watch my father,' Edward warned, tongue in cheek. 'He's kissed the Blarney stone.'

'That I have,' Jack admitted. 'During a trip back to the dear old sod from where our family came. We're descended from kings, you know. The kings of old County Clare.'

'Is there an Irishman who isn't descended from a king?' another male voice mocked.

Sadie focused on the speaker who was clearly related to Edward and Jack. Shorter than Edward she judged, and certainly younger. She knew this had to be Courcy.

From the opposite side of the room, an attractive girl leapt to her feet and came over to Sadie. Sticking out her hand she said, 'Welcome to Clare. I'm Erin.'

Erin's face was frank and open and dominated by startling china blue eyes. Her hair was a cascade of auburn curls that fell to her shoulders. She had a narrow waist, full bosoms and exhuded friendliness.

'I'm pleased to meet you,' Sadie replied, shaking hands with Erin.

'Edward has been telling us all about you,' Jack said. He shook his head. 'You've had a hard and difficult life, I'm afraid.'

Sadie glanced down at the floor.

'A hard and difficult life,' Jack repeated sympathetically. 'But you must look on the positive side and think how character building it must have been.'

Character building! Sadie thought, that was a laugh. If that was character building she could have well done without it. But she did take on board the point Jack was making.

Jack glared at his sons and daughter. 'I just hope it makes you three appreciate what's been handed to you on a plate. Everyone in this world isn't born with a silver spoon in his or her mouth, you know. Far from it!'

Sadie liked him for saying that. He may be wealthy, but had a sense of perspective unlike some people she'd heard and read about.

'We were simply the lucky ones,' Courcy said in a rather supercilious tone. He then turned to face Sadie directly.

'Can you really plough a straight furrow as you told Miss Dobson you could?' he queried mockingly.

Sadie turned her attention to him, noting that he was the only male present still sitting. 'Yes, I can,' she replied.

'Fascinating!'

'Edward told us how you lost all your clothes in the tornado. Would you be insulted if I offered you some of my older ones?' Erin asked Sadie.

Sadie gazed at the smart black dress Erin was wearing, which was far nicer than anything she'd ever owned.

'We are both a similiar size,' Erin went on.

'I'd be delighted to accept anything you can spare,' Sadie said appreciatively, her tone one of gratitude but, as with Mrs Ritter, completely without subservience.

'Great. That gives me the excuse to do some shopping!' Erin smiled, and clapped her hands in glee.

The clothes had been offered out of the kindness of Erin's heart and not just as an excuse to buy herself more, Sadie judged.

'Would you care for a drink?' Edward asked her.

That threw Sadie, she didn't know what to reply. She was an employee, after all.

Guessing her quandary, Jack said, 'It's all right, Sadie. In this house we treat our staff as friends rather than simply people who work for us. We're fairly liberal in that respect.'

'Yes, please then,' Sadie replied to Edward, thinking she was beginning to understand why Miss Dobson had spoken so highly of the Fitzgeralds. The angels had truly smiled on her when Edward had driven into her life.

'So, what will you have?'

Sadie glanced over to where Erin's drink stood on an occasional table. 'Sherry, please,' she replied.

'Show Sadie the painting of the house, Erin,' Edward said as he moved off to pour Sadie's sherry. 'When Sadie first saw Clare she said if she'd been an artist she'd have wanted to paint it, and I told her that grandfather had already had that idea.'

Erin beckoned Sadie over to a marble fireplace above which the painting in question hung. Sadie gazed up at the large canvas framed in gilt. 'The artist has certainly caught the spirit of the house,' she said.

'We've always thought it rather good,' Jack declared, coming to stand beside her.

There was a portrait on another wall Sadie now noticed, of a middle-aged woman. She knew instantly that the woman was Mrs Fitzgerald, and wondered what had become of her.

'Here you are,' said Edward, handing Sadie a schooner.

'Here's to your time at Clare, may it be a long and happy one,' Jack proposed.

They all drank to that, and as she was sipping her drink, Sadie caught sight of Courcy, still sitting, staring intently at her over the rim of his glass, a look that told her he found her attractive.

'Edward mentioned that these Trikhardt folk shot your dog,' Jack said.

Sadie's face clouded over. 'Yes, they did. Julius said Mischief was useless at hunting but that was just an excuse to get rid of him. He was a lovely dog, I still miss him.'

'A Dane, I believe?'

Sadie nodded.

Jack's face clouded with anger, as he loved dogs. 'The fella deserved what he got then. To shoot a dog is despicable, unless the beast needs putting down, that is.'

'Plenty of dogs round Clare,' Edward informed Sadie. 'We've got six of them.'

'All sorts,' Erin smiled.

'And all kept outside except for Smudge the Pekinese, who should be about somewhere.' Edward glanced around, but there was no sign of the peke.

'Smudge is a nice name,' Sadie smiled.

'And you called yours Mischief? That's a nice name too,' Jack acknowledged.

'Have you tried on your uniform yet?' Edward enquired.

'Not yet,' she replied.

'Well, I'm sure Mrs Ritter will make you after you have had dinner.' The staff always ate after the Fitzgeralds, and were even now waiting for Sadie to join them, as Edward was aware. They'd been requested to hold their meal until he brought Sadie down to them.

They made small talk for the next few minutes, until Sadie had finished her drink. Then Edward announced he'd escort her to the kitchen as she didn't yet know her way round the house.

'Was I all right?' she asked eagerly when they'd left the drawing-room.

'Very. They were all impressed with you, Father in particular. I can see you becoming a favourite of his.'

That pleased her tremendously.

Edward had been correct, Mrs Ritter did want Sadie to try on her uniforms after their meal. They only needed a few minor alterations which she did herself before going to bed.

In the morning she presented herself spot on time to start work.

★ ★ ★

Mrs Ritter stood in the door of the utility room and watched Sadie, whose back was to her, ironing. The girl had said she was well used to hard work, and so it had proved. There was nothing on which she could fault Sadie, whom she now considered a real find. Edward had done her a good turn in bringing Sadie Smith to Clare.

'How are you getting on with that lot?' Mrs Ritter enquired, stepping into the utility room.

Sadie glanced over her shoulder, but didn't stop ironing. 'Fine, thank you. I'll soon be finished here.'

'Right, join me in the kitchen when you have. We're having a dinner party tonight and I want to discuss the table with you.'

Discuss the table with her! Sadie thought that sounded very grand. She started to sing as she waded through what remained of the ironing.

As she went to the kitchen, she discovered Mrs Ritter laying out the best King's pattern silver cutlery. Mrs Ritter had already found out what Sadie knew, and more importantly didn't know, about housework. 'Would you like to set the table for this evening?' she smiled.

Sadie knew this was an important task, one Mrs Ritter normally reserved for herself. She was being honoured. 'Yes, please,' she smiled in reply.

'Dinner will be for ten,' Mrs Ritter went on. 'The family plus the Sturdevants, which makes six. Then there's Mr and Mrs Yaeger, their son, Carl and daughter, Phyllis. She's Edward's sweetheart by the way.'

That one word seemed to pierce Sadie's heart as though it had been an arrow fired from a bow. Sweetheart, she repeated the word in her mind. 'Is it serious between them?' she asked slowly.

'You bet. Those two met in school and have been mooning ever since. It's definitely a love match.' She dropped her voice to a conspiratorial level. 'And a good family match, too. The Yaegers own a department store in town and a cattle ranch. Each is a fine catch for the other if you get my meaning.'

Sadie suddenly felt sick. She'd told herself all along that she had no chance where Edward was concerned, but at the back of her mind, and in her heart, she'd secretly hoped . . .

Suddenly she put a stop to those thoughts knowing they would only upset her further.

'Are you all right, hon?' Mrs Ritter enquired. 'You've gone pale.'

Sadie shook her head. 'It's nothing.'

'Perhaps you'd care for a lie down? I can cope.'

'No, I want to do the table.' She took a deep breath. 'So, it's place settings for ten. Have you decided which dinner service to use?'

When Sadie came to lay the table she found that her hands were shaking.

Sadie had herself well and truly composed when the guests arrived that evening. Edward looked splendid in his black tie, she thought, he might have been a film star. As for Erin, the gown she was wearing made her green with envy. The gown was silver overstitched with sparkling silver thread and braid. It was low cut, then fell away under the arms. It had a slit on the left side that snaked halfway up Erin's thigh. The total effect was stunning.

When she saw Courcy he had a strange, lop-sided smile on his face. As she passed him, she thought she smelt alcohol and wondered if that was his problem.

The Yaegers arrived shortly after the Sturdevants. He white haired and loud, she blue rinsed and as plump as a Christmas turkey. Carl had a flat-top haircut and moved like an athlete, Phyllis was honey blonde with a golden tan and an excellent figure. Sadie hated her on sight.

Sadie was in charge of the champagne and soft drinks served in the drawing-room. Phyllis drank coke, as did her brother. And the only time Phyllis actually looked at Sadie she stared right through her as though she wasn't there.

At one point Edward smiled at Sadie, but she didn't smile back. If he'd asked her later why, she'd have said it was because she was on duty which she knew would be a lie.

When dinner was announced Sadie watched Phyllis leave the room, her small bottom wiggling sexily inside her tightly fitting dress. She paused to say something to Edward, who laughed and then took her by the arm.

Sadie imagined an outsize hat pin. How she'd love to have taken that and stuck it . . .

She smiled in satisfaction at the picture that conjured up in her mind.

It was Monday morning, Sadie's day off. She'd been for a long walk and was now returning to Clare. She was passing the stables when Erin appeared from behind them.

Erin called out. 'This your day off?'

Sadie nodded.

'What have you been doing?'

Sadie told her.

'And what are you going to do now?'

'I don't know. I haven't decided.' She laughed. 'The truth is I'm at a bit of a loss not being used to having time to myself. I'll think of something though.'

'I'm going into town. Want to come?'

'With you?' Sadie exclaimed.

'Sure. Father's at home all day so we can get Sam to drive us. What do you say?'

Sadie didn't have to think twice, this would be her first opportunity to visit Bald Rock Falls. 'Yes, please,' she replied eagerly.

'OK! Just let me get changed and we'll be on our way.'

Sadie, who was in jeans, decided she, too, would change. It was a chance to wear one of the pretty dresses Erin had so kindly given her.

After changing they met up again by the front door and went out to the garage where Sam, the chauffeur, was waiting for them.

Sam was a man in his late thirties who lived for cars, Jack's Cadillac being his pride and joy. Erin and Sadie got inside, and settled back as the Caddy drove off.

'Care for a drink?' Erin asked.

Sadie was taken aback. 'What sort of drink?'

Erin opened a cabinet built into the partition between themselves and Sam to reveal a well-stocked bar. 'Whatever you fancy. Scotch or Canadian whiskey? English gin? Russian vodka?'

Sadie giggled, thinking a bar in a car was the height of luxury. 'I'm not much of a drinker,' she confessed.

'Suit yourself. I'm going to have a gin and tonic.'

Sadie thought it was really far too early in the day to have alcohol. There again, the whole thing was such a novelty. 'I'll have a small one then,' she said, changing her mind.

'Good girl.'

Erin poured Sadie's drink and handed it to her. 'Now what about a cigarette?'

'I don't smoke.'

'OK.'

Erin lit a cigarette, then settled back in her seat, and grinned at Sadie. 'Don't look so worried, you won't get into trouble. Nor will I.'

Sadie glanced at Sam watching them in the rear-view mirror. He didn't appear anxious or disapproving, merely keeping a friendly eye on his passengers.

'Here's how!' Erin toasted Sadie. 'So how are you enjoying Clare?'

'Very much, thank you.'

'I like you, we all do,' Erin stated. 'I guess you and I could be girl-friends, eh?'

'I *work* for your father,' Sadie pointed out.

Erin shrugged. 'So what! This is Canada remember, we don't have all the class hang-ups that you do in Britain. There's far more equality out here, which is why it's an ace place to be. I don't think you inferior as a person just because you work for us, hell no! If anything I admire you for doing a job damn well.'

'Does Mrs Ritter say I do the job well?' Sadie probed.

'She thinks the sun shines out of your ass. Says she's never had such a hard worker, or one so bright.'

Sadie flushed with pleasure.

Erin gulped down more gin and tonic, then puffed contentedly on her cigarette.

'Are you going to work eventually?' Sadie asked out of curiosity, as Erin had left school earlier that summer.

'Why bother? There's no need for me to do so. Nor do I want to go to university and study like Courcy. The only thing I'm really interested in is finding myself the right husband, which I'll do when the time is ripe. By that I mean I don't want to get married too soon, I want plenty of fun and games before I tie the knot.'

'Have you anyone in mind?' Sadie asked.

'There are a few I've got my eye on. Contenders you might say.'

Sadie forced herself to put the next question, dreading the answer. 'When do Edward and Miss Yaeger plan to marry?'

'Couple of years, I guess. She's a cute little filly, eh?'

Sadie's reply was a thin, tight smile.

'What about you?'

'Me!' Sadie exclaimed. 'I don't have anyone.'

'I'm sure you will soon. You aren't exactly ugly, you know.'

Sadie stared into her glass, and saw Edward's face staring back at her. Behind Edward, Phyllis Yaeger was leering in triumph.

'Have you ever had a beau?' Erin asked.

Sadie shook her head. 'There was no time for anything like that on the farm. It was just work, work and more work.'

'What about the guy who was sent there with you, and then ran away?'

'Robbie! He and I were . . . like brother and sister, very close, but in a platonic way.'

'Was he good looking?'

Sadie pursed her lips. 'Yes. He had a slightly cheeky face when younger, but grew out of that. I would certainly call him attractive. And he was intelligent, and I mean intelligent. He was a real brain.'

Erin finished her drink and decided she would have another. Sadie declined when asked if she wanted her glass freshened.

'Doesn't your father mind you drinking?' Sadie enquired.

'Not as long as I don't abuse the privilege. He'd sure as hell get mad if I fell down drunk though. Then he'd paddle my butt just like he used to when I was a kid.'

Erin was a lot rougher in speech than Edward, Sadie thought. But then Edward was very gentlemanly in both speech and manner.

'What about smoking?' Sadie further asked.

Erin shrugged. 'I don't think he likes it, but he doesn't object either. He knows I'd only smoke behind his back if he did.'

'May I ask a personal question?'

'Sure. Shoot!'

'What happened to your mother?'

Erin's face darkened, and she became sad. 'She died

227

seven years ago from cancer. It was diagnosed, and then within a few months she was dead. It really cut Father up, and us.'

'I'm sorry,' Sadie muttered.

'Yeah! We all miss her, Father most of all, I guess.'

Erin fell silent then, and reflective, till they entered Bald Rock Falls. Then she brightened up again.

'Where do you want dropping off, Miss Erin?' Sam asked.

'Yaeger's store. You can park in the lot out back, OK?'

'Yes, miss.'

Sadie gazed out at Bald Rock Falls which was clearly far larger than Peterawa. She spotted a movie house which excited her, and all sorts of interesting stores.

'Here we are,' Erin declared as the car drew up outside the Yaeger building. They both climbed out, and Sam drove away.

'I adore shopping,' Erin smiled.

'I can't say I've done all that much of it.'

'Of course,' Erin nodded, thinking of Sadie's previous circumstances. 'Then you'll enjoy today. I promise you.'

Inside they passed several perfume counters, which caused Sadie's senses to reel. How gorgeous! she thought, nose twitching with delight.

They spent several hours in the store during which Erin bought a great many items and Sadie a few minor ones. It both intrigued and amazed Sadie that Erin had her own personal account which she charged everything to and which, Erin informed her, was settled at the end of every month by Jack. How lovely to be able to shop that way, Sadie thought wistfully, with a rich father to pick up the tab.

'Now how about lunch?' Erin suggested. Then, when she saw Sadie's slightly doubtful expression, she added, 'My treat, of course.'

Yaeger's boasted a restaurant which was clearly popular with the ladies of the town. They were fortunate in finding a table for two in a secluded corner, and they settled for that.

'It's busy,' commented Sadie, gazing about.

'A great meeting place for morning coffee, lunch and afternoon coffee. I use it a lot.'

Sadie wondered if Phyllis Yaeger might put in an appearance, but as it transpired she didn't.

They ate a leisurely lunch, washed down by a half bottle of Californian wine, followed by coffee.

'Would you mind if I walked round some of the streets?' Sadie requested.

'Yeah, of course. We'll drop our packages off with Sam, and then do just that.'

Erin was an excellent and enthusiastic guide, and showed Sadie completely round the town centre, pointing out things of interest *en route*. Then they decided it was time to go home.

They were halfway back when Erin suddenly gestured out the car window, and up at the sky. 'Edward!' she exclaimed.

Sadie slid across, and craned her neck to get a look. There it was, a scarlet coloured Gipsy Moth flying at several thousand feet. She had the mad impulse to wave, which was, of course, daft. It was the first time she'd seen the aeroplane Edward had told her about.

'I'd love to be able to fly,' Sadie said.

'Would you?' Erin queried in surprise.

'Oh yes. It must be a fantastic sensation being up there all by yourself, almost a holy feeling.'

'Holy!' Erin repeated, thinking that a strange word to use. But she could see what Sadie was driving at.

'I wonder where he's been?' Sadie mused aloud, never taking her eyes off the Moth.

'Up-country at one of our logging operations. I heard

him talking to Father about it over breakfast,' Erin explained.

How exciting! Sadie thought. She wondered if Edward could see their car, and what he was thinking about. Phyllis Yaeger? Jealousy coursed through her.

She watched the Moth descend, then disappear as it landed.

Erin started to chatter about her eighteenth birthday in the fall, and what she was going to ask her father for as a present.

Sadie forced herself to listen. But in her mind she was visualizing the scarlet Moth, with Edward inside.

Sadie humped a basket of washing outside intending to peg it out. She stopped, still holding the heavy basket, when she spotted the two riders in the nearby paddock. One was Edward, the other Phyllis Yaeger.

They were both laughing as Edward completed a sequence of complicated manoeuvres, then it was Phyllis's turn to do the same. She was an accomplished horsewoman, Sadie noted, looking good on a horse, and stylish with it.

Phyllis completed her manoeuvres, and the pair of them laughed again. Then Edward brought his mount alongside Phyllis's and, leaning across, kissed her on the lips.

Sadie swallowed hard, but didn't look away. When the kiss was over Phyllis grabbed Edward and returned his.

Not a snowball's hope in hell, Sadie thought, placing her basket on the ground. When she glanced up again Edward and Phyllis were riding at full gallop round the large paddock, he chasing her.

I hope she falls and breaks her lovely neck, Sadie thought, and immediately regretted it.

Edward and Phyllis, obviously enjoying themselves and one another's company, were still careering round the paddock when Sadie had finished her task.

As she entered the house, she slammed the door behind her.

Sadie suddenly experienced the creepy sensation that she was being watched. She whirled round to find a smiling Courcy staring at her.

'Hello,' he said.

'Hello,' she replied, and went back to polishing the silver.

'Hope I didn't give you a fright. I've been standing here for a good few minutes without you noticing.'

She didn't reply.

He came closer. 'Imagine big brother coming across you in the aftermath of a twister. Just like him!'

Sadie didn't respond to that either.

'He was a hero at school, you know. Edward Fitzgerald, star of field and track! All the girls idolized him. He simply snapped his fingers and he could have had any one of them.'

Courcy turned a wooden chair round and sat on it, resting his arms and head on the top of its back. 'Do you mind if I sit here?' he asked.

'No.'

'I thought we should get to know one another better. Don't you think that's a good idea?'

He made her nervous. She felt like a mouse confronted by a snake. Come to think of it, that was exactly what he reminded her of, a snake. 'What are you studying at university?' she asked by way of making conversation.

'Philosophy,' he smiled.

'Philosophy!'

His smile widened. 'That surprises you. Don't you see me as the philosophical type?'

'I don't know.'

'Yes, you do. You're just being polite. That's something I find most annoying about brother Edward, he's always polite. I find it nauseating.'

She glanced at Courcy. 'It sounds to me like you don't care for your brother very much?'

'Not so!' he protested. 'I mean,' he continued sarcastically, 'who could fail to like Edward? Everyone likes Edward.'

Except you, she thought. Courcy appeared to be jealous of Edward.

'Are you a virgin?'

She stopped polishing, shocked to the core. 'What?' She couldn't believe what she'd heard.

He slowly lifted one eyebrow. 'I said, are you a virgin?'

'Yes, of course I am.'

'You sound outraged that I should ask.'

That was precisely what she was. She resumed polishing.

'Sorry if I offended you. I didn't mean to. Anyway, you would probably say it was none of my business. I just wondered, that's all. I can be very curious at times. Particularly when the subject of my curiosity is as pretty as you. You are, you know, very pretty.'

Her nervousness increased. 'Are you really studying philosophy?' she queried, changing the subject.

'Nope. I only said that to impress you. I would like to impress you.'

'Why?' she heard herself ask.

'Because I find you most attractive. The first time I saw you, you made my heart flutter.'

He was trying to verbally seduce her! she thought in alarm. A cold shiver coursed up and down her spine.

'So what are you studying?' she queried.

'You at the moment. And satisfying studying it makes too.'

How silky and practised his words were. And how confident he was. How often had he come out with that line? she wondered. And what would she do if he tried anything on? Scream? She glanced at him and he was still smiling, his eyes filled with amusement and something else. What? Desire, she decided.

'Nice legs, very important that in a woman,' he said. 'Phyllis has nice legs, don't you think?'

Now why had he brought up Phyllis! She suddenly realized that she'd started to polish a small bowl that she'd already polished. She was becoming confused.

'Legs and backside,' he went on.

She flushed.

Courcy gave a low laugh, well aware of how disconcerted she was. He found that appealing.

'I told Edward once, that Phyllis has a lovely ass, and he wasn't pleased at all. He got quite angry actually. Don't you agree?'

'I can't say I've ever noticed,' she lied.

'It's gorgeous. But know something?'

'What?'

'Yours is better. And sexier. Far more so.'

This has gone far enough, she thought, laying down the polishing materials. 'Excuse me,' she murmured, and left the room.

His mocking laugh followed her.

Heather listened intently, nodding every so often, as Sadie related what had passed between her and Courcy. It was that evening and she was in Heather's room having coffee and cookies.

'Yeah, figures,' Heather said when Sadie came to the end of her tale. 'He would make a play for you now that Mary-Anne has gone. Damn!'

'Why damn?'

Sadie queried.

Heather gave her a strange smile. 'Because I was hoping it would be me he'd make a play for.'

'You?'

'Yeah, I think he's real cute. But he'd never look at me while Mary-Anne was about.'

233

'You mean there was something between them?'

'I should say. That's why she left, because she was pregnant by him.'

This was news to Sadie. 'I see.'

'She wanted to marry him, but Courcy would have none of that. She was paid off and told to go. There was a terrible scene here the day she left. I've never heard a woman scream and shout so much. It was sheer murder. But Courcy wouldn't be moved. Stupid bitch.'

'Why stupid bitch?'

Heather lit a cigarette. 'Mary-Anne never said, but it's my belief that she let herself get pregnant in the hope of trapping him into marriage. But she should have known Courcy better.'

'And you still . . . fancy him?' Sadie asked, amazed.

'Sure. Only I have no illusions about him. Nor marriage plans. I'd settle for just getting him into the sack, that's all.'

Sadie stared at Heather who, despite her dumpy figure, wasn't at all unattractive having a sweet, angelic, face. 'He sounds to me like a bit of a womanizer,' she probed.

Heather laughed. 'Bit of a womanizer! That's putting it mildly. He screws around like you wouldn't believe. He's first cousin to a jack rabbit.'

'And what about Edward?'

'He's different entirely. Chalk and cheese those two. I'm sure Edward's sleeping with Phyllis, but no one else. He's the loyal, faithful type, quite unlike his brother.'

'And knowing that you'd still go to bed with Courcy?'

'Damn right! He's exciting. He buzzes. And he certainly makes me buzz, *and* boil. But then I've always been attracted to bastards. A flaw I suppose.'

Sadie considered all these revelations, and it aroused vivid memories of Julius, which she rapidly put to the back of her mind. She tried not to think of Edward in

234

bed with Phyllis Yaeger. The two of them together like that made her feel sick. 'I got the distinct impression that Courcy doesn't care for Edward,' she said slowly.

'He's jealous of him. Edward is a natural golden boy and winner, which sticks in Courcy's craw. That's why Courcy won't work in the family business when he leaves university. That would mean playing second fiddle to Edward which would be plain poison to him.'

'So what will he do?'

'He plans to become a lawyer. He should do well at it too with that velvet tongue of his. He could charm the knickers off a nun.'

'Not this nun,' Sadie promised.

'He'll keep on trying. You can bet on that.'

Sadie sincerely hoped he wouldn't. She would just have to make it clear to him that she wasn't interested, nor ever likely to be.

'He's persuasive,' Heather warned. Then shivered. 'I only wish he'd try a little of his persuasion on me. It wouldn't take much for me to get on my back for him.'

Sadie was somewhat shocked at the crudity of that statement. 'What did Mr Fitzgerald say about the Mary-Anne business?' she queried.

Heather shrugged. 'I don't know, that was strictly between him and Courcy. But it would have been him that ensured Mary-Anne got a handsome pay-off. Whatever else you can say about the old guy you can never call him mean. He's generous to a fault.'

Sadie sipped some of her coffee. She was pleased she'd had this conversation with Heather, she'd learnt a great deal. Including the fact Edward and Phyllis were probably sleeping together.

She felt sick again.

Summer turned to autumn and soon it was Erin's birthday. She had been given a brand new MG sports car. Having

235

been taught how to drive by Sam, she was now forever zooming round the countryside. She and Sadie had become good friends and often spent time together.

Snow would be coming soon, Sadie thought, one Monday morning while she was out for a stroll. It was her day off and she was contemplating whether to go and see *Employee's Entrance* starring Loretta Young and Wallace Ford, and wondered if Erin would like to go with her.

Suddenly she realized she was close to the hangar where the Moth was kept and, although she'd often seen it in the distance, she'd never actually visited it before. On impulse she decided to do so now.

The doors were open, the Moth's cowlings off, with Edward on a ladder tinkering with the engine. She was about to turn away, not wishing to disturb him, when he glanced up and spotted her.

He called out to her.

She entered the hangar and stood beside the ladder. 'I was out for a walk and found myself here. I thought I'd look in.'

'Sure. Why not?' he grinned.

She nodded at the engine. 'What's wrong?'

'Nothing much. A small problem that I'll soon have fixed.'

'You're your own mechanic then?'

'Yeah. And fully qualified. I like fooling around with engines, it gives me a great deal of pleasure.'

Sadie could understand that. She stepped back a few paces and perused the plane. 'She's a beautiful machine.'

'Yeah, I think so too.'

'Is she difficult to fly?'

He shook his head. 'Not really, once you've mastered the basics, that is.'

'It's a British plane, isn't it?'

'Designed by De Havilland, yes, but this particular baby

was built in the States by Moth Aircraft Corporation.' He frowned. 'Are you interested in planes?'

'I find them fascinating. Not that I know much about them, but I wouldn't mind learning.'

He was intrigued, a woman interested in planes! 'Would you care to come up here and have a look at the engine?' he asked.

'Yes, please!' she replied eagerly.

She joined him up the ladder, and he proceeded to explain the mechanics. He was impressed by how quickly she grasped things, and by some of the questions she asked.

'Ah!' he exclaimed, discovering the fault he'd been searching for.

Sadie watched silently as he fixed it. When that was done they both climbed back down the ladder, he wiping his oily hands on a rag on reaching the floor.

Edward was looking puzzled, but the look soon cleared as the answer came to him. 'Of course, this is Monday. Your day off.'

She nodded.

'What are you going to do?'

'I was contemplating that when I found myself out here by the hangar. I thought I'd ask Erin if she'd like to go to the movies this evening.'

'What about now, for the rest of the day?'

She pulled a face. 'Nothing, I'm afraid.'

'Want to come up-country with me? The round trip, including time on the ground, should take about four hours.'

Her jaw dropped and she gawped at him. 'You mean . . . in the plane?'

'Yeah, of course. There's a spare suit and helmet you can use.'

Her face lit up with amazement and excitement. 'There's nothing I'd like more,' she blurted out.

It pleased him to see how thrilled she was. 'You're sure now? You really want to go up?'

'Oh yes!' she breathed. 'Oh yes!'

'OK then. The plane's gassed and ready to go, so all we have to do is get suited up.'

He led her to the back of the hangar where the suits hung on pegs, and handed her one, instructing her how to put it on. When she'd done that he gave her a heavy flying jacket and told her to slip that on. Finally she received a helmet and goggles.

When they were both suited up they returned to the plane which she helped him manoeuvre outside. He slid the chocks into place, then assisted her into the front cockpit. He plugged her head-set in, explaining that they would be able to talk during the flight by means of the Gosport tube connecting both cockpits. That done he strapped her in securely, asked her if she was comfortable, and then jumped back down to the ground.

Sadie took a deep breath, desperate to be airborne. What an unexpected piece of luck this was. She was trembling all over from excitement and anticipation, quite beside herself that this was actually happening.

Edward scrambled up into the rear cockpit where he busied himself with the instruments and controls, then he leapt down to the ground again and made his way to the propeller.

The engine caught and roared into life on the third swing, and a smiling Edward gave Sadie the thumbs-up sign, which she returned.

Once more in the rear cockpit, with head-set plugged in, Edward pulled the chocks free, by means of ropes attached to them, and hauled them into his cockpit and stowed them away.

'You OK?' he asked Sadie.

'Yes.'

'Then let's go.'

The Moth trundled forward, and gradually began to

pick up speed. Elation swept through Sadie as the little plane left the ground, and began to ascend. She watched the ground fall quickly away beneath them.

They flew over Clare, then banked to head northwards. They passed the town of Big Rock Falls on their left, then the plane descended as Edward brought them swooping over the Falls after which the town was named.

Sadie had seen the Falls from the ground, but they were even more spectacular from the air. A precipice of water fell to a white roar that danced and twisted madly to eventual peace in Lake Baldy several miles upstream. The rock over which the Falls tumbled was unusual for that part of the country as it was composed of compressed sand and gravel deposited there by a primeval Ice Age glacier.

'Good fishing on Lake Baldy, lots of walleye, pike and yellow perch. Used to go there often when I was a kid,' Edward said.

They skimmed over the lake, then started to ascend again, Edward levelling out the plane at two and a half thousand feet.

Sadie sat mesmerized by the great, and often majestic, natural beauty which now passed beneath them – enormous forests, winding rivers and creeks; canyons, gulleys, and snow-tipped mountains where the snow never melted.

They passed fingers of rock pointing skywards like some prehistoric monuments, a herd of galloping deer, scared by something, perhaps by the passing of their plane. And once they saw the small speck of a black bear ambling down to the river where no doubt it was hoping to catch itself a meal.

'It's wonderful,' Sadie said, voice filled with awe.

Edward smiled to himself, knowing exactly how she felt. He could remember only too clearly the magic of his own first flight.

A little later Sadie gasped at what loomed ahead. An

island of trees, set in a jade green river, rose out of a swirling mist and floating on the river were thousands upon thousands of felled, debranched, trees.

'That's where we're heading,' Edward informed her, adding, 'the river's the Abitibi by the way.'

They dived into some mist, strands of which floated by like wisps of white cotton candy. Then they were underneath the mist and turning towards a prepared landing site. Edward made a perfect landing, taxied the Moth into position and killed the engine.

Sadie closed her eyes, thinking that had been the most enthralling experience of her entire life. She couldn't wait to fly off again.

A man came striding towards the plane, waving to Edward as he got closer.

'Can you unplug yourself?' Edward asked Sadie.

'Of course.'

Sadie climbed from the cockpit and jumped to the ground where she was joined by Edward.

'That was wonderful,' she said. Taking off her helmet, she shook her hair free.

'Hi, Ed!' said the man, shaking his hand.

'Patsy, I'd like you to meet Sadie, a friend of mine.'

A friend of his, not employee! Sadie smiled at that.

The hand that grasped Sadie's was huge and rough, the fingers calloused. 'Pleased to meet you, Sadie.'

'And I'm pleased to meet you,' she responded.

'Patsy Kernan's our logging boss on this operation,' Edward explained.

'I presume you could use some coffee?' Patsy suggested to them.

'Wouldn't say no,' Edward replied.

'Then let's go to my hut. And the plans are there, too.'

Sadie was left in the dark as to what those plans were, but as they walked to his hut she gleaned from their conversation that they were to do with some new complicated machinery Patsy intended to have built.

The hut was crude and contained a wood stove, rocking-chair, desk and bed, the latter unmade. There was an enamel pot on the stove from which Patsy now poured coffee into three tin mugs.

'I have sugar but no milk, I'm afraid,' Patsy apologized to Sadie.

'Sugar's fine,' she replied.

The coffee was far stronger than she made, but it was somehow exactly right for that environment. It soon warmed her up after what had been, despite the heavy flying jacket, a cold journey.

'Here, Ed,' said Patsy, going to his desk where he unrolled a series of drawings and spread them flat. Edward studied the top drawing for a few moments, then began firing questions at the logging boss.

Sadie finished her coffee and laid her mug down. 'I think I'll wait outside while you two talk,' she said.

Edward turned to her. 'Have a look round, I'm sure you'll find it interesting. There are plenty of crew about if you want to ask anything.'

The first thing to catch her eye as she left the hut was a small locomotive hauling half a dozen flat cars towards the river, each piled high with debranched trees held in position by chains.

The next thing was an overhead wire contraption along which individual large trees, and sometimes two or three smaller ones chained together, passed along.

Everywhere was a hive of industry with men going about their various tasks. They all appeared cheerful enough, she thought, which meant they must be happy in their work.

One giant with an enormous beard and whiskers wolf-whistled at her, but it seemed good natured, not in any way threatening.

Not far from Patsy's hut was a compound where, Sadie correctly presumed, the loggers slept and ate.

She went down to the river's edge and stared out at the island covered in trees that she'd seen from the air. It reminded her of a Chinese plate she'd admired in a magazine.

She glanced out over the trees floating on the Abitibi, and wondered how long they would remain there before being moved on.

She inhaled deeply, thinking how clean and incredibly fresh the air was here. It made her positively glow inside.

Sadie set about exploring further, keen to discover all there was to see. It was a huge logging operation, she now realized, and was told by a passing logger that it stretched miles inland. The camp she was now in was merely the tip of the iceberg.

Felled trees came to the camp by means of locomotives and various skidding procedures. It was explained to Sadie that skidding meant the gathering together of felled trees at convenient places for onward transport. There were two types of skidding: ground skidding, achieved by endless chains and other devices and high skidding such as the overhead wire contraption.

About an hour later Edward joined her, as she stood watching a gang of men at work. 'How are you doing?' he asked.

'Fine.'

'Learnt anything?'

'I now know what skidding is, or yarding, as it's sometimes called.'

His face broke into a delighted grin.

'And that,' she said, pointing to a V-shaped wooden construction on trellisses, 'is a flume.'

He laughed. 'Ten out of ten!'

'Have you finished your business here?' she enquired.

He nodded. 'I thought we'd grab some lunch first before flying back.'

'Suits me. I'm starving.'

At that point a steam whistle blew announcing that the midday meal was now being served.

'What's on the menu?' she asked as they made their way to the compound.

'Bear stew.'

She came up short. 'You're kidding?'

'Yup. Just pulling your leg.' He paused for a moment, then said with a twinkle in his eyes, 'It's really rattler pie.'

'Ugh!' she exclaimed, screwing up her face. 'The very thought of eating snake turns my stomach.'

The canteen was the largest hut in the compound, and it was rapidly filling with raucous loggers. There were several meal shifts Edward told her, and this was the first.

Men greeted Edward as if he was one of them, the same giant who'd wolf-whistled at Sadie thumping him on the back and nearly sending him sprawling.

There was a choice of either casserole, or meat loaf or a fish dish. Sadie chose the fish which was delicious. She and Edward sat at a long refectory-type table with Patsy and certain others who settled down alongside. On the table plates were loaded with white bread and corn bread, the latter a great favourite of Sadie's.

'Plain but wholesome,' Patsy smiled at her.

The loggers' table manners left a lot to be desired, but that didn't bother Sadie. She liked these people, and felt at ease in their company.

The loggers ate voraciously, consuming vast quantities of food. Sadie was hardly surprised, theirs was an intensely physical job. Caught up in it all she herself ate more than she would have done normally.

'How do you feel?' Edward asked her when they were outside the canteen.

'As if I might burst. You certainly feed them well.'

'It pays us to do so. It would be a bad mistake on our part to skimp in that department.'

243

She saw the sense in that. 'Mr Fitzgerald's policy?' she queried.

Edward nodded. 'And one I wholeheartedly agree with. We feed them well, pay them well and, in return, they work damn well. It's a good arrangement all round.'

Patsy came to see them off. Sadie settled herself into the front cockpit and plugged in while Edward swung the propeller. Final goodbyes were shouted above the roar of the engine. Then they were off.

Edward circled above the camp before setting a course for Clare. If anything Sadie enjoyed her second flight even more than the first.

Sadie sat staring out of her bedroom window at a full moon dominating the night sky. She hadn't suggested going to the movies with Erin after all, her day had been complete as far as she was concerned.

Flying with Edward! Just to think about it brought a lump to her throat. What bliss those two flights had been! And what stunning scenery! She saw again the island of trees, rising out of a swirling mist. And floating on the river, kissing and nudging one another, thousands upon thousands of debranched trees.

She smiled softly, recalling Edward's delighted grin when she'd mentioned skidding, and told him what a flume was. The scene in her mind was so vivid and real she could almost smell that air like heady wine.

Being in a plane and flying had seemed the most natural thing in the world to her. Incredibly exciting, it was as if she belonged in a cockpit.

She remembered the vibration of the plane in flight, and the ever-present reek of engine oil. And the other odours, that of leather, and wood, and fuel.

She touched her stomach, still full from the meal she'd eaten in the loggers' canteen. And almost laughed out loud at an extremely filthy, but hysterically funny, joke she'd overheard.

A scarlet Moth, the same colour as the ribbons Edward had given her and which she'd never yet worn in her hair, keeping them for a special occasion.

Suddenly it dawned on her how she might fly again. If Edward would agree, that was.

Chapter Five

Things were a bit hectic round the house for the next few days after that, so Sadie bided her time, waiting to catch Edward in a relaxed, receptive mood. Her opportunity came when she found him alone one evening sitting in the drawing-room drinking a glass of brandy.

'Help me service the Moth!' he exclaimed in astonishment when she'd made her request.

'I appreciate that at the moment I know nothing about the mechanical side of the plane, but I am a quick learner, and very practical. I used to mend and repair all manner of things around the farm.'

'But why?'

'Several reasons. One is that I need a hobby, something of interest to occupy my spare time. And the other is I thought if I was helpful to you, you might reward me with more flights in the plane.'

He understood now. 'You've been bitten by the bug, eh?'

'If you mean the flying bug, yes. I'd do almost anything to go up again.'

He sipped his brandy, and thought about it. He managed perfectly well by himself round the hanger and with the plane, but nonetheless help would be welcome, especially if it was as enthusiastic as Sadie's promised to be.

'I don't know,' he swithered.

'At least give me a trial? I won't take offence if you decide I'm more of a hindrance than a help.'

'And you really are good with your hands?'

'Yes,' she assured him.

A female trainee mechanic! The idea amused him. And he certainly couldn't deny that she was good company.

'It would mean me teaching you everything, right from scratch,' he said.

'As I said, I'm a quick learner.'

He could well believe that. 'What sort of hours did you have in mind?' he queried.

'I have Sunday afternoons and all day Monday free. I could come over to the hangar then. And I have three evenings a week when I'm also free, I could also come over during any or all of those.'

'That's all your time off,' he said.

'Not really. You're bound to be away or doing something else sometimes. And I can't see you allowing me to do much without being supervised for some while to come.'

That was certainly true, he thought.

'Please, Edward?' she pleaded softly.

How could he refuse? It would be churlish of him to do so.

'All right,' he agreed, 'but you start at the very bottom, sweeping the hangar floor and making coffee.'

'I'll sweep it as clean as a whistle and make enough coffee to float a battleship,' she promised eagerly.

He laughed, and so did she.

'It's a deal, *apprentice*,' he said, extending a hand.

They shook on it.

Sadie was singing quietly to herself as she did the weekly household accounts.

'You sound happy,' Mrs Ritter smiled from the doorway where she'd been standing for the past few moments.

Sadie glanced up. 'Aren't I always?'

Mrs Ritter came over to Sadie's side and glanced down at the figures she had been working on. 'Any problems?'

'Nope. Everything appears to balance.'

Mrs Ritter did a few, quick mental calculations, checking Sadie's sums, all of which were correct. 'Your doing this takes a load off my shoulders,' she confessed.

'I rather enjoy it,' Sadie said.

'How about you taking over the ordering as well? Think you could manage that?'

'I don't see why not. It's straightforward enough.'

'I'll show you my system, then no doubt you'll improve on it,' Mrs Ritter said, wryly. She'd learnt long since that Sadie was a past master at making things more efficient.

'I've just come from speaking with Mr F,' Mrs Ritter went on. 'There's a new girl starting next Monday.'

Sadie laid down her pencil. 'As what?'

'Maid. It'll make matters easier all round, including more time off for you and Heather.'

More time off was good news, Sadie thought. Time she could spend out at the hangar with Edward.

'We don't really need another maid,' Mrs Ritter continued, 'but Mr F is taking her on as a favour to someone.'

'What's her name?'

'Jerelene Wilkerson. And I thought you would train her.'

'Fine,' Sadie agreed. Although Heather had been there longer, she was the one Mrs Ritter always turned to first.

They started to discuss which bedroom Jerelene would be put in and what duties she initially would be given.

'The yellow handled screwdriver,' Edward grunted to Sadie, who picked it out and handed it to him. He paused to wipe his forehead, leaving a streak of oil behind.

Sadie watched him intently, occasionally asking a pertinent question when she didn't fully understand what he was doing.

Edward patiently answered her questions, and was pleased with her rapid progress. There was no doubt that

248

she had mechanical ability, and would eventually, with proper tuition, make a first-class mechanic.

'Now hold this,' he said.

She leant forward, and did as instructed. For the space of a heartbeat they smiled at one another, then he resumed working.

Later he gave her a job to do all by herself which she successfully completed without referring to him once.

Sadie plumped up her pillows, then continued reading the Moth's manual which she was slowly going through from cover to cover.

Now what was a flange? she wondered, reaching for the dictionary. When she had the answer she again buried her nose in the manual.

'Hi, hon!' Phyllis Yaeger called out to Edward as she entered the hangar.

Edward glanced round, and frowned. 'What are you doing here?'

'I was at home and got bored and thought I'd drive over and see you. They told me at Clare you were out here. Anyway, what sort of greeting is that?'

He'd been squatting, and now came to his feet. 'Sorry, I just wasn't expecting you, that's all.'

Phyllis went to him, took his face in her hands, and kissed him deeply. She murmured as they kissed.

Jealousy tore at Sadie as she gazed on. Jealousy she had no right to feel, she reminded herself. Edward was her platonic friend after all, nothing more.

Phyllis broke off the kiss, then pecked Edward on the tip of his nose. 'Did I ever tell you you're the cutest guy in Bald Rock Falls?'

Edward cleared his throat and nodded to where Sadie was. Phyllis looked over and saw Sadie, not having previously been aware of Sadie's presence.

'You know Sadie, from the house,' Edward said.

Phyllis stared at Sadie, her expression gradually hardening. 'What's she doing here?'

'Sadie's become my apprentice mechanic. And damn good she is, too.'

Phyllis's gaze travelled from Sadie's face, down over her stained overalls to her booted feet, then all the way up again. 'Apprentice mechanic? You never mentioned it.'

Edward shrugged. 'It just never came up.'

'And how long has she been your . . . apprentice mechanic?'

'How long is it now, Sadie?'

'Four months,' Sadie stated quietly.

'I see,' Phyllis said, and suddenly smiled. Turning to Edward she went on, 'I didn't know you needed an apprentice mechanic?'

'I didn't really. But Sadie professed an interest, and so here she is. Of late I've begun to wonder how I managed without her.'

'How interesting!' Two falsely smiling eyes bored into Sadie. 'Attractive little thing, isn't she? I've never noticed her before.'

Sadie glanced down at the floor.

'And those overalls!' Phyllis laughed scathingly. 'Straight from the Rue de la Paix, are they?'

Edward frowned. 'They're work overalls, same as I wear. What's wrong with you?'

Phyllis rounded on him. 'Nothing darling, except hunger, that is. Why don't you get changed and take me out to dinner?'

Edward wiped the palms of his hands on his own overalls. 'Sure. We're finished here anyway.'

'Then we'll go to the house where you can change, and I'm sure Sally won't mind clearing up here. Will you, Sally?'

'*Sadie*,' she corrected Phyllis, knowing full well that getting her name wrong was intentional.

'Oh, I'm sorry, Sadie. Will you, dear?'

Patronizing bitch, Sadie thought. 'Not at all.'

'OK then. Come along Edward, I'm getting hungrier by the minute.'

'Just a sec'.' Edward struggled out of his overalls and tossed them over a nearby set of steps.

'I'm all yours,' he then said.

Phyllis linked arms with him, and marched him towards the hangar doors.

'Night, Sadie!' Edward called back over his shoulder.

'Good night!' she replied.

When they were both gone her anger turned to amusement. She wasn't the only one who'd been jealous.

Phyllis had been pea green.

Phyllis laid her flushed cheek against the polar bear rug she and Edward were on, and sighed with pleasure and satisfaction. 'That was extraordinary,' she said.

Edward ran a finger down her naked back, making her shiver. 'I thought so, too. I wish your folks would go away on vacation more often.'

'We have a whole week. Count your blessings.'

He parted her hair and kissed the nape of her neck, then the swell of a breast. 'I do, I assure you.'

She laughed softly, then rolled over to lie on her back, and stared at him.

'You're beautiful,' he stated.

She smiled and let her head loll sideways so she could stare into the log fire in front of which the rug lay. Heat from it washed over her, while another sort of heat warmed her insides. 'Edward?'

'Yeah?'

'I've been thinking.' She made an animal sound at the back of her throat as he teased a nipple with his teeth. 'About that girl.'

'Which girl?'

'The one at the hangar.'

He stopped what he'd been doing, and sat up. 'Sadie?'

Phyllis snaked a hand between his legs and took hold of him. 'I want you to tell her this apprentice nonsense is over, and that she's not to come by the hangar any more.'

When Edward didn't reply Phyllis gently squeezed.

He continued gazing at her, his eyes slightly hooded. 'Why?' he queried quietly after a while.

'Because I've asked you. Isn't that enough?'

'No, it isn't, I'm afraid.'

A flash of irritation crossed Phyllis's face, vanishing when she smiled. 'Oh come on, don't be a pooper. She's nothing to you.' Edward continued to regard Phyllis thoughtfully. 'I wouldn't exactly say that. She's a friend.'

'She's a housemaid!'

'That's true. But she's also become a friend and someone I like.'

'You said yourself you didn't need an apprentice.'

'I also said I'd begun to wonder how I'd managed without her.'

Phyllis's lips thinned, and she released him. She sat up so that they were now eye to eye. 'Is there something between you two? Is that it?'

'There's nothing between Sadie and myself. I give you my word.'

'I just don't want her about you so much, the two of you alone for God knows how many hours together.'

'We work, that's all,' Edward stated flatly.

'Yeah, sure. But she's a woman and an attractive one at that. I don't like the set-up. I don't like it one little bit.'

'Sadie gets a great deal of pleasure out of helping me with the Moth, and even more from flying with me occasionally. I'm not going to take that away from her for no reason.'

'But there is a reason!' Phyllis exclaimed hotly.

'Which is?'

'*I'm* asking you to do it!'

'I've already told you, that isn't enough.'

252

Phyllis took a deep breath. 'Then let me put it this way. I demand that you get rid of her from the hangar and don't take her up any more.'

'You *demand*?' he queried softly.

'Yeah, damn right. You *do* love me, don't you?'

'What's that got to do with it?'

'Everything I would say.'

Edward studied Phyllis, aware this had turned into a row that was about far more than Sadie Smith, a row he'd known would happen one day. Phyllis had been spoilt rotten from birth, and consequently had grown up wilful and selfish. During the years they'd gone out together they'd never clashed head-on, but it had been a certainty that eventually they would. And the result of that clash would decide who wore the pants in their relationship. Edward had no intention of it being Phyllis. If he gave in to her demand now it would be a watershed he'd regret for the rest of their lives together.

'I love you, Phyllis, but Sadie remains my apprentice,' he stated emphatically.

Phyllis was furious by his refusal and it showed. She had to fight back the urge to slap him.

She rose to her feet. 'I want to go to bed,' she said.

Her tone and manner made it clear to Edward that he wasn't invited to join her. 'I'll go then,' he replied.

'Lock the front door on your way out.'

He watched her flounce out of the room, upset in some ways, but in no doubt that he'd done the right thing.

Once he dressed, he left, locking the front door on his way out as she'd told him to.

Several large freezers and certain household items bought in bulk were kept in the basement. Sadie had already been through the freezers and was now in the middle of checking the other supplies when a hand was suddenly placed full on her bottom.

She yelped and jumped with fright. Whirling round she found Courcy, who'd returned home for the Easter break the previous day, smiling wickedly at her.

'It's even sexier than I remembered,' Courcy said.

She didn't have to ask what he was referring to. 'Don't ever touch me like that again,' she hissed indignantly, remembering vividly another occasion when her bottom had been touched. She could almost smell Julius's bad breath.

'Aw, come on, I was just being friendly, that's all. A little pat on the bottom isn't anything to get riled about!'

'I meant what I said. Don't ever touch me like that again.'

'There's something about you,' he smiled, shaking his head. 'I don't know what it is, but it's something special. I kept thinking about you all the while I was away, and that's no lie.'

Courcy took a sip from the glass he was holding.

'A bit early in the day for that, don't you think?'

He shrugged.

Sadie turned again to the contents of the carton she'd been counting.

Courcy edged closer. 'Do you find me repulsive, is that it?'

She didn't answer.

'Most women like the way I look. They find me handsome.'

She didn't answer that either.

Courcy swayed, and realized he was rapidly getting drunk. He hadn't drunk all that much really, he told himself, but, as Sadie had pointed out, it was still early in the day. What he'd had was affecting him far more than the same amount would consumed at night. 'Most women,' he repeated, and had another sip from his glass.

She couldn't resist the jibe. 'Including Mary-Anne, I presume?'

'Ah! You heard about that?'

'I heard.'

'She threw herself at me,' he slurred. 'What was a red-blooded guy to do?'

Sadie knew it was true, Mary-Anne had thrown herself at him. Heather had told her so.

'She was nice,' Courcy reminisced, his bleary eyes becoming introspective with memory, and his mouth curving upwards. 'But with aspirations that were her undoing.'

Sadie wrote some figures on to her notepad, desperate to restore some normality to the situation.

Courcy drained his glass, and considered a refill. 'Fancy a drink?' he asked.

'No, thank you.'

'Suit yourself.'

He was quickly back, his glass filled to the brim. He muttered when he spilled some, and took a long draft to ensure that didn't happen again.

'I did think about you a lot when I was away,' he said.

'I can't imagine why.'

He chuckled. 'You would if you were a man. Particularly this one.'

Sadie moved on to another carton, and started counting.

She froze when whisky fumes reached her nose. She could hear Courcy's breathing directly behind her.

'How about a kiss?' he asked thickly.

She moved away. 'No. Now buzz off and don't annoy me.'

He came close again. 'Just one little kiss?'

'I said no.'

'Know what? I think you're playing hard to get.'

'I am playing nothing of the sort. I simply wish to be left in peace to get on with my job.'

Courcy had a deep swig of his drink. He was enjoying this, it was marvellous entertainment. He gazed lecherously at the roundness of her buttocks and the trim legs beneath.

Sadie was acutely aware of his presence, and wondered if she should temporarily abandon this job and return to it later. She'd press on, she decided, it was urgent that some of these orders were placed.

Courcy had another swig. 'Are you *still* a virgin?' he asked.

She ignored that.

'I'm just curious, that's all. There aren't too many of those your age in this neck of the woods. No, sirreee!'

'I suppose you've seen to that,' she snapped.

'I've opened my fair share,' he leered. 'And I'll tell you something, Mary-Anne wasn't one of them.' He then roared with laughter, after which he had a gulp from his glass leaving it almost empty again.

'I'm sure you're playing hard to get,' he husked, only vaguely aware that his mind had gone numb, his head reeling.

Reaching out he placed a hand on her arm. 'Just a little kiss, eh?'

She pushed his hand away. 'I've had enough of this. Now leave me alone!'

Common sense and good judgement deserted him. 'Oh, I've had enough of this too.'

He tossed his glass away and grabbed her. Pulling her into his arms, he tried to kiss her but she struggled violently to fend him off.

She beat his back with her fists, at the same time twisting her head from side to side. He was far stronger than he looked, and easily managed to keep her pinioned.

Unable to kiss her mouth he settled for her neck, sucking hard with the intention of giving her a love bite. She attempted to knee him in the crotch, but he blocked her knee with a leg.

'Stop it! Stop it!' she screamed.

Courcy dropped an eager hand to her backside which he tightly gripped.

Sadie glimpsed Edward a split second before he hauled Courcy off her. Edward hit his brother hard in the face, knocking Courcy flying. Courcy landed on his own backside with a jarring thump, to sit there bemused while blood from his nose flowed down his front.

'Bastard!' Edward growled at him.

Sadie, sobbing with relief, leant up against a brick pillar for support. That had given her the fright of her life. Thank God Edward had intervened.

'Thank you,' she said to him. 'Thank you so much.'

'Are you OK?'

'I will be in a moment.'

Edward crossed to his brother and stared down at him. 'Get up!'

'You're not going to hit me again?' Courcy struggled to his feet. 'I think you've broken my nose.'

'Too bad. You stink of drink,' Edward accused.

'And you just stink. You had no right to interfere, you son-of-a-bitch.'

'Jesus, you were almost raping her!'

'She was *enjoying* it.'

'That's a lie,' Sadie stated.

'Of course it is,' Edward said. 'Any idiot could see that what he was doing was against your will.'

'Then the right person did see,' Courcy jibed.

'You want me to hit you again, little brother? Because if you don't watch your tongue, I will. Now apologize to Sadie.'

'What!'

'Apologize, or take the consequences.'

'You always were a bully.'

'And you always were an asshole. Now apologize.'

Courcy tried to outface Edward, but couldn't. He wilted before Edward's more powerful personality. Then he muttered something unintelligible.

'She didn't hear that,' Edward told him.

'I said I'm sorry. OK!'

'Is that all right, Sadie?' Edward queried.

She nodded.

'You can go, then. But let me say this, Courcy, if I ever find you trying anything like that on with her again, then God help you. I'll beat the living daylights out of you. Understand?'

'Yeah, yeah.'

'I mean it.'

'Why the good Samaritan act? It wouldn't be you're interested in that direction yourself? A little piece of ass on the side, eh?'

Edward's face contorted with disgust. 'You've got a mind like a sewer. I did what I did because you were way out of line.'

'Way out of line!' Courcy mimicked in a heavily mocking tone, and barked out a laugh. He hastily retreated when Edward advanced on him.

'Some day you're going to get your come-uppance, and I only hope I'm around to witness it,' Courcy said nastily, and started to leave.

'Wait!' Edward commanded, causing Courcy to stop and face him. 'The reason I came looking for you is that Father wants to talk to you. You'll find him in the drawing-room.'

'I hope he won't mind waiting while I get cleaned up first.' And with that Courcy sauntered from the basement.

Edward looked at Sadie, who smiled her gratitude at him. 'I think I can safely say he'll never try anything like that again. He's too scared of the consequences,' Edward said.

'I hope you're right.'

'Not a very pleasant experience, I'm afraid. I truly am sorry it happened.'

'It wasn't your fault it did.'

'No, but he is my brother. And you do work for our family.'

Sadie swept her hair from her face. Her heart was still beating wildly, and she was weak at the knees. What she needed more than anything was a cup of coffee and a rest.

'I also owe you an apology,' Edward went on.

'Whatever for?'

'Swearing like I did. Most unlike me.'

It was, she agreed. 'Forget it. Understandable in the circumstances.'

'It's just that Courcy made me so angry. When I saw what he was doing, I just exploded.'

'I can assure you I've never ever given him any encouragement. Quite the contrary.'

There was a sudden awkwardness between them, neither knowing what to say next.

'I guess I'd better get on then,' Edward mumbled. 'Will you be out at the hangar tonight?'

'Try and stop me!'

He grinned. 'Good. I'll see you there.'

'I'll come upstairs with you,' she said, thinking about the coffee. She'd finish her job later.

'I hope you won't mention this to my father. It would upset him dreadfully,' Edward said as they mounted the stairs.

'Of course not.'

The awkwardness returned, and they went up the rest of the stairs in silence.

Sadie gazed down at a series of small lakes she and Edward were flying over. A breeze was blowing causing the deep blue water to ripple, and the tops of the trees to sway.

'Would you like to take the controls?' Edward asked via the Gosport tube.

She thought she must have heard incorrectly. 'I beg your pardon?'

'I said, would you like to take the controls?'

Excitement rose in her. 'Can I?'

259

'Now just listen carefully while I explain how to handle them.'

A few minutes later she was piloting the Moth at a little over a thousand feet, getting used to the aircraft and how it responded.

'How am I doing?' she asked hesitantly.

'Great.'

'It feels . . .' She trailed off, lost for words.

'I understand,' he told her. And she knew that he did.

She flew the plane for fifteen minutes and loved every second of it.

Edward was talking with Carl Yaeger and his friend George when Phyllis materialized out of the throng to join them. 'I want a word with you, in private,' she told him.

'Sure. Where?'

'Come with me.'

Edward and she made their way through the party-goers to the lobby beyond. There Phyllis was stopped by her Uncle Bart who demanded a birthday kiss from her.

Phyllis laughed. 'You're an old roué, Uncle Bart,' she teased.

'Less of the old if you don't mind. I'm not sixty yet.' And with that he pecked her on the cheek.

'It's a smashing party,' Edward said as they continued on their way.

'I can't speak for anyone else, but I'm certainly enjoying it.'

'And so you should being the birthday girl!'

She took him into her father's den, and closed the door behind them.

'What about my birthday kiss?' Edward demanded, a twinkle in his eye.

'I thought I'd already given you one.'

'Then how about another?'

They kissed passionately for a few minutes and then she broke away from him. 'Would you like a drink?'

'Brandy?'

'Armagnac. I'll join you.'

He watched her pour their drinks, thinking she looked fabulous in the new pale green gown she was wearing.

'So what's this word then?' he asked.

She came over and handed him a glass. 'Thank you again for my gift, they're lovely.' The gift she was referring to were a pair of antique ruby drop earrings.

'I'm glad they met with approval.'

'Oh, they most certainly did,' she smiled.

Phyllis tasted her armagnac, then said, 'It's about gifts I want to speak to you.'

She hesitated, then continued. 'My folks have given me the most wonderful gift, a tour of Europe, to last between four and six months, depending on how we get on. And by we I mean myself and Cousin Lisbeth who is coming as chaperone.'

'Tour of Europe?' Edward repeated, momentarily stunned.

'Yeah, they'd like me to do it before I get married and settle down. I think it's a marvellous idea.'

Edward took a deep breath, trying to adjust to this new, and completely unexpected, situation. 'When would you—?'

'Early August,' she interrupted. 'Sailing from New York. We'll do England first, then go over to the Continent, ending the tour in Italy.'

She sighed. 'Me in Italy. Can you imagine it?'

'Should be some trip,' he acknowledged.

'Naturally I'll write all the time. And send photographs.'

Early August he thought, less than two months away.

'Are you happy for me?' she demanded.

'Ecstatic.'

She came up to him and pouted. 'You will miss me?'

'Dreadfully. I shall probably go into decline until your return.'

261

'As long as it's not terminal decline,' she teased in return.

'I'll try not to die,' he promised her, pretending to be deadly serious.

She kissed him, a kiss both hot and urgent.

'We'll get engaged when you get back and set a date for the wedding,' he said when they finally parted.

'Yes,' she breathed.

He gazed deep into her eyes, recalling the row they'd had over Sadie. Things had been cool between them afterwards, but that had soon blown over. He'd succeeded in establishing himself as the dominant partner in their relationship, something he'd felt was important, especially where Phyllis was concerned.

'Then let's seal the deal,' he said.

This time he kissed her.

Sadie tapped on the closed drawing-room door, wondering why Mr Fitzgerald had sent for her.

'Come in!' he called out.

She entered to find Mrs Ritter already there, with Mr Fitzgerald standing beside her. The two of them clearly had been deep in conversation.

'Ah, Sadie!' Jack beamed, and beckoned her over.

Had she done something wrong? If she had she couldn't think what it was.

'And how are you today, Sadie?' he enquired benignly.

It wasn't a ticking off, she was sure of that now. 'Fine thank you, sir.'

'How long have you been with us now?'

She did a quick, mental calculation. 'Fifteen months, sir.'

'And you're happy here?'

'Very, sir.' What on earth was all this leading up to?

'Good,' he nodded. 'Let's all sit down, shall we?'

Sadie now was utterly confused.

'Mrs Ritter has nothing but praise for you, Sadie. Says you are extremely capable.'

'Thank you, sir. Mrs Ritter,' she responded.

'Which brings me to the bad news. Mrs Ritter is leaving us, retiring directly after Christmas.'

Retiring! This was the first she'd heard of it. And why? Surely Mrs Ritter was too young for retirement.

'I'm afraid it's a case of having to retire,' Mrs Ritter explained. 'I've been diagnosed as having a bad heart.'

'I am sorry,' Sadie sympathized.

'The doctor tells me I can still have a full-term life as long as I sit back and take things easy from now on, which of course means giving up work.'

'Where will you go?' Sadie enquired.

'I have a married sister in Calgary who has written to say that she and her husband would be delighted to have me to stay. So that's what I'll do.'

'All of which means I'm going to need a new house-keeper,' Jack said. 'And Mrs Ritter has recommended you.'

That rocked Sadie. 'Me?' she queried softly.

'I know you're young for the position, but Mrs Ritter assures me you can do the job and that you'd have the respect and loyalty of the other staff.'

Jack paused, then added, 'Naturally it would mean a lot more money for you.'

What a marve'lous opportunity, Sadie told herself.

'There are no aspects to the housekeeper's duties that you haven't already mastered,' Mrs Ritter stated.

'If you're offering me the job, then I accept,' Sadie said.

Jack smiled broadly, as did Mrs Ritter, who now rose and came over to Sadie. 'Congratulations,' she said, extending a hand.

They shook hands, then Mrs Ritter took Sadie into her arms and hugged her. When she let Sadie go Sadie saw she was crying. At that moment Sadie was feeling rather emotional herself.

'Congratulations,' Jack beamed, and also shook Sadie's hand.

'I really am sorry to hear about your heart,' Sadie said to Mrs Ritter.

'Let's look on the bright side, it'll give me the chance to put my feet up and do all manner of things I've wanted to do for years, and have never had the time.'

'I'm going to miss you. We all are,' Sadie said.

'And I'm going to miss everyone here, and Clare itself.'

'We'll have you back for vacations, at my expense,' Jack promised.

'I'll look forward to that,' Mrs Ritter smiled through a haze of tears.

'Just take it easy and do it in your own time,' Edward said to Sadie via the Gosport tube. She was about to make her first unassisted landing.

She was apprehensive, but not nervous. She circled the Moth round the hangar, glanced at the rev counter, made a few mental calculations, and started in on her final approach.

The ground rushed to meet her, then there was a jolt as the plane's wheels kissed the ground. She throttled back and the plane slowed considerably. She taxied it round, bringing it to a stop in front of the hangar, and seconds later killed the engine.

'Well done,' Edward said.

'Did I make any mistakes?'

'Not one. It was a perfect landing.'

She flushed with pride at her achievement.

'A few more of those and I think you're ready to go solo. How do you feel about that?'

'I can't wait.'

He laughed, her keenness always delighted him. She was a most committed pupil.

'Tell you what,' he said. 'Let's go into town and celebrate.'

'You mean you and I?'

'Of course.'

She flushed again, though this time not from pride. 'What sort of celebration do you have in mind?'

'A drink. A meal perhaps. What do you say?'

'I'd love to.'

They put the Moth away, then returned to Clare to change. When they were both ready they drove to Bald Rock Falls.

'I reckon we'll go to Cindy's. I think you'll like it,' Edward said.

Sadie had heard of Cindy's, but had never been there. It was the town's most prestigious restaurant and bar. 'Fine by me,' she replied.

They sat at the bar where they ordered Martinis and their meal. Handing back the menu, Sadie gazed about her, thinking the pink and black decor bold but attractive.

'You did really well today,' Edward said.

'Thank you.'

'In a way I'll be sorry when you get your licence. You've been a pleasure to teach.'

'You're a good, and patient, teacher.'

They smiled at each other, then both concentrated on their drinks.

'Hi Ed! Long time no see.'

A young man about Edward's age, slim and swarthy, stood by their table. There was a certain Italian look about him.

'Hi yourself, buddy boy!' Edward replied, rising from his stool. The two men shook hands.

'Phil, I'd like you to meet Sadie Smith. Sadie, this is Philip Mandela.'

She shook hands with Philip, noting that he had a strong, firm handshake.

'Where have you been hiding? I've never seen you in Bald Rock before.' Philip queried.

'I get in from time to time.'

'You work around here, huh?'

'For the Fitzgeralds. I'm their housekeeper.'

Philip whistled. 'Ain't they the lucky ones!'

'So how's business?' Edward demanded. Then, by way of explanation to Sadie, he added, 'Phil's an architect. One of the brightest and most exciting around.'

'If you want a home designed, come to me,' Philip smiled. 'And business is real good.'

'Glad to hear it,' Edward said.

'And with you?'

'We're getting bigger all the time.'

Philip nodded his approval. 'You folks just here for a drink?' he asked.

'Drink and a meal.' Edward then went on to explain about Sadie learning to fly, and that they were celebrating her first unassisted landing.

'No kidding!' Philip exclaimed. 'How about that!'

'She'll be going solo soon,' Edward added.

Philip stared admiringly at Sadie. 'I could never pilot a plane myself. Don't have a head for heights.'

'Don't you ever fly?' Sadie sounded amazed. How could anyone be scared of flying?

'Sure. But only in the big commercial jobs, and always in an aisle seat.'

Sadie laughed, she liked Philip Mandela. He was funny.

They chatted until it was time for Edward and Sadie to move over to their table, at which point Philip left them saying he had to meet a client.

The meal was delicious, the outing a huge success. When Sadie got back to Clare she was quite tipsy.

Sadie woke with a start remembering something she'd forgotten to do. 'Damn!' she swore. That order had to go off with Sam first thing in the morning, which meant she'd have to go downstairs and write it out now. A glance at her bedside clock told her it was just coming up to one o'clock.

She got out of bed reprimanding herself. If she had an excuse it was that the day had been a particularly busy one.

266

Jerelene had been sick, yet again; Erin had entertained at home and Mr F had brought some unexpected guests back for dinner. On top of it all, Courcy was home which always made life more difficult. He was such a demanding man!

She slipped on her robe and stuck her feet into a pair of mules, quietly closed the bedroom door behind her and made her way along the hallway. She came up short outside Heather's door as she heard a low moaning from within.

She frowned. Was Heather ill? There it was again, a low moaning as if Heather was in pain.

She gently tapped on the door, and waited. She tapped again, fractionally louder, but there was still no response.

The moaning intensified, followed by a long, drawn-out groan. Heather *was* ill, Sadie decided, reaching for the door handle.

'Heather . . .' The word died in her throat as she was confronted by an unexpected scene. Courcy was crouched over Heather, the pair of them naked and on their knees.

Sadie stared, appalled. No wonder they hadn't heard her tapping. They were totally caught up in each other.

Courcy glanced up and saw Sadie. He stopped moving and a broad grin creased his face. 'Well hello! Have you come to join the party?'

For a split second Heather's startled eyes gazed into Sadie's, then she gave a muffled scream and buried her head in the bedclothes. Courcy laughed, quite unperturbed by Sadie's intrusion.

Sadie slammed the door behind her and fled downstairs.

'Sadie! Sadie, please!'

Sadie halted and waited for Heather to catch up.

'I really am sorry about last night,' Heather apologized, her face stricken with worry.

'I only came in because I thought you'd been taken ill. That's what it sounded like from out in the hallway.'

Heather bit her lip. 'Are you going to fire me?'

'No.'

Heather's shoulders slumped in relief. 'Thank you, Sadie. I appreciate that.'

'It's none of my business what goes on between you two as long as you're discreet and it doesn't interfere with your work.'

'We will be and it won't,' Heather promised.

'Well, at last you've got what you wanted, Courcy into your bed. You've always said you found him cute and very attractive.'

'I'm wild about him, Sadie.'

'Just don't go and get pregnant. Remember what happened to Mary-Anne.'

'I understand the situation. He's only seeing me for the fun. But what the hell! I'd rather that than nothing at all.'

'Is he . . . with other women?'

'You bet. He's never said, but I know he is. He's got quite a string at the university, and one or two in Bald Rock Falls.'

'You're crazy,' Sadie said. 'That sort of set-up wouldn't suit me at all.'

Heather didn't answer that. She liked Sadie enormously, but privately she thought her a bit of a prude. But then, she'd never been told about Julius.

'Thanks again,' she said.

Sadie hurried away.

Jerelene popped her head round the door of Sadie's office. 'There's a man to see you,' she said to Sadie, and giggled.

'A man?' Sadie queried, laying down her pen.

'He's very nice looking. Determined to see *you*.'

Sadie frowned. 'Did he give a name?'

'Mr Mandela.'

Philip! Edward's friend from Cindy's. She was suddenly confused, not quite sure what to do. She'd have to speak to him, but where? Standing up, she smoothed down her dress and patted her hair.

She glanced at her watch. The kitchen should be free, she'd have him taken there.

Jerelene giggled again once she'd received her orders, and scuttled off.

Now what could Philip Mandela want? Sadie wondered as she went in to the kitchen and put on the coffee. Perhaps it was something to do with Edward, she tried to kid herself, knowing in her heart of hearts it was she he'd come about. She hadn't failed to notice the way he'd looked at her.

'Hi there!' said a smiling Philip from the open doorway, Jerelene hovering behind him.

'Hello. Come in. I'm just about to make coffee. Will you join me?'

'That would be swell.'

She went to the door and closed it firmly, much to Jerelene's disappointment.

'It's nice to see you again,' she said.

'And you. How have you been?'

He was nervous, she noted, which surprised her. She wouldn't have thought Philip the type to be nervous around the opposite sex.

'Fine,' she replied. 'And busy.'

'They work you hard?'

'It's that sort of job.'

As she was pouring out the coffee, the door flew open and Heather shot in. 'Oh sorry!' Heather exclaimed, spotting Philip. She hesitated, then said, 'I'll do what I was going to later.' And with that she left them, closing the door behind her.

'Busy house,' Philip remarked.

'Yeah. There's always something going on. I like that.'

He smiled, and so did she.

'I was wondering . . .' He cleared his throat. 'I guess you must get time off. How about us going out together?'

She'd known this was coming. 'You mean a date?'

'Yeah. I asked Ed who told me there wasn't a guy in your life at the moment.'

She flushed. 'No,' she mumbled, 'there isn't.'

'Me neither. I mean there isn't a female currently in mine. So how about a date?'

She certainly found him attractive. 'What do you have in your coffee?' she asked, playing for time.

'Nothing. I take it black. Well, Sadie?'

She took a deep breath and said, 'What time I do have off is nearly all spent out at the hangar.'

There followed a hiatus during which he regarded her quizzically. 'Are you saying no?' he queried quietly after a while.

She was flustered, and further confused. All she could think about was Edward.

'Surely you can fit in one date?'

Of course she could. She was being downright stupid. Why shouldn't she go out with him? Go on, say yes, she urged herself.

'Thank you for asking, but . . .'

'*But* no dice, eh?'

'It was very kind of you to ask me. Thank you.'

There was another silence which he finally broke by saying, 'If you ever change your mind call me. My apartment number is in the book and so is my office one.'

'I'll remember,' she replied with a weak smile.

'I'll take a rain check on the coffee if you don't mind.' He held up a hand. 'And don't worry, I can let myself out.'

She slumped against a chair when he was gone. Why hadn't she accepted! He'd only asked for a date after all, where was the harm? She'd probably have enjoyed it.

'Stupid,' she muttered to herself. But if he'd returned and asked again he'd still have got the same answer.

Sadie gazed out over pale blue mountains surrounded by a slightly deeper shade of blue sky. The tops of the mountains were snow clad, and there were white streaks of snow in some of the valleys and crevasses.

'Sadie?'

She roused herself from her reverie. 'Yes, Edward?'

'I bumped into Philip Mandela yesterday who told me you refused him a date.'

She glanced at her watch. According to her calculations they should arrive at their destination in fifteen minutes. 'That's right,' she replied.

'I must say I was surprised. He's a terrific guy.'

'Yes, he is,' she agreed.

'I know it's none of my business, but do you mind if I ask why?'

She fought back the impulse to snap his head off. 'Why I didn't go out with him?'

'Yeah.'

She chose her words carefully. 'I suppose what it boiled down to was that I simply wasn't interested. So why waste his time?'

'I see.'

No, you don't, she thought.

'He was very disappointed.'

'Edward?'

'Yeah?'

'I don't really want to talk about this. The guy asked me out. I refused. End of story. OK?'

'OK,' he repeated.

Her heart was hammering, Sadie noted, and her palms sweating.

In the rear cockpit Edward was staring intently at the back of her head. Sadie knew he was staring at her. She could feel it.

Her heart beat even faster.

Sadie had been waiting to get Mr Fitzgerald on his own, and now was her chance. It was quite late one night, Edward was away on a trip, Courcy out on the town and Erin in bed fast asleep. When she entered the drawing-room she found Mr Fitzgerald sitting on a Chesterfield gazing morosely into a large glass of whisky.

'Excuse me, sir, can I speak to you?' she requested.

Mr Fitzgerald immediately brightened. 'Sadie! Come in, my darling, and join me in a glass of something.'

'I don't think I should, sir.'

'You're off duty, aren't you?'

'Officially. Though what I want to talk to you about concerns the house.'

'But you are officially off duty. So what will you have?'

His eyes were slightly glazed, and Sadie thought he might be drunk. Perhaps she should postpone her chat?

'Sherry, please,' she replied.

'Sherry it is,' he said, moving towards the drinks cabinet. 'Could never stomach the damn stuff myself, far too sweet for my taste. Marion used to drink it though.'

He stopped to stare at the portrait of his dead wife hanging on the wall. 'It's the anniversary today,' he stated quietly.

'Beg your pardon, sir?'

'Of her death, Sadie. Of my Marion's death.'

'I am sorry, sir,' she said sincerely.

'You would have liked her, and she you.' He took a deep breath. 'I still miss her dreadfully. You would think the pain would diminish after a while, but it doesn't. At least it hasn't with me. There's not a day goes by that I don't think of her and smile at some memory or other. It was a perfect marriage, only spoilt by her dying when she did.'

'You were very lucky then.'

He rounded on Sadie, and frowned. 'Lucky?'

'That you had what you had together, even if it was cut prematurely short. As I understand it that's more than many people have.'

He thought about that, and nodded. 'Very true. You're a wise young lady, Sadie Smith.'

'I wouldn't have bothered you if I'd known what day it was,' Sadie said when he handed her a schooner.

'That's all right. Do me good to talk for a bit rather than just sit here brooding.' He raised his own glass. 'But first a toast, to absent friends!'

She knew he meant his wife by that, but she'd never known Marion Fitzgerald. She thought of Robbie Hendry instead.

'Now, what can I do for you?' Jack asked.

'I want to get rid of Jerelene,' Sadie stated bluntly.

Jack raised a bushy eyebrow. 'Why do you want to do that?'

'Because she's lazy, unreliable, and generally more trouble than she's worth. We'd be better off without her.'

Jack took a sip of his drink. 'I took her on as a favour to someone.'

'I know that, which is why I'm here. Otherwise I'd have fired her ages ago.'

'Is she really that bad?'

'Heather and I are forever going round redoing jobs she's supposedly done.'

'In other words she's incompetent.'

'Exactly, Mr Fitzgerald.'

He was resisting her, unwilling to comply with her request, as she'd anticipated. 'Can I ask you one question, Mr Fitzgerald?'

'Sure. And I think we've known each other long enough for you to call me Jack.'

She smiled. 'OK, Jack. If one of your workers at the mills was as I've described Jerelene, what would you do?'

Her question had a certain deviousness that appealed to him. 'Fire the son-of-a-bitch, of course.'

'I imagined you would.'

'But we're talking about a girl here, the daughter of someone who once did me a good turn.'

273

'You've more than repaid your debt to him. Jerelene's been given a fair chance, she certainly can't complain about that. But it's a chance she's consistently messed up. We're better off without her, believe me.'

'All right,' he relented. 'You want me to tell her?'

'No. I'm the housekeeper, I will.'

He approved of that. 'Know something Sadie, you've got fine management potential. I'm continually impressed by the way you run Clare. Mrs Ritter was good, but you're better.'

'Thank you . . . Jack.'

'A first-class managerial mind, that's what you've got. The ability to run things smoothly.'

'You're very kind.'

'Not kind, Sadie, stating fact.' On an upbeat note he asked, 'Do you mind if I smoke?'

'Not at all.'

He produced a leather cigar case, took one out, clipped the end, then lit it. 'Is Courcy back yet?'

'I don't believe so.'

Jack shook his head. 'That boy worries me, always has. He doesn't take after me, and certainly not after his mother. I have nightmares that he'll come to a bad end one day.'

'I'm sure he'll be all right.'

Jack puffed on his cigar. 'He isn't working enough at university, his results are poor. Did you know that?'

'No, I didn't.'

'Yeah, too busy running around drinking and womanizing to get his nose down. I expect him to sow a few wild oats, wouldn't be natural otherwise. But with Courcy it isn't a few, but a whole goddamn fieldful.'

Despite herself, Sadie grinned.

'He still sleeping with Heather?'

That shook her. 'Yes, he is.'

'I wondered if you knew or not.'

'How did you find out?'

274

Jack smiled knowingly. 'I have my ways and means. I'm a lot smarter than Courcy realizes.'

He pointed his cigar at Sadie. 'To begin with I thought it was you he was doing the business with, then I found out it was Heather.'

Sadie blushed.

'Has he ever given you any trouble?'

'There were a few incidents,' she replied truthfully. 'But Edward sorted it out in the end.'

Jack's face lit up. 'Now there's a son to be proud of. Edward is the sort of son every man dreams of.'

'He is different, a breed apart,' Sadie agreed.

'He's a real ace.'

'And good at business, so I'm told.'

'Yeah. Firm, but fair. The workforce think the world of him, but then who doesn't?'

Courcy, Sadie might have said, but didn't.

'I know it's a sin to favour one child above the others, but I have to confess that Edward has always been the apple of my eye.' Jack paused, and a look of sheer love and adoration came over his face. 'He reminds me so much of Marion. There are times when I look at him and see a male version of her.'

'And what about Erin?' Sadie asked quietly.

'She's always been an easy kid. Even as a babe she hardly gave us any trouble. Erin will do fine in life, I have no doubts about that.'

Jack finished off the contents of his glass and strode to the drinks cabinet where he poured himself another large one.

'But tell me about you, Sadie, what are your hopes and plans? Much as we'd love you to stay I can't imagine you remaining at Clare for the rest of your days.'

'I certainly don't have any plans, not for the immediate future anyway,' she replied slowly. 'I suppose I eventually hope to get married and raise a family.'

'That all?'

'For the moment anyway.'

He nodded. 'What about Scotland? Would you ever like to return there?'

'Not to live I shouldn't think. I feel completely settled and integrated here. I would like to go back sometime, out of curiosity if nothing else. I do still have family there, after all, though whether I could ever find them is another matter.'

'You've sure had a tough childhood, Sadie, but come through it with credit. You've got more guts and determination than many I can think of. I raise my glass to you!'

She coloured slightly at this praise. 'Thank you, Jack.'

'Whoever gets you as a wife will be a damned lucky man. And I'm not just saying that, I mean it.'

She had a sip of sherry to hide her embarrassment.

'Did I ever show you the sports photographs I took of Edward when he was at school? He excelled at sports.'

'No, you haven't.'

'Would you like to see them?'

'Please.' There was nothing she'd have liked better.

For the next thirty minutes they went through the photographs together, Jack singing Edward's praises.

For Sadie it was a blissful half-hour.

Edward was delighted that a letter had arrived from Phyllis. She'd started off well, writing almost every day, but the spaces between letters had begun to get longer as she got more caught up in her trip. It was now just over a fortnight since her last one. Pretty stamp, he thought, as he ripped open the envelope.

She was having an amazing time, he read, she and Lisbeth were currently in Rome where they were sightseeing from morning to night. In fact they were having *such* an amazing time they had decided to stay on. They intended remaining another month or two. She'd already wired her father who'd agreed to fund them.

She hoped he was well, and how was everyone else at Clare? She'd write again soon, love Phyllis.

Edward frowned. This was the shortest letter yet, hardly more than a note really. Another month, or even two. She must be enjoying herself! He was disappointed, of course, but there again, this was the trip of a lifetime for her.

So she wouldn't be home till the Spring. If she agreed they'd announce their engagement right away and wed in the fall, October say.

He read the letter through again.

Sadie was sitting at her vanity table brushing her hair when there was a knock on the door. 'Come in!' she called out, thinking it would be Heather, but it was Erin whose eyes were shining like beacons.

'I had to come and tell you,' Erin announced breathlessly, plumping herself on the edge of Sadie's bed.

'Tell me what?'

'I'm in love. And I mean in *love*.' She wrapped her arms around herself and rocked from side to side. 'I can't begin to describe how it feels.'

Sadie laughed. 'Who is he?'

'Marty O'Hara. He comes from an Irish family as well.'

'Marty O'Hara,' Sadie repeated. 'And when did you meet him?'

'Tonight. On a hayride. We were talking, and sort of snuggled up close, and talked some more. And then, like the proverbial bolt of lightning, we both fell head over heels.'

'Just like that!' Sadie commented drily.

'Yeah, just like that. I've read about falling in love like that. I mean, it's fairy-story stuff, isn't it? But it actually does happen, and it happened to us tonight.'

'What does this Marty do?'

'He's a banker.'

'You mean he owns the bank?'

'No, but he has a good position with them, and is well respected. He's very ambitious.'

'I see.'

'Aren't you excited for me?'

Sadie went across to Erin, knelt down, and took Erin's hands in hers. 'I couldn't be more pleased.'

'You're the first person I've told. I was determined about that.'

'I'm honoured.'

Erin sighed. 'Marty! Isn't that such a romantic name?'

'What if he'd been called Fred?' Sadie teased.

Erin laughed. 'I don't know! But he is called Marty, and I think he's gorgeous, and adorable, and he simply makes me melt inside.'

Sadie had never known Erin so enthusiastic about a young man before or declare she was in love. Perhaps this *was* the real thing, only time would tell. 'When are you seeing him again?'

'Tomorrow night, we're going to the movies.'

'What's on?'

'Who cares!'

'As long as the two of you are together?'

'Precisely.'

'And when do we get to meet Marty?'

'I'm going to ask Father if he can come by this Saturday, maybe for dinner. What do you think?'

'I think that's a good idea. But as the pair of you have only just met I'd advise you not to let your father, or anyone else in the family, know the strength of your emotions. That might colour their attitude towards Marty. Let them meet him, get to know him, and then allow it to grow from there. That way, should either of you change your mind about the other, you're not left with egg on your face.'

Erin thought about that. 'Yeah, I guess you're right. Play it slow and easy with the family, huh?'

'That's how I'd do it,' Sadie nodded, then added, eagerly, 'What's he like? Tell me every single thing about him. I'm dying to know.'

Erin needed no further urging. Sadie listened intently, occasionally interrupting with a question, as Erin rattled on.

The colour of Marty's hair, his eyes, what sort of clothes he preferred, where he lived, the make of his car, his attitude towards, his philosophy on . . .

Edward watched the Moth slice through a woolly mass of cloud and then begin its final approach. He glanced over at the tower where Sadie's performance was being scrutinized by the Qualified Flying Instructor judging her. As far as he was concerned the QFI would be hard pressed to fault Sadie. But then you never knew with QFIs, they had a reputation for being difficult and contrary individuals.

The Moth made contact with the runway, settled perfectly, and started to slow down. Edward smiled, thinking he couldn't have executed a better landing himself.

The Moth taxied along the tarmac, then swung into a side-lane where it eventually stopped. He watched Sadie climb down from the machine, pause for a moment, then head towards the tower where she would be given the verdict.

This was the last hurdle in getting her licence. She'd already passed all the necessary certificates leading up to this moment.

Edward stayed where he was, as they'd agreed. She would come to him when the QFI had finished with her. He looked down at the bulky brown paper parcel at his feet and smiled.

Five minutes became ten, and he began to worry. Had she failed after all? Then there she was, hurrying towards him.

As soon as he saw her face he knew what the verdict was.

'I passed!' she whooped, whirling her arms in the air.

He laughed, and applauded her. 'I knew you'd do it. I was certain of it.'

'I was as nervous as a kitten beforehand, but once I was up it vanished and it was plain sailing, or I should say, flying after that.'

'I've got something for you,' he said, picking up the parcel and handing it to her.

'For me?'

'A gift from the whole family for passing.'

Sadie squatted down and placed the parcel back on the ground. Inside were a beautiful hand-made leather flying suit, a sheepskin jacket, a helmet and some goggles.

'Oh Edward, thank you!' she exclaimed.

Then, without thinking because she was so overcome, she leapt to her feet and kissed him full on the mouth.

She blushed furiously the instant she realized what she'd done. 'I'm sorry about that,' she mumbled.

He regarded her strangely. 'Why? I enjoyed it.'

A hiatus fell between them during which she refused to meet his eye. What an insane thing to do! she raged inwardly. Imagine just kissing him like that.

'Why don't you go inside and change into your new gear?' he suggested softly. 'Then we'll have a cup of coffee and fly home.'

'Thank you again, Edward,' she answered. 'The whole outfit is a splendid gift, and much appreciated.'

'We thought it was what you'd like most.'

'I won't be long,' she said, scooping up the parcel and holding it against her.

Edward stared at Sadie as she walked away, the slightest of frowns on his face. Then he was greeted by someone who knew him and the frown disappeared as he and the man fell into conversation.

★ ★ ★

Edward's expression was one of utter disbelief as he read Phyllis's latest letter, and the last he'd receive from her.

She was married to a Count Antonio d'Astozi, she now the Countess d'Astozi. They'd met in Paris from where he'd followed her throughout the rest of her tour. He'd proposed in Venice, she'd accepted, been introduced to his parents and had a sumptuous wedding shortly afterwards. At the time of her writing this letter they were just off on their Caribbean honeymoon.

Sorry, Edward . . . sorry . . . the same word ran through the letter, repeated continuously. She'd been unfair to him, stabbed him in the back, let him down dreadfully, but it would never have worked out between them after she'd met Antonio who was the only man for her.

They were madly in love and planned to live in Italy after the honeymoon. There was a family home in Rome, a villa and estate in Tuscany, and another villa and estate in the Romagna. The d'Astozis were fabulously wealthy, part of the Italian aristocracy, and could trace their genealogy back to the twelfth century.

Please forgive me, she pleaded.

Edward looked up from the letter, and shook his head. The duplicitous bitch! How long had she known she was going to get married? Long enough to get her parents out there for the wedding. This explained the Yaegers' sudden departure for Europe some weeks previously.

And why hadn't she let on before now? He knew the answer to that. She hadn't wanted to tell him in case anything went wrong and she didn't marry this Antonio. But now that she was married, it was fine to give him the kiss-off.

Rage welled up in Edward, rage he fought to control. He tried to read the letter again, but couldn't. A jumble of indecipherable letters stared back at him.

He took several deep breaths, and then rushed off to the hangar. At least in the Moth everything would be quiet, peaceful and serene.

En route he barged past Sadie who wondered at his dark, thunderous expression. Later that evening she heard about the letter from Erin.

A few days later Edward and Sadie were servicing the Moth. They'd been working for several hours, rarely speaking, when she decided to broach the subject.

'I was sorry to hear about you and Phyllis.'

Edward stiffened, then relaxed again. 'They're a handsome race, the Italians,' he said, thinking of Philip Mandela.

Sadie paused. 'I'm sure it wasn't that. Couldn't possibly have been.'

He smiled at the compliment which cheered him enormously. 'Thank you.'

Sadie wondered whether to pursue the conversation. She didn't want to intrude into his privacy, but there again she was his friend.

'Perhaps it was the title,' Edward mused. 'Some women find them irresistible, I'm told.'

'Only snobs.'

Edward laughed. 'Well, Phyllis is certainly that. A snob *extraordinaire*. I can just imagine her wallowing in being a Countess.'

'The Countess what?'

'The Countess d'Astozi. Very grand, eh?'

'Very,' she agreed, tongue in cheek.

This time they both laughed which told her she'd succeeded in lifting his spirits.

'Know something?' he said. 'Maybe, in the long term, Phyllis did me a good turn marrying someone else.'

'Possibly,' Sadie said very quietly.

'Anyway, good luck to them! I wish them all the very best, and I hope it works out for them. Now let's get back to work. There's still a mountain to get through.'

'Yes, boss,' she replied, and gave him a mock salute.

It had been gloomy and oppressive in the hanger before that, but now the atmosphere was considerably lighter.

Edward even hummed a jaunty tune which made Sadie smile.

'He almost bit my head off, and for nothing!' Miss Dobson complained bitterly to Sadie.

'I know,' Sadie replied placatingly. 'But Edward is going through a difficult time. You must appreciate that.'

'I do appreciate it. But there was no need for him to be so rude. Honestly, you never know where you are with him nowadays. One moment he's nice as pie, the next Attila the Hun.'

His moods had vacillated a great deal since the final letter from Phyllis, Sadie thought. He was up and down like a Yo-Yo.

'He'll get over it, just give him a chance,' Sadie said.

Miss Dobson sniffed and clattered a saucepan in the sink.

'We'll all just have to be patient with him,' Sadie added.

'I never see him getting cross with you,' Miss Dobson accused.

That was true enough, Sadie thought. It appeared she was immune to his bad behaviour.

'Lucky me,' she replied, with a smile.

Heather popped her head round the kitchen door. 'Mr F wants to know what's for dinner tonight?'

'Veal and spaghetti bolognese,' Sadie and Miss Dobson replied simultaneously. 'With a chocolate roulade to follow,' added the cook.

Heather vanished.

'It's a good roulade, too,' Miss Dobson told Sadie.

'I'm sure. We can always rely on you to turn out the very best.'

Miss Dobson relaxed at this praise, as Sadie had intended. 'I'd better get on then,' she said.

Later that afternoon Sadie found Heather in tears, Edward had been rude to her too.

'Edward, I want to speak with you!' Jack's voice called out.

Sadie, sitting in her office, glanced up from the pile of receipts and invoices she was going through. Jack had sounded angry and upset.

'Yeah?' Edward replied.

'This can't go on, Edward. You've got to get a grip of yourself.'

'What can't go on?'

'I've just had a call from Rocky telling me you almost caused a walk-out.'

'The guys were . . .'

'The guys were wrong according to Rocky, but so was the way you handled the situation. Jesus Christ, Edward, this simply won't do!'

Sadie chewed on the end of her pencil.

'OK, Father,' Edward answered contritely.

'It's this Phyllis thing, isn't it?'

'I guess. It started out as that, and then . . . I honestly don't know. Everything just seems to have gone to pieces.'

'You're not yourself and that's for sure.'

'I'll try harder, Father. I promise. I don't mean to go around like a bear with a sore head, it just happens.'

'Do you miss her?'

'Who?'

'Phyllis, dumbass.'

'Yes and no. That's the crazy thing. In fact, I think I'm actually pleased she's gone off with someone else.'

There was a pause, then Jack said, 'Listen, I've got an idea. Why don't you and I take a break together. Why don't we go on a fishing trip like we used to when you were young?'

'A fishing trip?'

'Sure. I'll rent a cabin, and we can stock it full of food and beer.'

'But the business . . .'

'The business can get along without us for a little while. It won't fall apart overnight just because neither you nor I are there. So what do you say?'

There was another pause, then Edward replied, 'Yeah, let's. A fishing trip together sounds great.'

Jack laughed and Edward joined in.

Sadie smiled as she listened to them walk away, the two of them making plans. Hopefully a break would do Edward the world of good.

Sadie stood at a window watching lightning flickering across a muddy grey sky. Rain lashed against the window. She wondered how Edward and Jack were faring, and hoped they were all right. She imagined them sitting in front of a roaring log fire drinking cans of beer and smiled.

'Hi!' said Erin, joining Sadie.

Sadie noticed that Erin had on her hat and coat, 'Going out in this weather?' she asked in surprise.

'You bet. I have a lunch date with Marty which I have every intention of keeping. He said the Roundabout Drugstore at twelve thirty, and that's where I'll be waiting for him.'

'The Roundabout Drugstore?'

'Yeah. Marty loves burgers drenched in ketchup, and the Roundabout makes the best burgers in town. He has lunch there almost every day.'

Sadie laughed. She'd met Marty on a number of occasions now and liked him enormously. He and Erin were a natural couple, a fact Jack himself had commented on.

'So, how are things going between you two?' Sadie asked.

'They just get better and better. We have our arguments, but who the hell doesn't? You know, I just can't imagine life without Marty now. He's become part and parcel of me, and me him.'

Sadie clasped Erin's hands between her own. 'I'm so happy for you. And envious, in the nicest possible way.'

'So when are you going to step out with the guys? You must get offers?'

'I had one the other day as a matter of fact,' Sadie said.

'Oh! Who?'

'A man I deal with in town. He asked me for a date.'

'And?'

Sadie pulled a face. 'He's nice, but not my type.'

'So who is your type?'

'That,' declared Sadie, wagging a finger at Erin, 'would be telling.'

'I worry about you sometimes,' said Erin, suddenly serious.

'Well, don't.'

'I couldn't bear to think of you ending up as an old maid. What a waste!'

'Let's hope it doesn't come to that,' replied Sadie, laughing. 'Now you'd better hurry if you're not to be late.'

Erin glanced at her watch, and squealed. 'Bye!' she cried, flying off down the corridor.

An old maid! Sadie shuddered at the thought.

'They're back!' Heather announced to Sadie. 'I just saw their car drive up.'

Had the vacation done the trick? Sadie wondered as she made her way to meet them. She prayed that it had.

She met Jack and Edward coming through the front door. Edward was smiling and there was a sparkle in his eye that hadn't been there before.

'You should have seen this one pike I caught,' he said to Sadie. 'I swear the monster was this size!' And with that he held his hands as far apart as possible.

Jack winked at her. 'A little exaggeration, I would say. But it was a big fish.'

'Big! It was a regular Moby Dick,' Edward protested.

Sadie laughed. Moby Dick indeed!

Jack rubbed his hands together. 'It's marvellous to be home again. Though I have to admit, we did enjoy ourselves. Didn't we, Edward?'

'We most certainly did.'

'We ate trout, which tasted out of this world. They simply melted in your mouth,' Jack informed Sadie.

'You caught lots?'

'Dozens. There are some in the car which I've asked Sam to take to the kitchen. I hope the staff will have them for supper.'

'Miss Dobson will be pleased,' Sadie said. She knew lake trout were a favourite with the cook.

'And how are you, Sadie, miss us?' Edward demanded.

'I'm fine. And miss you? We hardly realized you'd gone,' she joked. The truth was she had missed him, but then she always did when he was away.

'Well, that puts us in our place,' Edward said, tongue in cheek, to his father.

'I'll tell you what I could use, and that's a hot bath and a cup of coffee,' Jack stated.

'I'll have the coffee brought up to your room,' Sadie said.

He nodded. 'Great.'

'I think I'll have a hot bath, too. Then go to the mills and see what's what,' Edward stated.

He was looking better, Sadie thought. There was a buoyancy about him that had been absent of late.

It seemed to her that the break had worked. Edward appeared his old self again.

Jack started upstairs, and then turned back to address Sadie. 'By the way, we've decided to have a dinner party on Saturday night. I'll give you the guest list later. There should be about a dozen of us.'

'Right,' she replied.

'A hot bath it is then,' Jack declared, and continued upstairs.

'Would you like some coffee, too?' Sadie asked Edward.

'No thanks. Have you been taking care of the Moth for me?'

'Of course. Treating it as if it was a baby.'

'I'll go out and see it this evening. Will you be joining me?'

Wild horses wouldn't keep her away from the hangar she thought. 'I'll be there,' she replied.

'Good.'

He smiled at her, and she returned his smile.

'Hot bath,' he muttered, and followed Jack.

Sadie studied the guest list Jack had given her. Who was Miss Stella Du Lac? And what a fancy name, sounded like a film star.

Erin and Marty would be present, she noted, pleased that Marty had been invited. She'd place him beside Stella Du Lac whoever she was.

Sadie was on hand to take the guests' wraps when they arrived, and invited them to go through to the drawing-room where the family were waiting. Heather was there serving drinks, and would later wait at table, as would she.

Marty was the first to put in an appearance, eager to be with Erin. Then came the Richmonds, followed by Henry and Rebecca Winkelstein, and after them Miss Stella Du Lac.

Stella Du Lac had titian coloured hair, creamy skin, a fair-sized bosom and curvaceous hips. Her eyes were amber which contrasted strangely, and compellingly, with her hair. Sadie judged her to be about the same age as Edward.

When dinner was announced everyone trooped through to the dining-room where Edward promptly rearranged the place settings, sitting himself beside Stella. The two of them immediately fell into deep and private conversation.

As the evening progressed, Sadie couldn't help but notice the intimacy between the two, and again wondered just who was Stella Du Lac? Whoever, Edward was certainly entranced by her.

After the meal everyone retired to the drawing-room where some of the furniture was pulled back and the gramophone put on. Edward and Stella were soon dancing cheek to cheek.

Sadie saw it all when she brought in a fresh decanter of port, and it made her writhe inside. After that she contrived to pass the drawing-room door a number of times, and on each occasion Edward was with Stella, either dancing or sitting talking to her.

Midnight found Sadie drinking tea by herself in the kitchen. Was Phyllis gone only to be replaced by Stella Du Lac? It seemed so, Sadie thought bitterly.

Stella Du Lac, what a stupid pretentious name!

When she later made her way up to her room the gramophone was still playing.

'So, who's Edward's new girl-friend, this Stella Du Lac? And is that her real name?' Sadie asked Erin the day after the dinner party.

'Shhh!' said Erin to Smudge the Pekinese who, for some inexplicable reason, had started to bark.

'Stella? She was at school with Edward, a grade behind him, and one of his many admirers. She lost out to Phyllis but has, it seems, succeeded Phyllis now that Phyllis isn't around any more. As for the name, it's French. They are an old French family who go back quite away. According to them the original Du Lac was a fur trapper.'

'Are they rich?' Sadie further enquired.

Erin shook her head. 'Not like we are, or the Yaegers. Her father owns a small wholesale business where she works as a secretary.'

Sadie beckoned to Smudge who trotted over and jumped on to her lap where she began stroking him.

'It was a terrific dinner party. Marty and I thoroughly enjoyed ourselves,' she added, buffing a nail.

They weren't the only ones, Sadie thought, so did Edward and Stella.

She did her best to cover up the mixture of emotions she felt.

Sadie was replacing the oil filter-cap when Edward and Stella appeared in the hanger. She stood at their approach and wiped her hands on a rag, wishing she didn't look such a sight.

'Hi Sadie, everything OK now to take the Moth up?' Edward greeted her.

'Yes.'

'Sadie is a marvellous mechanic. Quite outstanding really,' Edward said to Stella. 'She has enormous natural talent.'

'I'm impressed,' Stella smiled.

'Oh, I forgot, I don't believe the pair of you have actually been introduced, though of course you know one another by sight. Stella, this is Sadie, Sadie, Stella.'

'I won't shake,' Sadie said when Stella extended a hand. 'Oil,' she added by way of explanation.

'Housekeeper and mechanic, quite a combination,' Stella smiled, trying to be friendly.

Stella was wearing a well-cut pair of slacks, a silk blouse and a cream silk jacket. Sadie thought she looked a million dollars.

'I'm going to take Stella up for a spin,' Edward went on. 'She's never flown before.'

'It's an unforgettable experience,' Sadie said to her. 'One trip aloft and I was hooked.'

'Sadie flies too. I taught her,' Edward told Stella.

Stella looked from Sadie to Edward, then back again at Sadie. 'He's right, you are clever.'

For a moment Sadie thought that might be a dig, but it wasn't. It was a genuine compliment. 'Thank you,' she muttered. It had been easy to dislike the haughty Phyllis Yaeger, but that just wasn't the case with Stella. If anything she liked Stella, which made matters much worse.

'We'll get suited up at the back of the hangar,' Edward said to Stella, and led her in that direction.

As they walked away Edward whispered something to Stella that made her laugh and clutch on to his arm. After that she kissed him.

Sadie glanced away, not wishing to see any more. She went outside the hangar and gazed up at the sky. For some reason she found herself thinking of Robbie and wondering yet again how he was and where he was. She still missed her great childhood friend and knew she always would.

'Can you give us a hand here, Sadie,' Edward called out from the hangar.

She went back inside and together they manoeuvred the Moth out of the hangar and into a take-off position.

Edward helped Stella, who was giggling, into the front cockpit, then climbed into the rear where he gave Sadie the thumbs-up.

Suddenly a terrible fear clutched Sadie as she stared at Edward, she felt he was about to embark on something incredibly dangerous. It was as though she was seeing him in another place and in a different aircraft.

Then, the fear lifted, leaving her shaking her head in wonder.

'Sadie?' she heard Edward say.

'Sorry!' she replied, and hurried to the propeller, which caught on the second swing.

She watched the Moth taxi forward, then pick up speed. It gracefully left the ground, racing skywards.

She shook her head. This just wasn't going to do, she told herself. She returned once more to the hangar where she began putting some tools away.

Sadie emerged from the hardware store where she'd placed an order which would be delivered to Clare the next day. She had one other call to make.

'Well, hello, how are you?'

It was Philip Mandela. Sadie shielded her eyes from the bright sun and smiled at him. 'I'm fine, how about yourself?'

'OK. Just off for lunch. Care to join me?'

She hesitated.

'We could go to Cindy's.'

That would be nice, she thought. She was in no great rush to get back. 'You're on,' she nodded.

He lifted both eyebrows. 'Must be my lucky day!'

She laughed at that, and took the arm he crooked at her. 'How's Eddy boy?' he enquired.

'Working hard.'

'Playing hard, too, I hear.'

'If you're referring to his new girlfriend, they have been seeing a lot of one another.'

'Is it love, do you think?'

She could feel the base of her neck turning red. 'I really don't know. He doesn't discuss his lovelife with me. I'm an employee, after all.'

'And also a friend from what I was led to understand?'

'Friend or otherwise, he doesn't discuss his lovelife with me.'

'Speaking of lovelife,' he smiled, 'how's yours?'

'What sort of question is that?' she retorted, pretending outrage. 'How's yours?'

'Somewhat blank at the moment.'

'You surprise me,' she jibed.

'Why?'

'I would have thought you'd be up to your neck in women.'

He laughed. He'd been nervous the day he'd come out to Clare to ask her for a date, but there was no sign of that now. He appeared totally relaxed, and certainly in good humour. She was enjoying his company.

They arrived at Cindy's and went to sit at the bar. 'I'm hungry enough to eat an entire steer all by myself,' Philip declared.

'That's hungry,' she acknowledged, straight faced.

'What about you?'

'A small steak will be quite sufficient.'

He stared at her, his gaze frank and admiring. 'I like you. I liked you the moment we met.'

'And I like you, too.'

'But you wouldn't go out with me? Turned me down flat when I asked.'

'Perhaps you should ask again.' She inwardly gulped realizing what she'd said.

His eyes narrowed as he continued staring at her. 'I hope you're not some sort of tease?'

Before she could reply, the bartender asked if they were ready to order. They both said they'd have Martinis to start with, then chose their food.

'Wine?' Philip asked her.

'Only if you're having some.'

He ordered a bottle of Chianti.

'I wouldn't say I was a tease,' Sadie said picking up their previous conversation.

'Good. I hate them.'

He passed her a bowl of potato chips, and she had one. 'I heard you passed your flying licence. Congratulations.'

'Thank you.'

'Do you bowl?'

There was an alley in Bald Rock Falls, but she'd never been to it. 'No,' she answered.

'Pity. Bowling's fun. I go at least once a week. It sure is relaxing.'

'I know Erin goes occasionally. She says it's fun too.'

Their Martinis arrived.

'Did you mean what you said?'

'What was that?'

'Perhaps I should ask again.'

She glanced into her glass, and saw Edward in the hangar whispering to Stella, who then clutched his arm and kissed him.

'Well?'

She looked up, and smiled. 'Do you want to ask me out again?'

He studied her, bit his lower lip, then replied, 'Yes.'

'So ask.'

'Will you go out with me?'

She nodded.

'OK then. It's a date!'

His obvious pleasure and enthusiasm amused her.

'So where will we go? And when?'

'How about bowling? I could make it Saturday night.'

'Bowling on Saturday night it is then. I'll pick you up about eight.'

'About eight,' she repeated. 'I'll be expecting you.'

He raised his glass in a silent toast, and she did the same.

They both drank, sealing the date.

'How about coming up to my apartment for a night-cap?' Philip suggested to Sadie as they left the movie house. This was their fourth date.

She glanced at him, unsure.

'I make a real mean Martini. The best in town.'

'Is your apartment far from here?'

'Just a couple of blocks.'

294

She thought about it as they walked to his car. 'OK,' she finally agreed.

They drove in silence to his apartment building where he parked in the residents' car-park. He took her hand as they made for the entrance.

She was curious to see his apartment as this would be the first apartment she'd ever been into.

Philip opened the door and snapped on an overhead light. In the hallway he flicked another switch which lit up a number of table lamps.

There was a lot of chrome and glass about, while the easy chairs and Chesterfield were of a well-padded light brown fabric. Apart from the table lamps there was a standard lamp which caught her eye.

'What do you think?' Philip demanded.

'Design the decor yourself?'

'Of course.'

'Very nice.' She was being polite, it wasn't really her taste at all. The only thing she liked was the standard lamp, which she thought was lovely. 'How many rooms are there?'

'This, the kitchen which is tiny, a small bedroom I use as a second office and my own bedroom. Want to see round?'

'Love to.'

'I'll make the Martinis before I give you the tour,' he smiled, taking her coat.

There were a number of pictures on the walls that Sadie now looked at. She didn't know much about art, but these seemed pleasant enough, if rather unexciting.

'How long have you lived here?' she asked as Philip mixed the drinks.

'Only a short while. This particular building is handy for work.'

Sadie went to the window to discover a large section of Bald Rock Falls spread out below her. 'Good view,' she commented.

'It's better in the daytime. The view is the reason I took a top-floor apartment rather than one lower down.'

He came across and handed Sadie a glass. 'Try that and tell me if I was boasting when I said I made a mean Martini.'

She had a sip and winced. 'It's certainly strong.'

'Yeah. Only way for a good Martini to be. I just sort of wave the vermouth at it.'

She had another sip.

'Well?' he demanded.

'Excellent. I award you a brownie point.'

He laughed. And then surprised her by kissing her quickly on the mouth. They had kissed several times before when saying good night.

'The grand tour,' she said.

'OK. Kitchen to begin with.'

He hadn't been joking, it was tiny. 'Do you do much cooking?'

'A bit. Mainly Italian stuff that I learnt from my mother. Perhaps I could cook for you one night?' he suggested.

'Perhaps.'

He took her from there to his office. The walls and ceiling were white, the carpet grey. On the walls were several framed drawings of his. Instead of drapes there was a Venetian blind at the window.

'Do you work here a lot?' she enquired.

'It all depends how busy I am, and how urgent things are. It varies tremendously.'

From there they progressed to his bedroom which, to her amazement, had claret coloured walls and a midnight blue ceiling with gold stars on it. The bed was a four-poster, hung with heavy brocaded gold curtains. The carpet matched the blue of the ceiling while the furniture was imitation Louis Quinze.

'Neat, eh?' Philip said.

She thought it positively ghastly.

'The bed is a genuine antique, cost a fortune,' he informed her, his voice filled with pride.

'Most unusual,' she replied evasively. The drapes she noted were claret coloured also, but with a gold thread running through the material.

'And that's the apartment,' he declared, switching off the concealed lighting.

'Interesting,' she murmured, settling down in his Chesterfield.

'I'll put some music on then freshen your drink,' he said.

'One of these is enough,' she replied. Two and her head would be spinning.

The record he chose was a romantic piece ideal for lovers. He smiled at her, gazing into her eyes across the room as he dimmed the lights.

He refilled his own glass, then came to sit beside her on the Chesterfield. He placed a hand on her face, and slowly dragged it down her cheek. He kissed the same cheek, then repeated the kiss again and again.

'All right?' he queried softly.

She murmured in reply. It was nice.

He kissed her neck and she felt a tightening in her chest, a constriction in her throat.

He gently nipped her neck, then kissed the spot he'd nipped. He did that several times, travelling from the base of her throat to the underside of her chin.

'Be careful. I don't want to spill my drink,' she said.

His answer to that was to take her glass and place it on the floor with his alongside. 'Now you don't have to worry,' he husked, returning to her neck.

No man had ever done this to her before, she thought, as he nibbled an ear. She gave a little gasp as his tongue slid inside it.

'That's tickly,' she whispered.

She closed her eyes, enjoying the sensations she was experiencing. If only it had been Edward, she thought dreamily.

Philip's mouth found hers, and he took her into his arms. His tongue crept into her mouth to play with her own. She tensed when a hand came to rest on her thigh.

'It's OK, honey, relax,' he whispered. Then his lips were once more on hers, his tongue again in her mouth.

She wondered what Edward was like to kiss? Would he have put his tongue inside her mouth as Philip was doing? Edward . . .

His hand left her thigh and then began slowly caressing her breast.

Philip's breathing became heavier and faster. His hand went from her breast back to her thigh and up inside her dress to clutch at her bottom.

Suddenly, with a resounding clarity, she knew this was wrong. Not for moral reasons, but because it was Philip making love to her and not Edward.

'No,' she said, and attempted to push his hand away.

'It'll be all right, I promise,' he panted.

'I said no!' she repeated harshly, and shoved his shoulders back.

He stared into her eyes, and she could see the passion reflected in his. They burnt with desire.

'God, I want you, Sadie. I want you more than anything,' he said, and grabbed her again.

She pushed him to one side and jumped to her feet. She was trembling, her emotions jumbled. All she knew was that it was Edward's arms she wanted to be in, not Philip's. Philip was merely a substitute. Black despair engulfed her because she knew that Edward would never be hers.

'I'm sorry,' she apologized. 'It's no good.'

Philip's face was contorted with frustration as he, too, came to his feet. 'What's wrong, Sadie?'

She shook her head. 'Nothing, I mean, it isn't your fault.'

'Then what is it?'

She smoothed down her dress, then did the same to her hair. 'Will you take me home please, Philip.'

'I rushed you, is that it? I tried to go too far too soon.'

Her heart was thumping, she realized. God, what a mess! Why, oh why, did she have to feel like this? 'There isn't anything wrong with you, or what you did. It's me,' she told him.

'I don't understand.'

She certainly wasn't going to explain to him. No one must ever know her secret for it would be humiliating if it ever got back to Edward, and it would mean she'd have to leave Clare. 'It's not important,' she said. 'Now could you please get my coat.'

'Sadie,' he pleaded, grasping her arm. 'Please stay.'

'No, I must go.'

'I didn't mean to offend you.'

'You didn't. As I said, it's me. Now please let's just leave it at that.'

He could see she was resolute, and that there was no point in arguing further. His shoulders were drooping as he went out to the closet.

'Will I see you again?' he asked as he helped her into her coat.

'Let's play it by ear, shall we?' she prevaricated, knowing that she'd never go out with him again.

'Can I call?'

'Sure.'

'I have become very fond of you in the short time we've been dating. I want you to appreciate that.'

'You're sweet,' she said, and pecked him on the cheek.

Was she being a fool? she wondered as they drove back to Clare. Probably, she decided. But she just couldn't let one man make love to her while it was another man she was visualizing in her mind. She was simply in love with Edward Fitzgerald, as deeply in love as a woman can be.

And with that a profound sadness descended to mingle with her despair.

Chapter Six

Sadie was *en route* to speak to Miss Dobson about the forthcoming week's menus when she bumped into an excited Erin.

'Guess what?' Erin demanded, face ablaze.

'What?'

She flashed a ring at Sadie. 'Marty and I are engaged. Father's agreed to it and we're to have an engagement Ball at Christmas.'

Sadie exclaimed in delight, and quickly examined her friend's ring which was a square-cut diamond surrounded by rubies. 'It's a beautiful ring,' she proclaimed. 'And I know your marriage will be successful. You and Marty are simply made for one another.'

'I can't tell you how happy I am, Sadie. I'm bursting with it.'

They both laughed, and Sadie hugged her. 'It really is marvellous news. And an engagement Ball! Where's that to be held?'

'At the Country Club. We did consider having it here at Clare, but in the end decided the Country Club was more suitable.'

Sadie was pleased with that decision. A Ball at Clare would have meant an enormous amount of extra work for her.

'You'll come of course?' Erin beamed.

'If I'm invited.'

'You'll be one of the first to receive an invitation. I promise you.'

An invitation for her to attend a Ball. How wonderful! Sadie thought. But what would she wear? She'd have to buy a gown as she didn't own anything suitable for such a grand occasion. It would be expensive, but worth it.

'We're going to have an orchestra, a sea of champagne and French chefs brought in from Quebec,' Erin burbled on.

'How many will be going?'

'Hundreds.'

'And you say you're holding it at Christmas?'

'Christmas Eve, that's Father's idea. Anything sooner would be a rush, and anything directly after something of an anti-climax. At least that's how I feel. So we decided Christmas would be perfect.'

'And what are you going to wear?'

Erin's eyes sparkled. 'Father has told me to fly down to New York, spend a few days there and buy whatever I consider appropriate, regardless of cost. I can't wait to go.'

'I can imagine.' What a wonderful trip, Sadie thought, enviously. 'And what about a date for the wedding?'

'Well, I certainly don't want a long engagement, neither does Marty. We thought June perhaps.'

They chatted together for a few more minutes, then Sadie excused herself saying that Miss Dobson was waiting for her.

As none of the rest of the staff yet knew she was able to break the news to Miss Dobson and Heather who were as thrilled as she was.

Erin found Sadie alone drinking coffee in the kitchen. 'That's just what I came for. Mind if I join you?' she asked.

'I'll get you a cup and saucer,' said Sadie, starting to rise.

'Sit down! I'll get it myself.'

Erin glanced at Sadie and frowned. 'What's wrong with you? You've got a face long as a pole.'

Sadie sighed. 'I'm trying to find a gown for your Ball. I've been through Bald Rock Falls with a fine toothcomb and can't find a thing. At least nothing in my price range. I think I'm going to have to resort to making a gown myself.'

'Yaeger's is the best store, and they don't exactly have the widest of selections,' Erin commiserated.

'It's OK, I'll manage something,' Sadie smiled ruefully, and shrugged.

Erin had a sip of coffee, and considered Sadie's problem. 'Maybe I can help,' she said a few seconds later.

'How?'

'You and I are more or less the same size, so why don't you borrow one of my gowns?'

'I couldn't, they're so expensive,' Sadie protested.

'Don't be an ass!' Erin admonished, plonking her cup back on its saucer. 'Come and have a look. I insist!'

Sadie was tempted, knowing that Erin had some gorgeous dresses. 'I suppose just looking won't do any harm,' she replied reluctantly.

'It'll be fun. Now come on!'

Out in the corridor Erin linked arms with Sadie and together they made their way to her bedroom where Erin threw open her built-in wardrobes.

Lemon, peach, lavender, all the colours of the rainbow it seemed. 'I never realized you had so many gowns,' Sadie commented in awe.

'Well, you must know the amount of parties and functions I attend. The number has just grown over the years. Now how about this one?' And with that she removed a pretty pink organza gown from the rack.

Erin held the gown against Sadie and studied the effect. 'A possibility, what do you think?'

'Let's go over to the mirror,' Sadie said. She studied herself carefully.

'I don't think it's me somehow,' she declared eventually.

'Maybe not.'

They went back to the row of gowns, and this time Erin extracted an off-white number with leg of mutton sleeves.

Sadie didn't care for that at all and muttered something about white just not being her colour.

Sadie spotted a gown right at the very end of the row, and liked it immediately. 'What about this?' she said, taking it from the rail.

The gown was made of black velvet, plain in cut and design, and, in Sadie's opinion, different and effective because of that. Its very simplicity attracted her.

'Can I try it on?' she asked.

Erin, smiling crookedly, replied, 'Go ahead.'

Sadie swiftly slipped into the gown and zipped it up. It fitted her so perfectly it might have been tailor made for her.

'You look good in it,' Erin stated softly.

Sadie detected an odd note in Erin's voice. 'What is it?' she asked.

'That gown,' Erin replied. 'It was my mother's, the last she ordered before she died. I hung on to it as a keepsake, but have never worn it. I never could somehow.'

'Your mother's?' Sadie repeated, and reached for the zip. 'Of course it's out of the question that I . . .'

'No!' Erin interjected, stopping Sadie's hand. 'If that's your choice then it's yours for the Ball.'

Sadie hesitated. 'Are you sure? I mean, what about your father?'

'He won't object. In fact, quite the contrary, I'm sure he'll approve.'

Sadie was still uncertain. 'I don't want to cause any offence.'

'You won't,' Erin assured her. 'Now take that along to your room and keep it there till the Ball.'

'You're a pal,' Sadie smiled, kissing Erin on the cheek.

'And you're a good one to me,' Erin replied.

Now she'd need the right shoes, Sadie thought, and began to speculate about those.

She'd look for them in Yaeger's just as soon as she had some free time.

* * *

'How do you feel now?' Sadie asked Heather, sitting on her bed.

'Weak, but better thanks.'

'And your tum?'

'Still rumbling occasionally, but the worst is over.'

Heather had been stricken with gastro-enteritis the previous day, and had been either in bed or on the toilet ever since. The doctor had been and had given her some medicine.

'Rotten way to spend Christmas Eve, I'm afraid,' Sadie commiserated.

'Have they all gone?'

Sadie nodded. 'A little while ago. There's just you and I left.'

Heather placed a hand on Sadie's. 'You must go and join them. I won't have you missing the Ball because of me.'

'I'm not leaving you alone,' Sadie smiled. 'You need someone to look after you.'

'No, I don't. I told you, I'm better.'

'Not that much better. You're still as white as a sheet.'

'I'm better enough to manage the toilet if I need it. I'll be perfectly all right on my own.'

Sadie was desperately disappointed at missing the Ball, but there was no choice in the matter with Heather ill. Miss Dobson, bless her, had volunteered to be the one to stay behind, but she wouldn't hear of that insisting it was her responsibility as housekeeper. Anyway, she knew how much Miss Dobson had been looking forward to the Ball, even more than herself which was saying something.

Heather reached for the glass of water by her bedside, and took a sip. She had been forbidden anything other than water until the doctor saw her again, which he was due to do the following day.

When Heather had finished with the glass Sadie took it from her and replaced it on the bedside table, then plumped up Heather's pillows.

She wondered how they were all getting on at the Ball. Erin had looked radiant when she'd left with Marty, Edward so handsome it had made her knees go weak.

'Sadie?'

She brought her attention back to Heather.

'I mean it, you must go,' Heather insisted.

'But . . .'

'Listen to me! I'm OK to stay here on my own. You're making an unnecessary sacrifice.'

Was Heather telling the truth? It would be awful if she went off and Heather took a turn for the worse. Could you have a relapse with gastro-enteritis? She didn't know.

'There's one thing I really regret about all this,' Heather said wistfully.

'What's that?'

'The Ball would have been my one chance to dance with Courcy. If he'd asked me to, that is. You never know with Courcy, he's such a shit.'

'And yet you're mad on him?'

'Stupid, isn't it? But there we are.'

'Did he stop by and see you before he went?'

'No. I hoped he might, but he didn't. He's taking some girl called Noni, I believe.'

Love, Sadie thought. What a strange illogical thing it was. If only the heart would listen to the head, but it never seemed to where love was concerned.

'Now go and get changed,' Heather told Sadie, wagging a finger at her.

Sadie was in two minds. There was certainly a marked improvement in Heather, but marked enough for her to chance the Ball?

Sadie relented. 'As long as you're absolutely . . .'

'I am,' Heather interjected.

'Absolutely?'

'Absolutely!'

'You're not just saying that because . . .'

'No!' Heather exclaimed in exasperation. 'Now please go!'

She would risk it, Sadie decided, elated at the thought she wasn't going to miss the Ball, after all. Erin had been so upset when she heard she was staying behind, as indeed had Jack. They'd be delighted that she'd put in an appearance.

'OK,' said Sadie, rising from the bed.

Heather smiled her approval and relief. 'You can tell me all about it in the morning. I'll want to know everything, including what Courcy's date looked like.'

'You won't be worried about being left in the house all by yourself?'

'Not in the least. It'll take a lot more than that to spook me.'

'I'll leave your bathroom light on, just in case you have to get in there in a hurry.'

'Good idea,' Heather acknowledged.

Sadie turned on the light, had a final word with Heather, then hurried along to her room.

She began running the bath, after which she laid out her things while it filled. Luckily she wouldn't have to wash her hair as she'd done that earlier.

Emerging from the bath she dried and powdered herself, then put on her brand new underclothes. Then she started on her make-up, which Erin had taught her to do.

Although she didn't use make-up very often, she was nonetheless clever about applying it. That evening she took even greater care than usual and when she finally finished she was pleased with the result.

She then put on her stockings, and after them the black velvet gown. The shoes she slid her feet into were plain and simple like the dress.

Now for her hair which she'd decided to wear up. She hummed as she arranged it on top of her head, with a few curls cascading down her back.

She then went to survey herself in the bathroom mirror. The overall effect was fine, but a trifle severe. She needed something to lift the black, she thought. A brooch perhaps, or a chain?

She tried a gold chain she'd bought herself the year before, but that didn't quite do the trick. And she didn't have a brooch. Perhaps she could borrow one from Heather – she had a wide selection.

She was walking towards her bedroom door when she suddenly had an inspiration. Crossing to a drawer instead she opened it and took out a cardboard box which she placed in front of the mirror.

Inside the box, lying on tissue paper, were the two scarlet ribbons that Edward had given her. Taking out one she tied a small bow at one end, then wove the ribbon into the back of her hair, securing it with a pin. She did the same on the other side with the other ribbon.

The ribbons fell to shoulder length and couldn't have been more perfect in complementing both her hair colour and that of the dress.

She was now ready. She collected her wrap and nipped down to the garage.

She shivered as she drove, until finally the car's heaters warmed up the inside. She enjoyed driving, having been taught by Sam, the chauffeur, but nowhere near as much as flying.

She arrived to find the Country Club ablaze with light, the car-park jammed full. Eventually she found a space, parked and hurried to the club's main entrance.

She checked in her wrap, paused to take a deep breath, then walked towards the main reception hall.

Jack was in the middle of his speech, his audience captivated by his Irish eloquence and humour, when Sadie entered through the elegant doorway. He saw the dress she was wearing, and for several seconds time rolled back for him.

First one pair of eyes turned to see what Jack was staring at. Then another followed, until Sadie found every person there gazing at her.

Then, with a slight shiver, Jack recovered himself and resumed his speech, finishing with a joke that earned him a huge collective laugh and rapturous applause.

Sadie, burning with embarrassment, wondered what all that had been about. It was as though a spotlight had been turned on her.

Through in the adjoining ballroom the band struck up. Jack immediately went over to Sadie and kissed her hand.

'Will you have this dance with me?' he asked, somewhat dewy eyed.

'Thank you.'

As they headed for the ballroom Sadie became aware of Edward watching her, the strangest of expressions on his face. She thought to smile at him, but didn't because he appeared to be quite distant.

The orchestra was playing a waltz. Jack took her into his arms, and off they went.

'Sorry about that,' Jack apologized. 'It was the dress that did it. For those few moments it was as though Marion was standing there and not you.'

Sadie now understood. 'But I thought your wife had never worn this dress?'

'Not publicly. But I was there, shortly before she died, when she bought it in Toronto. In fact that was our last outing together before the end. I can see her now, clear as day, standing there having tried it on, asking me what I thought. That was the image I saw when you walked through that door.'

'I shouldn't have worn it,' Sadie said.

'No, no! I'm pleased you did. And may I be the first to say how beautiful you look. Absolutely ravishing.'

'Thank you.'

He smiled at her. 'The young men will be falling over themselves to get to you tonight,' he predicted.

Half an hour later found Sadie dancing with Dean something or other; he had snapped her up the instant she'd come off the floor with her previous partner. Dean was chatting about skiing when she noticed Edward staring at her, as he danced with Stella Du Lac. When he realized she'd seen him he quickly glanced away.

'I really must sit down,' Sadie declared at the end of that dance, much to Dean's disappointment.

'Perhaps I could get you a drink?' he offered.

'A glass of champagne would be nice.'

He escorted her to another room where the bar was situated and left her while he went for the drinks.

'Hi!' said Courcy, coming up to join her.

'Where's your date?'

'Gone to the can.' He looked her up and down, and shook his head. 'Stunning. That's what you are tonight, Sadie, simply stunning!'

'That's kind of you.'

He raised an eyebrow. 'Not kind, merely a statement of fact. A rose, if not exactly among thorns, then among a bunch of weeds.'

She laughed. 'Hardly that!'

'Naw, I'm serious. The weeds all looked great till you walked in. You're a classy act, Sadie, you've left all the others standing.'

Courcy bowed low, a mocking bow but a genuine one at the same time. 'May I have the pleasure?'

'There's a young man who's gone to fetch me a drink.'

'So?'

'It would be most impolite of me not to be here when he returned.'

Courcy laughed softly. 'Always the lady, huh! But then that's part of your charm. In other words you're turning me down?'

'I didn't say I was.'

'But you are?'

'Why not try again later?'

He smiled crookedly. 'Maybe I will.' And with that he sauntered off.

By the time Dean returned with their drinks she'd refused three other requests to dance.

'How come I've never seen you around before?' Dean enquired as they sat down.

'I don't know.'

He was still talking when Edward came up to them. 'Would you care to dance, Sadie?' he asked.

Irritation flashed across Dean's face. 'She's already with me,' he protested.

'Sadie?' Edward smiled.

'Perhaps again later,' Sadie said to Dean, handing him her glass. She rose, took Edward's arm, and they made for the ballroom.

'So Cinderella did get to the Ball, after all?' he said as they walked.

She laughed. 'Yes, Heather's much improved.'

'And you are Cinderella, too. I've heard quite a few people talking about you since you made that spectacular entrance.'

'That was Jack's doing, not mine.'

'But why? I mean, what was it all about?'

'Ah!' he sighed when she'd explained to him. 'I understand now.'

Her heart beat wildly when he folded her into his arms – this was a moment she'd dreamt of.

'Are those the scarlet ribbons I bought you?' he asked as they waltzed.

'Yes. This is the first time I've worn them.'

He gazed into her eyes, making her melt inside. It suddenly seemed that her legs might be incapable of supporting her.

'Why tonight then?' he queried.

'I thought they went with my dress. Or I should say, your mother's dress.'

'They do,' he replied softly. 'Very much so. You look extremely glamorous tonight, Sadie Smith.'

'So does Stella,' she jibed in reply.

He smiled, but didn't comment on that.

When the dance came to an end they both applauded. 'Another?' he asked.

There was nothing she wanted more. This time it was a polka which meant there was less conversation between them. But it didn't matter to Sadie whether they spoke or not, just to be with Edward was enough.

'I'm afraid I must get back to Stella,' he said sadly when that dance was over.

'Of course.'

He lingered, reluctant to go.

'May I have the next dance, please?' a young man eagerly asked Sadie, materializing as though from nowhere. His face was shining with expectation.

Sadie nodded her acceptance.

'Enjoy the rest of the evening,' Edward told her, then strode away.

He knew he wouldn't.

'Courcy came to see me earlier and told me you were the belle of the Ball,' Heather said to Sadie.

'He did!'

'He said that up against you all the others paled into insignificance.'

'I'm flattered.'

'And what was his date, Noni, like?'

'Pretty, but not as much as you. I wouldn't say you have any real competition there.'

'You wouldn't lie to me, Sadie?'

Sadie made the sign of the cross over her left breast. 'Cross my heart and hope to die if I'm not telling the truth.'

'What sort of dress was she wearing?'

Heather listened wide eyed as Sadie recounted all she

could remember of the dresses that had been worn, of whom she'd danced with, and what they'd said.

However, she didn't mention Edward. That was private as far as she was concerned.

'Sadie!' Edward called out. It was one evening, and he had just returned home.

She stopped and turned to smile at him as he hurried to her side.

'I, eh . . . I stopped in at the mills earlier and had a thought while I was up there. You've never been to them, have you?'

She shook her head. 'No.'

'Well, they're starting up again the day after Boxing Day and I wondered . . . well, I wondered if you'd like to see them in operation?'

She considered that. 'How do you mean?' she asked slowly.

'I'd take you round. Show everything to you and explain how the whole operation works.'

Now why should he suddenly want to show her the mills! Unless they were an excuse . . . for what? Not merely to be alone with her, they had lots of that in the hangar.

'I think you'd find them interesting,' he went on.

She was sure she would. Particularly if he was acting as her guide.

'I'm not certain I can get away. What with Heather still in bed.'

She watched his face fall, which caused something to quicken inside her. 'There again, Heather should be up and about by then. If it was only for an hour say, and we went at the right time of day . . .'

'Whatever time you choose. That's entirely up to you,' he interjected swiftly.

Excitement was rapidly building within her. She sensed this was a new departure, a change in their relationship. 'All right then, thank you,' she replied.

'Just let me know when it's convenient and we'll arrange to meet up then.'

'OK. Fine.'

He beamed at her, then strode away leaving Sadie to stare after his retreating back.

Sadie had a mad impulse to jump into the air. Control yourself, she told herself. You could be wrong, adding two and two and getting five.

She prayed to God she was right.

'This is the saw mill,' Edward said, opening the door and ushering her through.

The din was deafening. Noise seemed to have become a physical entity hammering at her eardrums. Sadie positively wilted under the onslaught.

Edward laughed at her pained expression. Putting his mouth close to her ear, he shouted, 'Amazingly you get quite used to it after a while.'

Sadie found that hard to believe. How could you ever get used to this bedlam!

Edward beckoned her to follow him. He showed her all the machines and explained their different functions. Sadie was amazed by their efficiency.

Eventually they came to an office area where Edward ushered her inside. She gasped with relief because the office was sound-proofed.

'I've never heard anything like that in my life,' she declared when Edward had shut the door behind him.

'It is a bit ferocious when you're not used to it,' he admitted.

'A bit!' she exclaimed. 'More than that.'

He grinned at her. 'So, what do you think? Apart from the noise, that is.'

'It is interesting. Where do the planks go from here?'

'They get trucked to the railway station at Bald

Rock Falls, from where they're freighted to their destination.'

She looked through a pane of thick glass at the men going about their tasks. 'Do you get many accidents?'

'We're very safety conscious, a hobby-horse of my father's. But despite that there is always the odd accident. A man was decapitated only last year.'

Sadie's hand went to her mouth. 'How horrible!'

'It was certainly that. He was a good man, too, one of the best and a long-term employee of ours.'

'What happened?'

'A high-tension wire snapped. He wouldn't have felt a thing which was some consolation to his widow. The usual accidents we get here are loss of fingers or entire limbs, mostly arms. You'd be surprised how easy it is to lose one of those.'

Sadie could well imagine.

'The main offices are in the pulp mill which we can go over to now,' Edward said.

They left that office area by way of a door to the outside from where they made their way to the adjoining mill. 'Not so much noise here,' Edward told her as they went in.

'Now,' said Edward, stopping Sadie in front of a huge machine, 'woodpulp is achieved through two different processes. The first is called mechanical pulping, the pulp made by filing logs against a revolving grindstone under a stream of water. The resulting pulp contains much fibre debris and is used for newsprint and the cheaper grades of wrapping paper. Understand so far?'

'I think so,' she nodded.

'The second method is called chemical pulping. I won't bore you with the details, but the end result is a far finer grade of pulp that can be used for making high-quality papers.'

'The chemical process takes out more impurities?' Sadie queried.

'Precisely! It's more expensive, of course, therefore we charge more for chemical pulp.'

That all seemed fairly straightforward to Sadie, though as Edward had said he'd left out the long and complicated details of the chemical process. She now began to quiz him on these as they moved around, and Edward was delighted at how quickly she picked up and understood his explanations.

They stopped for coffee in the small office complex where a number of men and women were dealing with the paperwork.

'It's hot out there,' Sadie said, sipping her coffee.

'The chemical process requires heat which, of course, raises the overall temperature inside the building. In mid-summer it can be murder. Luckily these offices are air conditioned.'

There was a happy atmosphere among the office workers, Sadie thought, gazing about her. But it was something she'd noticed throughout the mill.

'Thank you very much for the tour, I thoroughly enjoyed it,' she said to Edward as they were leaving and walking towards the Cord.

'My pleasure.'

Edward appeared preoccupied while Sadie shot him the occasional glance out the corner of her eye.

'I've been invited to a New Year's party and wondered if you'd care to come with me,' he said as they reached the car.

She turned to face him. 'A New Year's party?'

'Yeah, a buddy of mine in Harrisfield is holding it.' Harrisfield was an outlying district of Bald Rock Falls.

Elation raced through Sadie. She'd been right, after all! 'Are you asking me for a date?'

'Yes,' he answered softly, his eyes boring into hers.

Sadie felt her legs start to go weak. Finally, after all this time he'd asked her out. It was a dream come true. 'What about Stella?'

315

'I'm not seeing Stella any more. We broke up the night of the Ball.'

'In which case I'd love to go.'

His face broke into a broad smile. 'Great!'

Edward was waiting for her in the drawing-room where they'd arranged to meet. He stood up as she came into the room.

'You look fabulous,' he declared.

'Thank you.' He looked fabulous himself, she thought.

'Like a drink before we leave?'

She saw he had a partially-filled glass on the table he'd been sitting beside. 'Please. But something soft,' she smiled in reply.

'Coke OK?'

'That would be lovely.'

When he handed her the glass their hands touched and it was as though an electric current passed between them. It was obvious that Edward had felt it too.

'Does Jack know you're taking me out?' she husked.

'I mentioned it.'

'And he doesn't object?'

Edward looked surprised. 'Why should he?'

'I am a family employee, after all.'

'He approved if you want to know. He thinks very highly of you, we all do.'

'Just so I'm aware of the situation.'

They made small talk for a few minutes, then went to the garage and picked up the Cord. As they drove to Harrisfield the electricity returned and seemed to spark between them.

The house was large and old-fashioned, the party in full swing when they arrived. They were given paper hats and drinks, after which Edward took Sadie round introducing her to everyone.

Sadie had wondered if Philip would be there, and was glad he wasn't. That might have proved something of an embarrassment.

'This time I get to dance with you more than twice,' Edward said, taking her into his arms. A gramophone was playing.

And me with you, she thought, but didn't say anything.

It was a merry party with lots of games and laughter, Sadie and Edward danced and danced, and in between talked about all manner of things. They couldn't have been more at ease with one another. They were dancing a slow waltz when Danny their host, burst into the room and excitedly announced that it was striking midnight.

They stopped dancing and looked into one another's eyes, and it was the most natural thing in the world for them to kiss.

As they kissed, Sadie felt she was drowning, and the only person she saw in her mind was Edward.

The musical was on tour prior to opening in Toronto, and Sadie and Edward had flown up to Timmins to see it. Sadie had been flabbergasted when Edward had suggested flying to see a show and then staying overnight in an hotel! She'd laughed when she'd accepted, thinking it a wonderful idea.

'Well worth the effort,' Edward declared as they left the theatre. It had been a splendid show.

Sadie turned her collar up against the cold. 'I'm glad we're not flying back tonight,' she said to him. 'That would have spoilt it somehow.'

'Can't fly in the dark, after all. And anyway, staying over gives me the opportunity to buy you the best dinner Timmins has to offer.'

He flagged down a cab and they climbed inside. Edward then gave the cabbie the name of a restaurant.

'Thank you for that,' Sadie smiled at him.

'The night's young. Thank me later.'

317

She lifted her face to him and kissed him.

'Hmmh!' she murmured when the kiss was over.

'I know just what you mean by that,' he said.

The restaurant was in a back-street and called the Moulin Conan. They went down a short flight of steps and through a door straight into a warm, romantic atmosphere. A gypsy violinist was playing, the tune sad and melancholic.

'Have you been here before?' Sadie asked, and immediately wished she hadn't. If he had been here with either Stella or Phyllis she didn't really want to know.

'No, I haven't,' he was able to answer truthfully. 'But it comes very highly recommended. The food is supposed to be out of this world,' he added.

A smiling owner appeared.

'I have a booking. The name is Fitzgerald,' Edward said.

'Ah *oui*, M'sieur Fitzgerald!' the owner enthused. 'Come zis way if you please.'

There was a gorgeous smell, Sadie noted, wine, cigars, a hint of garlic. Miss Dobson would have adored it.

Their table was secluded and beautifully laid, with a crisp, white linen cloth on the table, and a small vase of fresh flowers.

'An aperitif before your dinner, m'sieur?' the owner asked.

Edward glanced at Sadie, who nodded. 'Please,' he replied.

Sadie gazed about her. There must have been twenty tables, perhaps a few more, and most of them were occupied. Waitresses carrying trays laden with food and dirty dishes moved effortlessly among the tables. When she brought her attention back to Edward she found him staring at her.

'Shall we choose?' he suggested.

She wanted to touch him, and sensed that he felt the same. She lowered her eyes to study the menu which was in both French and English.

She went from one dish to the next, but was unconcerned about what she ate. It was quite enough to be here alone with Edward.

'Who recommended the restaurant then?' she enquired.

'A friend of Father's mentioned it recently. Said it was a real find and the next time I was in Timmins I was to be sure to visit it.'

Pork? Beef? Excitement had killed her appetite, but she would have to have something or Edward would be disappointed.

'What do you fancy?' she asked.

'The gigot thing.'

She looked that up and discovered it was lamb.

'And you?' he queried.

She felt like saying *him*. And suddenly had a vision of him served on a platter with an apple in his mouth, which made her giggle.

'What is it?' he demanded.

She shook her head. 'Nothing.'

'It must be something!'

She tapped her nose. 'Secret. And that's how it's going to stay.'

'We can't have secrets from one another,' he teased.

'Why not?'

'Because I want to know everything about you, including what you're thinking.'

She smiled.

'Everything,' he repeated, reaching out and touching her hand.

'Women always have secrets,' she told him. 'It's part of their feminine allure.'

He crooked his little finger round hers. 'God, you're lovely,' he said throatily and was about to elaborate on that when the wine waiter approached with their aperitifs. Reluctantly they disengaged little fingers.

'So what will you have?' Edward asked Sadie.

'Gigot also.'

'Right then.' He studied the wine list, and ordered a bottle of Heidsieck Monopole Diamant Bleu champagne to start with, followed by Margaux claret.

'You'll get me drunk with all that wine,' she protested when the waiter had left.

'Perhaps I intend having my wicked way with you,' he further teased.

'You'd better not!'

'No,' he said softly, his mood abruptly changing, 'that would spoil everything.'

He looked down and then raised his glass in a toast. 'To us,' he declared when she'd raised hers.

A waitress descended on them then, and they ordered. They both chose oysters to begin with and then the gigot.

'Why?' she asked.

He frowned. 'Why what?'

'You've never said. Why did you suddenly start asking me out?'

He thought about that. 'It was the night of the Ball obviously. You walked into that hall and . . . it was as if I was seeing you, the real female you, for the first time. It wasn't just that you were beautiful, but more than that. I think I've felt this way about you for a long while, but stupidly didn't appreciate it. Does that make sense?'

'I don't know, but I understand.'

'Maybe it was because you were only a kid when we first met, and that you were around the house and hangar all the time. You became like a second sister, I suppose. I was always vaguely aware of how attractive you were, yet somehow never equated that attractiveness to me.'

'You had Phyllis, after all.'

'Yes,' he nodded. 'I had Phyllis. I was committed there.'

She couldn't resist, if not exactly sliding the knife

320

in, then jabbing him with its point. 'And then you had Stella.'

He looked miserable and uncomfortable. 'Stella was OK. I'd never say a word against her. But then that night of the Ball I suddenly knew who I really wanted.'

'I knew long before that,' she said softly.

'You did? And you never said anything?'

'How could I in the circumstances?'

He could see her point, and began to understand some of the agonies she'd been through on his account. 'Is that why you never went out with other men?'

She nodded. 'With the exception of Philip Mandela. You want the truth?'

She might be making a mistake here, she told herself, but decided to plunge on regardless. 'I stopped dating him because he wasn't you.'

He didn't know how to reply to that, so hooked his little finger again with hers instead.

They remained like that, silent, until the champagne arrived. Sadie laughed with pleasure as the waiter popped the cork, then watched the bubbles fizz as the wine was poured into their glasses.

'Another toast,' Edward proposed when the waiter was gone.

She lifted her glass in expectation.

'To the future.'

Our future, she felt like saying, but didn't. She mustn't push too much, but rather let things take their natural course. 'The future,' she repeated, her eyes sparkling almost as much as the champagne.

Their meal was delicious; Sadie had never had oysters before and was thrilled by the novelty. The gigot was superb and Sadie felt that even Miss Dobson would have been impressed.

As they ordered their coffee, Edward took Sadie's hand.

'How did it take me so long?' Edward wondered in amazement, gazing into her eyes.

'Maybe it just wasn't right up until now. Who knows about these things?'

'It's certainly right now,' he said.

'Yes,' she agreed.

The gypsy violinist came over and played to them as they drank their coffee, the most perfect touch to a blissful evening.

When they arrived outside Sadie's hotel bedroom door to say good night their mood had completely changed. A certain shy coyness had grown up between them.

'An early breakfast and then home to Clare,' Edward said, taking her hand in his.

'You said to thank you later, therefore I'll do so again now. Thank you.'

'I enjoyed every moment of it.'

She took a deep breath, then said, 'Edward?'

'Yeah?'

'I don't want to rush into anything.'

'What do you mean?' he queried with a frown.

'I think you and I very easily could. I'm not saying we'd regret it, but rather that's not how I want things to happen. I want our relationship to develop slowly.'

'Are you talking physically?'

She nodded.

'OK. If that's what you want.'

'It is,' she said, and squeezed his hand. 'I just feel in my heart that's the way we should proceed.'

'I understand,' he replied, and kissed her lightly on the tip of her nose.

She took his head between her hands and kissed him on the mouth, a kiss full of tenderness and affection. 'Now I must go in,' she breathed when the kiss was over.

'I'll meet you in the dining-room for breakfast. Seven OK?'

'I'll be there.'

When she went into her bedroom she might have been walking on air.

But they didn't fly back to Clare next morning, for when Sadie woke she found that a blizzard was raging, and had been doing so for hours.

She met up with Edward at breakfast, after which they went out to the small airport where they were told that the weather forecast was pretty bleak. Flying was out of the question.

'So, what do we do?' Sadie queried as they returned to the hotel.

'Make the best of it, I suppose,' Edward replied, then added, mischievously, 'Hell, we could be trapped here for weeks!'

She snuggled up close to him. 'I think I could learn to like that.'

'I think I could too.'

When they reached the hotel they reviewed the situation.

'I suggest we go shopping. I'd just love to buy you all sorts of things,' Edward said.

Shopping! Saddie thought it funny that a man should suggest that. 'You're on,' she agreed. 'But I don't know about you buying me things.'

'I've heard all about you Scots being independent,' he teased.

'And I've heard a lot about you Paddies.'

'Paddies!' he repeated, pretending outrage. Then, in a mock Irish accent. 'Begorrah, are you insulting me race, colleen!'

Sadie laughed at his appalling accent.

He took her by the hand and yanked her to her feet. 'Let's go and do that shopping, huh?'

He glanced quickly around, saw they were alone and kissed her on the mouth.

They found a department store not far from the hotel and dived inside. 'God, it's cold out there,' Sadie commented, shivering.

That gave Edward an idea. 'I know the first thing I'm going to buy you. Come on!'

'A fur coat!' she exclaimed a few minutes later when he told her what he had in mind.

'Sure. Why not?'

'They cost the earth.'

'Not the earth, only money. And you're forgetting we Fitzgeralds are a very rich family.'

'But a fur coat, Edward!'

'Not just fur, but mink or fox. Which do you prefer?'

Mink or fox! What a lovely decision to have to make. Her mind spun at the thought.

'Or perhaps something else. Ocelot say?'

Ocelot! She almost burst out laughing at the absurd idea of someone wanting to buy her, Sadie Smith, the same Sadie Smith who'd slaved on the Trikhardt's farm for three dollars a month, an ocelot coat.

Edward saw her face fall. 'What is it?' he demanded.

'We'll never get a fur coat back in the Moth, will we? I mean, I don't want to risk damaging it in any way.'

'Don't worry about that. When it's time for us to leave I'll have the hotel pack it and send it back to Clare.'

The assistant fussed over Sadie as though she was the Queen of Sheba. It was madam this, and madam that, and would madam care to . . . Sadie adored it.

In the end she chose a dark mink coat that matched her complexion and hair, the price of which she didn't even dare think about. Edward then insisted she had a hat to match, which she did. She wore the coat and hat away from the department, Edward carrying her old coat in a bag.

'Now how about some perfume?' he asked as they walked past various perfume counters.

'The coat and hat are more than enough!' she protested.

'Nonsense. Remember, you're my girl now. Nothing but the best for you. Besides,' he wagged a finger at her, 'would you deprive me of the pleasure of giving you things?'

'Ah!' he exclaimed a moment later, having spotted a particular perfume. ' "Joy", the most expensive perfume in the world I'm told.'

'And who told you, Phyllis?'

He smiled. 'Jealousy doesn't become you, Sadie. You're far too nice for that. If you really want to know it was my mother's favourite.'

'I'm sorry,' she mumbled, feeling ashamed.

'There's no need to be. But just let me say one thing, whatever was between Phyllis and me, and Stella and me, is dead. Forgotten. I swear to it. OK?'

'OK,' she nodded.

'Right then.'

Sadie sniffed an open bottle of 'Joy', liked what she smelt, and dabbed a drop on her wrist. 'What do you think?' she asked, holding her wrist up to Edward.

'Very you,' he pronounced.

'Are you sure?'

'Positive.' To the assistant he said. 'We'll have a bottle of the largest size.'

'You're going overboard,' Sadie hissed to him when the assistant's back was turned.

'I don't care. I want to go overboard.' He stopped to think. 'Now how about shoes?' he queried as they moved away from the perfume counter.

'I have a pair,' she riposted.

'You know what I mean.'

'Edward, this is getting ridiculous!'

'Yeah, great, ain't it?'

She had to agree. In fact it was more than that, it was mind blowing.

She didn't care for any of the shoes in that store, so they went to a shoe shop, but she didn't particularly like anything there either. They then moved on to another department store where she found three pairs that took her fancy.

'It feels like Christmas,' she said as they left the shoe department.

'Christmas, New Year and vacation time all rolled into one.'

'Now I must buy you something,' she said.

'Me!'

'I insist. Just as you've insisted on buying me presents, so I now insist on buying something for you.'

'You don't have to do that, Sadie.'

'I know. But there again, you didn't have to buy anything for me.'

'That's not the point. I can afford it.'

'And I'll buy you something I can afford. Deal?'

'Deal,' he agreed. And, despite the fact that they were in a popular store, he kissed her on the mouth.

In the event they settled for a silk tie which she declared suited him admirably. From the way he went on about her gift, you would have thought it had cost a million dollars instead of four ninety-five.

They did a little more shopping, and then it was time for lunch. 'Know what I'd like to do?' Sadie said to him.

'What?'

'Go to a diner. Remember that was what we did the day we met? You took me to one for dinner.'

'A diner it is then,' Edward enthused, thinking it would be amusing to see Sadie sit down in a diner dressed in a mink coat and hat. It appealed to his sense of humour.

Outside the blizzard had intensified, the snow thicker than ever. The floor of the diner was awash with melted snow. The other customers, from what Sadie could make out, seemed to consist mainly of manual workers and truck drivers. Several of these gave her a strange look as she walked to a secluded booth.

'Coffee to start with,' she said to Edward, rubbing her frozen hands together. She then decided to have pizza, followed by English muffins, which were a great favourite of hers. Edward chose pizza and cherry pie.

She smiled at him when he'd sat again after placing their order.

He reached across and stroked the mink. 'That coat really suits you. Makes you look terrific.'

'You mean I don't without it?' she teased.

'I didn't mean that at all, as you well know.'

'I think I might wear it in bed tonight,' she declared, further teasing him.

He raised his eyebrows. 'I'd like to see that!'

'You'll just have to use your imagination.'

'Aww!' he pouted, his tone as light hearted and full of fun as hers.

She took one of his hands in hers, and kissed his fingertips. 'Thank you again for everything. I do appreciate it,' she said, serious once more.

His eyes shone as he stared at her. 'I told you earlier that we're a very wealthy family. Well, there are some things money can't buy, and meeting a girl like you is one of them.'

Sadie purred with pleasure.

He freed the hand she'd been holding to enfold hers. He then copied her gesture by kissing her fingertips.

'What will we do after lunch?' she asked.

'I don't know. We can't exactly walk the streets or sightsee in this weather. More shopping?'

She laughed. 'Don't tempt me! How about a movie?'

'Sounds good to me.'

'And this evening?'

'Let's eat, drink a little and talk.'

She couldn't think of anything nicer.

Sadie woke, and smiled to herself thinking of the previous evening. They'd decided to stay at the hotel for dinner and afterwards they'd managed to find a sitting-room where, as luck would have it, they'd been left alone. Edward had brought a bottle of wine with them which they'd slowly drunk while they talked in front of a log fire.

They'd both been amazed when midnight had struck, the time had simply flown by. Edward had kissed her good night outside her bedroom door, a kiss she could still feel on her lips.

She sighed with happiness, then slipped from her bed and got dressed. She was just leaving her room when Edward appeared.

'How would you like to go tobogganing?' he asked.

'Tobogganing!'

'As you've probably noticed the snow has stopped, but I've just spoken to Father on the telephone who tells me it's falling heavily round Clare. That means we've got more time to ourselves and I thought we might go tobogganing.'

'But I haven't any clothes for that!'

'Neither have I, so we'll buy some.'

She thought that totally outrageous. 'And what about a toboggan?'

'I'll buy one of those as well.'

'You really are unbelievable!' she declared, and kissed him.

'Well, do you want to go?' he demanded.

'Of course. It sounds marvellous.'

'OK. Let's get a large, hot breakfast inside us. Then we'll buy what we need.'

She linked an arm through his. 'Tobogganing it is then.'

Sadie shrieked as the toboggan careered down the mountainside, half of her frightened to death, the other half thoroughly enjoying herself. Edward, sitting behind her, gripped her even more tightly.

They were heading for a huge tree. Edward grinned wolfishly as he waited for the last possible moment before altering their course. The huge tree whizzed by only feet away.

Sadie could hardly breathe, she was so exhilarated. The toboggan's metal runners hissed over the ice and snow, a hissing that gradually diminished as the ground levelled out. They had slowed down considerably when Edward decided to tip the toboggan over.

Sadie shrieked again as she was thrown from the toboggan to go tumbling and sprawling in the snow. When she finally came to a halt her eyes, her mouth and her ears were full of it.

Edward, laughing, came and squatted beside her. 'Are you still alive?' he joked.

Her answer to that was to ram a fistful of snow into his face.

'Beast! You did that on purpose,' she accused.

'Guilty,' he admitted, wiping the snow away.

She glared up at him, but it soon dissolved into a warm smile. 'I thought I was going to have heart failure at one point,' she said.

'Fun, isn't it?'

She nodded.

He grasped her wrist and pulled her upright. She stumbled, and he grabbed her to him.

'To make amends for that tumble you're going to have to let me fly the Moth home to Clare,' she said.

'OK.'

They gazed into one another's eyes. Then suddenly she was being kissed, and kissing in return.

'Oh Sadie, oh my darling,' he murmured when they'd finally finished.

Hand in hand they strolled back to their hired car, dragging the toboggan behind them. And sitting on the car's rear seat they ate a picnic that the hotel had packed.

'It's afternoons like this that you remember for the rest of your life,' Sadie said to Edward.

'Yes,' he replied simply. This was an afternoon he'd never forget.

Edward's brows were furrowed in concentration as he read the *Toronto Star*. The civil war in Spain was proving to be a protracted, bloody business with no end in sight.

But it wasn't Spain that worried him so much as the rest of Europe. The way the journalist had described it was that 'Europe was a powder keg with Spain the lit fuse'.

'Edward!'

He glanced up to see Sadie floating on her back and waving to him.

'Come on in, the water's lovely!' she shouted.

'Meet you halfway!' he shouted in reply. He removed his sunglasses, then ran to the lake and plunged in.

He swam like a fish, Sadie thought, as Edward headed towards her. Suddenly he disappeared underwater.

She laughed, knowing what that meant. Stopping, she trod water, waiting for what was coming next.

Strong hands grabbed her legs and pulled her down. Down she went, and still further down. Edward's grinning face peered into hers, then he let her go and they both went shooting to the surface.

This time they both trod water. 'No more,' she giggled. 'One ducking a day is enough.'

'Spoilsport!'

'Race you to the towels,' she challenged, and set off as fast as she could, well aware that she didn't have a chance.

He teased her by doing backstroke and making rude faces at her as she strove to keep up. She got something of her own back though when they reached the lakeside because she managed to grab Edward's trunks which she then yanked down exposing part of his backside.

She still didn't win however, and he managed to throw himself on to his towel a full couple of seconds before she reached hers.

'Do you want to eat?' he asked when they'd both stopped laughing.

'Not yet. Later.'

330

'A cold beer then?'

'A few sips of one would be nice.'

He took a bottle from the cold box they'd brought, opened it and handed it to her. He watched her as she drank.

'Hmmh! Hits the spot,' she murmured, handing the bottle back.

He had several deep swallows, then put the bottle to one side. Focusing on Sadie he placed a hand on her side. He drew her towards him, and kissed her throat. Sadie closed her eyes, enjoying the twin sensation of his mouth kissing her, and the sun beating against her face. She kept her eyes closed as first one strap of her costume was pushed down over her shoulder, then the other.

Edward freed her breasts which were bigger than he'd imagined. He'd never tried to go this far with Sadie before, and now he felt overwhelmed by his love for her. It was July, and they had been stepping out together for six and a half months.

He gently caressed one breast, then the other. She sucked in a breath as he kissed both nipples in rapid succession.

'Why don't you take your costume off altogether?' he suggested, his voice suddenly dry and tight.

Her eyes slowly opened. 'What for?' she husked in reply, realizing that it was a daft question even as she asked it.

'I want to make love to you properly.'

She went very still inside. 'Somebody might come.'

He shook his head. 'Not a chance, Sadie. We're on a small island in the middle of a lake, and it can only be reached by boat. And you know that all the boats round here have outboards on them so we'd hear anyone a mile off.'

That was true enough, she thought. 'I don't want to get pregnant Edward,' she replied softly.

He touched a breast, cupping it. Desire, and love for her, consumed him. 'Marry me and it wouldn't matter if you did,' he croaked.

Marry! The word made her shiver all over. Her heart pounded while blood thudded in her ears. Marry! She repeated the word mentally, savouring it beyond belief. 'Is that a proposal?'

He nodded. 'Yes. Will you?'

Stunned, bursting with excitement, she took his face in her hands and kissed him on the lips. 'I would be honoured to become Mrs Edward Fitzgerald.'

'Then we're engaged?'

'Engaged,' she agreed, and shivered again.

'Oh, Sadie!' He wrapped her in his arms and hugged her tight, acutely aware of her breasts squashing against his chest.

'You're sure now?' she whispered.

'I couldn't be more so.'

He tugged her to her feet, then slowly pulled down her costume till it fell down. 'Ahh!' he breathed, staring longingly at her naked body.

She hooked her fingers into his trunks, and moments later they were round his ankles. He stepped out of them, and she out of her costume.

'You do know I'm a virgin,' she said.

He nodded, and taking her by the hand drew her down on to the towels.

Soon they were one.

'What?' Jack queried.

'I said we're engaged,' Edward shouted into his ear. They were in the sawmill where the din was awful.

Jack beamed. 'Did I hear right, *engaged*?'

Sadie nodded.

'By all that's . . . congratulations!' he roared. 'I couldn't be more pleased. But, for Christ's sake, let's get out of this racket.'

They followed him in to the office area, which was empty, and there they could at last talk.

'When did this happen?' Jack demanded.

'Earlier today. We both wanted you to be the first to know.'

'I couldn't be more pleased,' Jack repeated. Taking Sadie by the hand, he kissed her on the cheek. Then, to Edward, he added, 'You've got yourself a real fine woman, son. You couldn't have done better.'

'Nor could I,' smiled Sadie.

'We should go out and celebrate,' Jack proposed.

'Later Father. I'm going to take Sadie into town now and buy her a ring. I can't wait to do that.'

'Buy the best. Money's no object.'

'I will, Father. The best for the best.'

Sadie blushed at that.

'We'll have a special meal tonight, with champagne,' Jack said. 'I'll call Miss Dobson, explain what's happened, and tell her to pull all the stops out.'

'See you later then,' Edward said.

'Couldn't be more pleased,' Jack repeated yet again, and smacked a fist into the palm of his other hand.

'I told you he'd be delighted,' Edward said as they hurried to the Cord.

Sadie had had nagging doubts that he might not be because, despite how highly he regarded her, she was still staff, after all. But those doubts and fears were now dispelled. Jack had accepted her into the family, so there wouldn't be further problems in that direction.

'How about that beauty?' Edward queried, pointing to an engagement ring in a showcase they were standing in front of.

Sadie stared at the ring in question, thinking how simply magnificent it was. It immediately stood out from all the others.

'How much . . .?' she started to say.

'You heard Father, money's no object. We'll look at that one if you please, Mr Zupet.'

Zupet the jeweller nodded his enthusiasm, removed it from the velvet cushion it was embedded in and handed it to Sadie.

'The setting is platinum,' he explained as Sadie slipped it on the appropriate finger.

The central diamond was rectangular in shape with a yellow glint inside it. It was surrounded by smaller diamonds, supporting it, and showing it off, the way the *corps de ballet* do a principal ballerina.

'It's out of this world,' Sadie murmured in awe, hardly daring to think what it cost.

'Only arrived in last week,' Zupet informed them.

Edward had known the moment he'd seen it that that was the one for Sadie, providing she liked it, of course. A glance at her face answered that question.

'Well?' he demanded.

'It's a ring royalty would be proud to own,' she breathed.

'Shall we have it?'

She looked at him, her eyes glowing with excitement. 'Oh, yes please.'

'Done!' he declared with a smile to Zupet.

'Now how about the fit?' Zupet fussed.

The ring was slightly too large, which Zupet said could soon be fixed. He asked if they could come back in a couple of days, which didn't suit Edward at all. He wanted it fixed there and then. Seeing how adamant he was, Zupet told them to return at closing time and he'd do his very best to have the ring ready.

Zupet then measured Sadie's finger, after which she and Edward left the store.

'Happy?' he asked her.

'Ecstatic. What a ring! It's the sort of engagement ring every girl dreams of.'

'Good. As long as you're happy. Now I want to take you some place.'

'Where?'

'You'll see when we get there,' he added mysteriously.

They drove out of town towards Clare, but instead of going direct to the house turned off about half a mile from it along a dirt track.

Sadie was intrigued, where on earth were they going? And why? She tried to winkle it out of Edward, but he remained tight lipped, and clearly amused, about the matter. Finally they drew up overlooking a narrow shining river winding its way through verdant pastureland.

'What do you think?' Edward demanded.

'Think of what?'

'Come on,' he said, and got out of the car.

She joined him on the edge of the track staring out over the river and pastureland.

'I've always liked this place,' he stated.

'It's very nice.'

'You get trout in that river, which is called Silver River by the way. The Indians named it long ago.'

Silver River, what a lovely name, she thought.

'Well protected here from the weather,' Edward went on. 'Good tree screen over there which shelters it from the northerlies, and those small hills opposite are a natural barrier when the wind is blowing the other way.'

Sadie was completely at a loss. 'Edward, what is this all about?'

'I thought I'd build our house right there,' he said, pointing.

She stared at him. 'Our house! But what about Clare?'

'One day, when Father dies, Clare will be mine, or ours, and we'll go and live in it. But Father is only fifty-six, still a relatively young man, who could live for another twenty years or so. I don't want to live with Father, and Courcy, don't forget, while trying to have a home life and bringing up children.'

Sadie began to understand what Edward was driving at. Living as a married couple at Clare would certainly have its difficulties.

'And what if Father married again?' Edward went on. 'He's always maintained he never will, but who knows about these things? He's still fit and healthy, after all.'

If Jack did remarry that definitely would present problems, Sadie thought, for then Clare would have two mistresses. 'No, you're right. I can see that now,' she said to Edward.

'Clare will be ours, and ours alone, in time. But until then, with your approval, we'll live here.'

It was a lovely spot, Sadie thought. 'What sort of house did you have in mind?'

'I don't know. I thought I might consult Philip Mandela about that, see what ideas he could come up with.' Edward glanced at Sadie. 'Would it bother you if I brought Philip in on this?'

'Not in the least. I'd hate to deprive him of a commission just because we went out together a few times.'

'OK then,' Edward nodded. 'I'll make an appointment and see Philip as soon as possible.'

What a day! Sadie thought. First of all she'd been proposed to, then bought an engagement ring that would turn every girl for miles around green with envy, and now was having her own house built for her.

When they returned to Zupet's he had the ring waiting for them, and it now fitted perfectly.

All the way back to Clare Sadie kept looking at it, amazed that such a ring was on her finger.

How did that saying go? My cup overflows. Hers truly did.

'It's brilliant!' Erin squealed when Sadie showed her the ring. They'd returned home to find Erin and Marty waiting for them, Jack having called them with the news and told them to come over for dinner.

'Wow!' was all Marty managed to say.

'At the back of my mind I thought that we might just have to go to Toronto to get something suitable, but Zupet came up trumps,' Edward said.

'Very nice. Very nice indeed,' Courcy commented drily, peering over Erin's shoulder. He was back on summer vacation from university.

Sadie moved her hand slightly and the yellow glint became a lance of yellow light.

'Zupet always did run a first-class store,' Jack said, popping a bottle of champagne. 'There again, there is money in Bald Rock Falls as he well knows.'

'Like us and the Yaegers for example,' Courcy smiled, which earnt him frosty looks from both Jack and Edward.

'So, when's the wedding to be?' Erin demanded eagerly.

'We haven't discussed that yet.'

'It won't be till our house is ready,' Edward told his sister.

Jack had poured champagne which he now began handing round, starting with Sadie. 'Which house?'

'The one we're going to build out at Silver River.'

Jack stopped and stared at Edward. 'What's wrong with Clare?'

'We want to be on our own. Not having to share with you and Courcy.'

'And what's wrong with me?' Courcy demanded jocularly.

'Where would you like me to begin?' Edward replied drily.

To give Courcy his due he laughed at that, seeing the truth in what Edward had said. 'So it's going to be me and the old man when you move out,' Courcy smiled when he'd finished laughing. 'That should be fun.'

'I'll sure miss you round the house,' Jack said to Sadie. 'You're a ray of sunshine.'

'When do you plan to start building?' Marty asked Edward.

'No idea yet. We'll have to consult Philip Mandela first, then plans will have to be drawn up, and so on.'

'Quite a while then,' Courcy mused, staring into his glass.

'Could be,' Edward said.

'Well, speaking selfishly, that pleases me,' Jack declared, which raised a laugh all round.

'A toast,' Jack proposed, raising his glass. 'To the newly engaged couple, Edward and Sadie. May their union be a fruitful one, and may they have many long and happy years together!'

With the exception of Edward and Sadie everyone else drank to that.

'To Sadie! The girl for me,' Edward toasted, raising his glass.

Sadie blushed as they drank.

'And to Edward, the guy who snared her!' Courcy toasted, raising his glass.

Sadie glanced at Courcy, thinking she'd heard a hint of pique or jealousy in his voice. From Edward's expression he'd obviously thought the same.

'To Edward, my future husband!' Sadie said, changing the toast diplomatically.

'Someone refill these glasses,' Jack instructed when that toast was over.

'I'll do it,' Sadie said, making for the ice bucket.

'No, you won't!' Jack stated sharply, bringing her up short. 'Erin will.' He gestured to Erin, indicating she should take over.

'But it's my . . .' Sadie started to protest.

'That's precisely what it's not,' Jack interjected. 'If you're to be my future daughter-in-law, then you can't remain on here as housekeeper. That would be unthinkable.'

'But she will remain in the house?' Edward protested.

'Of course. But not as an employee. As from today she's a guest. Tomorrow we'll advertise the position in the *Bald Rock Clarion* and other newspapers.'

'But how will you manage until the new housekeeper is installed?' Sadie enquired.

'You'll do the job, but not as an employee. Can't have that. You'll be helping out as a friend and future member of the family.'

'That OK with you?' Edward asked Sadie.

'What? Losing my job or helping out till the new house-keeper arrives?'

He grinned at her. 'Both, I suppose.'

She shrugged. 'Sure.'

'That's settled then,' Jack growled.

'I'll arrange the necessary advertisements,' Sadie said to him, to which he nodded his agreement.

Erin went round refilling their glasses. 'I think it's marvellous you're going to be my sister-in-law,' she said to Sadie.

'They must come to dinner soon,' Marty chipped in. Their house was on the outskirts of town which Jack had bought them as a wedding present.

'We'd like that,' Edward smiled in reply.

'You're the only one left now,' Erin said to Courcy as she refilled his glass.

'I'm in no hurry to tie the knot. No hurry at all,' he told her.

'Now what about an engagement party? You're going to have to have one of those,' Jack said to Sadie.

She recalled Erin's, the turning point of her romance with Edward.

'How about the Country Club again?' Jack suggested.

Sadie looked at Edward, wanting him to decide.

'Country Club's fine by me,' Edward said. 'That's if Sadie's happy?'

She nodded, not really caring where the party was held. All that mattered, as far as she was concerned, was that she and Edward were engaged. The rest was icing on the cake.

After a while they all trooped through to dinner where it transpired Miss Dobson had quite outdone herself.

★   ★   ★

Later that night Sadie was brushing her hair and thinking of Heather. Heather had been overjoyed to hear of her engagement to Edward, but at the same time upset knowing that Courcy would never propose to her. Although she idolized Courcy she was under no illusion that she was anything more than a convenience for him, one of many.

She wondered if Heather would now, in the light of her engagement, leave the Fitzgeralds' household? If she'd been in Heather's shoes she certainly would have done. But there again, she and Heather were complete opposites in their attitudes towards life.

She stopped brushing when there was a tap on her door. 'Come in!' she called out.

It was Edward, with yet another bottle of champagne. He smiled at her as he closed the door quietly behind him.

'Father's asleep and snoring,' he said, glancing around. It was the first time he'd been in Sadie's room.

'And what about Courcy?'

Edward shrugged. 'Around somewhere.' He crossed to where she was sitting. 'So how does it feel to be an engaged lady of leisure?'

'I don't think I've taken it all in yet,' she answered truthfully. 'So much has happened since this morning, it's left me somewhat bemused.'

He laughed softly. 'I know exactly what you mean.'

'Thank you again for the ring, Edward. It really is superb.'

'Not nearly as superb as you,' he said, and lightly kissed her on the lips.

'And while we're thanking one another,' he went on. 'Thank you for this afternoon.'

She knew he was referring to their love making. She smiled, and continued brushing her hair.

'How about a drink?' he asked, waving the champagne bottle at her.

'Not for me. But you go ahead.'

'I stupidly forgot to bring some glasses. Do you have any here?'

'There's one in the bathroom. Use that.'

Edward found the glass, popped the champagne and filled the glass halfway up.

'Not even a sip of bubbles?' he cajoled, offering her the glass.

'OK then, just a sip,' she smiled.

When she'd had her sip he bent and kissed her, tasting the champagne she'd just drunk.

Electricity and urgent desire flowed between them, causing him to place the glass down and pick her up into his arms. They continued to kiss, the kiss becoming more and more passionate.

He slipped a hand underneath her robe and stroked her breast. When he touched her nipple she groaned while still kissing.

'God, I love you,' she said, tearing her mouth from his.

'And I love you.'

'Do you want to stay the night?'

'That's what I hoped you'd say.'

'I thought so. Wait a moment.'

She hurried to her door, and locked it, then turned off all the lights other than her bedside one.

He came to her as her robe whispered to the floor, his robe falling beside hers. Her night-dress was next, followed by his pyjamas.

She smiled when he entered her, and continued smiling till the sensations that exploded within her changed her expression to a look of sheer incredulity.

Erin puffed on a cigarette, then had a swig of Tom Collins. She and Sadie were in one of Toronto's leading fashion houses where they were being shown a selection of gowns and dresses.

'We'll have lunch after this in the Savoy Grill. It's named after the famous one in London,' she said to Sadie.

Sadie glanced down at the notes on the two gowns she'd so far considered for the engagement Ball. She'd really have preferred to wear the black velvet one she'd worn to Erin's Ball, but felt she couldn't wear it twice.

Jack himself had suggested the shopping trip to Toronto, and that Erin should accompany her. Erin had jumped at the opportunity.

Another model made an appearance, the gown she was wearing was deep blue taffeta studded with *diamanté*. It was low cut at the front, and positively plunged at the back.

Sadie hated it.

'Tell you what,' Erin said, leaning closer. 'What do you say we go to a night-club tonight?'

'Just the two of us?'

'We'll be safe. Don't worry. And we could have a sauna at the hotel beforehand.'

A sauna! Sadie liked the idea of that. She wasn't so sure of the night-club however.

'There is a concert on. I would appreciate going to that if we could get tickets,' she said to Erin.

'Good music at the night-club.'

'Better at the concert,' Sadie countered.

Erin laughed. 'OK, you win. We'll see if we can get tickets.'

The next model appeared, sporting a close fitting, pillar-box red gown that puffed out at the ankles.

Not for her either, Sadie thought.

'You're going to have to say hello to Phyllis and her husband, it would be rude of you not to,' Sadie said to Edward. They were at their engagement Ball at the Country Club which was just getting into full swing. The d'Astozis had arrived a little earlier and were now in conversation with Helen and Charles Tinniswood, old friends of Phyllis's.

The d'Astozis had turned up in Bald Rock Falls the

previous week to spend some time with Phyllis's parents. When Sadie had learnt this, she'd insisted they be sent an invitation, something Edward hadn't been at all keen on. But she'd argued that it was the proper thing to do. She wanted Phyllis to see how happy Edward was, and that he wasn't carrying any secret torch for her.

'Shit,' Edward swore.

'Not afraid to meet the count, are you?' she teased.

'Don't be ridiculous. I just find it . . . well, difficult considering the circumstances.'

'That's all in the past, over and done with. And if any embarrassment should be felt it should be on her part, not yours. And she clearly doesn't or she wouldn't have accepted our invitation.'

That made sense, Edward thought.

Courcy came up to them, his eyes betraying the fact that he'd been drinking heavily. 'Thought I'd ask my future sister-in-law for a dance,' he requested. Then, ever so slightly insolently, 'That's if it's OK with you, big brother?'

'I see you've been swimming in the sauce again,' Edward retorted.

'Me!' Courcy exclaimed in affected surprise.

'Yeah, you. You look it, and stink of it.'

Courcy held up his fists. 'Them's fighting words! Apologize or take the consequences.'

It was clearly only a joke, but Sadie didn't want it to go any further nonetheless. You never knew with Courcy whose moods were mercurial. What might be a joke now could be serious thirty seconds hence.

'Stop being silly, Courcy,' she admonished lightly. 'And I'd be delighted to dance, only later. We still have some guests to welcome.'

He dropped his fists. 'It's always later with you, Sadie. Never now,' he said, suddenly a little boy.

'Well, this time I promise. We shall dance before the end of the Ball. OK?'

'OK,' he said, and bowed low.

Sadie steered Edward in the direction of the d'Astozis.

'I sometimes wonder about him,' Edward muttered.

'How do you mean?'

'If he's all there. There are occasions I'm convinced he's got a screw loose.'

Sadie quite agreed with that. There was also a dark side to Courcy that frightened her, as it had the day he'd cornered her in the basement. She shuddered at the thought.

They were stopped several times *en route* to the d'Astozis who were now talking with Phyllis's brother Carl and his partner for the evening. But eventually they reached them.

Phyllis had seen their approach and tensed, Sadie noticed. Edward was also tense, she could feel it in his arm.

Phyllis went quiet when they reached her party, and beamed at them. 'Congratulations to the two of you!' she gushed, and threw herself at Edward to kiss him on the cheek. She then shook Sadie's hand and kissed her cheek also.

Sadie stared at the count, thinking Phyllis certainly hadn't married him for his looks. He was small, thin and in his early thirties, she judged. He had fine, aristocratic features and delicate white hands. There was a touch of grey in his hair which looked as though it had been set. His eyes were black, glittering and predatory. They reminded Sadie of Anna Trikhardt. But above all he was arrogant.

'Allow me to introduce you,' Phyllis burbled on. 'Darling, this is Sadie Smith who has become engaged to my old school friend, Edward Fitzgerald. Sadie and Edward, this is my husband, Count Antonio d'Astozi.'

'Pleased to meet you,' Sadie said as the count extended a hand.

'Delighted,' the count smiled, shaking hands cursorily

with Sadie. 'Such a beauty! Signor Fitzgerald is indeed a most fortunate man.'

Insincere, Sadie thought. She could detect it in his voice and eyes.

'I am that. *Most* fortunate,' Edward stated levelly.

Sadie knew that had been meant for Phyllis, and smiled inwardly. Was it her imagination or had Phyllis put on weight, particularly round that famous *derrière* of hers? It wasn't her imagination, she decided gleefully. The pasta was having its effect on Phyllis.

'And may I congratulate you both on your marriage. Canada's loss is Italy's gain,' Edward said, not to be out-done in the gallantry.

Phyllis clutched at her husband's arm. 'We're over here for a while because Antonio has always wanted to see Canada and the States. He also has some business to attend to.'

'And what sort of business is that?' Edward queried.

The count's eyes became hooded. 'This and that. Nothing of interest. Speaking of it would only dull such a sparkling occasion.'

Phyllis laughed brittly, and touched a beautiful diamond and emerald necklace she was wearing.

She'd done that to draw her attention to it, Sadie guessed correctly. Well, she was damned if she was going to admire the goddamn thing. The necklace no doubt was part of the d'Astozi jewels.

'Such a large country, Canada,' the count said. 'It seems to go on and on for ever.'

'Yes, it is a large country,' Edward agreed.

'It makes our countries in Europe seem so little by comparison.'

'Little perhaps, but simply overflowing with history and culture. Isn't that so, Antonio?'

Sadie decided she didn't like the count at all. He was a creep, Phyllis was welcome to him. Come to think of it, Phyllis was a creep, too. They deserved one another.

'Why you could spend a year in Venice and still never get round all the museums, galleries, theatres and other places of interest,' Phyllis went on.

'Really?' Sadie smiled.

'And as for Roma!' Phyllis exclaimed, clapping her hands. 'Roma is simply the centre of the universe.'

'The centre of the universe. My, my!' Sadie smiled, trying not to sound bitchy.

'We have a family home there,' Phyllis bulldozed on. 'And a villa and estate in Tuscany, and the same in the Romagna. We make our own wine, don't we, Antonio?'

'The family brand, d'Astozi wine,' he confirmed.

'I'm surprised you have time for that, what with all those houses and villas to take care of,' Sadie said innocently.

Phyllis frowned. 'I don't actually make the wine myself. We have people to do that.'

'Oh! How silly of me,' Sadie replied.

'And how are things in Europe?' Edward said to the count. 'Volatile from what I read.'

The count's eyes became hooded again. 'If you are referring to Spain, who knows how that will end? Certainly not I.'

'The Italians are involved, I believe,' Edward said.

'So I understand. We have been helping General Franco who is an admirable man.'

'And a Fascist like your Mussolini.'

The count's lips thinned. 'As I am myself, Signor Fitzgerald. I am a loyal supporter of Il Duce.'

'And you agree with his policy of giving armed assistance to a man who is rebelling against a democratically-elected government?' Edward continued softly.

'Democratically elected maybe, but a government composed of communists, socialists and worst of all, anarchists. It is right that Franco tries to overthrow such a rabble.'

346

'But a democratically-elected rabble all the same,' Edward said.

The count shrugged.

'I think it's time you and I danced,' Sadie said to Edward, gripping him firmly by the arm.

He knew he was being taken away before he went any further. Just as well, he thought. He didn't want anything happening which might spoil the party for Sadie.

'Of course. Shall we?' Then to the count, Phyllis, and the silent Carl and his partner, 'If you'll excuse us. Enjoy yourselves.'

He and Sadie took the dance-floor where he swept her into his arms.

'The guy's a creep,' she said.

'You noticed?'

'How could I fail to.'

'I should have known he'd be a Fascist.'

'But one who lives at the very centre of the universe,' Sadie said, tongue firmly in cheek.

Edward stared at her, then slowly began to laugh.

Sadie was *bored*. Since Mrs Wilson had taken over as housekeeper she had nothing to do all day except lounge around the house or work on the Moth. And there was only so much she could do on the Moth. Looking after it, when Edward insisted on doing his share, was hardly a full-time occupation.

She'd flown a great deal of course, but even that was beginning to pall somewhat.

The trouble was she wasn't like Erin who could happily spend an entire day doing absolutely nothing. If only she could read, but she'd tried that and got bored with that as well.

'Damn!' she muttered. It would be hours yet before Edward was home. She would have liked to have gone and chatted with Miss Dobson in the kitchen, but wouldn't in case Mrs Wilson was there. Nothing was ever said, but she knew Mrs Wilson was uncomfortable when she was about, presumably feeling she was snooping or checking up on her.

What she could do was drive into town in her new car, a present from Edward, and go shopping. Except there was nothing she needed to buy.

Or she could visit the beauty parlour? For what! Her hair was fine as were her nails. And she certainly didn't need a facial.

'Damn!' she muttered again.

She'd write to Janet Bone, she decided, the two of them having kept in touch over all these years. Then she recalled she'd already written to Janet, who was currently being courted by a nice young man called Gary. Sadie was waiting for a reply.

She sighed. What to do! How she wished Jack hadn't made her give up her job which she missed dreadfully. The resulting inactivity was driving her out of her mind.

She was *bored* witless!

Edward finished the newspaper article, then reread it. There had been an Agreement at Munich between Chamberlain, Daladier, Hitler and Mussolini, so it seemed that the threat of Europe erupting into war was over.

Thank God for that, Edward thought grimly. From what he had understood, Europe had been teetering on the very brink of it. And if Britain went to war so, too, would Canada and the rest of the Empire.

'Edward, where are you?' Sadie called.

'Coming!' he answered.

He skimmed through the rest of the article, then tossed the paper aside.

And soon Europe, possible wars, and Agreements at Munich were completely forgotten.

★ ★ ★

'Work in the mills, but why?' Jack, thoroughly surprised, demanded.

'Because I need something to do,' Sadie explained. 'I'm going crazy the way things are at the moment.'

'And you say Edward agrees?'

'He does. But tells me I also need your permission.'

Jack poured himself a scotch and soda. 'How about you, my dear? A sherry perhaps?'

'No, thank you.'

Jack had a sip of his drink, and thought about her request. 'You don't like being a lady of leisure then?' he queried.

'Hate it. Maybe it would be different if I was born to it, but I wasn't.'

'And what about when a family comes along?'

'If I was working I'd reconsider the situation when that happened.'

'And what if I say no?' Jack asked softly.

'I won't go against you, Jack. But I can't believe you'd wish me to remain unhappy.'

'This has nothing to do with you and Edward has it?'

She laughed. 'Nothing whatever. I love Edward and he loves me. But I only have him for a short part of the day. The rest of the time I'm sitting around twiddling my thumbs.'

'What about coffee klatches? Surely you've been invited to some of those?'

She could see he was teasing her. 'Jack! Sitting around drinking coffee and gossiping for hours on end isn't my idea of a productive day. I've tried it with Erin and some of her friends, and find it one big yawn.'

'But why the mills?'

'Simple, it's the family business and where Edward is. I'd be interested to learn about it so that will be another bond we have between us.'

Jack wagged a finger at her. 'You're a smart kid. I

349

realized that the first time we met. You've got a brain in - your head, same as Edward. The pair of you are going to - make one hell of a team.'

He downed his whisky and soda. 'OK then, you can work at the mills for as long as you want. There's a junior clerical post vacant at the moment, that suit?'

'For now,' she answered with a broad smile.

This time when he offered her a drink she accepted.

'Tell me something,' asked Sadie as she and Edward climbed out of the Cord, on her first day in her new job, 'once inside do I have to call you sir?'

'Damn right!' Edward replied, knowing she was teasing him. 'Either sir or Mr Fitzgerald.'

'And which do you prefer?'

He pretended to consider that. 'Tell you what, I'll have sir in the mornings and Mr Fitzgerald in the afternoons.'

She went round the car to join him. 'And what about at night when you come to my room?' she whispered.

He winked at her. 'You can call me anything you like just as long as you let me in.'

She slipped a hand into his and they went into the pulp mill's small office complex where she was introduced to everyone.

They turned out to be an amiable bunch whom Sadie got on with without trouble. By the end of the first day she'd settled in and become one of them.

'Mr Mandela to see you,' Kate, the new maid, announced, showing Philip into the drawing-room where Sadie was sitting waiting for Edward to join her.

Sadie rose and shook hands with Philip whom they'd been expecting. 'Good to see you again,' she said.

'And you. As arranged I've brought over some drawings for you both to look at.'

350

'Edward will be right down. In the meantime can I get you anything?'

'Not for me, thanks.'

Philip propped the large leather case containing the drawings against a chair, then they both sat and smiled at one another. 'I guess I should take this opportunity to congratulate you. I haven't seen you since the engagement was announced.'

'Thank you.'

'I never figured . . . you and Edward.'

'Funny how things turn out,' Sadie replied smoothly.

'Yeah!'

'Do you still make a mean Martini?'

'The meanest in town,' he replied, and they both laughed.

'Who are you currently seeing?' Sadie enquired.

'Her name is Diane Wunch. We get on real well together. Possibly because we have the same sense of humour.'

Sadie had vaguely heard of Diane Wunch, through Erin she thought, but she couldn't remember anything about her.

'Think it might end in marriage?' Sadie asked.

He shrugged. 'Who knows! It might.'

She smiled suddenly, remembering Philip's awful bedroom. She pictured the four-poster bed and wondered how often Miss Diane Wunch had been in it. If nothing else it had certainly looked comfortable.

'What is it?' Philip asked, referring to her knowing smile.

Sadie roused herself. 'Nothing. Nothing at all.'

Philip jumped to his feet when Edward came into the room. 'Hi Ed boy, how are you!'

'Fine Philip. And yourself?'

'Couldn't be better.'

'Glad to hear it. Let's have a drink and then you can show Sadie and me what you've come up with.'

Philip opened his case while Edward busied himself with the drinks. Sadie was excited to see what Philip had produced, because he had been more or less given a free hand.

Philip laid the first drawing on a convenient coffee table, and the three of them grouped themselves round it.

'Your brief was a one-off, none of the Cape Cods or ranch types . . .' Philip began by saying.

Sadie stared intently at the drawing, trying to imagine it in three dimensions. More drawings followed the first, with different angles, interiors, exteriors.

'What do you think?' Sadie asked Edward when they'd perused the final drawing.

'I like it. You?'

She smiled at Philip. 'Me too.'

Philip's expression showed how relieved he was at this positive verdict. He was a superb architect, just as Edward had claimed, Sadie thought, pity about his taste in bedrooms though. It was going to be a fine house, Sadie thought, when their discussion finally came to an end. It would be a joy living there.

'That's it then!' declared Philip. 'You have both agreed the finalized plans, so I can now go ahead and start building.'

'When will you begin?' Sadie enquired.

Philip gestured at the closest window through which thick falling snow could be seen. 'It'll be spring before we can start on the foundations and basement, I'm afraid. April perhaps, depending on the thaw, maybe May.'

Sadie's face fell. She hadn't thought about the weather. But Philip was right, the ground would be like iron until the thaw came.

'So when would you reckon to finish?' she asked.

'Late summer, early autumn should do it. Unless we run into any snags that is, but I don't foresee any.'

Sadie was disappointed to hear this because she knew Edward was adamant that they didn't get married until the house was ready and they could move into it when they returned from their honeymoon.

Philip left them shortly after that, and when Edward returned from seeing him to the door he found Sadie poring over the copy plans. He immediately gathered her into his arms and kissed the nape of her neck.

'Late summer, early autumn seems such a long way away,' she murmured.

'It'll soon roll round.'

She turned to face him. 'It's just that I want to get married as soon as possible.'

'Sure. But let's do everything properly. Anyway, in the meantime what's the difference? We work together, we live in the same house, and most nights we sleep together.'

All of which was true, she thought. 'It's still not the same,' she replied, nuzzling him.

'Now we know when the house is going to be ready, shall we set a date for the wedding?'

Her face lit up. This was something she'd been dying for. 'Any suggestions?'

'Once the house has been finished it still has to be decorated and finished. All of which takes time. So I wondered, how about getting married on Christmas Eve?'

'Why not! I only wish it could be this Christmas Eve.'

'So do I. But it's not as though you're fast becoming an old maid. You'll be coming up to twenty-one when we do marry, just the right age in my book.'

'And we will have all those nights in bed together before then,' she demurred.

'Of course.'

'And what about a honeymoon?'

'Would the West Indies appeal?'

'Very much,' she replied, her eyes shining at the prospect. 'It's only a pity we couldn't fly down in the Moth.'

He thought about that, then shook his head. 'Wouldn't like to chance it at that time of year. But what we could do is hire a plane down there.'

'That would be fabulous!' she enthused.

'The West Indies it is then, and a hire plane. I can hardly wait.'

'Me neither.'

He kissed her, after which they went back to studying the plans and talking about what life was going to be like in their brand-new house by Silver River.

Jack was delighted when they told him the date of their forthcoming marriage, and promised them it would be the biggest wedding ever seen in Bald Rock Falls.

'Do you fancy doing a bit of management?' Jack asked Sadie whom he'd summoned to his office.

'Management?' she queried in surprise.

'I've discussed it with Edward and we both agree. You've picked up an awful lot very quickly, so much so there's no reason why you shouldn't take over some of his responsibilities, which are increasing all the time, thanks to the current boom. Normally I'd just give you a better job, but as you're capable, and soon to be part of the family, I've decided to promote you to management.'

Sadie beamed with pleasure. It was true she had learnt a lot in a very short while, but then it really wasn't a tremendously complicated business once you had grasped the basics. 'When do I begin?' she asked.

Jack chuckled at her enthusiasm. 'Go and fetch a chair. Starting now you'll spend a week at my elbow while I teach you and explain some of the finer points. After that, you'll move in and share Edward's office with him. Any objections?'

'None at all.'

'I didn't think there would be,' he smiled.

'I'll be right back,' Sadie said, and left to fetch a chair.

* * *

'There you are, she's officially yours,' said Philip Mandela handing Edward the house keys.

Sadie gazed at the newly completed house thinking it was even better than she'd expected.

'She's a beauty and no mistake,' Edward commented.

Sadie went to Philip and kissed him on the cheek. 'Thank you for giving us a truly wonderful home. We both appreciate all the efforts you've made on our behalf.'

'Shall we have another look around inside?' Edward suggested to Sadie.

Philip, gratified by his success, left them to it.

Edward and Sadie entered their office together, already talking business.

'I'll have to fly up-country tomorrow,' Edward said. 'Remember Patsy, the logging boss you met on your first flight? Well, he's got an on-site problem that needs sorting out.'

'Give him my regards. I only wish . . .' She paused, and smiled ruefully. 'I only wish I could go with you. But that's impossible, what with work here and getting the house ready . . .' She trailed off, and shrugged.

'You're the one who wanted to be kept busy!' Edward chided her.

'I am not complaining. It would just have been nice, that's all.'

'Yeah, I would have liked it too.'

Edward flicked on the intercom and asked for some coffee to be sent through. He then hung up his jacket and switched on the radio.

Sadie sat at her desk and pulled a folder in front of her which she was going through when Edward suddenly said, 'Sshh! Listen!'

'I will repeat that,' the radio announcer said. 'War has been declared between Britain and Germany, to take effect from 5 p.m. Greenwich Mean Time. Despite valiant last minute efforts by . . .'

Sadie was stunned.

'Shit!' Edward swore softly.

Sadie glanced at the calendar. It was 3 September 1939.

Jackie, who'd made their coffee, came in carrying two mugs on a tray. 'Have you heard, Mr Fitzgerald . . .?' she started to say excitedly.

'Yes,' he interjected, 'just now on the radio.'

'Does that mean Canada will also go to war?'

'Yes, as sure as eggs are eggs. We'll be up to our necks in it before we know where we are.'

Sadie suddenly felt like being sick. War had been looming, but everyone had been deluding themselves that it wouldn't really happen, that those concerned at the highest levels would see sense.

She sat back in her chair, all thought of work gone. War! She visualized it as an evil black beast crouching over Europe, blood dripping from its fangs and talons.

They sat and listened to the extended news bulletin, and were joined by Jack halfway through. Gradually they did all get down to work, but no one's heart was really in it.

One word was reverberating round in everyone's mind: War.

Sadie and Edward lay in her bed having just made love. It was a week now since the war had been declared, a week during which the British liner *Athenia* had been sunk by submarine, and the RAF had raided the entrance to the Kiel Canal and bombed several German warships. It had also seen the first enemy air raid on Britain while Russia had begun to mobilize.

'I'll have to go to New York shortly for more fittings. I hate taking time off, but there is no other option, I'm afraid,' Sadie said. The fittings she was referring to were for her wedding dress and trousseau which were being designed by Oliver Chantelle, *the* top New York designer.

'Huh?' Edward queried, lost in thought.

Sadie repeated herself.

'Oh! Yeah, sure.'

She rolled on to her side to smile at him. 'What's wrong? Got something on your mind?' Then, when he didn't reply. 'Can I help?'

Again he didn't reply. 'Is it about work?' she further probed, wondering what it could be.

Edward gave a long sigh, pushed his hands through his hair, then sat up in bed. 'There's no way I can say this without hurting you,' he stated.

Fear suddenly clutched Sadie. 'What?'

'I'm going to England to join the RAF.'

She stared at him, appalled. 'The RAF?' she repeated in a dull, dead tone.

'I won't be dissuaded,' he declared emphatically. 'My mind's made up.'

'But what about our wedding? The invitations are all ready to be sent out, everything's arranged.'

'The wedding as planned will have to be scrapped. We'll have a civil ceremony just as soon as we can, followed by a few days at Niagara Falls. I'll leave directly after that.'

'Directly after . . .' She was stunned, unable to think. 'But why not wait? Surely you can . . .?'

'Now is more important than later,' he cut in sharply. 'Britain needs every trained pilot it can get at the moment. Look at it this way, if Britain and her Allies are strong enough at the beginning, perhaps this thing can be nipped in the bud. If not, it could drag on for years.'

A look of resolution came over his face. 'Hard as it is, for both of us, Sadie, I intend to go. I know it's the right thing to do.'

'If you must you must,' she muttered.

He clasped her face in his hands. 'I must.'

Edward going to join the RAF! Minutes before she'd had every happiness before her, now she had only worry and fear. 'Are you sure I can't make you change your mind?' she pleaded desperately.

He shook his head. 'I wouldn't have spoken to you about it unless I was determined. I shall leave as soon as we return from our honeymoon.'

Sadie sobbed, and fought back the temptation to hit Edward. What a stupid man! Stupid and dearer to her than life itself.

'I'm sorry,' he said.

'Not half as much as me.'

'You must understand I'm doing what I believe is for the best.'

'Damn Adolf Hitler to eternal perdition!' she swore hotly, while equally hot tears rolled down her cheeks.

'Honey, I . . .'

She pushed him away when he tried to embrace her, then dashed the tears from her face. 'I need time to get used to the idea, that's all,' she husked.

'Do you want me to go back to my own room?'

'Yes!' Then, 'No.'

Directly after the honeymoon, she thought miserably. What would that be in reality? About two weeks, she reckoned. And then how long before she saw him again?

'I'd have to go before long anyway . . .'

'Shut up!' she hissed. If only this were a dream. Despite the warmth of the bedclothes she was frozen. The horrid taste of bile rose into her mouth and made her grimace.

'If you were me would you behave differently?' he asked softly.

'Of course I would! But then I'm not you, I'm a woman and we have more sense.'

He laughed at that. 'I could never deny you're a woman, Sadie. You're certainly all that.'

'And you're all male which includes having no brain,' she retorted.

He caught her hand and held it to his chest. 'One big comfort to me is the knowledge that if anything untoward did happen, and there's always that possibility, then as my wife you'd be financially secure for life.'

God, what a thing to say! She didn't give a damn about being financially secure. What she wanted was him alive, safe, and here with her.

Pulling her hand from his she got out of bed and went in search of a handkerchief. She mopped up her tears and then washed her face in the bathroom.

She picked up a comb, considered using it, then tossed it aside. What did it matter what she looked like!

'Are you all right?' Edward asked, appearing beside her.

'Oh, I'm fine. Never better,' she replied sarcastically. 'I mean, what do you expect? I've just been told out of the blue that as soon as my husband returns from our honeymoon he's going off to war where he'll possibly get his ass shot off. Why shouldn't I be all right?'

'I know it's a surprise.'

'Surprise!' she exclaimed. 'That's the understatement of the century.'

She brushed past him and went back to bed, pulling the bedclothes up round her chin.

'I'm cold,' she complained.

He hesitated at the other side of the bed. 'Shall I join you?'

'Why not? You were before.'

He climbed in beside her. 'I knew you'd be angry and upset. I expected that.'

'Edward?'

'Yes?'

'Will you please shut up and stop talking like a complete and utter fool.'

She started to cry again, and dabbed at her face using her handkerchief, her emotions see-sawing from self-pity to cold fury.

'I'm sorry,' he repeated.

Reaching out she switched off the beside light, plunging the room into darkness. She then lay down, staring up at the ceiling. Her memory then recalled various scenes from the film *All Quiet on the Western Front* which she'd seen some while previously in Bald Rock Falls. Dead men in grotesque positions, men with limbs blown away, men screaming in agony, men . . .

She didn't know how long she lay there racked with fear, but eventually she became aware of Edward snoring gently beside her.

She wasn't cold any more, and a strange, almost ethereal, calmness had overtaken her. He was going, and there was nothing she could do about it. She just had to accept it. Considering the problem, she finally fell asleep in Edward's arms.

When she woke next morning she knew what she was going to do. She would accompany Edward to England and stay near wherever he was based. That way they wouldn't be apart.

Edward told Jack their plans at breakfast.

'What!' Jack exclaimed, sounding utterly horrified. 'The RAF? Where the hell did that hare-brained idea come from? And a civil ceremony? Not what was planned!'

Jack threw his fork down with such force that it bounced off to go skidding along the table where it ended up against a jar of maple syrup. 'What do you think of the RAF nonsense?' he demanded of Sadie.

She shrugged. 'You can imagine.'

'I'd prefer to go now rather than later,' Edward went on. 'After all I . . .'

'What do you mean now rather than later? You don't have to go at all! We didn't have conscription in the last war and we won't have it in this!' Jack exploded, his face going puce.

Edward stared at his father. 'It's a matter of honour, duty and obligation. Of course I must go, there's no question about it.'

'Bullshit!' Jack roared in reply. 'There's every question about it. What about the business, eh? What about that?'

'You'll manage without me.'

'I don't want to manage without you. I want you here. I want you both here.'

Jack rounded on Sadie. 'Can't you make him see sense?'

'I've tried,' she replied softly. 'But he's determined to go. His mind's made up.'

'This is crazy,' Jack choked.

'I want to be there at the very beginning which is why I'm joining the RAF. If it wasn't the RAF, it would be the RCAF,' Edward stated.

'He'll see action sooner with the RAF,' Sadie explained.

'I don't want to hear any more!' Jack declared vehemently, jumping to his feet and knocking his chair over.

'It's important to me, Father. This is something I feel I must do,' Edward told him.

Jack glared at his son. 'I've never thought you a fool, Edward, but I do now.'

'You're upset, Father . . .'

'Damn right I am!'

'But I'll only be one of thousands of young Canadians flocking to the Colours . . .'

He was sounding like a third-rate political tub-thumper, Sadie thought in despair.

'Hitler can't be allowed to do as he pleases. Nor can Fascism be allowed to run rampage through Europe. They both must be stopped. You know that's true!'

'Sure,' Jack conceded. 'But why by you, my son and heir?'

Edward smiled ruefully. 'Every soldier, sailor and airman who gets caught up in this will be someone's son, and many of them heirs.'

'But I don't care about them, I only care about *you*!'

'Aren't you being a bit selfish, Father?'

'I forbid you to go,' Jack ordered Edward, in a tight voice.

'You know you can't do that, Father. I'm twenty-six years old, not a kid any more.'

'Then I'll disinherit you.'

'No, you won't,' Edward replied patiently.

Jack balled his hands into fists, wishing he could think of some argument or threat that Edward would listen to. He was filled with despair and terrible anguish. Edward, his son, his dear darling son, going off to fight in a war. It didn't bear thinking about.

Edward rose from the table. 'If you'll excuse me I have some calls to make.'

Sadie also rose. 'And I have one wedding to cancel and another to organize.'

Side by side they walked to the door, and had almost reached it when there was a sudden muted cry behind them, followed by a gasping sound. They turned to find Jack bent over, clutching his chest.

Edward frowned. 'Father?'

Jack looked at them through eyes that were bright with pain. He'd gone very pale, while his forehead had become beaded with sweat.

Jack staggered, then pitched headlong, crashing to the floor.

Edward and Sadie sprinted to his side. 'What is it? What's wrong?' Edward demanded.

Jack tried to reply, but couldn't.

'I'll call an ambulance,' Sadie said, jumping to her feet. She rushed off to the nearest telephone.

'Hurry!' Edward said, quite unnecessarily.

Jack groaned, and clutched his chest even tighter.

'What's taking them so long!' Erin said angrily, looking yet again at her watch. She'd been at home when Sadie had called and had hurried straight to the hospital.

Edward fidgeted, finding this waiting unbearable.

'Shall I get some more coffee?' Sadie offered.

They both shook their heads, too anxious even to consider her suggestion.

A few minutes later the door opened and Dr McKenzie entered.

'How is he?' Edward demanded.

'A very sick man. Your father has suffered a severe heart attack, Mr Fitzgerald,' McKenzie replied.

'But he'll be OK?'

'Ask me that again in a couple of days' time when I'll have a better idea.'

'Can we see him?' Erin asked.

'That's out of the question, I'm afraid. You'll be able to see him in a couple of days' time when, hopefully, his condition will have stabilized somewhat.'

Sadie took Edward's hand and squeezed it.

'Is there anything further we can do?' Edward enquired.

'Nothing for the moment.'

'Poor Father,' Erin muttered.

They talked to McKenzie for a little longer, then left.

Edward brooded silently during the drive back to Clare. Eventually Sadie spoke, voicing what they were both thinking. 'What happens now?'

'I don't know,' he answered quietly. 'I honestly don't know.'

There was another period of silence, then she said, 'You mustn't blame yourself or feel guilty.'

Edward didn't reply.

Sister Choi came into the ante-room where the family were waiting. Courcy had raced back from university the minute he had heard the news. It was the second day after Jack's heart attack.

'The doctor says you can see Mr Fitzgerald today, but only for a few minutes.'

'His condition has stabilized then?' Edward asked.

Sister Choi nodded. 'We are very pleased with him. He is making good progress.'

A general sigh of relief went up. This was just what they'd wanted to hear.

'There is just one thing,' Sister Choi went on. 'Mr Fitzgerald has given us strict instructions that his son Edward is not to be allowed into his company.'

Edward's face fell. 'Not allowed . . .' he repeated, and trailed off.

Sister Choi stared Edward straight in the eye. 'I'm sorry, but those are his wishes which we have to comply with.'

Edward looked at Sadie, then back at Sister. 'That's OK, I understand.'

'He was most emphatic about that,' Sister said in an apologetic tone.

'You guys go on, I'll wait for you here,' Edward told Sadie, Erin and Courcy.

'I'll stay with you if you want?' Sadie offered.

He shook his head. 'That's not necessary. Besides, you want to see Father and I know he'll want to see you.'

'Are you sure?'

'Yeah, I'm sure.'

Sadie kissed Edward, 'I'll speak to him,' she whispered.

And she did, but to no avail. Jack was adamant. He didn't want either to see or to speak to Edward again unless Edward changed his mind about the RAF.

Sadie stared at Edward sitting morosely in their office holding his head in his hands, deep in thought.

She went over and kissed the top of his head.

Edward, only now aware of her presence, immediately sat up straight. 'How is he?'

'Off the danger list.'

'Thank God for that!'

'I tried again, but he still refuses to see you.'

Edward pulled a face. 'And he won't. Father can be as obstinate as a mule when he wants.'

She sat on a chair by the side of Edward's desk. 'He's still weak, of course, but doing fine. McKenzie himself told me how pleased he was with him. Responding excellently were McKenzie's exact words.'

'Good,' Edward replied.

There was a slight tension between them, so Sadie said, 'We've got to talk.'

'About the wedding?'

'And the RAF.'

'Yeah, I suppose so,' Edward said quietly.

'You still want to go, don't you?'

He nodded. 'I consider it *that* important. The situation hasn't changed over there, after all. But there's Father, and this place. How can I go while he's laid up? Who would manage the business?'

'I could,' she volunteered. 'I'd cope somehow.'

He stared at her. 'I have to admit, the thought had occurred to me.'

'If you're to go, it's the only solution. Providing you think I'm capable, that is.'

'I know you are. I'll have no qualms about leaving the business in your hands. You might find it a little scary to start with, but that will quickly pass.'

Her heart was heavy within her at the thought of not travelling to England with him, after all. 'I'll join you later, when Jack's better,' she said, praying that it would be very soon. Every day parted from Edward would be torment.

'Which leaves the question of marriage,' he said. 'Sadie . . . I mean . . . How can we in the circumstances? It would be completely wrong in my opinion, tasteless.'

Despite herself she had to agree. 'We'll postpone it then?'

'I think that would be best.'

'Till England?'

'Till England,' he nodded.

It would be tasteless, she thought. Even if Jack was off the danger list, he was still extremely sick. And there was no point in asking Edward to wait until Jack was out of hospital, he wanted to go now when, as he saw it, he was needed most.

'I'll make this up to you, I promise,' Edward said.

'How?'

'Well, for starters I could buy you an expensive lunch.'

'And then?'

'Why don't we discuss that over the lunch?'

'Deal,' she declared, rising to her feet.

'Sadie,' he said, taking her in his arms. 'Thank you.'

She felt like crying, instead she smiled.

Sadie, Erin and Courcy all went to the station to see Edward off. Despite pleas from the three of them Jack still steadfastly refused to see Edward before his departure.

'There's the train,' said Courcy, pointing along the track to where a distant speck had appeared.

The dreaded moment of parting had almost arrived, Sadie thought, feeling utterly miserable.

'Oh, here!' exclaimed Erin, remembering what she had in her coat pocket. She pulled out a small parcel and handed it to Edward. 'It's a white silk scarf same as I've seen wartime pilots wear in the movies. I thought you'd like it.'

He kissed her. 'Thanks, sis.'

'I'm going to miss you, Edward. You've always been around, and now . . .' She trailed off as words failed her.

'And I'll miss you.'

Erin grabbed him, held him tight. Then, reluctantly, she released him.

'I'll say *au revoir* also,' Courcy said, offering him a hand.

'Goodbye, Courcy. Work hard and try to lay off the sauce, not to mention women.'

Courcy laughed. 'You and I have had our differences, Edward, but I'm told all brothers do. I wish you the very best and ask God to bring you back safely to us again.'

Edward was touched by that for he and Courcy had never been particularly close. 'Are you sure you don't want to come with me?' he teased.

'Hell, no! I'm a coward. One hundred per cent, chromium plated coward.'

The two men embraced, then Edward turned to Sadie who'd promised herself she wouldn't cry, at least not until he'd gone.

'Well, this is it,' he said.

'I'll attend to your bag,' Courcy told Edward, and moved off a little way, taking Erin with him, to give Edward and Sadie some privacy.

They stared at one another, their last few minutes ticking away as the train hurtled closer and closer.

'You'll write,' she said.

'Often. I swear to that. I'll have a letter ready to post as soon as we dock in Southampton,' he promised her.

'I'll be expecting it. And I'll write the instant I have an address.'

She glanced towards the approaching train, and there it was, just outside the station.

A lump leapt into her throat. And, despite herself, there were tears in her eyes.

'Sadie?' he whispered.

'What?'

'Never forget I love you.'

'I won't.'

'You mean so much to me.'

But not enough to keep you here and stop you from volunteering, she thought. 'And I love you,' she whispered instead.

Somehow she was in Edward's arms, his eager mouth on her responsive one. Then the kiss was over and he was disentangling himself.

'I have to go now,' he said.

'Yes.'

There was one last lingering look between them, then he ran up the steps to the nearest carriage where Courcy had already given his bag to the attendant.

Edward disappeared, then reappeared smiling at a window to wave at them.

They all waved back, and as Sadie waved tears coursed freely down her face.

'Give 'em hell!' Courcy shouted, and punched the air.

Train doors were slamming now, and somewhere a whistle blew. There was a great hiss of steam near them, followed by another further down the train.

Edward blew kisses at Sadie who blew some back. The train then began to move slowly off, taking Edward from her into God alone knew what perils and danger. She wanted to chase after it, but was rooted to the spot. And then it had left the station, gathering speed with every passing second.

Courcy took a deep breath, then turned to Sadie. 'I've got an idea. How about I take you both into town and buy you the biggest ice-cream sundaes sold in Bald Rock?'

Sadie realized he was trying to be kind, and appreciated that. And funnily enough, right now there was nothing she would have liked more.

'Sounds delicious,' Erin enthused.

They were both doing their best to be kind, Sadie thought. 'OK, ice-cream sundaes it is,' she agreed through streaming tears.

Courcy took one of her arms and Erin the other as they left the station and made their way to the car.

'How do you feel this evening?' Sadie asked Jack who was sitting up in bed reading a Jack London novel.

He growled in reply.

'Like that is it?'

'I'd like a Scotch.'

'So would I. Let's go and get one.'

He blinked in amazement.

'I spoke to Dr McKenzie on the telephone this afternoon and he's given me the go-ahead to get you back on your feet. So we're going to go downstairs, together.'

Jack looked uncertain.

'Well, it is what you want, isn't it? To be mobile again.'

'Yeah, of course.'

'Right then.'

She took his robe from the wardrobe and tossed it across the bottom of his bed. She then pulled back the bedclothes. 'OK?'

He laid his book aside and nodded.

She could see how nervous he was, but that was to be expected after his confinement. 'Now don't worry, you can hang on to me,' she said.

He swivelled round, and dropped his feet to the floor. Sadie knelt and helped him into his slippers.

She raised him upright, then helped him into his robe which was a beautiful purple colour. When it was tied she hooked an arm round his. 'We'll just have to be careful on the stairs, that's all,' she said.

He placed one foot in front of the other and tottered. He swore out loud.

'This won't be easy,' she told him.

'I know that!' he muttered crossly in reply.

His illness had been a terrible ordeal for him, Sadie thought, as they slowly made for the door. Jack was a man who liked being up and busy. Lying in bed was anathema to him. It had taken a great deal of energy on her part, and Erin's, who'd been an enormous help, to keep his spirits up. They had a nurse, Miss Tripp, who came in during the day, who was efficient, if somewhat clinical, in her approach.

Jack paused at the door to catch his breath. 'Damn hard work this!' he complained.

'Before you know where you are you'll be leaping about like a ballet dancer.'

Jack threw back his head and roared with laughter at the image that conjured up. 'You're the best tonic there is, Sadie,' he said when he'd finished. 'Just the sight of you cheers me.'

'Thank you, kind sir.'

'You will give me that Scotch now, won't you?'

'A promise is a promise.'

'Then let's go.'

The next day to earn his drink he not only had to walk down to the drawing-room, but also to amble all the way round it.

Within a week he was able to walk without Sadie's assistance.

One day the following April found Jack frowning as he studied Sadie. Preoccupied with his own problems he hadn't realized how thin and haggard she'd become.

'I think it's you who now needs to see a doctor,' he said.

He startled her for an instant, then she smiled, 'I'm fine. Really I am.'

'You look dead beat.'

She ran a hand through her hair. 'Well, I won't pretend life's been easy recently. From morning to night it's just one thing after another.'

'And on top of everything there's the worry about Edward?'

She didn't reply to that.

He made a decision. 'I'm going to restart work on Monday. Give me a few days to pick up the reins again and then you can skedaddle over to England which is where you want to be.'

'Are you sure?' she queried, trying to keep the excitement out of her voice.

'I'm sure. And don't worry, I'll pace myself. I have no intention of overdoing things.'

'You'll have to get the go-ahead from McKenzie first.'

'I know within myself that I'm up to it.'

'I won't go unless you do,' she stated emphatically.

He smiled at her. 'You win, as always. I'll make an appointment to see McKenzie tomorrow.'

She was suddenly filled with happiness, feeling as though a thousand cares and worries had dropped from her shoulders. England! At last! England and Edward.

The following day McKenzie agreed to Jack's return to work, and she began making the necessary bookings and reservations.

Chapter Seven

Sadie stared out the cab window as it wound its way through the busy dock area. Her ship, *TSS Bartholomew*, was berthed at pier eight, but she'd instructed the cabbie to take her to pier twenty-one, the pier she'd disembarked at all those years and heartaches ago, when she'd first arrived from Scotland.

'Here you are, lady,' the cabbie announced, stopping his vehicle alongside a huge stack of wooden boxes, all of which were stencilled with the words '*machine parts*'.

She spotted the sign identifying 'Pier 21' which she recalled vividly from the day of her landing.

'Wait here,' she ordered the cabbie, and got out.

Then, she remembered, an ice-cold wind had been howling, in complete contrast to the present slightly muggy, calm that prevailed.

There was the passageway that they'd passed along *en route* to the high-ceilinged hall over to her right. In that hall they'd been split up into three groups by the man called Schroeder. Faces of those she'd travelled with came flooding back to Sadie, so real it was as though she was actually seeing them. Where were they all now? And how had they fared, that smashing band of pals? Janet was the only one she kept in touch with but, even so, she hadn't ever seen her from that day to this.

She spoke the names out loud, picturing each individual face as it was inscribed on her memory. 'Janet, Fiona, Jean, Elspeth, Kate, Isa, Minnie, Beth . . .' until at last she ran out of names.

She stood there for some while, recalling events and conversations now long in the past.

Eventually, so moved she could hardly speak, she returned to the cab whose driver took her to pier eight and *TSS Bartholomew* which she then boarded.

Early next morning *Bartholomew* left its berth and headed out to sea where it waited until the full convoy had formed.

That afternoon the convoy started its journey across the Atlantic, destination England.

'The Isle of Wight!' an excited passenger cried, pointing to a strip of land that had appeared off *Bartholomew*'s starboard bow.

Excitement surged in Sadie. England! It might not be Scotland, but she felt she was home nonetheless.

They passed the Needles and entered the Solent. It had been an uneventful crossing for which Sadie, and everyone else, was most grateful. Word had it that another convoy travelling in the opposite direction hadn't been so fortunate, three of its ships had been hit by German torpedoes.

They passed Cowes and turned into Southampton Water where several warships rode at anchor. The name of the closest was *Avenger*, Sadie noted, as they steamed on past.

There was a great flurry on board now, passengers and crew hurrying to pack up before they docked. Sadie was content to remain where she was as she had done all her packing prior to coming up on deck.

Southampton itself was now visible, the dock area bustling as the land crew prepared to deal with the incoming convoy bringing much needed foodstuffs and supplies.

Sadie looked up when she heard the drone of an aeroplane, and watched a solitary Lancaster fly overhead. What a beautiful plane, she thought, with a strange elegance for a machine that size.

The business of docking took longer than she'd expected.

But finally, at last, *Bartholomew* was tied up and the gang-planks in place.

Sadie was one of the first down and into Customs and Immigration where she spent a further half-hour before being allowed through. Once released she hurried to the waiting cabs and jumped into one.

'The Excelsior Hotel,' she instructed the cab driver. Jack had recommended the hotel as it had been used previously by friends of his.

As they were leaving the docks she caught sight of a newspaper board carrying the headlines: National Government Formed: Churchill Prime Minister.

So there had been a change of government, she thought, and wondered what implications that carried. From what she knew of Winston Churchill he would prove to be a far stronger and more aggressive leader than the outgoing Chamberlain.

The Hotel Excelsior turned out to be a large, imposing building whose windows, like most others in the city, were heavily taped against bomb attack. The cab driver carried her bag inside where she paid him, adding a generous tip for which he gratefully thanked her.

There was no trouble renting a room, something she'd worried about, and before long she had settled in. There was hot water when she tried the tap, so she promised herself a bath after she'd phoned.

'Could you get me the Red Lion pub in Duxford, please? That's in Cambridgeshire,' she asked the switch-board operator when she came on.

A few minutes later she was talking to Mrs Williams, the Red Lion's landlady.

Sadie spent the night in Southampton, and the next morning travelled up to London where she changed trains, catching another one for Cambridge. On arriving in Cambridge she hired a cab and asked the driver to take her to Duxford.

How different the countryside was here to Canada, so green and lush, she thought, as the cab bowled along. She liked it very much.

'Spits!' the driver said to her over his shoulder, and pointed to the sky.

There were three of them, flying parallel to the road they were travelling along. Sadie knew Edward wouldn't be piloting one of them, he flew Hurricanes.

Duxford was a pleasant village, its houses and cottages quaint. The Red Lion had a thatched roof and a white-and-black timbered exterior. To Sadie it was reminiscent of a fairy-tale. Edward had often mentioned the Red Lion in his letters, which was how she knew about it, but he had never described it.

'Good food at the Red Lion, and a fair pint of bitter,' the cab driver informed her as she got out.

Sadie's first impression was of wood and brass, the latter gleaming. The furniture was composed of settles, high backed and sided wooden chairs, refectory tables, some of the latter with chairs alongside, others with benches. There were old pictures and prints on the wall together with a multitude of horse brasses.

Sadie paid off the driver, then went to the bar behind which stood a middle-aged lady with dyed blonde hair. Several regulars were sitting at the bar, farm-hands by the look of them, who gazed curiously at her.

'I'm Miss Smith. I rang yesterday,' Sadie said to the woman.

The woman's face brightened into a smile. 'I thought that's who you must be. I'm Mrs Williams. Pleased to meet you.'

They shook hands across the bar. Then Mrs Williams said, 'Your room is all ready and waiting. Would you like something here, or do you want to go right up?'

'Right up please.'

'Albert, will you take the lady's case, please,' Mrs

Williams asked one of the farm-hands who immediately slipped from his stool and picked up Sadie's bag.

Sadie followed Mrs Williams into a side passage, and then up some carpeted stairs that creaked. Her room was at the end of the landing.

'Toilet there, bathroom next to it,' Mrs Williams explained, pointing to the relevant doors.

The room was bright and airy, with a friendly, homely atmosphere about it. The double bed was covered in a thick, rust-coloured quilt.

Sadie went straight to the window and gazed out, smiling at what she saw.

'Overlooking the aerodrome as you asked,' Mrs Williams said with a frown, longing to know why Sadie wanted to overlook the aerodrome.

'This is all very nice,' Sadie said, turning from the window and gesturing about her. 'Thank you.'

'And you don't know how long you'll be with us?'

'Some while, I hope.'

Mrs Williams nodded at that. 'Will you be wanting supper? I've prepared a lovely hot pot.'

'That sounds fine.'

Mrs Williams nodded again. 'I'll leave you to it then.'

Sadie took a deep breath as she shut the door, then returned to the window and stared out at the aerodrome where Edward was stationed. She could see several tiny figures moving around inside and her pulse raced to think that one of them might be Edward.

She unpacked after that. Then she decided to go for a walk before supper.

'Going out?' Mrs Williams smiled when she reappeared in the bar.

'Just for a short time.'

'The hot pot will be ready when you return.'

Outside it had started to drizzle, but that didn't bother Sadie who found it refreshing. She walked in the direction of the aerodrome, passing a number of villagers *en route* who all, without exception, said hello to her. It was certainly a friendly place, she thought.

She stopped at the perimeter fence surrounding the aerodrome, then walked along its length until she came in sight of a barred entrance guarded by two RAF policemen.

She retraced her footsteps then, enjoying the walk, and all the new sights and sounds.

Back at the pub Mrs Williams sat her at a table, and placed a hot bread roll and pat of butter beside her. 'Baked that roll myself, and the butter is from a nearby farm,' Mrs Williams informed Sadie.

'They both look lovely,' Sadie replied.

'Call me Ma. Everyone does.'

Sadie smiled. 'OK then, Ma.'

'That's the ticket,' Ma said, and bustled off to fetch the hot pot.

Sadie tasted the roll and butter, both of which were delicious; the butter had a creaminess to it that she wasn't used to.

Ma brought a plate of steaming hot pot to Sadie's table and set it down in front of her. 'I hope you'll find that to your liking,' she said, wiping her hands on her apron.

'I'm sure I will.'

'What about a drink to go with it?'

Sadie thought about that. 'Do you have any cider?'

'We have indeed.'

'Then I'll have a glass of cider, please.'

Sadie took her time over the meal, she was in no hurry after all, finishing up with a nice pot of tea and some cheese and biscuits. She was on her final cup of tea when Ma came over carrying a cup of her own.

'Mind if I join you?' Ma asked.

'Please do.'

'Do you smoke?' Ma queried, offering a packet of Players.

'I don't, thank you.'

Ma lit up, then studied Sadie through a haze that had formed in front of her. 'Are you American?'

'Canadian, by adoption, that is. I was born in Scotland,' Sadie replied.

'And what brings you over here?'

Sadie didn't see why she shouldn't say, it was hardly secret after all. 'To meet up with my fiancé. He's in No. 66 Squadron.'

'Ah!' breathed Ma. The mystery was solved. 'When you asked for a room overlooking the aerodrome I thought it had to be something like that. Knew it wasn't your husband though, you're not wearing a wedding-ring.'

'There would have been if it hadn't been for the war. We were due to get married last December, only Edward decided to join the RAF instead.'

'Would that be Edward Fitzgerald? He's Canadian.'

'Yes. He doesn't know I'm coming, so it'll be a surprise. I know he and his friends come in here most nights, so I thought I'd be sitting here waiting the next time he does.'

Ma laughed. 'Some surprise all right! He's a nice young man, Edward, I like him. There again, most of them are nice young men.'

'Edward often mentions them in his letters, and this pub, of course. He's said repeatedly how much he enjoys it here.'

'They've had some great nights, the lads from No. 12 Group. Singing, drinking, party games, all sorts. They're my best customers.'

Ma paused, then asked, 'When did you arrive in England?'

'Yesterday. I spent the night in Southampton, then came straight up here. I can't wait to see Edward again. It's been about eight months now.'

Eight months at that age was a lifetime, Ma thought. She remembered how much she'd been in love when engaged to Cyril, a love that had lasted until the rat had run off with Polly Elmwhite, a barmaid they'd employed. Last she'd heard the pair of them were managing a pub somewhere in Dorset. Ah well! She had her Harry now. It wasn't exactly love, but a lot better than having no one. And as she'd always told herself, Harry was kind and that went a long way.

'What time do they usually come in?' Sadie enquired.

Ma snapped out of her reverie. 'Never before eight. The first of them normally appear then.'

'Then at eight I'll be sitting waiting,' Sadie said.

'All the way over from Canada in wartime to see your fiancé, that's so romantic!' Ma sighed. She had some champagne in the cellar, good stuff kept for special occasions. Well, to hell with expense, she decided, she was going to give the couple a bottle of it on their reunion.

Edward Fitzgerald's face was going to be a picture, she thought. She mustn't miss the moment when he spotted Sadie.

What shall I wear? Sadie wondered as she went upstairs to change quickly. The trouble was she hadn't brought much with her, not wanting to be encumbered by luggage.

She considered her wardrobe, but nothing seemed quite right. Her navy blue skirt was a great favourite, but would it seem too formal? There was always the new cream linen fitted suit which she'd never worn, but Sadie felt that was too dressy. Alternatively she could wear her pink floral dress with its fitted bodice and scooped neckline. That might do, she thought.

Or there again . . .

The clock behind the bar finally struck eight.

Sadie was as nervous as the proverbial cat on a hot

tin-roof. She'd been to the lavatory four times in the last hour, and now she needed to go again.

No, I don't, she told herself. It was all in the imagination. Grit your teeth and bear it, she thought.

She glanced over at the bar and there was Ma smiling at her, which she followed with a wink.

A few minutes later the door opened and two airmen came in, the pair of them laughing raucously. They ordered pints of bitter, and proceeded to chat with Ma who'd served them.

The door opened again, this time to admit a group of locals. When they'd been attended to they sat at a table adjacent to Sadie's.

Another airman came in, followed by another, and three directly after that. These joined the first two, all of them standing or sitting at the bar.

Sadie had a sip of her gin and tonic. She was so keyed up with excitement she felt like an overwound spring. Without realizing she was doing so she kept touching and patting her hair.

More airmen came in and were greeted loudly by those already present. When they'd been served some of them went over to a dartboard in a corner and started up a game.

When it reached a quarter past eight, Sadie began playing a game of her own, that the next person through the door would be Edward. Again and again she was disappointed as the pub rapidly filled.

Half-past eight found her with an empty glass, contemplating having another drink. The trouble was she didn't want to be up at the bar when Edward arrived, but sitting to the side, out of the way. She'd hang on, she decided, she didn't really need another drink anyway.

Just before a quarter to nine a whole gang of airmen came bursting in, but Edward wasn't one of them.

A ginger-haired airman smiled at her, which she pointedly ignored. With a shrug he carried on the conversation he was already involved in.

Ma came over carrying another gin and tonic. 'Have this on the house,' she said, placing it before Sadie and collecting up the empty glass. 'How do you feel?'

Sadie made a face. 'Where is he?'

Ma looked at the door, thinking this might be one of the nights when he didn't come in, and hoped that wasn't the case. How cruel for Sadie if it was.

'Pecker up! He'll be along,' Ma said confidently, and retreated behind the bar where her Harry was trying to keep up with the demand to be served.

There was a roar from the area surrounding the dartboard, as someone had won. That was followed by loud cries of, 'It's your turn to get them in, Julian!'

At nine o'clock some of the airmen began to leave, shouting 'Goodbye!' and 'See you tomorrow!' as they went.

Quarter past nine became half-past, and then a quarter to ten. When the clock behind the bar struck the hour Sadie knew Edward wasn't going to show up that night.

She'd hang on anyway, she thought, and did until Ma called last orders. Then she rose to go upstairs. 'Tough luck,' sympathized Ma, coming up to her as she was about to climb the stairs. 'But he's bound to be in tomorrow night. You could still phone the 'drome you know, and tell him you're here.'

Sadie considered that, then shook her head. 'I've been planning this surprise for so long it would be a shame to spoil it now. No, I'll wait until tomorrow night and try again then.'

'Is there anything you'd like? A cup of tea, or a sandwich?'

'No, thank you, Ma.'

'How about another drink? I can serve you as you're stopping here.'

'I won't bother with that either.'

'Right then. See you at breakfast, luv.'

'Damn!' Sadie swore when she was in her bedroom. 'Damn! Damn! Damn!'

She had a terrible night's sleep, tossing and turning and waking up every half hour or so.

When morning dawned, and it was time to get up, she felt utterly exhausted, as if she hadn't been to bed at all.

The bar clock tinged eight.

Here we go again, Sadie thought. She wasn't as nervous as she'd been the previous night, as she had spent the day preparing herself for another disappointing evening.

She thought of the planes she'd watched that day, a great many of them coming and going from the 'drome. She'd seen two flights of Hurricanes take off which had brought her heart into her mouth. Had Edward been flying one of them? She must ask him. All six Hurricanes, much to her relief, had returned safely.

She glanced again at the evening paper lying in front of her. The war was going badly for Britain and her Allies. It was now almost certain that Holland would fall while the gallant Belgian army was taking an awful hammering.

The solitary ray of sunshine was Churchill, the general image he projected was as a reborn King Arthur back to save England in her time of peril.

The first airmen arrived, the same two who'd been first the previous evening. They again went up to the bar, ordered pints of bitter and engaged Ma in conversation.

Then some of the darts players appeared, a threesome followed by another threesome, and soon a game was in progress.

An old man with only one arm came in, ordered a bottle of brown ale and went off into a corner to drink it.

Quarter past eight became half-past and Sadie began to experience an awful sinking feeling. Was this going to be a repeat of the night before? Surely not!

A crowd of airmen came in together, all laughing, joking and larking among themselves. Two young women were next, and they joined the darts players whom they evidently knew.

Quarter to nine came round, then the hour. Sadie stared morosely into her glass thinking that her big surprise was turning out to be a resounding flop. It looked like she was going to have to telephone the 'drome after all.

At ten past nine, with the pub in full swing, the door opened once more and in strolled the ginger-haired airman who'd smiled at her the previous night and with him . . .

Her spirits leapt to see that face she knew so well, and which she'd missed so much. Edward had arrived at long last.

'Two pints of best and a brandy, please, Ma,' Edward said to Mrs Williams, wondering why she had such an odd expression on her face. 'Are you all right?'

'I'm fine,' Ma replied, her smile one of secret knowledge. 'And you?'

'Never better.'

'Is that a small brandy or a large?'

Edward frowned, puzzled. Ma knew perfectly well he always drank small measures. 'Small, please,' he answered.

'Are you sure about that?'

What was going on? 'Perfectly.' And why was she now smiling like some goddamn cat who'd just swallowed a bowl of cream and the family goldfish?

'Suit yourself,' Ma said, placing the pints before them.

383

Edward paid for his drinks, and sipped his bitter. Then he continued talking with Charlie Benson who flew in the same flight as him.

Sadie finished her drink, then rose and walked over to stand behind Edward. 'Excuse me, can I get to the bar?' she said.

He moved. 'Certainly. There you . . .' The words caught in his mouth which then fell open.

Sadie smiled. 'Buy a girl a drink?'

Ma chuckled to herself. Edward's expression was even better than she'd anticipated. That alone was well worth a bottle of champagne.

'Sadie!' Edward croaked, unable to believe his eyes.

'In person.'

'But . . . but . . .' He swallowed. 'What are *you* doing here?'

She laughed, thoroughly enjoying herself. 'I came to see you. What else?'

'Jesus Christ!' he swore, and flung his arms round her.

'I take it you two know one another?' a bemused Charlie Benson said.

'Know one another. This is my fiancée from Bald Rock Falls!' Edward explained.

Other people had stopped to stare, some smiling, some whispering among themselves.

'This is just . . . incredible! I'm asleep and this is a dream, it has to be,' Edward said.

Sadie's reply was to tenderly kiss him on the lips. 'Now that's no dream, is it?' she declared.

There was a pop! and a champagne cork flew across the pub. 'This is on me,' Ma said, pouring champagne into two glasses she'd set on the bar.

'It's my fiancée from Canada!' Edward yelled to those watching and listening.

'I wanted it to be a surprise,' Sadie said to him.

'It sure as hell is that all right. I'm . . .'

384

Sadie laughed again, feeling euphoric, as did Edward.

'A toast to the reunited couple!' Ma proposed, waving a tot of whisky in the air.

Edward and Sadie each took a glass of champagne, and toasted one another. Then the whole pub erupted into a spontaneous cheer.

'Let's go and sit by ourselves, shall we?' Sadie suggested.

'Yes.' Turning to Charlie he said, 'Excuse me, won't you?'

'Of course,' Charlie smiled. 'And if I may say so, Edward, you have impeccable taste in women.'

'Thank you, kind sir,' Sadie responded.

'Nothing kind about it. It's the truth.'

'Thanks, Ma,' Sadie said, indicating the champagne bottle. She had been moved by the landlady's generous gesture.

'My pleasure, luv. My pleasure entirely.' .

Edward picked up the bottle and followed Sadie back to the table where she'd been sitting.

'I'm stunned,' he stated as they sat. 'I mean . . . you just appeared like a genie out of a bottle.'

Sadie liked the image that conjured up. 'You've lost weight,' she said, thinking how much thinner his face was. 'Don't they feed you well?'

'The food isn't bad. Not what I'm used to mind, but palatable enough. But how did you get here?'

She then launched into a detailed account of the last eight months, how desperately lonely she had been at Clare without him, but how preoccupied she had been both with Jack and the everyday running of the mill. Edward was delighted to hear that his father was so much better and was touched that he had suggested that now he was back at work, it was high time Sadie followed Edward to England.

'How is Father? Has he forgiven me yet?'

'He's OK, but I wouldn't say he's forgiven you.

You must know how much you mean to him. He is still devastated by your leaving.'

Edward's face hardened. 'I'm doing the right thing, Sadie. I'm in no doubt whatever about that.'

Sadie then told him all about her crossing aboard TSS *Bartholomew* and that she'd arrived in Southampton two days previously.

'It's so good to see you,' he said, clasping her hand and squeezing it. 'I want you to know I've missed you every bit as much as you've missed me.'

They both glanced up as six airmen stopped at their table.

'Come on Edward lad, introduce us to your fiancée,' one of them requested.

Edward stood. 'Sadie, this is Nick Marston whom I've mentioned in my letters.'

Nick pumped Sadie's hand. 'Don't believe a word of what he's said, I'm sure it was all a terrible exaggeration.'

Sadie laughed. 'He spoke highly of you actually. In fact, he spoke highly of all his friends. A "top-hole bunch" he called you.'

'She's a stunner. I envy you, Edward,' another airman said, grinning at Sadie.

'And this is Jeremy Passmore-Thomas. A Blundell's man, as he's forever telling us,' Edward said.

Sadie shook with Jeremy. 'What's Blundell's?' she queried.

'A public school in Devon, mentioned by Blackmore in *Lorna Doone*,' Jeremy informed her.

Sadie was then introduced to the rest of the chaps. Two of them, Rupert Griffiths and 'Miffy' Moxon, kissed her on the cheek.

'Now, can you guys please leave us alone? We've got a lot to catch up on,' Edward pleaded at last.

'Trust you to want to hog her to yourself,' Jeremy complained.

'Well, she is my fiancée, after all!' Edward retorted.

'Couldn't you share her just a little? I mean, she is such a corker,' Nick said.

'There will be no sharing, and that's that!' Edward replied, feigning outrage.

'Pity!' Nick muttered.

'All right, come on you shower, let's give these two lovebirds a chance,' Rupert said. 'Last back to the bar buys the next round!'

There was a stampede to the bar where it fell to Miffy to pick up the tab.

'They're all great guys. Stand by you through thick and thin,' Edward smiled to Sadie now they were alone once more.

'It's obvious how fond you are of them. And they of you.'

'We're all close in No. 66, it's that sort of squadron.'

He reached out and grasped her hand. 'God, it's good to be with you again. I still really haven't taken it on board that you're actually here and not still in Bald Rock Falls. How is the old place?'

'More or less the same.'

She twisted her hand, and squeezed his. 'Everyone sends their love, and they're all looking forward to the day when you return.'

He smiled to hear that. 'How long have I got you for?'

'I don't know, I didn't put a time limit on my visit. I suppose it all depends.'

'So I might have you here for some while?'

'You might,' she smiled. 'If that's what you want.'

'You know it is, Sadie.'

They gazed into one another's eyes, she acutely aware of the electricity sparking between them.

'I love you,' he whispered.

'I love you,' she whispered in return.

'Now tell me everything that you didn't find space

for in your letters. Doesn't matter what, I want to hear everything regardless of how trivial.'

Sadie laughed. 'I hardly know where to begin. But let me see now . . .'

Edward listened enthralled, occasionally asking a question which Sadie answered to the best of her ability.

The time flew by, and all too soon Ma was calling last orders.

'Where are you staying?' Edward queried, realizing he didn't know even that yet.

'Here, at the pub. Ma's rented me an exceptionally nice room.'

'I'll come and see you tomorrow. I've got the day off because our planes have been called in for a full maintenance.'

'So we can spend the whole day together!' she exclaimed.

'Yes, you couldn't have timed things better. I'll call for you about ten, OK?'

'I'll be ready.'

He then had a thought. 'Tell you what, there's some nice countryside round here. If the weather's nice why don't we have a picnic?'

'Sounds terrific. But where will I get a picnic?'

'Ask Ma to make us one, of course. I'm sure she will.'

'I'll do that then.'

The people were leaving the pub now, the numbers dwindling with every passing second.

'I wish I could kiss you.'

'You'll have plenty of opportunity to do that tomorrow. You're just going to have to wait.'

They both rose. 'Goodbye for now.'

'Goodbye.'

Then, not giving a damn who saw, he pecked her on the lips and then he strode from the pub without looking back.

Sadie felt quite weak inside, and deliriously happy. She couldn't have been more pleased.

'I'll be delighted to,' Ma replied when Sadie asked if she'd make them a picnic. 'Any preference?'

'None I can think of.'

'Right, leave it to me,' Ma beamed.

'And thanks again for the champagne.'

'Don't mention it.'

Sadie made her way to the bed where, in complete contrast to the night before, she slept like a log, dreaming of her and Edward together.

The day dawned bright and clear, the sky a pale blue dotted with fluffballs. After a hot bath, Sadie went down to breakfast which that morning she had with Ma. Ma was full of questions about Canada and Bald Rock Falls, listening sombre faced when Sadie told her about her childhood, and life with the Trikhardts.

After breakfast Ma excused herself and went off to make up the picnic, and Sadie went to buy a newspaper. The main story was that the Dutch Queen, Wilhelmina, had arrived in London having fled from her own country.

Edward arrived promptly at ten to find Sadie sitting patiently waiting for him.

'The picnic,' Sadie declared, indicating a lidded wicker basket standing on the table beside her.

'Oh, good-o! I'll go and pay for it.'

Sadie smiled to hear him say good-o, he sounded just like an Englishman. 'Don't worry about that, I've told her to put it on my bill.'

'But I should pay,' Edward protested.

'In a way you will. Jack gave me a considerable amount of money before I left to take care of expenses. He was anxious that I came.'

'That's OK then.'

Edward picked up the basket and they both shouted to Ma in the rear that they were off.

'Where do you have in mind?' Sadie asked when they got outside.

'A little secluded creek I know that isn't far away. We can drive there,' Edward replied, pointing at a car parked by the kerb.

The Morris was old, and dented in several places. By no stretch of the imagination could it ever have been called a thing of beauty.

'Not exactly the Cord, is it?' she smiled.

'It's reliable, and easy on the gas. Besides which, I like it.'

Sadie got into the front passenger seat, and was immediately aware of how much smaller the car was than the saloons she was used to. There was something about it, though, that she found appealing. It had a distinctive personality of its own, she decided.

The Morris started up without any trouble, and they were off. They chatted as they drove, and every so often, unable to help herself, Sadie reached out and touched Edward.

'Here we are!' he announced a short time later, drawing the car into the side of a country lane. Sadie hopped out, and before long Edward was guiding her across rough grass on to a narrow path that eventually brought them out on to the bank of a meandering stream.

'And how did you find this place? Not with some other female, I hope?' Sadie teased.

'It was Jeremy who brought me here, actually. It's an ace creek for trout fishing,' Edward replied with a smile. 'I've tried it on several occasions using Jeremy's rods which he's kindly said I can borrow at any time.'

They found a grassy knoll which was quite dry, and sat down. Sadie gazed at a weeping willow, some of whose drooping branches almost touched the stream, and thought how idyllic a spot it was.

'How about that kiss now?' Edward asked softly.

She turned her face to him, sighing as his lips met hers. This was what she'd dreamt about during those long months of parting, being in Edward's arms again.

They kissed and kissed, and continued kissing, neither wanting to break contact with the other.

Sadie closed her eyes as he gently stroked first one cheek, then the other. She sighed again when he kissed the tip of her nose, and each eyelid in turn.

'Oh Sadie!' he murmured, clasping her face with both hands.

She opened her eyes and smiled at him.

She took his hands, and brought them down into her lap. 'I did all the talking last night. Now it's your turn. How's the war been for you these last few weeks?'

'Same as before. Nothing much happening. We fly out, go through our paces as the CO calls it, then fly back. What we're waiting for, what the whole country's waiting for, is the big offensive that's bound to come. We all know it's going to happen, the only question is when.'

'And then it's war for real?'

'Very much so.'

A shiver of fear ran through her. Fear for him, Edward, the man she loved. 'And nobody has any idea when this offensive will take place?'

He shook his head. 'The Nazis continue to surge forward, rolling up everything and everyone in their path. Some optimists among the British and French still hope to hold them in France, but the realists, of which I'm one, know there isn't a snowball's chance in hell of that.'

'And you'll be in the thick of it?'

'Bound to be. Germany has to win the air before it can cross the Channel, and that's where Britain's fate, for now anyway, will be decided.'

Edward picked a blade of grass and tied it in a knot which he then pulled tight. 'Ever heard the word blitzkrieg?'

Sadie shook her head.

'Well, blitz means lightning and krieg war. Lightning war. It's a surprise and swift method of attack that the Nazis have so far used with devastating effect. That's how they'll attack Britain, and when they do the RAF will be waiting for them.'

'Is there any chance they'll beat you and win the war in the air?' Sadie asked softly.

'Let me put it this way, they have far more aeroplanes than us, but we have the Spitfire and the Hurricane which are better than anything they've got. That difference in performance could tip the balance in our favour. All we can do is fight like fury and pray to God.'

A mood of melancholia had descended on them. They both sat staring into the slowly moving water, lost in their own thoughts. Eventually it was Sadie who roused herself.

'Does a cup of tea and a sandwich appeal?' she asked.

'Good idea.'

'There are some bottles of beer here, would you prefer one of them?' Sadie queried on opening the picnic basket which was crammed full. Ma had certainly done them proud.

'Please. And can I make one request?'

'Sure.'

'Let's not talk about the war any more?'

'OK,' she smiled.

A few minutes later he had her laughing, and soon he was, too. The war wasn't mentioned between them again that day.

The moment Edward entered the pub Sadie knew from his face that something had happened.

'What is it?' she asked as he sank into the chair beside her.

'Jeremy's dead.'

She caught her breath. 'Dead? What happened?'

'Simple really. I suppose any of us could have done it. During some low flying he flew into a cloud only to discover, too late, that the damn thing was sitting on top of a hill.'

Edward shook his head. 'The weather here is what makes flying in this country so incredibly hazardous. It's completely different to what we were used to in Canada. You can be up for an hour and during that time experience everything from blazing sunshine to snow.'

Sadie thought of Jeremy Passmore-Thomas who'd grinned at her, and who was now dead.

'The first fatality in our squadron,' Edward said. 'Good old Jeremy, the Blundell's man. We're going to miss him.'

And he wouldn't be the only fatality either before all this was over, Sadie thought grimly. And she prayed fervently that Edward wouldn't be one of them.

'Can I get you a drink?' she asked.

'No, I'd rather have a walk.'

'I'll get my coat,' she said.

When Sadie returned she found Edward surrounded by some of the other chaps, Nick Marston, Rupert Griffiths and Miffy Moxon, all sunk in gloom and talking about Jeremy.

Edward made his apologies when he saw Sadie, then rose and came across to her.

'Terrible,' Ma said to them from behind the bar, Miffy having told her what had happened.

'Yes,' Edward agreed.

He took Sadie's arm, and they left the pub, wandering aimlessly around.

They walked in silence for a while, then Edward said, 'I'd give anything to be able to go to bed with you right now.'

'I can't take you back to my room in the pub,' Sadie replied quietly. 'Ma would certainly find out, and I just don't want that.'

'I understand. It's a pity though.'

Sadie thought so too. But self-respect refused to let her use her room at the pub.

After a while they returned to the Red Lion where they joined in what had become a wake for Jeremy.

Jeremy Passmore-Thomas, the Blundell's man, deceased.

'Rent a cottage!' Ma exclaimed.

'Do you think you could help me?' Sadie asked.

Ma resumed polishing a glass. 'I don't know. I'll have to think.'

'There's nothing wrong with my room here, it's just that it now seems to me that my own place would be preferable.'

Ma put the glass away, and started on another. Of course Sadie was right, pub rooms were fine as far as they went, but over a period they did leave a lot to be desired. Especially, and here she smiled inwardly, when the young lady in question had a fiancé who was as desperately in love with her as Edward obviously was.

'There isn't much comes up in Duxford. People tend to stay put round here,' Ma said.

'There must be something, surely?'

Ma's brow creased in thought.

Harry popped his head round the corner. 'I'm just going out for a few minutes. I'll bottle up when I get back. All right?'

'Make sure it is only a few minutes. It's not long till opening time,' Ma retorted. 'And where are you going anyway?'

She got no answer to the latter, Harry having already fled. 'Men, honestly!' she exclaimed in annoyance. Then, softening, 'But what would we do without them, eh?'

'A cottage, or house, or anything self-contained,' Sadie said, bringing Ma back to the subject under discussion.

'Wait a minute!' Ma said, stopping polishing. 'There

is a cottage available. Though not in Duxford, but a few miles out. It's on Fred Lowe's farm and was rented to old Mrs Sumsion until she died last year. As far as I know it's still lying vacant. I certainly haven't heard of it being let again.'

'What's it like, have you been inside?' Sadie asked eagerly.

'I haven't been inside, but would imagine it was fairly basic, which means an outside convenience.'

Sadie shrugged that aside, she wasn't in the position to be choosy. 'Does this Fred Lowe come in here?' she asked.

'Occasionally, but only that. He isn't much of a drinker. Would you like me to telephone him and set up an appointment for you to see the cottage?'

'Please!' Sadie exclaimed, clapping her hands.

Ma glanced at the clock behind the bar. 'No point in doing it now as he'll be with his cows. Dinnertime would be our best bet. I'll telephone him then.'

'Do you know how big it is?' Sadie queried.

'A kitchen, bedroom and parlour would be all, I should think. You'll have to furnish it, of course, but I could help you there. So that wouldn't be a problem.'

'When you do ring would you ask if I can view it this afternoon?' Sadie requested.

Ma laughed at her impatience, but knew the reason for it. 'I'll do that,' she agreed.

The appointment was made for four o'clock that afternoon.

Fred Lowe was waiting for Sadie and Ma when they arrived at Sweetbriar Cottage having walked the two miles there from Duxford. Fred was in his mid-fifties with broad shoulders, powerful-looking arms and a typical weather-beaten countryman's face. He shook hands with both of them, having eyed Sadie suspiciously up and down, then ushered them inside.

Basic was the right word for the cottage. There was no gas, or electricity and the convenience *was* outside. It was also damp, Sadie thought, sniffing the air. Perhaps it just smelt that way because it had been unoccupied for so long. The cottage was empty except for a double bed in the bedroom.

'Did Mrs Sumsion die on that?' Sadie asked, indicating the bed.

Fred's eyes twinkled, and for a moment he considered pulling the posh young lady's leg, then decided against it. 'No, she didn't. She was outside when she keeled over and expired there and then.'

That was a relief, Sadie thought. The bed, apparently clean and certainly comfortable, could stay.

'Now about rent,' said Fred, and named a sum that brought an instant rebuke from Ma.

'You're a highway-robber, Fred Lowe. My friend will have none of your cottage at that price!' Ma declared.

He pulled a face. 'It's a fair rent. A man's got to show a profit, after all.'

'Fair, my backside. Now name a proper sum or we're on our way. There is another cottage available,' she lied.

'Another cottage? Whose? Where?' Fred demanded, now flustered.

Ma tapped her nose. 'That's for us to know and you to find out. Well?'

Fred dropped the rent to one that met with Ma's approval.

Ma turned to Sadie. 'What we haven't asked yet is whether you want it or not?'

'I do,' Sadie stated emphatically. The cottage left a lot to be desired, but she would do her best to make it into a comfortable home.

'Done then,' said Fred, who then spat on his right hand and extended it to Sadie.

A smiling Sadie, not in the least perturbed by a spat-on hand, shook hands with him.

'Done!' she agreed.

'I love it,' smiled Edward, having been given the conducted tour of Sweetbriar Cottage. 'But you're going to need transport living out here. I'll give you the car.'

'And what about you?' Sadie queried.

'There are plenty of bicycles round the 'drome. I can always use one of those.'

'Then I accept the car.'

'Which I give you on one condition.'

'Which is?'

He smiled mysteriously and took her hand. She knew right away what the condition was when he pulled her towards the bedroom.

'I just hope Mr Lowe doesn't pass by and decide to look in the window,' Sadie said as they undressed.

'He'll get a shock if he does.'

To their delight the bed creaked loudly which they both thought extremely funny.

Sadie arrived at the Red Lion for a bath, a facility Ma had kindly offered when she moved into the cottage, and which she'd gratefully accepted, to find Ma, Harry and several locals grouped round a wireless on the bar. Ma put a finger to her lips and beckoned her over.

'This is the BBC Home Service, here is the news,' the announcer said. 'In the House of Commons this afternoon the Prime Minister Mr Churchill said, "What General Vegas called the Battle of France is over, the Battle of Britain is about to begin . . ." '

When the news was finished, Harry switched off the set. 'I don't know about anyone else, but I'm having a large rum,' he said.

Ma nodded. 'Me too. Only make mine whisky.'

The Battle of Britain, Sadie thought. The offensive that Edward had talked about had finally arrived with the Fall of France.

'How about you?' a pale-faced Ma asked Sadie. 'Gin and tonic?'

'Please,' Sadie replied weakly. 'And I'll have a large one, too.'

When she picked up her glass she found that her hands were trembling.

'Here's to the Royal Air Force, and especially the chaps who come in here,' Harry toasted.

They all drank to that. But in Sadie's case it was to one of those chaps in particular, Edward.

Sadie was in the garden one afternoon weeding when Edward came cycling up. She immediately stopped what she was doing and rose to greet him.

'Got some time off then?' she said. He normally visited her in the evening.

'Yeah, a couple of hours. So I thought I'd spend them with you.'

'How are things at the 'drome?'

He shrugged. 'Quiet as usual. It's the squadrons down south who are seeing all the action.'

'How bad is it down there?'

'They're holding out, but just. The 'dromes are taking a hell of a pounding. On our side we're knocking them out of the sky, but still they keep on coming.'

'I've got a bottle of beer inside, would you like some?'

'Yeah, that would be nice.'

'I'll get it for you then.'

He caught her, and pulled her into his arms. 'What about a kiss first?'

She kissed him, still finding it thrilling.

'I'll come with you,' he said when the kiss was over. Hand in hand they strolled towards the cottage.

398

'You've done a remarkable job in such a short time,' he stated when they were inside. The interior of the cottage was totally transformed from an empty shell to a cosy, inviting home.

'I could never have accomplished half of it without Ma's help, she's been a true friend,' Sadie replied.

'Ma may have helped by lending you things, but you put it all together in your own personal way. And that's what makes it special.'

Sadie found the beer, unscrewed the top and hunted out a glass.

'Great,' he said when she handed him both glass and bottle.

Edward sat down, and Sadie started arranging some flowers she'd brought in earlier.

'They're pretty,' Edward commented, nodding at the flowers she was dealing with.

'Aren't they just! I'm told that all around here is covered in daffodils in the spring. I would like to see that.'

'Maybe you will.'

She glanced at him. She hadn't set a date for returning to Canada, it had been left completely open-ended and was, in fact, something they hadn't even discussed.

Edward sipped his drink, thinking how different it tasted to the beer in Canada. He'd never thought he'd get to like English beer, but now he was actually quite partial to it.

'I heard on the radio that the Luftwaffe has started bombing London,' Sadie said.

Edward nodded. 'At night-times only though.'

She heard something in his voice which made her look up. 'Is that significant?'

'Oh, yes. If only they'd do it during the day then they'd come within reach of 12 Group.'

'Which would mean you getting involved,' she stated, biting her lip.

'I didn't come over here to sit on my ass drinking beer!' he retorted hotly. Then he instantly regretted it.

'I'm sorry,' he apologized.

'It's all right. I fully understand your feelings. But you must also understand mine. The last thing I want is for you to get hurt, or worse.'

'Unfortunately people do in war,' he said quietly, staring into his glass, and seeing Jeremy Passmore-Thomas's face gazing back at him.

'Yes,' she agreed, just as quietly.

That night London was again bombed by the largest number of enemy aircraft yet.

The next day's newspapers reported that the devastation had been terrible, but that the Londoners remained in good heart.

One front page carried the picture of a young mother and son looking defiantly up at the sky. 'London Pride' was the caption.

Sadie was driving into Duxford to do some shopping and to call into the Red Lion for a chat with Ma when the first of the aeroplanes appeared from Duxford aerodrome heading south. The Spitfires led, followed closely by the Hurricanes.

Sadie stopped the car and stared up at the passing planes, counting the flights as they passed overhead. She soon realized this was no ordinary sortie, but something big, for the numbers she counted told her that every plane in the 'drome must have taken off.

When she reached the pub Ma greeted her with the news that for the first time London was being bombed in daylight.

Now Sadie knew where the planes, and Edward, were heading. London.

Edward banked his plane and brought the ME 109 into his sights. A quick burst and the 109 was trailing smoke.

He didn't wait to watch the 109 go down, but twisted out of the way in search of further quarry.

His stomach was tight with fear, the breath rasping in his throat. Yet at the same time he was exhilarated beyond belief.

A Heinkel loomed up and he raked that along its fuselage. Moments later the Heinkel burst into flames, and almost immediately its crew began to bale out.

Then a scream came over the r/t, followed by a choking crying, 'I'm going,' a voice he didn't recognize said. 'I'm go. . .' And that was that.

And still the aerial ballet continued, a macabre and magnificent dance of death during which both sides strove to dominate the other.

Sadie sat waiting patiently for Edward to arrive. Some nights he didn't come, being too exhausted to cycle to the cottage.

She heard his bicycle and rushed to open the door. He looked absolutely ghastly, she thought, as he slumped into an easy chair.

'Cup of tea?' she offered.

'Anything stronger?'

She brought out the bottle of brandy she'd got from Ma and poured him a large tot.

He downed the tot in one gulp and held out the glass for a refill.

'We lost Rupert today,' he said.

She handed him his refill. 'How?'

'He was concentrating on a Dornier and didn't see a 109 line up on him. His plane blew up.'

Edward knocked back the second tot, clearly devastated.

That was three of the chaps now gone, Sadie thought. Jeremy, Nick Marston who'd been killed on 12 Group's first day over London, and now Rupert.

Edward laid the empty glass on the floor, leant back

and closed his eyes. 'The more we knock down, the more seem to come. It's as if they have an inexhaustible supply of planes and pilots.'

'How about the Poles?' Sadie asked. He'd mentioned the Polish Squadron during his last visit.

'They're doing well, far better than anyone expected. They do chatter a lot on the r/t, but fight like lions. Their second squadron has been made operational, and a squadron of Czechs. Dowding's throwing everything at the Jerries that he can get aloft.'

'But they still keep coming,' she said, paraphrasing his words.

Edward nodded. 'They still keep coming,' he repeated.

She went and knelt beside him. 'Is there anything else I can get you?'

'No, just to be here with you is enough. That's all I want. To be with you.'

She took his hand and held it to her cheek. She was still holding it when his head lolled sideways and he began to snore.

When she heard the bicycle Sadie made for the door expecting it to be Edward. But it wasn't, it was Ma.

As soon as Ma stepped into the light and she saw the expression on Ma's face she knew why Ma had come. 'Edward?'

'Charlie Benson rang the pub and asked me to break the news.' She paused, then said sorrowfully, 'Edward was shot down this afternoon I'm afraid. Miffy saw it happen and Charlie saw him explode.'

Sadie didn't realize it, but she was grinning fatuously. 'There's no doubt then?'

Ma shook her head.

Edward dead, gone for ever. She'd never kiss him again, they'd never make love again together. Never . . . Never anything together again. She became dimly aware that Ma was speaking.

'What, Ma?'

'Why don't you sit down and I'll put the kettle on. I brought over some whisky if you'd like?'

'No . . . no whisky. And no tea either.'

'I'll stay with you as long as you wish. Harry's looking after the pub.'

Sadie found she was washing her hands, and stopped. Quite distinctly, as though he was there with them, she heard Edward laughing, the laughter ringing in her head like a peal of bells.

Edward dead. Of course she'd known it could happen, and had been prepared for it. Now, she realized she hadn't been prepared at all for the simple reason she hadn't believed it would actually happen. Others might die, but not Edward. He would survive. Only he hadn't.

'I'm so sorry. You know that,' Ma said.

'Yes. Thank you.'

'He was a fine young man. But there again, they all are. And terribly brave. Which is what you're going to have to be now.'

She would sit down, Sadie decided. It was as though time had somehow stopped, while everything, her thoughts, Ma's speech, Ma's movements, were in slow motion.

She would have to write to Jack which was going to be dreadfully difficult. What could she say? What words were there? None at all.

Edward! She wanted to open her mouth, throw back her head and shriek as loudly as she could, until she could shriek no more.

What was Ma saying now? Where were the glasses kept? Ma intended having a whisky.

'In there,' she replied, pointing.

'Are you sure you won't?' Ma queried, waggling a half-bottle at her.

'No, no, thank you.' She was certain that if she'd had some whisky she would have been sick.

And then somehow, she found herself sitting by the

range with Ma facing her, Ma's expression one of anxious concern.

'You don't have to stay, Ma. I'll be all right, honest,' she said.

Ma frowned, uncertain whether or not to believe her.

Sadie stood up. 'I assure you I'll be OK. In fact, if you don't mind I'd prefer to be on my own.'

Ma rose. 'I'll do whatever you wish, Sadie.'

'Thank you for coming, Ma. I was telling Edward only recently what . . .' She smiled ruefully, then continued, 'What a true friend you've been.'

'I'll leave the bottle, just in case,' Ma said.

'You take it with you. I have some brandy in the house if I feel the need.'

Ma crossed to where the half-bottle was standing and slipped it into her handbag. 'I'll pop by again in the morning to see how you are. You may want some company then.'

Sadie nodded.

'I'll let myself out, there's no need for you to bother.'

Ma went to Sadie and hugged her. 'I'm so sorry. So very, very sorry,' she husked.

Sadie sat down again when Ma had gone, and stared vacantly into space reliving memories of her and Edward. The day of the twister when they first met, his teaching her to fly, Erin's engagement Ball when she'd worn the black velvet gown and the scarlet ribbons he'd bought her in her hair.

It was late, well past midnight, when she finally roused herself and went to bed.

The tears came in the middle of the night, a night during which she hadn't slept a wink. She'd lain in bed staring out of the window, visualizing Edward's plane plunging earthwards in flames, and then blowing up in mid-air.

Again and again the scene was repeated, while she wondered what his last seconds had been like. Had he been conscious? Better if he hadn't. But if he had, had he thought of her?

'Oh, Edward,' she whispered as tears streamed down her face. 'Oh, my darling, my love.'

Yet again the plane plunged earthwards, and blew up in mid-air.

Two nights later there was the roar of a motor bike outside the cottage followed by a frenzied pounding on the door.

'I'm coming! I'm coming!' Sadie called out irritably as she hurried to answer it. She didn't look at all well. Her skin was pale, there were dark smudges under her eyes, while her cheeks had become sunken. Her hair was pulled back and pinned. It also needed washing, something she hadn't been able to bring herself to do.

It was Miffy, his face ablaze with excitement. 'Edward's alive!' he blurted out the moment she opened the door. 'The sod is alive and in St Thomas's Hospital in London.'

Sadie gaped at him. 'Alive?'

'He managed to bale out before the explosion, which none of us saw. And apparently there was some kind of mix-up in the hospital which is why the squadron has only now been notified that he's alive.'

Sadie heaved a sigh of relief. Alive! Edward was alive! 'There's no mistake?'

'No mistake,' Miffy confirmed. 'I raced out on the old motor bike to let you know as soon as I could.'

Sadie's thoughts were whirling. She had to go and see him, right away. She'd pack a bag and take the car, drive through the night.

'What about petrol?' Miffy queried when she told him what she planned.

'I have plenty here thanks to Edward. I'll put several cans in the trunk which together with a full tank should get me there and back. I've also got a number of coupons if I need to buy some more.'

'Do you know where St Thomas's is?'

'No, but I'll find it. Don't you worry about that.'

Then, with an exclamation of delight and relief, Sadie threw her arms round Miffy and kissed him solidly on the cheek. 'Thank you, thank you, thank you!'

'I've got a London A-Z in one of my motor-bike panniers, you can take that with you,' Miffy said when Sadie had disentangled herself.

'A-Z?'

He explained to her what that was and she agreed it would undoubtedly be a big help. She began to think what she might need to take with her while Miffy went out to fetch it.

How long would she be in London? She had no idea. It seemed better to pack more rather than less.

Miffy returned with a battered A-Z, showed Sadie how to use it and where St Thomas's was located. He also gave her a road-map and marked out the route to London. 'Is there anything else I can do to help?' he asked when he'd done that.

'Nothing, thank you.'

'Then I'll be on my way. Give Edward my, and everyone else's, regards.'

'I'll do that,' she promised, ushering him to the door.

She packed her bag in double quick time, and stowed it in the boot of the car. Then, working by lamplight, she topped up the Morris's tank after which she put two large cans of petrol in the boot alongside her bag.

She went back into the cottage and wondered if there was anything else she should do? She turned out all the lamps, then locked the door behind her. The car started straight away, and she was off.

It was a difficult drive because of the blackout and her headlamps being partially masked, so it took far longer than it would have done during the day. It would have made more sense for her to have waited until morning before leaving, but sense had nothing to do with how she felt. All that mattered was that she was on her way to Edward, an Edward miraculously alive when she'd thought him dead.

She skirted round Saffron Walden and headed for Bishop's Stortford. The next town she passed through was Harlow, beyond which she eventually came in sight of London.

The sky above the capital was fiery red in places, orange in others. It was as if a doorway had been opened allowing you a view into hell, she thought.

As she got closer she heard the explosion of German bombs, interspersed with the distinctive crack of ack-ack.

Searchlights scoured the heavens, occasionally picking out a German plane passing overhead. One such plane got hit by ack-ack and Sadie watched with satisfaction as it tumbled out of the sky.

She entered the outskirts of London to find the streets eerily deserted. She drove for a while, then drew over and consulted Miffy's *A-Z*. She was in Walthamstow she discovered, and from there plotted a course to Hackney and then Islington.

There was a lot of noise now, the sound of exploding bombs not all that far away. She pulled over to allow a fire-engine to go past. A policeman waved her down and told her she couldn't continue along the road as several houses had been hit, the rubble from which was completely blocking the street.

She backtracked, and then tried again, this time managing to get through Hackney into Islington. There she stopped again and consulted the *A-Z*.

There was a loud explosion near by, the force of which caused her head to go flying forward and smack against the steering-wheel. Small pieces of debris rattled against the car's roof while no more than six feet in front of her a standard lamp went crashing to the ground.

She wiped her face with her hand, relieved to find there was no trace of blood. She'd have a nasty bruise come morning, but the skin hadn't broken.

When she heard a whistling noise she ducked down, closing her eyes and gritting her teeth when that explosion, even louder than the last, went off.

She was getting out of there, she thought, engaging the car's gears. She shot away, speeding down the road for a half-mile or so before slowing to a more reasonable pace.

Because it was night the German planes were having it more or less their own way. Well, it wouldn't be like that when day broke bringing RAF fighters with it, she thought. Then the enemy would be given a dose of their own medicine.

Holborn was a shambles, rubble and holes everywhere. After several thwarted attempts she finally found a way that took her down to Aldwych and Waterloo Bridge.

Crossing the bridge gave her a panoramic view of London in the Blitz. It was a sight she knew she'd never forget.

Coming off the bridge she turned right into York Road which led into Lambeth Palace Road, and a few minutes later she was drawing into St Thomas's Hospital. Dawn was breaking as she climbed, thoroughly exhausted, from the car.

Sadie passed through Casualty where a great many people were waiting to be seen, all hurt in some way during the night's bombing. A trolley was hurriedly pushed past her by two elderly porters, one of whom was holding a transfusion bottle above the victim's head.

There was a very tired-looking man on Reception who listened patiently while Sadie explained why she'd come.

'Pilot Officer Edward Fitzgerald,' the man mused, consulting a sheaf of papers. He removed his glasses, rubbed his rheumy eyes, put the glasses back on again, and once more consulted the papers.

'I have an M. Fitzgerald, that wouldn't be him, I suppose?'

Sadie shook her head. 'His initials are E. J., Edward John.'

The man sighed, and continued his search.

'Got you!' he exclaimed with a smile at last. 'Pilot Officer E. J. Fitzgerald.'

'That's him,' Sadie acknowledged excitedly.

The man told her which ward Edward was on, and how to find it. She left Reception almost at a run.

'You can't see him till after breakfast, I'm afraid,' the night Sister said, having heard Sadie's request. 'It just wouldn't be fair on the other patients. Besides which, whatever the circumstances, Matron would have my guts for garters if I let you in now.'

Sadie's shoulders slumped in disappointment. 'Are you sure . . .?'

'Yes. I really am sorry,' the sister interjected firmly.

Sadie glanced at the glass-panelled doors beyond which was the darkened ward. 'So when is breakfast?'

'Seven thirty.'

She glanced at her wrist-watch, it wasn't that long to wait. 'Is there a seat somewhere?' she asked.

'Come with me.'

The Sister led Sadie out into the corridor where she pointed out a metal chair that had been pushed back into a small recess. 'It's the best I can do, because our normal benches have been appropriated for something or other,' she apologized.

'Thank you very much. This will do fine.'

The Sister left Sadie then, reappearing about ten minutes later with a cup of tea for which Sadie thanked her profusely.

When she'd drunk the tea she laid the cup and saucer on the floor by her chair, then settled down to pass the time. It positively dragged by, every second seeming a minute, every minute an hour. She forced herself to be patient, knowing there was nothing else for it.

The rattle of plates and chinking of cutlery announced the arrival of breakfast, which was brought to the ward on a wooden trolley propelled by a middle-aged woman.

The trolley disappeared into the ward to be followed by several young nurses who appeared from a nearby stairway.

Sadie yawned, and wondered where she could find a lavatory. She enquired of a passing porter who directed her to one not far away. As she passed the ward doors she looked in thinking she might spot Edward. But she was unlucky.

She was just sitting down on the metal chair again when Matron came striding out of the ward towards her.

'Miss Smith?'

Fiercesome, but kindly underneath. She might be a martinet but she has a heart, Sadie thought. 'That's me,' she replied, rising.

'You are Pilot Officer Fitzgerald's fiancée who's driven down from Cambridgeshire to see him?'

'I left the moment I heard he was alive. We all believed he'd been killed, you see.'

Matron's face softened. 'Yes, there was a bit of a muddle there, I'm afraid, our fault entirely. I can only say we've been under enormous pressure since the Blitz started, pressure that in certain instances has caused problems.'

'I understand,' Sadie smiled.

'Normal visiting hours aren't for some while yet, but you may go in now.'

Sadie's face lit up. 'Thank you very much.'

'You may tell the Pilot Officer that there will be a doctor along directly.'

Sadie nodded. 'I'll do that.'

Matron strode away and Sadie hurried to the ward

where she found Sister waiting for her. 'He's up on the left,' Sister smiled.

In the ward the breakfast things were being cleared away, and beds remade. Several cleaners were also polishing the floor.

Edward was sitting up in bed reading a book that so absorbed him he didn't notice her approach.

'Sadie!' he exclaimed, when he saw her.

She kissed him on the cheek, and wished it had been his mouth, having resisted kissing him there because of those watching.

Emotion welled up inside her, and tears crept into her eyes. 'We all thought you were dead,' she stated.

'Who? Me?' he joked. 'It'll take more than that to kill me.'

She indicated his bandaged shoulder. 'What happened there?'

'A bullet which thankfully passed straight through. It's put me out of action for a time though. I was concussed, though I can't quite remember when.' Then, in a completely different tone. 'What I do know is that I'm a very lucky man to be alive.'

'Nobody saw you bale out,' she told him.

'That's all a haze of confusion. I recall the plane being hit, then battling flames as I tried to get out, and the next thing I was on the ground with an ARP warden bending over me.'

'How's your concussion now?' she queried.

'A lot better than it was. I had one hell of a headache that has deteriorated to a muzziness which will hopefully disappear within the next few days.'

Love for him swelled within her. She wanted to take him in her arms and hold him close, to rain kisses on him, to lose her temper with him for causing her so much grief, to . . . to do a thousand and one things as a sign of her love.

'How did you get here?' he asked.

'I drove down overnight. The squadron was only notified yesterday evening that you were still alive, and Miffy kindly came to tell me as soon as he could.'

'Good old Miffy.' Edward smiled.

'I know you've described to me what was happening in London, but it was still something of a shock and eye-opener to see it for myself.'

'Yes,' he said. 'Last night was particularly bad. If anything the raids are intensifying.'

'You'll be out of it now, for a while at least,' she smiled, thinking how pleased and relieved she was about that.

They continued talking, and were still doing so when Sister entered the ward with a doctor.

'Oh, the doctor's here to see you,' Sadie said, remembering what Matron had told her.

'And how are you today, Pilot Officer?' the doctor enquired on reaching Edward's bed.

'OK, doc.'

'How's the shoulder?'

'Easier than yesterday.'

The doctor nodded. 'I think I'll have a look if you don't mind.'

Sister glanced around, caught the attention of a staff nurse, and beckoned her over.

'Do you wish me to go?' Sadie asked.

The doctor, somewhere in his late twenties, gave Sadie an appraising look. 'You're the fiancée that Matron mentioned, I take it?'

'Yes,' she replied.

'Are you Canadian too?'

'By adoption. I was born in Scotland, but I went to Canada as a child.'

'Interesting country. I'd like to go there one day.'

Staff and another nurse completed manoeuvring screens round Edward's bed which was what the doctor had been waiting for.

He turned his attention again to Edward. 'Let's have a look and see, shall we?'

Sister slipped Edward's pyjama top to one side and began undoing his bandage. She then peeled away the dressing underneath.

The doctor murmured his approval as he peered at the wound. 'I would say that is coming along very nicely indeed.'

'How long before I can be discharged?' Edward asked.

'What about your head?'

Edward repeated what he'd told Sadie.

'There's an MO at your aerodrome, I presume?'

'Oh, yes.'

The doctor nodded. 'And you drove down last night, I understand?' he said, addressing Sadie.

'Yes.'

'Then I don't see why Pilot Officer Fitzgerald can't be discharged and accompany you back up to Cambridge-shire. Normally I would have kept him in longer, but to be truthful we desperately need the bed.'

'So I can go today!' Edward exclaimed jubilantly.

'Just as soon as that wound has a fresh dressing put on it and is rebandaged. The thing to do is present yourself to the MO as soon as you get back, and he'll take it from there.'

'That's tremendous,' Edward beamed, looking at Sadie who couldn't have been more pleased.

The doctor and Sister left them, and a few minutes later they were joined by the same staff nurse who'd put the screens round who brought a fresh dressing and bandage with her.

'Going home then?' Staff smiled as she worked on Edward's shoulder.

'That's it,' Edward replied, thinking about not the 'drome but about Sadie's cottage. When he glanced at Sadie he knew from her expression she was thinking the same.

'There,' said Staff when she was finished, which co-incided with another nurse appearing, carrying Edward's uniform and laundered underclothes.

Edward stared at his uniform which was burnt and scorched in places. 'What about my flying suit?' he queried.

'That wasn't salvageable,' the nurse replied.

Edward looked at a grim-faced Sadie. 'As I said, I'm a very lucky man to be alive.'

Sadie shivered as she realized how close a call it had been.

'Would you care to wait in the corridor while the Pilot Officer gets dressed,' Staff requested of Sadie.

Out in the corridor Sadie touched the part of her forehead that had smacked against the steering-wheel and winced. A bruise couldn't be showing yet, she thought, otherwise someone would have commented.

Staff came out with another cup of tea. 'To keep you going,' she said, comfortingly.

Sadie was just thanking Staff when a plane droned low overhead. A few moments later there was an explosion which drew in a nearby window, and caused Sadie's cup to rattle in its saucer.

God, she was tired, Sadie thought. But she wasn't going to linger in London any longer than was absolutely necessary. The sooner she and Edward were away from here, the better. With planes dropping out of the sky not even hospitals were safe.

She didn't have long to wait before Edward emerged from the ward, smiling when he saw her.

'How do you feel now?' she asked.

'Dizzy. But I didn't tell them that in case they changed their minds. It's being on my feet again, I suppose. I'm sure it'll soon pass off.'

'Let's get to the car so you can sit down. Do you want me to take your good arm?'

'Please.'

They walked slowly, Edward having to stop once when his head started to spin. He sighed with relief when they reached the Morris.

'Dorniers,' he said, pointing up at the sky.

Off to their right a wave of these black planes was passing overhead. Evil-looking machines, Sadie thought. She could have cheered when a flight of Spits zoomed into view to fall upon the Dorniers.

'I wish I was up there,' Edward said quietly.

Sadie glanced at him. She didn't.

Sadie left London by the same route she'd used coming in, proud with herself that she managed it without any problem. She only relaxed when the capital was finally behind them.

'You must be whacked,' Edward said sympathetically.

She grinned at him. 'Why? Do you want to drive?'

'I wish I could,' he smiled in reply.

She *was* exhausted, and suddenly ravenous. She suggested stopping at a pub somewhere along the way, and that was exactly what they did. When they got back on the road again Sadie felt refreshed.

On reaching Duxford she drove to the 'drome where Edward got out. 'I'll meet you in the Red Lion at seven this evening by which time I should know what's happening,' he told her.

'Seven. I'll be there.'

'And Sadie, thanks for coming to London for me.'

'Wild horses wouldn't have kept me away once I knew you were alive.'

He bent into the car and kissed her on the lips, a kiss that exhilarated her.

'Till later,' he said.

'Till later,' she repeated.

He watched her drive off, and waited till she'd disappeared before going into the 'drome.

Arriving at the cottage Sadie parked the car and went inside where she slumped into a chair. Tiredness over whelmed her, an overpowering tiredness that made her eyelids droop.

Forcing herself to get up again she threw off her clothes, put on a nightie and tumbled into bed.

Within seconds she was asleep, a sleep in which she dreamt that Edward was in bed beside her.

'Well, that's that then,' Harry said as Ma switched off the wireless standing on the bar. 'Seems the Battle of Britain is over with our lot the victors.'

A cheer went up, after which a great deal of hand-shaking and back slapping took place.

Edward gazed about him and thought of those now dead. Jeremy, Nick, Rupert, 'Boy' Somerville, Tommy Baker, Ian Moresby, and others, some close friends, all comrades. And then he thought of how close he'd come to being numbered among them.

'OK?' Sadie queried, touching his good arm.

'Yeah, just thinking that's all.'

Sadie guessed what he was thinking, and why he was suddenly so sombre. The same thought had gone through her head.

'Let's sit down,' she suggested.

'What do you imagine will happen next regarding the war?' she asked when they were settled.

He made a face. 'I don't know. The Germans will continue to expand their conquests, I suppose, carving up what they can with the Italians. As for Britain, at this point that's very hard to say. Another Battle of Britain perhaps at a later date. As I told you before, the Nazis have to win the air before they can cross the Channel.'

Charlie Benson came in and waved, but didn't join them, presuming correctly that they wanted to be left alone. He, too, had been shot down, but had been fished out of the Channel unscathed.

'What did the MO say to you today?' Sadie asked.

'That my wound is healing just fine.'

'Do you think you're fit enough to go on a trip? And if you are, would the MO allow you to do so?'

Edward regarded her quizzically. 'What sort of trip do you have in mind?'

'I'd like to go to Scotland, not for long, simply a few days. But it seems ridiculous coming all this way and not going. Besides which I am dying to know what became of my family.'

Edward considered this. 'I'm up to the trip all right, as to whether or not the MO would sanction it, that's another thing. But I think he might.'

He paused, then went on, 'How would you contact your family?'

'I've given that some thought, and it seems to me the only way I could would be through the first Barnardo's Home I went to, the one called Babies Castle. I don't have its address, but the Barnardo's HQ must.'

'It's definitely worth a try,' Edward nodded. 'Why don't we find out where that HQ is and write to them.'

Sadie sipped her drink, and tried to imagine a reunion with her family. What would they be like? And what would they think of her? Would they even remember her?

'I'll start making enquiries tomorrow,' she said.

When Sadie saw the sign she pulled the car over so that she could gaze at it. 'Scotland', the sign proclaimed, she was about to return to her homeland. The thought gave her goose pimples.

'Return of the native,' Edward said, and smiled.

'After a long time,' she qualified.

Seconds later they crossed the border.

What a hard, grey city it was, Sadie thought, staring out of her hotel window. Hard and grey, yet somehow friendly, which she found reassuring.

'Come in!' she called out when there was a knock on the door.

It was Edward. 'How's your bedroom?' he asked, glancing about. 'Mine's OK.' They had considered booking in as Pilot Officer and Mrs Fitzgerald, then decided against it. Instead they'd booked two separate double rooms which meant that Edward could still spend the night with Sadie.

'I've no complaints,' she answered.

He looked into her bathroom, noting that it was larger than his, then went over and kissed her.

He glanced at his wrist-watch. 'We've been apart a full fifteen minutes and I missed you during every one of them.'

She smiled. 'And I missed you.'

He kissed her again. 'I thought we'd have dinner downstairs, then go and catch a show. There's one called *Swing of the Kilt* that's been recommended to me.'

She had to laugh at that, how Scottish could you get. *Swing of the Kilt*! It sounded perfect. 'I only hope we can understand it. I find their accents very broad,' she replied.

'Och hoots the noo, lassie!'

She laughed again, and this time kissed him.

'We've got time before dinner if you'd like?' he suggested, voice suddenly husky.

'Time for what?' she teased, knowing full well what he meant.

'You know,' he replied, playing along with her.

'Know what?'

'A little bit of . . .' He winked at her.

'Are you *sure* we've got time?' she further teased.

'Positive.'

It transpired they were so late for dinner they almost didn't get served. As for the show, although what was said on stage was mostly unintelligible, they nonetheless still found it hysterically funny.

'Do you remember it?' Edward asked.

Sadie stared at the large sandstone building situated

418

within its own grounds. 'Vaguely,' she murmured in reply. 'I have a feeling of *déjà vu*, as if I'm seeing something out of a long forgotten dream.'

She continued staring at the building, and seemed to recall looking at it with an older woman from almost the same place. Older woman? That would have to have been her mother. Was her memory real or imagined? She didn't know.

She tried to visualize her mother's face, but couldn't. A blur remained where the face should have been.

'Doesn't look like a castle,' Sadie mused, and again something jangled in her brain.

They drove through some lovely gardens, still immaculately maintained despite the war, and parked in front of the building's main entrance. As they climbed from the car a young woman dressed in a uniform similar to a nurse's appeared to greet them.

'Miss Smith?' the young woman queried.

'Yes.'

'Please come with me, Matron is expecting you.'

They passed a number of happy looking children as they followed the young woman. There was a good atmosphere about the Home, Sadie thought, smiling at two little girls walking along hand in hand.

They were shown into a small waiting-room where they were asked if they'd like a cup of tea.

'Nervous?' Edward asked when the young woman had left them.

'What do you think? This is my only hope of finding my family. If they can't, or won't, help me, then I'm sunk.'

Edward held up two crossed fingers. He was about to speak again when the door opened and another young woman entered. 'If you would come this way, Miss Smith, Matron is anxious to see you.'

Sadie glanced at Edward. Matron anxious to see her! Why should that be?

'I'd like my fiancé to accompany me. Is that all right?' Sadie asked the young woman.

'Of course.'

The young woman led them to a brightly lit office where Matron was sitting behind a desk. Matron immediately rose to stare at Sadie, her eyes shining.

Sadie gazed back with the realization she knew the matron. Then, with a shock, the penny dropped. 'Miss Tupper!' she exclaimed, 'Is it really you?'

Matron came round from behind the desk and warmly embraced Sadie. 'Sadie Smith!' she said, shaking her head. 'Sadie Smith!'

Matron held Sadie at arm's length. 'Here let me look at you. My, what a change, what a transformation.'

'Miss Tupper,' Sadie repeated, quite bemused at meeting up again with this woman she'd once regarded as a second mother. 'But Matron's name is Gore?'

'Gore is my married name,' Matron explained.

Sadie remembered Edward's presence. 'This is Pilot Officer Fitzgerald, my fiancé,' she said, introducing Edward.

'How do you do?' Edward enquired politely, shaking hands with Matron.

'Very well, thank you.' Then she turned back to Sadie, having noted Edward's accent. 'You mentioned in your letter that you'd returned from Canada, but not that you'd brought a fiancé with you.'

'I didn't bring him,' Sadie replied. 'Rather I came back to join him, as Edward had already signed up with the RAF.'

'I understand,' Matron nodded.

'We were on the brink of getting married in Canada when war broke out. Now marriage will have to wait till afterwards I'm afraid.'

Matron ushered them to chairs, waiting till they'd sat down before saying eagerly, 'Now tell me what's happened since leaving here, Sadie. I want to know everything.' To Edward she added, 'Sadie was always very special to me. We're not supposed to have favourites, but I just couldn't help it as far as she was concerned. I missed her dreadfully after she'd gone.'

Sadie smiled thinly, and began with the day she left Babies Castle. An appalled Matron listened as she related the time she'd spent with the Trikhardts.

'My God!' Matron whispered, putting a hand to her mouth. 'They really treated you like that?'

'Slave labour,' Sadie said. 'That's what Robbie and I were. Slave labour.'

'How awful,' Matron murmured.

'But then my circumstances took a decided turn for the better when the tornado struck, for that was when I met Edward.'

Sadie continued her story, bringing it right up to the point where she'd travelled to Duxford to be close to Edward, and finishing by explaining why she'd come to Babies Castle.

'I have your file here,' Matron said, opening a drawer in her desk and taking out a buff-coloured folder. 'I had it looked out after I received your letter.'

'So can you help me?' Sadie asked.

'It's against our rules for me to give you any information regarding your family. But in this case I'm going to break those rules, providing you promise never to divulge to anyone that I did.'

'You have my word,' Sadie said.

Matron opened the folder, glanced at a form on top of the contents, then wrote an address on to a pad.

She tore the top sheet off the pad, and handed it to her. 'That was your parents' address when you were committed here. It may be that someone in your family still lives there, or if they don't neighbours may know of their whereabouts.'

Sadie stared at the address, and as she did a huge lump came into her throat. 'Thank you,' she said quietly.

'It's the least I can do after what you've told me.' Matron shook her head. 'I feel in some way personally responsible for what has happened to you, as though it was somehow my fault.'

'How could it possibly be that?' Sadie smiled. 'My years here were marvellous because of you. You had no way of knowing what lay in store for me after I left here.'

'No matter. As I am part of the organization that foisted you on to those odious Trikhardts, some of the responsibility has to be mine.'

'No, Matron, you acted then, as I'm sure you still do, in complete good faith. The blame for what happened to me lies not on your shoulders but elsewhere.'

'I agree with Sadie,' Edward stated. 'You have nothing either to feel guilty or ashamed about. On the contrary, from what Sadie has said you have everything to be proud of, loving and caring for her as you did when she was in your charge.'

Matron bit her lip. 'I shall still write a report and send it to head office. This must be looked into. I shall insist on that.'

'But tell me about you now,' Sadie said. 'When did you get married?'

Matron's expression changed to one of sadness. 'I met Ronald through a course I went on, and we married shortly afterwards. In the event we only had three years together before he died of a brain tumour.'

'I am sorry,' Sadie said softly.

'At least we had three glorious years, during which I didn't work. After Ronald's death, I came back here and was made Matron when the previous one retired.'

They chatted for a while longer, Sadie and Edward taking tea with Matron, then it was time to go. Matron insisted that she accompany them to their car.

It was a tearful farewell, the former Miss Tupper kissing Sadie on both cheeks, and embracing her.

'I hope you find your family,' Matron said. 'God go with you, Sadie. I'll remember you always.'

'A nice woman,' Edward commented as they drove away.

Sadie stared down at the address she'd been given, which had never left her hand. What was she going to find there? Anything? Nothing?

They returned to the hotel to make enquiries about the address. Then they set out again after lunch.

It was a mean street, the tenements lining either side, old, grey and thoroughly wretched looking. Many had been daubed with chalked graffiti.

'What was the number again?' Edward asked.

Sadie consulted her piece of paper, then told him.

'Further along,' he said.

They parked the car outside the relevant close, and got out. When she reached the close mouth, Sadie wrinkled her nose, the smell emanating from within a combination of boiled cabbage and stale, human odour.

Sadie stepped into the close and, with Edward by her side, walked along it. They came to a flight of stone stairs which they went up studying all the nameplates on the doors they passed.

On the third landing the first door they came to said 'Smith'. Sadie's heart leapt into her mouth when she saw it.

'Well,' Edward murmured, looking at her.

'It could be another family with the same name,' Sadie said.

'Could be,' he agreed. 'The only way to find out if it's your family is to knock on the door and ask.'

Sadie stared at the brass nameplate which was old and scratched in several places. It certainly appeared to have been there for a long time.

She cleared her throat, struggled to control her nerves, then reached out and knocked. When there was no reply she knocked again.

'Seems there's no one at home,' Edward said after she'd knocked a third time.

Sadie knocked yet again, with the same result. 'Definitely out,' she declared, bitterly disappointed.

'Let's come back after dinner. Hopefully there will be someone in then.'

He took her by the arm and they started back down the stairs. They stopped at the window on the half-landing directly below and stared out.

'Not very pretty, is it?' Sadie said. She glanced up at him and smiled. 'I'm glad you're with me. I'd hate to be doing this on my own.'

'Moral support, eh?'

'Something like that.'

'Shall I tell you a secret?'

'What's that?'

He bent and whispered in her ear. 'I love you.'

She laughed. 'That isn't a secret. And I love you too.'

They continued down the stairs and out to where they had parked the car.

Edward looked at his watch. 'Half past seven, we should make a move,' he said. They were in a pub near the tenement block. It was a rough pub, but friendly nonetheless. Sadie was the only female present.

Sadie knocked back her whisky. 'I suppose we had,' she agreed.

'Nervous again?'

She nodded. 'I've got a stomachful of butterflies.'

'Understandable in the circumstances,' he sympathized, placing a comforting hand over one of hers.

He finished his drink, and stood up. Sadie followed suit. 'Goodbye,' he called out to the barman who gave them a wave in return.

They drove the short distance in silence and parked in the same spot as before.

A fat woman wearing a scarf tied round her head gave them a curious look as they passed her in the close. They climbed the stairs till they arrived once more in front of the door bearing the Smith nameplate.

'Good luck,' Edward smiled at Sadie.

She knocked, and moments later the door was opened by a slim, pale-faced woman whom Sadie judged to be in her late-twenties. A sister? Then she saw the wedding-ring.

'Does a Mr Smith live here?' Sadie asked.

The woman's gaze went from Sadie to Edward, and back again to Sadie. 'Aye,' she replied.

'Is he in?'

The woman nodded.

'Do you think I could speak to him, please?'

'Who will I say wants him?'

'Miss Smith.'

The woman frowned, then said, 'Wait here then.'

'It could still be another family with the same name,' Sadie said quietly to Edward, when the woman had vanished from sight. But in her heart of hearts she didn't believe it.

The man was slim like his wife and had a receding hairline. Sadie saw the resemblance straight away.

'Can I help you?' the man asked.

'I'm Sadie,' she said, her voice suddenly tight and husky.

'Sadie?'

'Sadie Smith. I think you might be my brother.'

Incredulity swamped his face. 'Sadie!' he whispered. 'Jesus bloody Christ.'

'Which brother are you?' she queried, tears now in her eyes.

'I'm Ken, the oldest. You were the youngest.'

'Hello,' she smiled, and stuck out a hand.

He took the hand, started to shake it, then pulled her into his arms and hugged her. 'Sadie,' he repeated. 'Sadie!'

425

The wife reappeared to stare at them, clearly wondering what was going on. 'Beth!' he cried out. 'This is my wee sister, Sadie, the one I've told you about.'

Beth came forward to smile tentatively at Sadie. 'He's often talked about you. The wee sister his ma gave away.'

'This is my fiancé, Pilot Officer Edward Fitzgerald,' Sadie said, gesturing at Edward.

'How do you do?' Ken beamed, letting Sadie go and pumping Edward's good hand. 'Been wounded, I see.'

'In the Battle of Britain,' Sadie proudly informed her newly-found brother. 'Edward flies Hurricanes.'

'A hero, eh?'

Edward coloured. 'Hardly that,' he protested.

'But listen, we can't stand talking here. Come away inside.' As Ken closed the door behind them he instructed Beth, 'Go and put the kettle on, hen.'

'There are so many questions,' Ken said to Sadie as he escorted them into the flat's kitchen, the only other room being a bedroom. 'For a start, why do you speak like a Yank?'

It wasn't the first time that mistake had been made, she thought.

'My accent isn't American but Canadian,' she explained. 'And that's because I was brought up there. I spent some years in the Home Mother put me into, then shortly after leaving there I was shipped over to Canada where I've been ever since.'

A little girl was sitting on a pouffe staring in awe at Edward, while an older boy was on the floor in front of the cavity bed playing with a box of lead soldiers.

'Canada!' Ken mused, shaking his head. 'Well, I never.'

'You might introduce me,' Beth, having now filled and put the kettle on, admonished him.

'Oh aye, of course. I'm sorry, it's just that I don't know whether I'm coming or going. This is so unexpected, completely out the blue. We never expected to hear from you again, Sadie, we thought you quite lost to us. Anyway, Sadie, I'd like you to meet my wife, Beth.'

The two women exchanged pleasantries, then Sadie was introduced to the little girl who was called Sandra and the boy whose name was William.

'Sit down, the pair of you,' Ken said, indicating a pair of easy chairs in front of the range.

'I'd like to stand for now, and just look around me,' Sadie replied.

'Certainly, if that's what you want. Will you sit, sir?'

Edward smiled. 'The name's Edward, and yes I will, thank you.'

Sadie stared at the cavity bed which she now vaguely remembered.

'This was the room you slept in, on a made-up sofa,' Ken said quietly. 'Ma and Da slept in that cavity bed, while the rest of us were in a pair of beds through in the other room. You were born with a bad hip and couldn't walk.'

'The Home arranged for me to be operated on, which was completely successful, as you can see.'

'You look fine, Sadie. I was thirteen and already working when Ma took you away. She cried for days afterwards, and repeated over and over again to anyone who'd listen that she'd done it for your own good. How much do you actually remember of everything?'

'Very little. I was only four, don't forget.'

Beth extracted a tin from a cupboard and opened it. 'William, have you been at the biscuits again!' she exclaimed angrily.

'I only had one, Ma. That's all there was,' William protested.

'I'm awfully sorry,' Beth apologized to Sadie. 'I'm

427

afraid you've caught us short, no biscuits, teabread or cake in the house to offer you. If only we'd known you were coming.'

'That's all right,' smiled Sadie. 'I understand.'

'It's a bit embarrassing though,' Beth persisted.

'It really doesn't matter,' Sadie reassured her. 'A cup of tea will be lovely.'

'Did you know Da was dying, and that was why Ma did what she did?' Ken went on.

'The situation was fully explained to me at the Home. How long did Da live for after my departure?'

'I can't remember the precise details now,' Ken replied. 'But Ma was pregnant and miscarried late into the pregnancy. Da passed away the following week.'

Ken sighed. 'The day Da died was a truly awful one. I've never seen a woman so distraught as Ma. The two of them were very much in love.'

'There's that photo you can show Sadie,' Beth suggested.

'Oh aye!' Ken exclaimed. 'I'll get it for you.' And with that he hurried from the room.

'It's their wedding photograph,' Beth said. 'One of those old brown things, but you can make them out well enough.'

Ken returned with the metal-framed photograph which he handed to an eager Sadie. 'That's them right after the ceremony. It was a church "do" as you can see, Ma married in white.'

The faces staring out at Sadie were those of two strangers. Her mother had been beautiful she noted, her father striking rather than handsome.

'What were their names? I've forgotten,' she asked.

'Ken and Louise. I was called after him and always got "young" Ken until his death.'

Louise, a pretty name she thought. 'What about my other brothers and sisters? Tell me about them.'

'Well, you'd better sit for that,' Ken said, and again indicated the empty easy chair.

After Sadie had sat down Ken did likewise on one of the wooden chairs surrounding the table. He'd no sooner done that than Sandra went to him and climbed up on to his knee.

'A real daddy's girl,' Ken said, stroking her hair.

'How old is she?' Sadie asked.

'Four. The same age as you when . . .' He broke off and smiled thinly. 'William is seven, a big boy. Aren't you, son?'

William nodded shyly.

'Both good children I'm happy to say,' Ken added.

Beth started to lay out cups and saucers, and wondered if any of the neighbours would have biscuits she could borrow. She decided against asking them, thinking that would be even more humiliating having already admitted to Sadie and Edward that they had nothing in.

'Anyway, back to the family,' Ken said to Sadie. 'As I've already told you I was the oldest, Tom came after me, Lena next, then Ian, Bill, Morag and finally you. Seven of us in all. Or . . .' and here his face clouded over, 'there were seven.'

'How do you mean?' Sadie asked softly.

'Before you went to the Home, Ian was sent to live with Auntie Joyce and Uncle Bobby, Morag to Uncle John and Auntie Liz. You were the third and last to go. Being farmed out as it were could well have saved Ian and Morag's lives, same with you in being sent to the Home.'

Sadie frowned. 'I don't understand.'

But Edward, listening grim faced, did. He could see what was coming.

Ken continued. 'TB, you may or may not be aware, is a communicable disease. Bill caught it, and Lena. Both died within a year of Father.'

That rocked Sadie. 'Was Bill the one who used to play a lot with me? I have dim recollections of him.'

Ken nodded. 'That's right. Bill was very fond of you.

We all were, you understand, but you and Bill were particularly close.'

Beth filled the teapot and set it aside for a few moments to steep. How sad Sadie looked, she thought, and how like Ken. There was no mistaking they were brother and sister.

'What about Ma?' Sadie asked.

'She soldiered on for a few years after Da, three to be exact. It was amazing that she never succumbed to TB, considering that she slept alongside Da up until the day of his death. But incredibly she didn't. She died of a heart attack.'

'How old was she then?' Sadie queried.

'Thirty-six, and looked fifty-six. I distinctly remember Dr McLeod saying it wasn't really a heart attack that killed Ma, but a bloody hard life full of pain and anguish that simply wore her out in the end.'

'Thirty-six,' Sadie repeated. How young that seemed! 'And how old was my father when he died?'

'Thirty-five.'

'Many died young round here,' Beth chipped in. 'And still do.'

Beth poured the tea. 'Sugar and milk, Sadie? And what about you, Edward?'

They both stated their preferences, then William piped up, 'Can I have tea too please, Ma?'

'Of course you can, son.'

'And me!' Sandra said.

'So what happened after Mom died?' Sadie asked.

'There was only Tom and I in the house then, and by that time, he too, was working. We managed to scrape by.'

'And where's Tom now?'

Ken smiled. 'Married also and living about a mile from here. He's an electrician in a shipyard which makes him exempt from being called up same as myself.'

'And what do you do?'

'I'm employed in a factory that was changed over to making munitions right at the beginning of the war. A few of the men have been released for the Forces, but because the work load is fairly heavy, they've retained most of the men.'

'So I can meet Tom then!' Sadie exclaimed excitedly, accepting the cup of tea Beth handed her.

'Oh aye, and Morag too. She's still single with a very good job in the Civil Service. Morag's done well for herself.'

'And what about Ian?' Sadie queried.

'He's a cook with the Royal Navy. Heaven alone knows where he is or when he'll be back.'

'I was thinking,' Beth said. 'Why don't we have a get together tomorrow night? Sadie could meet Tom and Morag then.'

'That's a good idea!' Ken acknowledged.

'Will they both be free to come?' Sadie asked.

'Aye, of course they will. Or if they aren't, they'll make themselves available. After all, how often does a long-lost sister suddenly pop up out of nowhere!'

All the adults laughed.

'Now tell us about yourself and Canada,' Ken urged.

This time Sadie played down her life with the Trikhardts, thinking there was no need for them to know the full truth.

It was late when she and Edward finally left the Smith's household and returned to their hotel.

'It went well, I thought,' Edward said when they were in bed together.

'Yes. Extremely so. I liked him a great deal. And Beth.'

'A nice couple,' Edward agreed.

'And tomorrow night . . .' Sadie smiled in the darkness. 'Tom and Morag.'

'You've got your family back at last,' Edward said, touching her bare thigh. 'I couldn't be more pleased for you, Sadie.'

'Thank you.'

Thirty-six and thirty-five, she thought, picturing the wedding photograph that Ken had shown her.

Later, when Edward was asleep, still thinking of her mother and father, Bill and Lena, Sadie began to weep.

'OK?' Edward asked Sadie, the two of them having just emerged from the car.

'Yeah.' She turned to Edward, eyes sparkling. 'Last night I was as nervous as a kitten, tonight I'm so excited I could burst.'

Edward laughed softly. She'd been in a buoyant mood all day, forever glancing at her watch to see what time it was, willing the hours to pass.

'Got the Scotch?' she queried.

He held up the bottle wrapped in brown paper. It was a malt, one of the best Scotland produced, the assistant had assured them.

'And the candy?' To get what Sadie wanted had been difficult to come by, but eventually they'd managed it.

'That's on the rear seat. You'll have to carry it.'

Sadie retrieved a huge box of chocolates and armed with that, Edward with the Scotch, they went upstairs.

The door opened almost immediately to reveal Ken dressed in a suit and tie. 'Welcome!' he beamed, and kissed Sadie on the cheek.

Beth came out to stand behind Ken. She was wearing a fetching navy blue dress splashed with large white polka dots. The make-up she had on made her look younger and more healthy.

'Everyone's here and dying to meet you,' Beth declared.

'To help the celebration,' Edward stated, passing the Scotch to Ken, who thanked him and politely said he shouldn't have bothered.

'And these are for you,' Sadie smiled, handing Beth the box of chocolates after they had kissed.

They went into the kitchen where three adults were standing, already holding glasses. Sadie knew the man must be Tom, and wondered which of the two women was Morag.

Ken, who was clearly enjoying himself, held up his hand. 'I shall now do the introductions. Sadie, this is your sister, Morag, who's a year older than you.'

Morag, who didn't seem to have the same family resemblance, came forward. 'Hello, Sadie,' Morag said, tears in her eyes.

'Hello, Morag.'

The pair of them fell into one another's arms, embracing each other warmly. 'I just couldn't believe it when Beth rang me at work today and told me. I just couldn't believe it,' Morag bubbled.

'And this is your brother, Tom,' Ken went on.

Tom was shorter than Ken, broad shouldered and barrel chested. He had a mole on his left cheek and a silly smile on his face. 'It's good to have you back, Sadie,' he said, voice thick with emotion.

'And it's good to be back. You've no idea how good!' she replied.

He threw his arms round her and Morag, and hugged the pair of them.

Tom's wife produced a scrap of hanky and blew her nose, following that with a large swig from her glass.

'I only wish Ian was here,' Ken said. 'That would have made it perfect.'

Tom kissed Sadie on both cheeks, and then she, almost overcome by the situation, kissed him back. When she tried to speak she found she couldn't.

'I think a toast is in order,' Ken declared.

'So much to talk about. So much to catch up on,' Morag said.

'Aye,' Tom agreed.

'I don't remember you, but Tom does. Don't you, Tom?'

'I can see wee Sadie dragging herself round this room as though it was yesterday. Wee Sadie who couldn't walk because of her hip and who vanished one day because Ma gave her away.'

'Terrible times, terrible times,' Morag said, continuing to cry.

'And you've come from Canada, I'm told?' Tom smiled, a glint of tears now in his eyes.

Sadie found she still couldn't speak, so nodded instead.

'A toast, I think,' Ken repeated.

'You haven't finished the introductions yet,' Beth chipped in. 'Senga, this is Pilot Officer Edward Fitzgerald, Sadie's fiancé.'

'Pleased to meet you,' Senga said, shaking hands with Edward. 'As you've probably realized I'm Tom's wife.'

'I'm pleased to meet you,' Edward responded.

'I thought it was some sort of joke when Beth came round this morning before I left for work,' Tom said. 'Our Sadie turning up at the door after all these years! Pull the other one it's got bells on, I told her.'

Sadie found her voice at last. 'No joke, Tom, as you can see.'

Edward stared at the kitchen table which had been covered with a clean white cloth. On it had been set out plates of sandwiches, biscuits and cakes, whisky, sherry, beer and glasses.

'But where are the children?' Sadie asked, suddenly realizing they weren't present.

'Through in the bedroom playing,' Tom replied. 'You'll meet our lass in a minute. But first I'd like you to meet my wife.'

When that was done, Ken got his way at last, and glasses were charged and passed round for a toast, others recharged.

When everyone was ready Ken raised his glass. 'To Sadie, whom none of us ever forgot, and whom we often talked about. Welcome home!'

'Welcome home!' the other Smiths chorused.

When she tried to reply, Sadie found she'd lost her voice again.

'I've been trying to analyse how I feel, and I think I've come up with the word that describes it exactly,' Sadie said to Edward as they drove back to Duxford.

'And what's that?'

'Complete. There's been a great gap in my life, hole if you prefer, that has been there as long as I remember. You can't imagine what it's like not having a family, having no one to call your own. I used to ache with a sense of loss when I was young which dulled as I grew older, but never left me.'

'And now the ache has gone?' Edward smiled.

Sadie nodded. 'I have a sense of belonging now that I never had before. It's terribly important to me.'

'All I can say is, because it meant so much to you, thank God we found your family. And that they turned out to be nice folks.'

'It's also a relief to know that what the Home told me was true, that Mom did turn me over to them for my own good. I always believed it to be true, of course, because I wanted to believe it. But I have to admit at the back of my mind there was always that niggle of doubt, that the story was just a concoction by the Home to make me feel better and more ready to accept what had happened.'

Edward stared at Sadie, thinking how much he loved her. He was wise enough to know that finding her family could only strengthen their love by making Sadie a fuller and happier person. And because of that he, too, was overjoyed, that they'd found the Smiths.

'Complete,' Sadie repeated, and nodded. 'That describes how I feel exactly.'

She started to hum as she drove, which made Edward smile.

Their trip north of the border had been a resounding success.

Chapter Eight

'We caught the final Heinkel over Aldeburgh Bay, Jonty put two bursts through his fuselage and down he went trailing smoke. And that was the end of another bandit.'

It was mid-April 1941, and Edward had been back flying since the previous December.

'Did the crew get out?' Sadie asked.

Edward nodded. 'I saw them do so, and splash down safely enough. The Navy would have fished them out before long.'

Sadie was pleased about that. She might loathe and detest the Nazis, but human life was human life after all.

'Talk of the Devil!' Edward exclaimed with a laugh, pointing at the pub door through which Jonty Porritt had just walked in the company of an attractive female in uniform.

'Over here, Jonty!' Edward called out. 'And it's your round, you son-of-a-gun!' Jonty was one of the replacements who'd joined 12 Group directly after the Battle of Britain. He and Edward had become fast friends.

Sadie was pleased to see Jonty, she liked him, and wondered who the woman was with him.

Jonty extended his arms like wings and rushed in at Edward, pretending to strafe him. Edward obliged by clutching his chest and falling over the table feigning dead.

'Idiot!' Sadie smiled. But she was well used to the airmen acting like overgrown schoolboys. In truth it wasn't that long ago since many of them had been at school. At twenty-seven Squadron Leader Fitzgerald, as he was now, was an old man amongst them.

The female in uniform joined Jonty at Edward's and Sadie's table. 'Allow me to introduce the lovely Gabrielle who's just delivered an Oxford to the 'drome, and who will be staying overnight here at the rub-a-dub,' Jonty said.

Edward rose, took Gabrielle's hand and kissed the back of it. 'Delighted,' he murmured.

'You don't have to worry about him, Sadie here has Edward well and truly ball and chained,' Jonty said to Gabrielle, who laughed.

When the introductions were over Jonty said he'd buy a round although, he gave Edward a mock scowl, he was certain it wasn't his turn.

'Jolly well is!' retorted Edward, affecting an upper-crust English accent, which made the others laugh. They didn't come more upper crust than Jonty, excluding royalty that is, whose family seat was somewhere in Nottinghamshire.

Sadie stared at Gabrielle's uniform which was new to her. Gabrielle was wearing a dark blue tunic and skirt, Air Force blue shirt and black tie, gold wings and stripes and black silk stockings and shoes.

'Please sit down,' Edward said, indicating a free chair. 'Brought in an Oxford, have you?' he smiled when she'd done so.

'Half an hour ago, too late to get a connecting flight back. I'll either do that tomorrow or else take the train.'

'Where are you flying out of?' he enquired.

'White Waltham. Do you know it?'

Edward shook his head. 'Never been there, I'm afraid.'

Sadie was intrigued. 'Excuse me,' she said. 'I've never seen your uniform before. Are you part of the RAF?'

'Yes,' replied Gabrielle. 'I belong to the Women's Transport Section of the Air Transport Auxiliary, the ATA.'

'They're ferry pilots,' Edward explained.

Sadie was even more intrigued. 'What exactly do you fly then?' she asked.

'Non-operational aircraft for now, but we have hopes of flying operational craft in the not-too-distant future.'

'You mean like Hurricanes and Spitfires?'

Gabrielle laughed at the expression on Sadie's face. 'Why not? A woman is just as capable of flying those as a man. All we have to do is convince the powers that be that we can.'

A shiver coursed through Sadie at the thought of flying a Hurricane or Spit. 'You'd never fly the big bombers though, surely?'

'Again, why not?'

'Lancasters and Wellingtons?' Sadie queried incredulously.

'Sadie flies herself,' Edward explained to Gabrielle.

'Marvellous. What have you flown?'

'Only a Gipsy Moth, I'm afraid. Edward owns one in Canada. In fact, he taught me how to fly.'

'And damn good she is too. A natural,' Edward stated.

Jonty rejoined them with the drinks. 'What's all this then?'

'Edward was just telling me that Sadie flies,' Gabrielle informed him.

Jonty raised an eyebrow. 'You do? I didn't know that. You've never said.'

'I suppose it just never came up,' Sadie replied.

'In my opinion a woman can fly the big bombers,' Gabrielle said, returning to that subject.

'Never!' scoffed Jonty.

'I have, quite off the record, taken the controls of a Halifax, so I do know something of what I'm talking about,' Gabrielle went on.

Jonty looked amused.

'How did you find it?' Edward asked.

'Very different to a Magister which is what I'd flown directly before that, but all right. It wasn't anything I couldn't handle.'

'But that was in the air. You neither took off nor landed it,' Jonty said.

Gabrielle shrugged. 'If you can drive a saloon then you're capable of driving a sports car, and if you can do that, then why not a heavy goods vehicle? It's all the same principle.'

'Let me put it this way, I'll believe it when I see it with my own two eyes,' Jonty mocked.

'Sadie mentioned Hurricanes earlier,' Edward said. 'They're pretty tricky to fly. Why, think of the training our guys have to go through before being posted.'

Gabrielle gave him a lazy smile. 'Your pilots are being trained to fight the enemy, which is one thing. All we have to do is fly it, safely, from A to B, which is quite another.'

Edward thought about that. 'I take your point,' he replied slowly.

'One plane you don't ever want to try and fly is the Airacobra, they're real sods. I took one up a while ago and nearly bought it. Nasty, vicious little aircraft,' Jonty said.

'I've heard others say that about them,' Edward nodded. 'Exactly what is it that makes them so difficult?'

They continued talking about aircraft and flying until time was called.

The ATA, Sadie mused, as she drove home to the cottage having dropped Edward and Jonty off at the 'drome. How interesting.

Sadie gazed out of the window at the rain lashing down. God, she was bored. Bored stiff! She'd hoped Edward would cycle out, but so far he hadn't put in an appearance. He probably would this evening though, he did manage to visit most evenings.

It wasn't the evenings that bothered her, but the days. They were interminable. There was nothing left to do in the house any more, except the usual dusting and cleaning which she soon got through. Once a week there was the washing and ironing, but again that didn't take very long.

She was sick of walking, having, it seemed to her, explored every inch of countryside thereabouts. Nor could she keep calling into the pub to chat with Ma, that wasn't fair on Ma as it invariably held her up.

Work in the pub? She had considered that, but the idea didn't really appeal.

Leaving the window she sat and picked up the morning newspaper. The news was bad, Yugoslavia had fallen to a Balkan blitzkrieg, and Athens had been taken by the Germans who'd pushed the British out in the process. The war wasn't going at all well for Britain and her Allies. And London had been heavily bombed again, so, too, recently had Liverpool, Belfast, Clydebank, Southampton, Portsmouth and Plymouth resulting in massive damage and loss of life. And here she was sitting twiddling her thumbs!

With a sigh she threw down the paper. She'd make a cup of tea, she decided.

When she glanced out the window she saw that the downpour had intensified.

'Join the ATA!' Edward exclaimed in surprise.

'Don't you approve?'

'Yes. I don't know. I mean, I haven't thought about it.'

Sadie took his hand in hers. 'Well, I have thought about it, a lot. It's time I got off my backside and did my bit. Why even old Mr Grimshaw who goes into the pub has joined the Home Guard and he's over eighty.'

'He hasn't!' Edward exclaimed again in surprise.

'He has. When I heard that I really felt ashamed. I've made enquiries about the ATA and they need every pilot they can get. And I'm a pilot.'

'But that would mean leaving here?'

'I'd keep on the cottage as I'll undoubtedly get back from time to time. Ferry pilots come and go at Duxford, you've told me that yourself. There's no reason why I shouldn't be one of them.'

'I suppose I . . .' Edward shrugged. 'To be honest I don't want you to join, but I suppose that's just me being selfish. There is a war on, after all.'

'And I may be Canadian by adoption, but I'm Scottish by birth. Since returning here I've come to view this as my war which my country is fighting. Besides which, I'm bored to distraction and need something to do! Something that is worthwhile, and delivering planes would be precisely that.'

'I didn't realize you were *that* bored,' he replied.

'Not when you're with me of course,' she stated, sensing hurt feelings. 'But I am when you aren't. I'm simply an active person, that's all, someone who needs something to do.'

He gathered her into his arms, and kissed her tenderly. 'I'll miss you.'

'And I'll miss you. But as I said, I'll be back from time to time. And if I keep on the cottage we'll be able to meet here when I do.'

'Romantic trysts?' Edward smiled.

'Exactly,' she smiled in return. 'The other thing is that I'm running short of money and have to start earning again.'

'Money isn't a problem,' he protested. 'I'll happily give you whatever you need.'

'I prefer to pay my own way, thank you very much.'

'But you are my fiancée!'

'And still independent. The ATA pays six pounds a week which will keep me on a financial even keel.'

'OK then, but at least let me pay for the cottage. I'd like to do that.'

She nodded her assent, not minding such an agreement. It was also a practical one as he would still be in the area whereas who knew where she'd be based.

'When will you join?' he asked.

'Right away. The sooner the better.'

'I'll bet you can't wait to get up in the air again.'

She smiled, he couldn't have been more right.

A week later she left for Hatfield in Hertfordshire.

'What did you learn to fly on?' McBrain, the ATA's Chief Flying Instructor, asked Sadie.

'A Gipsy Moth, sir.'

'Well, we've got Tiger Moths here, not all that different. Get kitted up and report back to me. You can take me for a spin.'

'Yes, sir.'

McBrain strode away, while a delighted, if somewhat apprehensive, Sadie returned to the locker rooms where her newly issued flying kit was stored.

'I'm going up with McBrain,' she said to Fiona Caldicott who'd befriended her on arrival.

'Don't let him put you off, he's a sweetie really. All bark and no bite.'

'A good flyer, I presume?'

'An ex-BOAC captain who's too old to be at the sharp end. And yes, he is a good pilot, and a stickler for procedure. So make sure you do everything by the book if you wish to impress him.'

Sadie made a mental note of that.

Sadie executed a smooth take-off, and started to climb. She smiled as she watched the ground fall away beneath her. How she'd missed flying!

She was slightly uncomfortable in her flying suit because of its military strangeness, but she knew she'd soon grow accustomed to it. The goggles she was wearing were of a type unknown to her, and were also strange.

When she reached two thousand feet she banked the Moth and embarked on a series of manoeuvres that culminated in a roll. She contemplated inverting the plane and flying upside down but, remembering Fiona's advice, decided against it thinking McBrain might consider that reckless flying.

She stayed up for twenty minutes, then brought the Moth in again, making a perfect landing. When she'd finished taxiing she switched off and got out.

McBrain jumped down beside her, and removed his goggles and helmet. 'You'll do,' he pronounced, and walked away.

Elation filled her, and joy. If the Moth had belonged to her she would have taken it straight back up again.

As it happened she was allowed to take it up again later in the day.

There were six of them flying in formation which was a hard thing to do when you had to fly, read a map, watch the ground, and keep in position all at the same time. It could only be done in perfect weather.

Sadie and other newcomers were learning the country, finding their way round solely by map reading and ground observation. A far more difficult thing to do in Britain than it had been in Canada where a railway track might run in the same direction for hundreds of miles.

The Moths weren't equipped with radios or any other navigational devices. Locating your destination rested fairly and squarely on the pilot's shoulders.

Jane Peebles was wandering again, Sadie noted. She waggled her wings to try and attract Jane's attention, and succeeded in doing so. Jane immediately closed up.

Sadie loathed flying in formation, but orders were orders. She glanced at the map on her lap, trying to pin-point precisely where they were.

Looking down she saw a canal. Now that shouldn't be there, surely! She found the canal on the map and realized they were a little further east than she'd thought.

The formation droned on.

'How are you, darling?' Sadie said into the telephone, Edward having just rung her.

'Fine. And you?'

'In the pink, as the girls round here say.'

'And what about the flying?'

'Hard work, but I'm enjoying it. I'm being sent to Upavon in a few days' time where I'll be flying two engine aircraft. I'm looking forward to that.' Upavon was where the RAF Central Flying School was sited.

'How long will you be there, do you think?'

'I don't know. Your guess is as good as mine.' She paused for a moment, then whispered, 'I do miss you, Edward.'

'And me you.'

'How's the cottage?'

'Just the same. I was up there yesterday, making sure everything was OK. I sat on the bed and thought about you.'

'I can imagine what you were thinking,' she giggled.

'That was part of it,' he confessed.

'How's the war going for you?'

He hesitated before replying. 'Busy. We've been over London again, and there's increasing enemy activity at this end. Jonty sends his regards by the way, and Miffy. They're well, too.'

'Will you write to me tonight?' she requested.

'I've telephoned!'

'But a letter is nicer in a way. You can read it over and over again, and sleep with it under your pillow.'

'I'll write then.'

'And so will I. Be careful, Edward.'

'I do my best about that, I can assure you. And you be careful, too.'

There was a slight pause, then Sadie stated quietly, 'I love you, Edward.'

'And I love you, Sadie. For forever and a day, as they say in the fairy-tales.'

She thought that lovely. 'Same here. For forever and a day,' she repeated.

'I'll have to go now,' he said.

From the tone of his voice she knew that he was smiling, and could just picture that smile, and the rest of his face. Her heart ached at being parted from him, but it was her choice, a choice she had no doubt was the right one, if hard.

'Goodbye,' she said.

'Goodbye, Sadie.'

When she'd hung up she took a handkerchief from her pocket and blew her nose. As she walked away from the telephone she prayed that it wouldn't be too long before she saw him again.

And for God to keep him safe.

Molly Kerrane came bursting into the Upavon Mess, and hurried over to the group of ATA females sitting in the far corner of the room.

'You'll never guess!' she said breathlessly.

'Guess what?' queried Jane Peebles.

'We're now allowed to fly operational aircraft.'

'Where did you get that from?' Sadie demanded.

'It's on the notice-board, orders from the very top.'

'Taking effect when?' Dorothy de Paula asked.

'Right away.'

This was wonderful news, Sadie thought. And precisely what every female member of the ATA had been waiting for.

'You're certain it's there in black and white?' Fiona Caldicott queried.

'Go and look for yourself if you don't believe me,' Molly retorted.

'That's it then!' said Lettice Bunbury, and whooped like a Red Indian.

A startled squadron leader glanced in their direction, wondering what was going on.

Jane jumped to her feet, grabbed hold of Dorothy, and began to dance.

Allowed to fly operational aircraft! Sadie drummed her feet under the table she was so delighted.

Two days later the female members of the ATA currently at Upavon were summoned to the Mess where they were to be addressed by the CO, Wing Commander Ledbetter.

They all stood when Ledbetter came striding into the Mess. 'At ease,' he growled on reaching them, and indicated that they could sit down again, which they did.

'I'll get straight to the point,' he said brusquely. 'The ATA has decided to open a new Ferry Pool at Hamble just outside Southampton, and you're all being posted there where your first officer will be someone called Mower. Hamble is to be an all-female pool whose job will be to deliver new Spits from the nearby aircraft factory at Chartis Hill and modified Halifaxes from the, again nearby, factory at Marwell. Any questions?'

Spitfires and Halifaxes! Sadie mentally drooled at the thought.

'When do we leave here, sir?' Daphne Rogers asked.

'Tomorrow morning at 0900 by which time you will have your kit packed and ready to go. An Anson will take you there. Any further questions?'

When there weren't any he strode from the Mess leaving an excited buzz behind him.

The Anson was flown by Jim Mollison, a famous long distance record breaking pilot of his day.

'Barrage balloons,' said Sadie, pointing through the cabin window. Jane Peebles, sitting beside Sadie, craned over Sadie's shoulder to have a look.

'Must be Southampton down there,' Sadie murmured.

'Yes, it is. I recognize it,' Jane confirmed.

Some of the barrage balloons were lowered as the Anson made its approach, passing along a lane that had been opened specially for it.

Shortly after that the Anson touched down. They'd arrived at Hamble which for most of them was going to be their home for the rest of the war.

They were met and taken to the Mess where they were introduced to their First Officer, Gabrielle Mower, the same Gabrielle whom Sadie had met at the Red Lion in Duxford.

'Temporary sleeping accommodation in the form of camp-beds has been arranged at the 'drome for now, but you're all going to have to find your own billets off site, I'm afraid,' Gabrielle announced. 'Something I'm sure you'll approve of as it will be far nicer for you living off-'drome.'

'You are the first arrivals at this new Ferry Pool, which I believe you've already been informed is to be an all-female one. There will be more arrivals in due course until we're eventually brought up to full strength. Any questions?'

Sadie's hand shot up. 'When do we start flying operational aircraft?'

Gabrielle smiled. 'Keen I see. I like that. There's a Spit being flown in tomorrow so we can get to know the machine. This' – she held up a card – 'is what's known as a handling note. On it are all the details relevant to flying a Spitfire. Everything you need to know is here, what you don't need to know has been left off. In other words it contains only the essential information to enable you to take a Spit from A to B. I will now hand these out and suggest you study them before tomorrow morning.

'Now, how about a nice cup of tea during which I can begin to get to know you.'

'Duxford, wasn't it?' Gabrielle said to Sadie a little later.

'That's right. You'd delivered an Oxford and had to stay overnight at the pub. You came in with Jonty Porritt to join myself and Squadron Leader Edward Fitzgerald, my fiancé.'

'I remember your fiancé saying you flew, and that you were a natural, as he put it.'

Sadie blushed. 'Don't forget he's very much in love with me,' she replied modestly.

'Well, we'll see,' Gabrielle smiled.

'You are responsible for me joining the ATA,' Sadie said. 'I'd never heard of it up until then.'

'And now we'll be working together.'

'Yes,' Sadie agreed, glad about that. She'd liked Gabrielle the night they'd met.

Once they'd settled into their temporary dorm the girls were released to go into Hamble where they immediately began making enquiries about suitable accommodation.

The Spitfire arrived exactly on time, coming in low over the 'drome and then circled before landing.

'Beautiful,' Dorothy de Paula, standing beside Sadie, murmured. Sadie knew she was referring to the machine and not the pilot's handling of it.

When the Spit had come to a standstill the pilot killed the engine and got out. Sadie was shocked when she realized he only had one arm. The pilot was in his late fifties and also a member of the ATA.

He and Gabrielle exchanged a few words, then he turned to the girls and grinned. 'So who's going to be the first to take her aloft?' he queried.

'Me!', 'I will!', 'Yes, please!' was chorused in reply.

'I think you're going to have to choose,' he said to Gabrielle.

Gabrielle wanted to be the first herself, but felt that would be pulling rank. She scanned the eager faces, and wondered who to pick.

'Sadie Smith, the honour's all yours!' she called out.

A concerted groan of disappointment went up from the others, while Sadie could hardly believe her luck.

'Digested your handling note?' the one-armed pilot asked her as he escorted her to the plane.

She nodded.

'Any questions or worries?'

'I don't think so.'

'Just follow the instructions and you won't get into any trouble. And make sure you thoroughly familiarize yourself with the cockpit before taking off. Don't feel pressurized because we're watching. All right?'

'I understand,' she replied.

'Good luck!' Gabrielle called out, and waved.

Sadie climbed aboard and settled herself in. Slowly, and with reference to her handling note, she went over the controls. When she was satisfied she understood those she mentally went through the take-off and landing procedures. Finally she was ready.

The Merlin engine caught and the propeller whirred into action. She eased the plane forward, manoeuvring herself into position.

She took several deep breaths, closed the canopy, and a few seconds later taxied into her take-off.

A thrill that was almost sexual ran through her as the Spit left the runway and started to climb. No fancy stuff, she reminded herself, everything was to be straightforward and simple.

Sadie marvelled at the machine as it cut through the air. She compared it to a true thoroughbred which was so responsive to the controls! Her only slight reservation was that the visibility was somewhat restricted, but that was easily remedied by simply swaying the plane in either direction.

She could have flown the Spit all day, so it was with the utmost reluctance that she brought it in to land again. She bumped fractionally on making contact with the ground, but it was nothing to be concerned about, and she was soon taxiing to where the others were standing.

'Flies like a dream,' she said to Gabrielle and the pilot on rejoining the group.

'No problems?' the pilot smiled.

'None at all.'

'Can I be next?' Jane Peebles piped up.

This time Sadie was among the watchers as the Spit, with Jane flying it, took off.

That evening Gabrielle announced that they would begin delivering the next day.

Sadie, Jane, Dorothy and Fiona were dropped off at Chartis Hill by an Anson which then took the others on to Marwell.

Sadie was interested to see one of these rural aircraft factories where the planes were made. The hangers were so skilfully camouflaged that anyone who didn't know they were there would never have spotted them.

Aircraft factories were a prime target for the enemy, and consequently newly assembled planes were moved as quickly as possible to what were known as Maintenance Units where they were then fully fitted out. It was the ATA's task to move the planes to the MUs, and then take the fully fitted aircraft on from there to the specific aerodromes.

The runway at Chartis Hill, as it was at all rural factories, was a strip of ground over which wire netting had been laid. It was a runway Sadie would come to know very well indeed.

The new Spits that needed to be delivered were brought out for the girls. They were all bound for the same MU in Lancashire, and the girls had agreed to fly in loose formation, but it wasn't to be as exacting as it had been in their training.

The girls set off enthusiastically.

This was the life, Sadie thought once she had taken off. If only Edward could see her now!

From Lancashire they went to Norfolk where they were eventually picked up by Anson and returned to Hamble.

The next day they went to South Wales, Kent, and then home again.

From there on in, weather permitting, they flew seven days a week.

Sadie was trembling with excitement as she brought the Spitfire in to land at Duxford where she was to be picked up later on by an Anson. She should have at least three hours with Edward, providing he was there, that was. She'd tried to telephone the aerodrome before taking off, but hadn't been able to get through.

She was aware of a group of airmen watching her as she sped along the runway, and was pleased with herself that she'd made a perfect, textbook, landing.

She taxied the Spit to where she thought would be a convenient place to park it, and there killed the engine. In other aerodromes she'd come to know precisely where they wanted their new aircraft parked, but this was her first official trip to Duxford.

She jumped down, took off her goggles and helmet, and shook her hair free.

'Good God, was that you?' a familiar voice exclaimed.

She turned to find Miffy Moxon staring at her.

'Hello, Miffy. How are things?'

He crossed over to her and shook her by the hand. 'Excuse me for being a bit incredulous. But you, a woman, flying a Spit! It makes the mind boggle.'

'Chauvinist!' she teased. 'We women of the ATA are

452

flying Spits, not to mention all manner of other fighter craft all the time now.'

'It was an excellent landing. Top marks.'

'Thank you,' she smiled. 'Is Edward around?'

'Somewhere. We're not long back from a sortie. Does he know you're coming?'

'Nope.'

'Then I won't spoil the surprise. You stay there and I'll root him out for you.'

Miffy wasn't gone long, returning with a mystified Edward, demanding to know what this was all about.

Edward's face was a picture when he spotted Sadie who rushed straight into his arms.

'I'll leave you two lovebirds alone then,' smiled Miffy as they kissed, and off he went.

'By all that's wonderful!' Edward gasped when the kiss was over. 'When did you get here?'

'Minutes ago. I'm delivering this,' she replied, indicating the Spit. 'Oh, it's so good to see you again!'

'And you. How long have you got?'

'Three hours plus. I can't be more definite than that.'

'Terrific. Let's go to the Mess and have a cup of tea.'

'I must sign the Spit over first. The formalities have to be observed, after all. Then we can have tea.'

'Who do you have to report to?'

She told him.

'Right, come on. We'll get this over and done with in double quick time.'

He looked tired, she thought. She'd thought Miffy hadn't looked all that great either. The squadron was having a harder time than he'd admitted to her in his letters and telephone conversations, she correctly guessed.

'How's Jonty?'

'OK. He's in the Mess playing darts at which he's become something of an expert.'

'And Ma?'

'Just the same. She never changes.'

'I'd love to see her,' Sadie said.

'Well, you can go and visit, but without me, I'm afraid. I can't leave the 'drome until stood down.'

'Then I'll stay with you.'

He bent and kissed her on the lips. 'How I've missed that,' he murmured.

'And I've missed you.' She shivered. 'I could eat you all up.'

That made him laugh. He felt exactly the same way.

They did what had to be done, then Edward took Sadie to the Mess where she was greeted loudly by those pilots she knew. Jonty went on one knee before her and swore that she was even more beautiful than he remembered, and how did a Canadian oaf like Edward manage to be so lucky? Wouldn't she please change her mind about Edward, and consider his suit?

'Bugger off, you randy bastard!' Edward said, which got him a great roar of approval.

Jonty came to his feet again and winked at Sadie. 'Well, if you ever do change your mind you know where to come.'

It was all good fun and Sadie was enjoying every moment of it, but she wanted to be alone with Edward, and knew he felt the same way. He suggested that she sat at a secluded table and said he'd join her there with the teas.

She smiled when he finally sat facing her.

He reached out and took her hand in his. 'Pity we can't get out to the cottage.'

'Pity,' she agreed, knowing what was in his mind.

'Maybe next time?'

'Hopefully.'

Time slipped by as they sat there deep in conversation. They were reminiscing about Canada when suddenly a klaxon blared. Edward immediately jumped to his feet.

'Have to go! It's a scramble,' he explained.

He pecked her on the lips, then went charging after the other pilots making a bee-line for their planes.

Sadie followed them outside and watched them take-off, Spits and Hurricanes all mixed up together. As they climbed the planes began to untangle themselves, forming into their various flights and squadrons. Then they were gone, the last machine swallowed up by cloud.

Sadie returned to the Mess where she ordered another cup of tea, intending to wait there for Edward.

Eventually the planes came back and landed, but none of the pilots got out. The planes were feverishly refuelled, and immediately took to the air again. Exactly the same procedure happened a second time, shortly after which her Anson arrived.

Hectic was hardly the word for it, she thought, as she walked out to the Anson. How many sorties were they flying a day? No wonder Edward had looked tired and wan.

At least she'd seen and talked with him, she thought, with satisfaction, if she'd arrived later she might have missed him.

A month later Sadie got another chance to deliver a plane to Duxford, this time a Hurricane that she brought from an MU in Leicestershire. It was shortly before dusk when she touched down, right on schedule.

She got out of the plane carrying her nightbag and rushed to sign the Hurricane over. That done she went in search of Edward.

Their reunion was as loving as the previous one, she throwing herself into his eager arms, and the pair of them kissing passionately.

'I'm not being picked up again till the morning,' she informed him.

'The cottage is waiting and ready,' he replied. 'Do you want to go straight there or drop in at the Red Lion first?'

She didn't have to think about that. 'Cottage first, pub later.'

He kissed her again, then squeezed her tight. 'Come on,' he said, almost dragging her to the Morris.

He drove, putting his foot down.

'You'll kill us going this fast!' Sadie complained with a laugh, for he didn't have the benefit of full headlights, as they were partially masked.

Don't worry. I've got eyes like a cat.'

'Well, just remember you don't have nine lives, that's all.'

He squealed to a halt in front of the cottage, and hopped out. Going round to her door he opened it for her. Hand in hand they went inside.

He lit the lamps, and while he was doing that she put a match to the made-up range which soon blazed into life.

'Wine or brandy?' he asked, rubbing his hands together.

'What sort of wine?'

'Sauterne or claret.'

'Claret, please.'

She ran her hands up and down his back as he opened the bottle. 'I've been dreaming of this almost since I left,' she confessed.

When he poured her wine he found his hand was shaking so much he spilled some from the glass as he was giving it to her.

'To us!' she toasted when he'd poured himself a liberal tot of brandy.

'To us!' he repeated, and they both drank.

'Bed?' he proposed.

'Bed,' she agreed.

It developed into a race as to whom could get their clothes off first. Sadie won, and squealed as she dived between the freezing cold sheets.

'We'll soon warm up,' Edward said, getting into bed and reaching for her.

'It's been so long,' she murmured.

They kissed, his hands moving over her, touching, caressing, while she did the same to him.

When it was over they rested in one another's arms where Sadie fell asleep, smiling contentedly. While she slept Edward stroked her hair wishing the moment would last for ever.

Eventually Sadie woke, and they made love again. Then she pronounced herself to be ravenous.

'Let's go and see what Ma has in her kitchen,' Edward said, kissing Sadie on the tip of the nose.

'I had a letter yesterday from Courcy,' Edward informed her as they dressed.

'How is he? And Jack?'

'Both fine, the business thriving. Jack is still mad at me of course, but always reads the letters I send Courcy according to Courcy.'

'And Erin, how's she?'

'The same, as is Marty.'

'No sign of a family yet?'

Edward shook his head. 'Apparently not. I only hope that guy is doing the right things.'

Sadie laughed. 'I'm sure he is. Erin would see to that.'

'Yeah, I guess.'

She should write to Jack again, Sadie thought, it was ages since she last wrote. The trouble was she had been so busy since joining the ATA.

'Miss Dobson sends her regards,' Edward stated a few moments later. 'And oh! Heather's left to get married.'

'Finally given up on Courcy?'

'Seems so.'

'Who's she marrying?'

'Courcy never mentioned him.'

Sadie was pleased about that, and hoped she was marrying someone nice.

'You look gorgeous,' Edward said, staring at her as she finished dressing. 'A real knockout.'

'Thank you.'

'Particularly by lamplight, it does something for you.'

'You mean it hides the lines?'

He took her into his arms. 'You don't have any lines as you well know.'

'I have! Several.'

He peered into her face. 'I can't see them.'

'They're there. I assure you.'

Staring back into his face she now saw that he had lines where none had been before. Lines that were deeply etched as though cut with a knife. It was hardly surprising, she thought, considering what he was going through.

Ma was ecstatic when Sadie walked into the pub, and insisted on opening a bottle of champagne. The evening developed into a riotous party which left them all with sore heads the following morning.

A morning that came round much too quickly as far as Sadie and Edward were concerned.

Sadie passed over Winchelsea in Kent, heading for Lydd where she was to deliver the Blenheim she was flying. At Lydd she was to pick up an Avro York that had to be taken to Herefordshire. There she would be collected by a Fairchild which would return her to Hamble. The single engine, four-seater, Fairchild was the other type of aircraft used by the ATA to taxi its personnel about the country, and was considerably smaller than an Anson.

She was flying at five thousand feet when she saw the speck appear on her starboard side, coming in off the Channel. Her heart leapt into her mouth when the speck grew large enough for her to identify it as a Messerschmitt ME-109.

Keep calm now, she told herself, diving the Blenheim and wondering what evasive action she could take. If only she'd had a radio she could have whistled up help! But of course she didn't. She was a sitting duck.

The Messerschmitt closed and began an attack run. Sadie threw the Blenheim first to one side, then the other. The Blenheim juddered as bullets smacked into its fuselage.

She was going to have to bale out, she thought, angry at the prospect of losing a precious plane. But what else could she do?

And what if the German machine-gunned her as she floated down? They had been known to do that. Well, if he did, it would be curtains for her.

She pulled the Blenheim into a steep climb as the Messerschmitt started another attack run. She levelled off, and was in the process of getting out of her seat when, as if from nowhere, a Spit went screaming past.

She fell back into her seat to reassess the situation, and could have cheered when she saw that there were three Spits in all.

'Oh, you lovely, beautiful, lads!' she muttered, chest heaving with relief.

The Messerschmitt tried to escape back across the Channel, but hadn't gone far when the Spits pounced. The Messerschmitt exploded in a bright orange ball that sent bits of debris scattering in all directions.

The Spits returned, one doing a victory roll as it went past the Blenheim.

Sadie waved them on their way.

Sadie woke feeling absolutely dreadful. It was April 1944 and the war had now been waged for four and a half long grinding years. She ran a hand over her forehead which she discovered to be wet with perspiration. When she attempted to get up, she was overwhelmed by nausea.

She laid her head again on her pillow, and sucked in a deep breath. It was strain and overwork of course, that was doing this to her, flying six days a week with only two weeks' holiday a year did get to you after a while.

Still, if it was bad for her, it was far worse for Edward and those who flew combat sorties and missions.

She struggled upright, and this time stayed that way. The queasiness gradually subsided to be replaced by heartburn. Getting out of bed she stumbled over to her dressing-table where she had some tablets which would soon deal with that.

She could hear Jane Peebles moving around in the next bedroom. She, Jane and Fiona Caldicott shared a pretty house in Hamble, that was painted pink and had a largish garden which one of the neighbours used for growing vegetables. In return he gave them free vegetables.

It was Fiona's turn to make breakfast that morning, but Sadie couldn't face the scrambled eggs and toast that were placed in front of her. Fiona ended up eating them while she settled for a cup of tea.

At twenty to nine they left the house and cycled to the aerodrome.

It had started to rain heavily halfway there, and it was still raining at ten o'clock. The girls were sitting in the Mess waiting to be given assignments.

'Think it might be a wash out?' Pat White, an American who'd come over to join the ATA, asked.

Sadie hoped so. A day at the aerodrome, or better still, back in bed, would suit her.

'Could be,' Dorothy de Paula said from the window where she stood staring out.

Bile suddenly shot up Sadie's throat to make her gag. She jumped from her chair and fled to the nearest lavatory where she was sick.

'Christ!' she mumbled to herself. Her forehead was covered in cold, clammy sweat, while her hair had gone lank.

She rinsed the foulness from her mouth, reapplied her lipstick with a trembling hand, then returned to the Mess.

'You look ghastly,' Molly Kerrane commiserated.

'I feel it,' Sadie replied, slumping back into the chair she'd so hurriedly vacated. She glanced over to where some of the girls were playing bridge, and wondered if she should go and have a word with the MO. She decided she would if she got any worse.

About an hour later Gabrielle entered the Mess. 'It's a wash out, I'm afraid,' she announced. 'The rest of the day is your own.'

Someone cheered.

Home to bed, Sadie thought. Normally she would have been disappointed not to be flying, but not that day.

She went home and crawled into bed where she fell instantly asleep. When she woke up again it was early evening and the rain had finally stopped.

'How do you feel now?' Jane enquired when she went into the kitchen.

'A lot better thanks. A little light headed though, but maybe that's from sleeping through the day.'

'Hungry?'

'Not in the least.'

'Tell you what,' Jane smiled. 'I'm going for a walk in the woods. Why don't you come with me?'

Sadie thought it was a splendid idea, and when Fiona heard where they were going she said she'd accompany them.

Everything was sharp and clear after the rain, the air filled with fragrant smells of all descriptions.

'Look!' exclaimed Fiona, pointing at a squirrel staring at them from the branch of a pine tree.

'He's gorgeous,' Sadie said.

The squirrel sat back on its haunches, waggled its forelegs up and down, then abruptly ran along the branch to disappear behind the trunk of the tree.

They were about to resume their leisurely walk when two soldiers suddenly materialized out of the undergrowth. The soldiers had smeared faces and vegetation draped over their tin hats and uniforms. They were two of the hardest, fittest-looking soldiers Sadie had ever seen.

The men stared at them, faces expressionless. Then one nodded to the other and they flitted away, vanishing soundlessly into some bushes.

'Who were they?' Jane queried.

'They had incredible tans, so they've not long come from somewhere hot,' Fiona mused.

'Desert soldiers?' Sadie wondered.

'If so why are they here at Hamble?' Jane said, raising an eyebrow.

'Something is definitely going on,' Sadie stated firmly. 'First we've had a huge build-up of small craft in the harbour, then the Americans arrive to build and equip a service base for these craft, and now desert soldiers.'

'What do you think it adds up to?' Fiona asked.

'What do you think?' Sadie retorted.

'Our return to France?'

'Could very well be,' Sadie nodded.

'But when?' Jane queried.

'Soon I would guess. Just think of the time of year. Next month perhaps, or the month after.'

They continued speculating about the future as they completed their walk in the woods and started back for their house. They were in open country again when Sadie said, 'Ssshhh! Listen!'

A light aircraft, Sadie thought. 'There!' she cried, jabbing a finger at the sky.

They stared in amazement as the tiny aircraft went over, not knowing what to make of it. Not an aircraft at all, more of an aerial torpedo, Sadie thought.

The drone that had caught her attention abruptly cut out and the aerial torpedo plunged earthwards. There was a loud explosion when it hit the ground.

After that the aerial torpedoes, which quickly became known as doodle bugs, became a regular feature over Hamble. The vast majority continued inland, but a few did fall on the village surrounds, though fortunately never on the village itself.

* * *

'Damn!' Sadie muttered. What was wrong with the skirt. Why wouldn't it do up?

She tugged again at the zip which travelled another couple of inches before stopping once more. And there it steadfastly, despite all her efforts, remained.

Sadie pulled the zip down, dropped the skirt to the floor and stepped out of it. Was she putting on weight? Going to a full-length mirror in her bedroom she studied herself in profile.

Now that she looked, maybe she was. Her tummy certainly seemed to have . . .

She went rigid as a sudden thought burst in her brain. Could it be? Could it possibly be that . . .?

She began to put two and two together.

'I've got a Spit for Duxford, do you want to swop with me?' Lettice Bunbury asked Sadie.

Sadie could have kissed her. For the past week she'd been doing her best to get a delivery to Duxford, but to no avail.

'Yes, please,' Sadie answered with a smile.

'Always glad to be of help,' Lettice said. 'I only hope you get a little time with your Edward.'

So did she, Sadie thought. So did she!

Sadie's luck was in, on landing at Duxford, and having handed over the Spit, she found Edward chatting in the Mess. He was naturally delighted to see her and went up to get them both a cup of tea.

'I've got some news,' she told him when he joined her at their secluded table.

'What's that?'

'I'm pregnant.'

His jaw fell open. 'But I . . . we always take precautions?'

'Well, we weren't careful enough. I've had it confirmed by a doctor in Southampton, I'm almost three months gone.'

463

Edward stared at her, and swallowed.

'I can get an abortion. I've made a few enquiries,' she said hesitantly.

'Is that what you want?'

'Of course not!'

'Me neither.'

'Then I'll have it,' she declared, eyes misting over. She'd become so incredibly emotional of late, something else that was now explained.

'We'd better get married as soon as possible,' he proposed.

She nodded. 'You speak to your CO and I'll do the same to Gabrielle this evening.'

'We'll get married locally, and spend our honeymoon in the cottage, all right?'

'I couldn't think of anything nicer.'

'Or we could go away?'

'No. A local civil wedding followed by a reception in the Red Lion.'

'As soon as possible,' he repeated, thinking she had her good name to protect. 'Will you tell Gabrielle it's a "must" job?'

'Only if I have to.'

'Same here with my CO.'

'OK then.'

'Are you going to be fit enough to fly in your condition?'

She laughed. 'I'm not that delicate a plant. I'll keep on flying as long as I can, or until they make me stop. Whichever comes first.'

Not caring who might be watching, he took her hand in his. 'And Sadie, I really do love you. You're everything to me. The sun, moon and the whole galaxy of stars.'

'And you're the same to me.'

When Sadie had gone Edward went straight to see the CO.

* * *

The wedding took place in Cambridge the following week. Jonty was one witness, Ma the other. Sadie was dressed in a dark grey suit for the occasion, Edward in his uniform.

When it was over they went to a restaurant for a meal, then motored back to Duxford where they dropped off Jonty and Ma whom they'd see again later at the reception.

'So how does it feel to be Mrs Edward Fitzgerald?' Edward asked Sadie as they drew up outside the cottage.

'Wonderful!'

She gazed down at the eighteen-carat gold band firmly ensconced below her engagement ring, and heaved a sigh of complete happiness. She was Edward's wife at last. How fast, with almost bewildering speed, everything had happened in the end.

They got out of the Morris and Edward opened the cottage door. 'Wait!' he instructed, holding up a hand. 'Let's do this properly, shall we?'

He lifted her off the ground, and cradled her in his arms.

She laughed with joy as he carried her inside.

'What are you doing?' Sadie asked as she dumped some shopping on the table. She'd just come from Duxford and coffee with Ma.

'Writing to Courcy to give him our news,' Edward answered.

'Well, don't send it off before I include a page for Jack.'

'OK,' Edward nodded, and continued writing.

Sadie began putting the shopping away. Only twenty-four hours left and then it was back to Hamble, Edward to the aerodrome. Their honeymoon leave had simply flashed by.

'Edward?'

'Yes?' he queried without looking up.

'Let's go to bed.'

'I'm busy. Later.'

She went to him and curled her arms round his neck. 'I want to go now.'

'Can't you wait till I'm finished?'

'No,' she replied, and poked her tongue in his ear.

'You're a shameless hussy, Mrs Fitzgerald.'

She smiled salaciously at him, and winked.

All resolve gone Edward tossed his pen aside, and rose to his feet. She took him by the hand and led him through.

The talk in the Anson had all been about the Allied landings in Normandy two days previously. From what reports they'd heard everything was going well, casualties less than feared.

Sadie had been the last to get picked up and couldn't wait to get home and into a hot bath. She was whacked having had a particularly rigorous day.

'We'll be flying replacement aircraft over there before long,' Lettice Bunbury burbled.

'Ooh-la-la, *la belle France*!' Jane exclaimed, and waggled her hips.

Sadie thought of the desert soldiers who'd been camped round Hamble, and the hundreds of tanks belonging to them, all of which had disappeared just before the invasion. The small craft in the harbour were also gone, they, too, now 'over there'.

The excited chatter continued until the Anson landed and came to a halt.

'Who's for a drink in the Bugle?' Dorothy asked as they disembarked.

'Not for me,' Fiona replied.

'Sadie?' Jane queried.

Sadie shook her head.

'Aw come on, kid!' urged Pat White.

'Not for me. I'll skip it this once,' Sadie replied as they walked across the tarmac.

She glanced over at a Tomahawk and wondered where that had come from. The Tomahawk was an American plane she hadn't so far flown, and didn't particularly wish to either as it had a nasty habit of 'ground looping' after landing, which meant it did a complete U-turn while still rolling at speed. So far she'd flown sixty-eight different types of aircraft, but other girls had flown more.

'Sadie, can I have a word?' Gabrielle called out as they entered the main aerodrome building where Gabrielle had her office.

'Of course.'

What was all this about? Sadie wondered as Gabrielle closed her office door behind her. And why was Gabrielle so tight faced? Was it some particularly difficult delivery she was being assigned for the next day? She hoped it wasn't the Tomahawk.

'Have a seat,' Gabrielle said, indicating a chair in front of her desk.

Sadie sat, and waited for Gabrielle to go on.

'It's bad news, I'm afraid,' Gabrielle said in a rush. 'Edward has been shot down.'

Sadie went cold all over. 'Shot down?'

'He's alive, but badly burnt.'

Sadie stared at Gabrielle who seemed to shiver at the edges. It was her eyes playing tricks on her, she realized. 'How badly burnt?'

'Pretty seriously. I don't know the details however.'

Sadie jumped to her feet, her tiredness forgotten. 'I must go to him at once. I'll borrow a car, I'll . . .'

'I already have a Fairchild standing by. Jim Mollison will fly you,' Gabrielle interjected. 'Edward's in hospital in Colchester. Jim will fly you to the nearby 'drome at Earls Colne.'

Thank God it was June and long light nights, Sadie thought, her mind racing. Earls Colne! It was a small aerodrome she'd heard of, but never been to.

467

'Transport has been laid on for you when you arrive there,' Gabrielle further elaborated.

'Right. Thank you. I'll leave now.'

'I'll accompany you to the Fairchild,' Gabrielle said, and had to hurry after Sadie who was already at the door.

Badly burnt, Sadie thought as she made for the Fairchild. Please God, his face had escaped. She'd seen some pilots who . . . She shuddered thinking of Edward like that.

Jim started up the engine when he saw her approach, and she quickly climbed inside. He gave her a grim look, but said nothing. Several minutes later they were in the air.

It was a short journey, but to Sadie it took for ever. As they flew she twisted her wedding-ring round and round.

As they descended, Sadie saw a car waiting by the side of the runway and correctly guessed it was for her.

As soon as the Fairchild had stopped, and it was safe to do so, Sadie shot out of the plane. The FANY driver confirmed that the car was indeed at her disposal.

'Get me there as swiftly as you can, please,' she said to the FANY, and climbed into the car.

The FANY did as she'd been requested, knowing the reason for Sadie's anxiety. When, on arriving at the hospital, Sadie rushed off with only a hastily mumbled thank you, she understood.

As Sadie hurried inside she was remembering another hospital. Everything had turned out all right then, hopefully it would do so again, she reassured herself.

Enquiries led her to Peasgood Ward and Sister Galsworthy, a thin, middle-aged, spinster type who exhuded a combination of efficiency and compassion.

'How bad are his burns?' Sadie demanded.

'Extensive, Mrs Fitzgerald.'

'And his face?'

'That, too, was burnt, I'm sad to say.'

Sadie rocked where she stood, while a sob escaped her lips.

'They can do marvels nowadays, Mrs Fitzgerald. You must console yourself with that.'

'Is he conscious?'

'The squadron leader is heavily sedated. That's normal procedure in cases like this.'

Sadie went back to twisting her wedding-ring. 'Can I see him?' Then, almost hysterically, 'I have to see him!'

Sister nodded her assent, and understanding. 'Come with me. You could no doubt use a cup of tea after your journey, I'll have one brought in to you. And how about something to eat?'

Eat! She could no more have eaten than . . . 'No, thank you, tea would be lovely though,' she replied, somehow managing a smile.

Sister took Sadie to a single room next door to her office where Edward lay swathed in bandages. There was a drip up, fixed to his left arm.

Sadie's eyes filled with tears when she saw him. Her beautiful Edward burnt, but at least alive. She wanted to rush forward and take him into her arms, clasp him to her bosom, tell him it was going to be all right. But of course she couldn't.

In a daze, she sat on the chair by his bedside and stared at him. She didn't hear Sister leave the room, or later, the nurse enter with her tea.

'Mrs Fitzgerald?' the nurse said tentatively.

Sadie was suddenly aware of her presence, having up to that point been totally focused on Edward. 'Thank you, thank you very much,' she said, accepting the cup and saucer.

She must have drunk the tea for when she looked again her cup was empty. She laid it on the floor by her chair and went back to staring at Edward.

He groaned once, and said something she couldn't make out. But for the main part he just lay there without moving, like some Egyptian mummy.

'Mrs Fitzgerald, this is Dr Pym who is looking after your husband.'

Sadie blinked and looked round to find Sister and a bald-headed doctor beside her. 'We only got married two months ago, although we'd been engaged for some years,' she said.

The doctor glanced at Sister, then back again at Sadie. 'Is there anything I can do to help?'

'He will live, won't he?' she queried, desperation in her voice.

'We're hoping so. He has a fifty fifty chance,' the doctor replied in a flat tone.

'You'll do everything for him that you can?'

'Of course.'

'I mean, money's no object. He comes from a wealthy family. His father would want the best for him no matter what the cost. As do I.'

'I understand,' the doctor said.

'Oh God!' Sadie whispered in anguish, and ground a fist into her mouth.

'Would you like me to give you something?' the doctor queried.

Sadie shook her head.

'Nothing powerful. A very minor sedative.'

'No,' she declared emphatically.

'How about a little food now, Mrs Fitzgerald?' Sister asked.

'I couldn't,' she mumbled.

'More tea then?'

'Yes. Yes, I could manage that.'

'And what about a wash and brush up? I'm sure my staff wouldn't mind you using their private facilities.'

'I don't want to leave him, not even for a second,' Sadie replied, voice cracked and riven.

Sister nodded that she understood.

'Can I stay here as long as I want to?'

'Yes, Mrs Fitzgerald,' the doctor replied.

That made her feel somewhat easier inside.

'We'll leave you for now then,' the doctor smiled. 'And I'll be back to speak to you again later.'

'I'll have your tea brought in,' Sister said, picking up the empty cup and saucer. 'And there will also be someone along shortly to change the squadron leader's drip.'

Outside the room, when the door was firmly shut behind them, the doctor said to Sister, 'I think he'll survive if he can just get through the night. So we must keep our fingers crossed.'

They parted, Sister going off to arrange Sadie's tea and Edward's new drip.

Sadie roused herself, having been on the point of dropping off. A glance at her watch informed her it was ten to three in the morning. She was completely exhausted, but it never entered her mind to leave Edward's side. She'd have to eventually, of course, but not yet.

She gazed at him, illuminated by a small side light. A nurse had given him an injection at midnight, and he was due another around four.

'Sadie?' The voice was a weak croak.

She was on her feet in a flash and bending over him. 'I'm here, Edward. Try not to speak.'

'Sadie?'

'You've been burnt, but it's all going to be OK.'

'I . . . love . . . you.'

'And I love you, darling.'

His head lolled sideways, and at the same time he gave a long drawn-out sigh.

She stared at him in horror. 'Edward? Edward!'

When there was no reply she ran from the room to find someone, and almost bumped into Night Sister who was about to start on her rounds.

'It's my husband, something's happened!' she exclaimed.

Sister brushed past Sadie and into the room where she went straight to Edward. It only took her a couple of seconds to establish what she'd feared.

'I'm awfully sorry, Mrs Fitzgerald,' she said sympathetically to Sadie.

'You mean . . . ?'

'Your husband's dead.'

Sadie couldn't believe that. It wasn't true. The Sister had made a mistake. 'He can't be . . . He just can't be!'

'Sit down, Mrs Fitzgerald and I'll . . .'

Sadie grabbed Sister's arm. 'He can't be! You're wrong! You're lying!'

'No, Mrs Fitzgerald,' Sister replied softly. 'I'm not wrong. He is dead. I'm dreadfully sorry.'

A blackness came over Sadie and she slumped to the floor in a faint. Luckily Sister was able to break her fall.

'Ashes to ashes, dust to dust . . .' The vicar's words reverberated round and round inside Sadie's head as if they were sounds rung out on a bell.

'Would you care to throw in some earth, Mrs Fitzgerald?'

She gave him a sickly smile, then bent and scooped up a handful of earth from the pile at her feet. She stared down at the oak coffin bound with brass, the best available, and thought of Edward lying inside.

No, not Edward, she corrected herself, Edward's body. Edward, her Edward, was elsewhere. In heaven she hoped.

She threw the earth into the grave and listened to it rattle on the coffin. Somebody had taken her by the elbow, supporting her. Jonty, she realized. Good old Jonty!

'Chin up!' he muttered.

What an incredibly stupid thing to say, she thought, and very English. Stiff upper lip and all that! Well, she wasn't the stiff-upper-lip type.

God, she would have done anything to get Edward back. Given an arm, a leg, run from there to Timbuctoo, whatever.

When it was all over she thanked the vicar who commiserated with her in a very professional, though sincere, manner.

'I'll drive you back to the cottage,' Jonty said when she'd finished with the vicar.

'And I'll come and keep you company,' Ma offered.

'If you don't mind, Ma, I'd prefer to be on my own.'

'Are you sure, Sadie?'

Sadie nodded. 'I really do want to be alone. For now anyway.'

'All right then,' Ma said, and squeezed her hand.

Other people came up to her then, mainly airmen from the aerodrome, friends and colleagues of Edward's, plus some village chums from the pub.

'He'll be sorely missed, for Edward was well liked and popular,' Jonty said as they drove from the cemetery.

Not nearly as much as I'll miss him, Sadie thought, feeling thoroughly wretched, while at the same time experiencing a profound sense of loss.

Jonty was talking again, but she'd ceased listening. She glanced up at the sound of an approaching plane, and watched a Hurricane pass overhead.

As it flew into the distance she imagined it was carrying Edward out of her life for ever.

Gabrielle had arrived at the cottage twenty minutes previously and was now sitting with a cup of tea balanced on her lap while she toyed with a piece of Madeira cake that had been a present from Ma.

'Which brings me to the purpose of my visit,' she said. 'Are you ready to return to work?'

Sadie shook her head.

'It might be the best thing. Stop you brooding.'

'I'll be honest, Gabrielle, I don't consider myself fit to fly right now. I simply can't concentrate.'

'I see.'

Sadie sipped her tea. It was two weeks now since Edward's funeral since which she'd hardly crossed the threshold. Ma had done what shopping she'd needed, and been kindness itself.

'When do you think you'll be ready?' Gabrielle asked.

'I don't know.'

'We do appreciate what you must be going through, how awful it must be for you.'

'I've had some lovely letters. Yours included.'

Gabrielle set her crockery on the floor. 'I'll arrange indefinite leave for you, which won't be a problem when I explain you don't consider yourself fit to fly.'

Sadie smiled. 'They wouldn't want to lose one of their precious aircraft, would they?'

'No, they wouldn't,' Gabrielle agreed, smiling also.

'It's good of you to visit me personally. I appreciate that.'

'Now I must be getting back,' Gabrielle said, rising.

'Did you come in a Fairfield?'

'Yes. Flew it myself which was a pleasure. Now I'm deskbound I don't have much chance of flying.'

Sadie considered driving down the road, but decided she couldn't face that. One of the airmen had brought Gabrielle to the cottage.

'I don't want to go to the 'drome if you don't mind,' Sadie apologized. 'But you can drive our Morris yourself and leave it there. Someone will soon bring it back for me.'

Sadie handed Gabrielle the car keys and then they went to the door together.

'Goodbye for now,' Gabrielle said.

'Goodbye. And give my love to the girls.'

'I'll do that.'

They kissed, after which Sadie went out to stand just

474

in front of the door from where she watched Gabrielle drive off.

It was a gorgeous day, the sky blue, the sun shining in the distance and somewhere a bird was singing.

Sadie went back into the cottage and closed the door behind her.

A few days later Sadie made up her mind, she was going to leave the cottage and Duxford and go somewhere else. She had no specific place in mind, just as long as it was somewhere else.

There were too many memories for her here. Everywhere she looked she saw Edward, heard his voice, remembered something they'd done together.

Nor did she need to worry about money. Edward had had an account in a bank in Cambridge containing a substantial amount of capital, which as his widow was now legally hers.

Widow, that horrendous word she hadn't yet been able to bring herself to say.

If she was careful that money would be sufficient until well after the baby was born.

She smiled at the thought of the baby. At least Edward had left something of himself behind. If it was a boy she'd call him Edward after his father, if a girl Edwina.

She'd go soon, she decided, the sooner the better and she'd never return.

Early the following week she got into the Morris and drove away, without any idea where she was going.

Chapter Nine

Clare!

Sadie gazed out of the cab window at the house Edward had brought her to all those years before. How well she remembered that pinky brown stone topped by a double peeked slate roof, and the Gothic arch of a door. It was marvellous to see it again. She couldn't have been more excited. 'Look, Edward,' she said, holding the baby up in front of her. 'That's our home. Your daddy's home.'

Edward gurgled as though he understood, which pleased Sadie enormously.

'OK,' she said to the cabbie, who pulled away from the vantage point she'd asked him to stop at.

What a surprise Jack and Courcy were going to get when they got in from work that evening. She couldn't wait to see the expressions on their faces, particularly Jack's.

There was snow and ice everywhere, a true Canadian winterscape. She'd forgotten just how cold it could be.

'Here we are then, lady,' the cabbie said, drawing up in front of the house.

He took her bags from the boot and placed them by the door, smiling broadly when she added a generous tip to his fare.

Ring or simply go in? she wondered as the cab drove off. Go in, she decided.

A maid was *en route* to the door as she entered. 'Could you bring my bags in, please,' she smiled.

The maid was startled and flustered at the same time. 'Are we expecting you . . .?' She trailed off, waiting to be given a name.

Sadie obliged. 'Mrs Fitzgerald. Mrs Edward Fitzgerald.'

The maid looked dumbfounded. 'Mrs Edward Fitzgerald?' she repeated.

'That's correct. Is Mrs Wilson still housekeeper?'

The maid slowly shook her head. 'No, she left. It's Miss Ramirez, now.'

Thank goodness for that, Sadie thought. It would make matters easier. 'And what about Miss Dobson, the cook?'

'She's still here, and in the kitchen right now. Shall I get her for you?'

'No, don't bother, I'll surprise her. Just bring my bags in and take them upstairs. I'll sort out which room I'll have later. And what's your name?'

'Donna.'

'Pleased to meet you, Donna.'

Donna seemed about to say something further, but didn't. 'I'll take care of those bags,' she muttered instead, and walked past Sadie, shooting her a strange sideways glance as she did.

Sadie, with Edward cradled in the crook of her left arm, went to the kitchen where she found Miss Dobson, older and now a little grey, preparing a meal.

Miss Dobson looked up from what she was doing, her face registering shock and amazement when she saw Sadie. She promptly dropped the fork she was holding.

'I'm back,' Sadie stated simply.

Miss Dobson opened her mouth, then closed it again.

Sadie crossed to the cook and kissed her affectionately. 'Say hello to Edward Fitzgerald,' she smiled.

'Sadie?' Miss Dobson finally managed to croak.

'In the flesh. How are you?'

Miss Dobson collected her wits. 'Fine, fine,' she replied, wiping her hands on her apron.

'I didn't write that I was coming because I wanted to surprise everyone. When do you expect Jack and Courcy home?'

Miss Dobson took a deep breath. 'Then you don't know?'

'Know what?'

'That Mr Fitzgerald is dead.'

That stunned Sadie. 'Dead?'

'Yes. Shortly after he received the news about Edward. He suffered a massive coronary.'

Sadness filled Sadie. She'd been extremely fond of her father-in-law. She was going to miss him.

'Courcy runs the business now,' Miss Dobson went on. 'He took over when Mr Fitzgerald passed away.'

Courcy in charge of the mills! Now there was a real turn-up for the books. Logical though when you thought about it, for who else was there with Jack and Edward both gone.

Baby Edward screwed up his face and started to cry. 'What time is it?' Sadie queried, glancing at her watch. 'He needs feeding,' she explained to Miss Dobson.

'Did you say his name was Edward Fitzgerald?' Miss Dobson queried.

'That's right, named after his father.'

'Our Edward?'

'Well, of course!' Sadie frowned. 'But you must know that we got married?'

Miss Dobson shook her head. 'I'm afraid I didn't.'

This was puzzling, Sadie thought. Why hadn't Courcy or Jack told her? How odd!

At which point a small, raven-haired Hispanic woman whom Sadie judged to be in her early thirties entered the kitchen.

'You must be Miss Ramirez. I'm Mrs Fitzgerald,' Sadie said.

'Pleased to meet you, Mrs Fitzgerald. You are obviously one of the family?'

'Edward's wife. But then you never met him. It was in your predecessor's time that he left for England to fight in the war.'

'And was unfortunately killed,' Miss Ramirez said, glancing at Miss Dobson who raised her eyebrows.

'Is my husband's old room free?' Sadie queried, bouncing baby Edward up and down.

'Yes. It's exactly as the day he left it.'

'Then that's the one I'll have.'

'Of course.' Miss Ramirez looked undecided, then said, 'Perhaps I should call Mr Courcy and inform him of your arrival?'

Her surprise had lost its attraction now that she'd found out Jack was dead. 'Why not!'

Miss Ramirez was clearly relieved to hear that. 'I'll call him straight away,' she declared, and hurried from the kitchen.

'Can I feed the baby here? Or would you prefer I use the drawing-room?' Sadie asked.

'Here's fine. Would you like a cup of coffee? And how about something to eat? I can quickly rustle up a sandwich if you'd like one.'

'A club sandwich? I haven't had one of those since I left.'

'A club sandwich it is then,' Miss Dobson nodded.

Sadie removed her coat, then settled herself into a chair. Soon Edward was sucking noisily and she was experiencing that dreamy feeling she always did when she fed him.

'Is he on solids as well?' Miss Dobson queried, buttering a slice of bread.

'He has been for some time now. I should have weaned him months ago, but . . .' Sadie shrugged and smiled. 'Call it my little foible if you like. I'll certainly do so shortly though.'

She was still feeding when Miss Ramirez returned. 'Mr Courcy is on his way,' Miss Ramirez informed her.

'What did he say when you told him?'

Miss Ramirez blushed. 'You really want to know?'

'Yeah.'

'He swore. A phrase I'd rather not repeat.'

Sadie laughed, thinking maybe she should have waited till he got in from work after all. 'Do we still have an account at Yaeger's?' she asked.

'Yes,' Miss Ramirez replied.

'Good. Does Donna drive?'

'Yeah. Her car's parked round back.'

'Then I'd like her to go to Yaeger's and get me a few things. A crib because I could hardly bring one of those over on the boat with me. And some heavier winter clothing which we'll both need.' It was January 1946, four months after the end of the war.

Sadie turned to Miss Dobson. 'Do you know if my mink coat is still here?'

'I believe it is.'

'I suppose it'll be all right,' Miss Ramirez said hesitantly, wishing Courcy would hurry up and get there.

'It will be, I assure you,' Sadie smiled. 'Now if you could find a pen and a piece of paper I'll tell you what I want.'

The list was drawn up and Donna duly despatched to Yaeger's. As soon as he'd been fed Edward fell asleep. With Miss Ramirez's help, Sadie made up a makeshift bed for him in the drawing-room, after which Sadie ate her sandwich and drank her coffee. She'd just finished when Courcy appeared.

He strode into the kitchen, stopped and stared at her. 'My God, it's you!' he exclaimed.

'Well, of course. Who did you expect.'

He digested that. 'We lost touch. Didn't know where you were.'

'That was my fault, I'm afraid.'

He looked at Miss Ramirez and Miss Dobson who were watching him and Sadie. 'We'll go through to the drawing-room and I don't want us to be disturbed.'

'Yes, Mr Courcy,' Miss Ramirez nodded.

In the drawing-room Courcy closed the door and then went straight over to the drinks cabinet. 'It's a bit early in the day for me, but what the hell! What about you?'

'No thanks, I've just had some coffee.'

Courcy poured a shot of Scotch and threw it down his throat. Then he poured himself another.

'Some things never change,' Sadie commented drily.

'I don't drink all that much any more. At least, not like I used to. But your turning up like this is something of a shock! A goddamn big one actually. I never expected . . .' He broke off on noticing the baby.

'Whose is that?' he demanded, thinking Miss Ramirez hadn't mentioned anything about a baby when she'd called.

'Mine,' Sadie smiled. 'Come and meet Edward, your nephew.'

'Nephew!' he exclaimed. 'Sadie, just what are you trying to pull?'

'How do you mean?'

'First of all Miss Ramirez tells me there's a Mrs Edward Fitzgerald in the house, who turns out to be you, and now you're saying that the baby is my nephew!'

'The baby is,' she replied quietly. 'And I am Mrs Edward Fitzgerald, or was. Technically I suppose I'm now Mrs Sadie Fitzgerald.'

'Bullshit!' he retorted.

'Are you saying that you didn't know Edward and I were married?'

'Of course I didn't.'

'But he wrote informing you. I saw the letter.'

Courcy shook his head. 'No such goddamn letter arrived at Clare.'

Now that explained why Miss Dobson hadn't known either, Sadie thought. 'Well,' she said. 'I think I will have that drink after all. Then we'd better sit down and talk.'

'What do you want?'

'Gin and tonic, please.'

She sat and stared at him as he poured her drink. He'd put on weight she now realized, which suited him. And his neatly clipped moustache had gone which was definitely an improvement.

'Here,' he said, thrusting a glass at her.

'Before we go any further, Courcy, I want to say how sad I was to hear about Jack. That was something I had no idea about.'

'We both wrote to you directly we received news of Edward, but our letters were returned marked "not at this address".'

'I went away you see, and didn't leave a forwarding address. I was very distressed, and confused at the time, as you can imagine. I subsequently suffered a breakdown which took me quite some while to recover from.'

Courcy crossed to where the baby lay and stared down at him. 'And you claim this is Edward's?'

'I don't claim, Courcy, he is.'

'Can you prove that?'

'I have his birth certificate naming his parents if that's what you mean.'

'And what about a marriage certificate?'

'I have that also.'

Courcy's lips thinned. 'I'd like to see both if you don't mind.'

'Sure. They're in one of my bags upstairs. I won't be a minute.'

He watched her leave the drawing-room, then returned to the drinks cabinet and poured himself a really hefty measure. 'Jesus Christ,' he whispered, his tone a combination of anger and despair.

When Sadie got back to the drawing-room she found a despondent Courcy gazing down at Edward. She handed him the documents in question which he carefully studied.

'I can have these checked, you know,' he said.

'Do so if you wish. You'll find everything's above board.'

'Or I could destroy them here and now,' he went on somewhat wildly.

'That wouldn't alter the truth of the matter, and I would only send off for copies.' She paused, then said gently, 'It came to me while I was upstairs why you're so upset. You thought you'd inherited, is that it?'

Courcy's shoulders slumped. 'I was provided for with a financial settlement. But Clare itself and the business, plus all our land and other holdings were to go to Edward. But with Edward already dead it all came to me instead.'

'Except Edward left a widow. And under the terms of the family trust Jack created some years ago, which Edward explained to me after our marriage, Edward's widow would become principal beneficiary in the event of his predeceasing Jack.'

Courcy barked out a laugh. 'It's crazy! You were the maid and housekeeper, now you own everything!'

'I don't see it that way, Courcy. But rather as someone holding it in trust for Edward's son who is fully entitled to what was his father's.'

Courcy had another swig from his glass, then went over to a chair and slumped into it. He sat there silently for a few seconds, then said, 'I apologize for being so awful to you just now. But it's not every day a man loses Clare and the rest just like that!'

Sadie, having retrieved her drink from where she'd put it before leaving the room, sat facing him. 'If it wasn't for little Edward I'd let you keep it, Courcy, for it would be far more your inheritance, by right of blood than mine. But I've got little Edward, and his future, to think about.'

Courcy gave a long drawn-out, painful sigh. 'So it's back to the law for me, I guess,' he said, smiling tightly at Sadie.

'How was that going?'

'OK, nothing startling. My practice had just began to build when the old man died. Then it was a case of either selling the business or running it myself. I chose the latter.'

'Which is what I'm sure Jack would have wanted.'

Courcy pulled a face. 'I don't know about that. He'd always envisioned Edward as boss, Edward being his favourite as you know. I was always the black sheep of the family, rather living in Edward's shadow.'

Sadie didn't know how to reply to that, for what he said was absolutely true. 'I've been thinking about Edward's letter, the one you never received,' she said, changing the subject. 'It might well have been lost at sea, the ship carrying it having been sunk. That was still happening then.'

'Sounds a likely explanation,' Courcy nodded.

'He wrote it on our honeymoon, or what passed for a honeymoon. We had two months of marriage, and then he was . . .' She broke off, and took another sip of her drink.

There was a silence, then Courcy prompted, 'You mentioned something about a breakdown?'

'I simply went to pieces after Edward died. I left Duxford and travelled north to Glasgow where I contacted my family again. They were supportive, but I soon realized I had to be alone. So I continued north until I came to the most beautiful place called Mallaig where I rented a house. And it was there, fifteen months ago, that little Edward was born.

'The baby began the healing process, and when the war was finally over I knew that I had to bring him back here where he belongs.'

'And is that healing process complete?' Courcy enquired softly.

'I think so. I still miss Edward dreadfully, of course, but I've now come to terms with his death.'

'Jack took it real bad,' Courcy said. 'The effect on him was terrible. Then one day he just dropped down dead from a coronary. I suppose his heart was weakened with his first heart attack before Edward left.'

Sadie thought of Jack, recalling how much he'd loved and doted on Edward. How she wished that he'd lived to see little Edward.

'I suppose you'll want me to move out,' Courcy said.

'Where would you go?'

He shrugged. 'I don't know. Find an apartment somewhere in town, I guess.'

'You'd miss Clare though, wouldn't you?'

'Naturally,' he smiled. 'It's been my home since I was born.'

She made a decision then. 'You're welcome to stay, but on one condition.'

'Which is?'

'No funny stuff with me. Your first pass will be your last.'

He thought about that. 'OK, it's a deal. Thank you.'

'I mean it, Courcy. You behave yourself, or you're out.'

'I understand, Sadie. And as I said, you've got yourself a deal.'

'The only thing is, you don't think folks will talk? I mean, you and I living here, sharing the same house.'

'Naw!' he said, shaking his head. 'Having Miss Ramirez and Donna also resident makes it OK. No one will talk, I promise you.'

'Good, because I wouldn't want that. Not just for my sake, but little Edward's.'

He laid the two certificates he was still holding on to a circular table beside his chair. 'What happened about your flying?' he asked.

'You mean me being in the ATA? They were very kind and understanding after Edward's death. They gave me indefinite leave, then a discharge when I wrote and told them I was expecting.'

'And you really flew Spitfires? I find that incredible.'

Sadie laughed.

'And you enjoyed it?'

'Loved every moment. Hard work at times, mind you, but terribly rewarding.' She paused, then added softly, 'I haven't flown since the day Edward was shot down. That was my last delivery.'

'Do you miss it?'

'Let's just say that I think about my time in the ATA frequently. But now, what about you and Erin?'

'What about me?' he queried.

'I take it you're not married yet?'

He shook his head. 'I date regularly, but nothing serious.'

Sadie did a quick mental calculation. Courcy was thirty that year, beginning to push on a bit. 'You can't keep playing the Lothario bachelor for ever,' she smiled.

He didn't answer that.

'So there's no one special?'

'No one.'

'Maybe you should have married Heather. She was madly in love with you.'

'Heather wasn't for me,' he replied. 'Not in the long term anyway.'

'But OK to take to bed once in a while?'

'Exactly,' he answered, and laughed.

He'd changed, she thought. He wasn't as raffish as he'd been, nor did she feel uncomfortable in his presence as she often had in the past. Was this the result of Edward's and Jack's deaths, she wondered? There again, perhaps he'd changed simply because he'd grown up. Whatever, she much preferred the new Courcy she was now talking to.

'And what about Erin and Marty?'

'She had twins last summer. Boys called Ricky and Gene.'

Sadie clapped her hands in delight. That was wonderful! She couldn't wait to see them and show off little Edward.

'I'll call her tonight,' Sadie said. 'Are they still living in the same house?'

'No, they moved into a larger property when they found out she was pregnant.'

'They could have taken over the house at Silver River. Unless other arrangements have been made there?' Sadie said.

'That house is still empty, in fact no one's even been inside since the last time you and Edward were there. And I did make that suggestion to Erin, but she wouldn't hear of it. She said that was yours and Edward's house and should remain as such.'

'Well, I'll never live there now so I'll have to think of what to do about it,' Sadie answered.

'If I were you I'd knock it down. A waste I know, but somehow, in my book anyway, the right thing to do.'

Sadie tended to agree with that, but she would consider the matter further before she made a decision.

She finished her drink and agreed to another when Courcy offered. He returned the certificates to her when he took her glass.

'We can go first thing in the morning to see Father's lawyer and start getting this thing sorted out,' Courcy proposed.

'You're being very good about this,' she said.

'Have I a choice? The law is on your side, any contesting action on my part would only, in the long run, be a waste of money. All I'm doing is bowing gracefully to the inevitable.'

'You must be bitterly disappointed,' Sadie said when he handed her back her refilled glass.

'Of course. I'd be lying if I said I wasn't. I was enjoying running the business, much more fun than being a dry as dust lawyer.'

She'd have to get someone to replace him, she thought. Then, why bother? 'You could continue running the business, as my manager,' she suggested.

He frowned. 'Your manager?'

'Sure! Why not? The only difference is that you

would be accountable to me, and on a salary rather than the company profit.'

He shook his head. 'Everything's happened so quickly. Why only an hour ago I was owner, now here I am discussing the post of manager.'

'Life's like that sometimes,' Sadie said. 'It was the same for me the day Edward died.'

'A decent salary though, I hope?'

She smiled. 'Your father always believed in paying fair rates, and so do I. We'll negotiate something suitable.'

'Then I accept!' he declared, raising his glass in a toast.

They both drank to his new post as manager.

Sadie turned away from little Edward now fast asleep in the crib Donna had bought at Yaeger's, and stared round what had been Edward's room.

There were several school medals tacked to one wall, and various trophies on another. She went to a chest of drawers on top of which was a photograph of him dressed in tennis gear representing his school in a match. As she gazed at it her eyes misted over.

She replaced the photo and picked up a smaller one in a brass frame, this one of him representing the school at track.

In a way the wardrobe was the worst of all, it contained clothes that even after all these years still smelt of him. She buried her face in a sports coat and wept.

Sadie was at breakfast next morning, Courcy having already left for the mills, when Erin burst into the dining-room.

She rose from her chair as Erin flew into her arms. The pair of them hugged and kissed one another.

'Let me look at you!' Sadie said, holding Erin out at arm's length.

'I got fat,' Erin pouted.

She had certainly put on weight, being far fleshier than she'd previously been. 'You're not that bad,' Sadie said kindly.

'I am. Having twins did that to me. But I diet and exercise and I am hoping to eventually get myself back to what I was.'

'And I'm sure you will,' Sadie smiled.

'You're just the same, lucky dog. A teensy bit older looking perhaps, but we're all that.'

'It's great to see you again, Erin. I can't tell you.'

'And I'm just so thrilled to be able to call you *sister-in-law*.'

Sadie's smile faded from her face, replaced by a bleak, haunted expression. 'Yes. Your widowed sister-in-law.'

'Oh Sadie, I am so sorry,' Erin whispered.

How often had she heard those sentiments? Sadie wondered. And always her mental response was the same, not nearly as sorry as she was.

'Would you like to see little Edward?' she asked.

'Would I! Lead me to him.'

But first of all Sadie had to stop and admire Ricky and Gene who were in a double baby carriage outside the dining-room. 'How big were they when they were born?' Sadie enquired, jiggling Ricky up and down. She could see both Erin and Marty in the boys.

'Ricky was six pounds, Gene slightly less. What about little Edward?'

'Just over eight.'

'A big boy,' Erin acknowledged.

'Just like his father.'

'It's still hard to think – ' Erin bit her lip – 'that I'll never see Edward again.'

'Yes,' Sadie agreed. 'There are times when I expect him to come walking in through the door, or find myself making a mental note to mention something to him.'

'Will you tell me all about Duxford? I'd love to hear.'

'Of course.'

'Now come on,' said Erin, scooping up Gene and addressing him. 'Let's go and meet little Edward, your cousin.'

'He's in the kitchen with Miss Dobson,' Sadie said, and led the way.

Erin stayed until late afternoon, and it was the most marvellous reunion. When she left it was agreed that Sadie and Edward would come to lunch at her house the following day.

Sadie stared at the scarlet-coloured Gipsy Moth, memory after memory connected with it tumbling through her mind. The paint had faded, and there was dust, dirt and cobwebs all over it, but nothing that couldn't soon be put right.

'Your daddy's aeroplane,' she told Edward, who gazed back at her from his stroller through eyes that were the image of his father's.

She walked round the plane, then climbed up and sat in the front cockpit. Lovingly she caressed the controls, itching to get airborne again.

She clambered back down to the ground where she decided she would start work on the machine the very next morning. She'd go over it from propeller to tail, giving it a full service in the process. Then she'd have it repainted, keeping it scarlet of course.

She took the Moth's manual back to Clare with her and she spent a number of hours studying it, refreshing her memory.

The Moth left the ground and began to climb, its engine purring like a contented cat. She'd done a good job there, Sadie congratulated herself, thrilled to be back in the air.

At five thousand feet she indulged in a few aerobatics, noting how the plane handled, and how she herself was a little rusty.

She flew out over Lake Baldy, and past the Falls, which were as magnificent and awe inspiring as ever. From there she flew over the town itself which had grown larger in her absence.

Leaving the town behind she flew low over Erin's house, turned and did so again. She smiled when Erin ran from the house to wave at her. She waggled her wings in reply.

She stayed up for as long as she could, reluctantly landing again only because she was almost out of fuel.

How glorious that had been! she thought. She was completely exhilarated.

Now she felt she was truly home.

One day the following July found Sadie nervously waiting in the drawing-room, every so often glancing at her wrist-watch. Edward was sitting on the floor playing with some soldiers and a cardboard box that he was pretending was a fort. The soldiers were kilted highlanders that Sadie had spotted in town and hadn't been able to resist buying because of their Scottish connection.

She started when Donna popped her head round the door. 'They're here, their car's just driven up,' Donna declared.

Sadie jumped to her feet. 'Come on Edward, let's go and meet them,' she said.

'Mom-mee,' Edward replied, and got up from where he'd been sitting. Smiling broadly he walked over and took her hand.

Sadie's heart was thumping as they left the room. This was the moment she'd been looking forward to ever since the telephone call she'd received the previous week.

She opened the large Gothic-arched wooden front door and stepped into brilliant sunshine.

The man getting out of the car was somehow very typically Canadian in appearance. The woman who'd been sitting beside him was already out and helping their three children from the rear seat.

Sensing Sadie's presence the woman turned and stared at Sadie, their eyes locking. Even though Janet Bone had aged, Sadie had no difficulty recognizing her. She liked the look of her husband, Gary Gorman, too.

The two women met halfway and fondly embraced, at the end of which both were crying.

Janet had rung Sadie to say she and her family were going to be passing that way on vacation and could drop by. Sadie had insisted that the Gormans spend the night.

'I can't believe it,' Janet said, clutching Sadie's hand to her bosom.

'Me neither.'

'Do you remember . . . ?' they both started to say at once. They broke off and laughed in unison.

'Come and meet Gary,' Janet said.

When all the introductions had been made, they went inside where Janet marvelled at the house and Sadie's elevation in the world. What a contrast to Sadie's circumstances when she'd landed in Canada, Janet commented.

Sadie laughingly agreed.

From there on in 'Do you remember . . . ?' was an expression used over and over again.

Sadie frowned as she read the October monthly profit statement. She'd wanted to give Courcy a fair chance, but it was nine months now since she'd appointed him manager which she considered long enough. The time had come for her to speak to him.

'Donna!' she called out when Donna passed the drawing-room door.

'Yes, Mrs Fitzgerald?'

'I believe Mr Courcy is in his room. Do you think you could ask him to come and see me.'

Donna nodded and went off.

Sadie sighed, and laid the statement on top of the previous ones. She hoped this wasn't going to turn nasty, but something had to be done.

'You sent for me?' Courcy said shortly afterwards, striding into the room, shutting the door behind him.

'I want a word.' She indicated the settee facing her, which Courcy sat on.

'I'm not at all pleased with the company's performance,' she said.

He crossed his legs and leant back. 'How so?'

'We are making a profit, but each month the margin becomes less and less. If it continues this way we'll eventually be losing money. What do you have to say to that?'

'Not my fault. Demand is down, and I've been having trouble with the workforce who just won't work as hard as they used to.'

'Why not?' she queried.

He shrugged. 'A post-war syndrome of some sort, I'd imagine. There's a great deal of unrest nowadays, a lot of folk unsettled. It's a general trend in my opinion.'

'You mean nationally?'

'Yeah. Same in the States. They, too, are having an upsurge in labour troubles from what I read.'

Sadie hadn't read anything of the sort. 'And why is demand down?'

'It went up during the war. Now that the war is over it's coming down.'

'You're talking about pulp?'

'That's right,' he confirmed.

'Why should there be less pulp needed just because the war is over? Did the war make that much difference to demand?'

'No other explanation for what's been happening.'

She considered that. 'Our prices are competitive, I take it?'

'Yeah, of course!' he snapped in reply.

Edgy, she thought. He didn't like this questioning. Why? Did he feel it was an assault on his ability and masculinity? Or was he covering up something? If it was the latter she'd find out.

'And how about quality?' she went on.

He shifted uncomfortably on the settee. 'I have to admit we've had problems there. But nothing I can't handle.'

'What sort of problems?'

'Some of our chemical pulp hasn't been up to scratch. Lousy maintenance of the machinery in some cases, sloppy workmanship in others.'

'And what have you done about that?'

'I gave the maintenance guys hell, kicked ass in other words, and fired a few who'd been sloppy. Things have now improved in that direction.'

'But the profit margin is still down?'

'I told you, demand isn't what it was. Things are different to when Jack and Edward were in charge. They wouldn't do any better nowadays than I am.'

Sadie could only wonder about that.

'I'm coming into work with you tomorrow, I want to go through all the books and see just what's what for myself,' she stated.

Courcy glared at her. 'Why should you want to do that?'

'You're not objecting, are you?'

He was immediately flustered. 'Hell no! Not in the least.'

'Good, it's settled then,' she smiled, thinking she'd get Donna to look after Edward for the day. Donna would like that, she adored Edward, who was very fond of her.

Courcy stood up. 'Are you finished with me?'

Sadie nodded.

'Right. And I won't be home for dinner tonight. I'm going out.'

'Have you told Miss Ramirez?'

'You tell her!' he said coldly, and stalked from the room.

Sadie stared at the open doorway through which Courcy had vanished. They'd just had their first quarrel, if that was the right word, since her return.

She had the definite feeling it wasn't going to be their last.

The next morning Sadie insisted they went to the mills in the Cord, and that she drive. She didn't want to put Courcy down, but this was her way of reminding him that she was the owner, and boss. That he was in her employ, and answerable to her. Nor was the point lost on Courcy.

On arrival they went straight to the small office complex in the pulp mill where Sadie commandeered a desk for her use, but not Courcy's desk as she didn't want to flout his authority in front of the staff, and began going through the order and account books.

It was soon clear that the rot had started shortly after Courcy had taken over from Jack. Gradually profits had begun to fall, orders diminish. Customers that had been buying from the firm for years were suddenly doing so no longer. All this applied to both mills, not merely the pulp output as Courcy had led her to believe. And why was Courcy having trouble with the workforce when neither Jack nor Edward had had any difficulty keeping them in line?

When Courcy went over to the saw mill on a job Sadie knew would keep him away for at least half an hour, she took the opportunity to collar Merv Ulvenes who'd been with the company for over twenty years.

'Hi Merv, how are you?'

He beamed back at her. 'Fine, Mrs Fitzgerald. To what do we owe the honour?'

She returned his smile. 'I'm looking for some answers, Merv.'

'Answers?'

'I want to ask you something, and I assure you that what you reply is strictly between us. OK?'

He nodded. 'Shoot.'

'What sort of manager would you say Mr Courcy is?'

Merv's smile vanished to be replaced by an overall nervousness. 'Mr Courcy's OK,' he replied hesitantly.

'Merv, come on,' she cajoled. 'It's important I know.'

Merv shifted uneasily from one foot to the other. 'Strictly between you and I?'

'Strictly.'

'He tries hard, I suppose, but he just ain't the man old Jack was. Or your husband come to that. The staff simply don't respect him the way they did old Jack and Edward.'

Sadie had guessed as much. 'There are bad relations between him and the staff then?'

'He upsets people, rubs them up the wrong way. Why we've had more staff turnover in the past couple of years than we've had in all my time here. Part of the reason is that he interferes unnecessarily, and often to the detriment of the task in hand.'

'I see,' Sadie said slowly.

'He's even put my back up on a few occasions, and heck I'm the easiest guy in the world to get on with!'

Which was true enough, Sadie thought. Merv was well known for his easy-going manner.

'Have you any idea why we've been losing orders?'

Merv shook his head. 'Can't help you there, I'm afraid. All I know is that our output has been steadily decreasing.'

'OK then, thanks a lot,' Sadie said, patting Merv on the arm.

'And this was strictly between you and me? I've only told you what I have because you're the owner after all.'

'Strictly between you and me, Merv,' she reassured him again. 'You have my word on that.'

The picture Merv had painted was one of incompetence and bad managership, Sadie thought, as Merv walked away. Things were beginning to make sense.

She decided she'd fly up-country the next day.

She flew up the Abitibi River to the site where Patsy Kernan was logging boss, the same Patsy whom Edward had introduced her to the very first time he'd taken her flying.

She landed the Moth and taxied to a halt. As she was taking off her helmet she spotted the unmistakable figure of Patsy coming towards her.

'Thought it must be you,' Patsy said when she'd jumped to the ground.

He pointed a finger at the Moth's fuselage. 'Haven't seen this baby since you and Ed went off to the war. I hear you did real good in that.'

His expression became one of sadness. 'I am sorry about Ed. He was a fine man.'

'Yes,' she agreed softly.

Patsy's expression brightened again. 'But I believe you've got a little boy!'

'That's right. I called him Edward after his father.'

'Ed would have liked that.'

Sadie took Patsy by the arm. 'Now how about some of that coffee of yours? Even Miss Dobson our cook can't make coffee as good as you do.'

Patsy laughed. 'The pot's on. All I got to do is pour.'

'So why the visit?' he asked as they headed for his hut.

'You do appreciate that I'm now the owner of the Fitzgerald business? On Jack's death it went to Edward, and on his to me as his widow.'

'Sure, I know,' Patsy nodded. 'Must have been one hell of a shock for Courcy when you turned up as you did, he thinking he'd inherited and all.'

'A shock indeed for him,' Sadie agreed. 'And it's about him that I'm here.'

'Oh?'

'Let's get that coffee first though.'

They went into Patsy's hut where, as he'd said, the pot was already on. He poured the thick black coffee into two tin cups, then waved a bottle of rum at Sadie.

'Not for me thanks,' she said. 'But you go ahead.'

Patsy handed Sadie her cup, then poured a liberal amount of rum into his own. 'You mentioned it was about Courcy that you're here?' he prompted.

'How are you finding him to work for at this end?'

Patsy brought his cup to his mouth, and studied Sadie over its rim as he drank. 'Not so good,' he said eventually.

'Why?'

'For one thing he keeps turning up and altering work procedures. That in itself is a major pain in the ass.'

'Why does he do that?' Sadie queried.

Patsy had some more coffee, then replied slowly, 'My guess is he's trying to be better than Ed and the old man, which he never will be.'

'He's still a Fitzgerald,' Sadie countered.

'Maybe so. But he isn't up to the same mark as his pa or brother.'

Sadie mulled over that. 'What else?' she asked.

'Lots of little things. Wages arrive late, supplies don't come in on time. Men leave and aren't replaced for weeks on end. And then there are those goddamn reports.'

'What reports?'

'At the end of every day, I'll repeat that, *every* day, I have to sit down and write a lengthy report on what's happened. I've come to hate those goddamn reports. And there's no use trying to be brief, all that happens then is that I get a letter instructing me to write in fuller detail. About the only item I'm allowed to leave out is when the men go to the can and what they do when they're there.'

Sadie laughed.

498

'Can you do something about them, Sadie? 'Cause if I have to keep writing them I can see me jacking it in and going to another outfit. It's only my loyalty to Jack and your Edward that has kept me here.'

'Don't leave Patsy, changes will be made,' she said.

'When?' he said desperately.

'Soon,' she promised him.

'You're what!' Courcy exploded.

'Taking over. From now on, I'll be running the business.'

Courcy took a deep breath. 'And why may I ask?'

'I think you know the answer to that.'

He tried to hold her gaze, but couldn't. He glanced down at the carpet instead.

'What you gave me the other night as reasons for the fall in our profit margins were really excuses for bad performance on your part.'

He shot her a filthy look. 'Demand for pulp is down since the war. There's no disputing that.'

'True, I grant you. But not down by a great deal. You've lost a lot of orders through not delivering on time.'

'There have been a few unfortunate incidents in relation to that,' he conceded.

'More than a few, Courcy. Firms have just got fed up with us and switched to mills who do deliver as agreed.'

'I initiated a new system that should have been an improvement on the old one. Unfortunately there have been teething troubles.'

'That's putting it mildly! The staff still find your new system thoroughly confusing. Nor are they helped by you continuing to tinker with it, trying to improve it further as I believe you're forever saying.'

Courcy crossed to the drinks cabinet and poured himself a large Scotch. He was furious with Sadie. Everything had been running smoothly until she'd reappeared.

He paused then, and took stock. No, it hadn't, he reluctantly admitted to himself. He'd only been pretending that it had.

'Damn!' he muttered.

'Pardon?'

He turned to face her. 'You don't have to worry about me making a fuss. I'll formalize the situation by giving you my resignation later tonight.'

She felt sorry for him then. How pathetic he looked standing there, like a little boy who'd just been given a dreadful school report.

'Come and sit down,' she said, indicating a chair adjacent to the settee she was on.

'I don't want your resignation,' she said when he'd sat. 'I'd like you to continue.'

'But taking orders from you.'

'Let's put it this way. I'll be the owner in charge of the business. You'll be my manager and second in command.'

'And what makes you think you can run the business better than me?'

'I know I can,' she replied softly. 'Don't forget I worked there when Jack and Edward were alive. I was taught the management side of things by Jack himself.'

Courcy thought about that, then shook his head. 'You can count me out. I'm going to reopen my law practice.'

'You mean quit?' She paused, then said 'I'll tell you this, Courcy, neither Jack nor Edward would have quit in similar circumstances.'

His face flamed. 'They wouldn't have found themselves in these circumstances,' he replied honestly.

'But they wouldn't have quit if they had. They weren't quitters, are you certain you want to be?'

When he didn't reply, she asked, 'Would your decision have been different if I'd been a man? Is that it?'

He looked directly at her, and this time did hold her gaze, 'I don't know, possibly.'

'I believe we can work together, Courcy, even make quite a good team.'

'You do?' he said, surprised.

'I do,' she confirmed. 'Your main mistake is that you've been going about certain matters the wrong way, trying to improve tried and trusted systems and practices. However, what damage has been done can and will be rectified. The company is still sound which is the important thing.'

'I really loused up, eh?'

She decided a little reassurance was in order. For she genuinely did want him to stay, something she felt she owed Jack. 'Let's look at it this way, you took over a company of which you had no practical working knowledge and proceeded to run it as best you could. If an accusation is to be levelled it's that you simply tried too hard, and have an awful lot to learn about labour relations. So what do you say?'

She'd won him over. 'I enjoy being at the mills, Sadie. I never imagined I would, but I do. Perhaps there's more of the old man in me than I thought.'

'Could be,' she smiled.

'OK then, we'll give it a try,' he said.

Next morning Sadie took control at the mills, leaving little Edward behind to be looked after by Donna who'd agreed to become his full-time nanny.

Sadie emerged from the Sinclair Building where the offices of R. W. Allmeyer were located, Allmeyer being one of the customers the company had lost.

It had been a difficult meeting with Allmeyer who'd been most reluctant to replace his business with Fitzgerald's, but in the end, with assurances and promises, Sadie had talked him into giving them another chance.

She stood shivering as an icy wind whipped down Yonge Street, and prayed that a cab would appear soon. When one stopped Sadie gratefully climbed into its warm interior.

She thought again of Allmeyer, and smiled at her success. One more company to see the next day and then she could leave Toronto and fly home to Clare. She hated being away overnight from little Edward, but there were times when it was necessary. She would be away again the following week as she had to go to Ottawa on a similar mission, trying to win back lost business.

On reaching the hotel she went up to her room where she stripped and had a leisurely wallow in the bath. Slipping into her dressing-gown she decided she couldn't be bothered going to the dining-room, so rang room service and ordered a meal to be sent up.

She put the television on, but there wasn't anything of interest showing, so switched it off again. Crossing to the window she stared out over the city and wished she had some company for the evening.

Even at Clare she was often lonely, spending a considerable number of evenings by herself once little Edward had been put to bed.

There was Courcy, but his new girl-friend was taking up a great deal of his spare time. And if they were in together, she usually went early to her bedroom not wanting to intrude.

She did see Erin of course, the pair of them regularly visiting one another. How the twins were growing! As was little Edward who was now two years old.

With a sigh she turned away from the window. Maybe there was something on the radio? she thought. She was more fortunate there, tuning into a comedy programme that always amused her.

When her meal arrived she ate it sitting propped up in bed. In the middle Donna rang to say Edward wanted a word with his mommy.

She felt better afterwards, their conversation had cheered her considerably.

The following day she was again successful in recapturing lost business.

'Pregnant again! That's wonderful news!' Sadie enthused, and kissed Erin on the cheek.

'Wonderful in some ways, not so in others,' Erin responded.

'Why's that?'

'Well, I am pleased to be adding to the family. And Marty, of course, is over the moon. It's just that I've only recently managed to lose all that weight I piled on with the twins, and now I'll be putting it back on again. Back to square one.'

Sadie felt for Erin, knowing what a titanic struggle it had been for her to regain her shape. 'As you're only having a single baby you shouldn't get so big this time round,' she said.

'Who says it's only a single baby? There's no certainty of that. Though naturally it's what we're hoping for. Two sets of twins would be too much to handle. At least for us it would be.'

'I'll keep my fingers crossed then,' Sadie smiled. 'Now how about some tea?'

'Please. But I won't be having sugar. That's something I'm going to cut down on right away.'

Sadie nodded her approval. She temporarily left Erin to go to the kitchen, only to bump into Lois *en route*, Lois being Donna's replacement.

'And no cake or cookies,' Sadie instructed, thinking of Erin. 'Just tea.'

When Sadie returned to the drawing-room she found Erin staring at a framed photograph of her and Edward taken outside the Red Lion pub in Duxford.

'The uniform certainly suited him,' Erin commented.

'Yes. I always thought that.'

'Makes him very dashing, and handsome.'

'He was handsome without the uniform,' Sadie said.

Erin smiled at her. 'I know that. I meant the uniform made him even more handsome.'

Erin lit a cigarette, and sat down. 'You should socialize more,' she said.

'I do socialize!'

'But not enough.'

'I socialize as much as I wish to,' Sadie countered, which was both true and untrue.

Erin decided to be more forthright. 'What I'm driving at, Sadie, is that it's high time you got yourself another man. Edward would have wanted that, I'm sure of it. And you have little Edward to think about, it's neither good nor healthy for a child to be brought up by a single parent. I appreciate that in some cases there's no alternative, but in your case there is. Why you're beautiful! And still relatively young, not to mention rich. If you gave them half a chance a legion of men would be falling over themselves to marry you.'

Sadie mentally pictured a legion of men clamouring at Clare's front door, and smiled. But the smile soon faded when she replied to her sister-in-law, 'I'm just not ready yet, Erin. Maybe sometime, but not yet.'

Erin wagged a finger at Sadie. 'As long as you're not thinking of doing a Queen Victoria! That would be a tragic waste.'

'I'll try not to do a Queen Victoria,' Sadie assured Erin, her smile returning.

At which point Lois and the tea arrived.

Sadie studied the profit sheet that had just been presented to her. Their profit margin had increased for the sixth successive month, and by a larger percentage over the previous margin than that over its predecessor.

She'd succeeded in turning the company round, Sadie congratulated herself, there could be no doubt about that.

She scribbled on a pad, and nodded at the result. By her calculations they would shortly be back at the point Fitzgerald's had been at when Courcy took over. And when it reached that point she wasn't going to be happy with that and rest on her laurels.

No indeed. She had plans.

'Expansion? Build our own paper mill?' a dumbfounded Courcy breathed. It was now a year since Sadie had assumed command at the mills, during which time they'd gone from strength to strength.

'Sure! We'll use our own pulp to make our own paper. If I'm right our overall profits should double.'

Courcy swallowed hard.

'And when that's established and working smoothly I have another idea I want to implement,' she went on.

'What's that?'

'Something an Oregon mill has successfully done according to an article I read. They are making and selling finished wood products at the mill itself.'

'What kind of wood products?' Courcy queried.

'Desks for one. Tables and chairs. Those sort of things.'

'But that's manufacturing!' Courcy protested.

'It's part and parcel of what was referred to in the article as an integrated mill. The processing of raw materials into finished, saleable goods is completed in one series of operations on one site.'

'But . . . but the investment of such a project would be enormous!'

'Though not beyond us, if handled correctly.'

Courcy contemplated all this, and shook his head. 'Jack would have been against it.'

'Why?' she demanded.

'I just know he would.'

'Baloney! Quite the contrary. Jack would have loved the challenge. He'd have been all for it, as would Edward.'

'Well, I don't agree.'

She studied him. 'Know what I think?'

'What?'

'That underneath you are, and always have been, a conservative with a small c. You're scared to take risks.'

He bridled at her use of the word scared in reference to him. 'I am nothing of the sort!'

'I say you are.'

'I've taken plenty of risks in my time.'

'Name one?'

He thought and thought, but couldn't.

'See!'

'Damn you, Sadie. Do you always have to be right?'

'I'm not,' she smiled. 'But I know I am about this.'

'But the capital needed . . .'

'I'll put up whatever's necessary as collateral against a bank loan,' she interjected.

'But not Clare itself? That's sacrosanct.'

'If the bank was to insist on Clare then Clare would go on the line.'

He was horrified at that. 'You wouldn't! You couldn't! What if the unthinkable happened and it all went wrong. What then?'

'It won't.'

'But what if it did?' he persisted, brow suddenly beaded with sweat.

'If the worst came to the very worst then I suppose I would lose the collateral,' she answered. 'But trust me, it won't.'

He prayed to God she was right.

Sadie had to be patient through the winter, but finally the day arrived the following spring when work began on building the paper mill.

'Mrs Fitzgerald, will you dig out the first scoop?' the foreman asked her.

506

This was something she'd been eagerly looking forward to. Leaving Courcy she went to a bulldozer with a mechanical scoop and climbed aboard. The operator was already on board, and standing to one side, waiting to instruct her.

'Easy really,' he said to her, and explained what she had to do.

With a clank the metal scoop descended and bit into the earth, to rise again leaving a hole behind.

A cheer arose from those watching, after which more bulldozers started up and began digging.

Sadie descended to the ground again and, eyes shining, returned to Courcy. 'Fun, eh?'

He nodded, but looked unconvinced.

'Come on. Loosen up! Days like this are to be enjoyed, so stop being a party pooper.'

Sadie stared out over the site of the paper mill, already seeing it built and functioning.

She shivered with excitement, and suddenly found herself covered in goosepimples.

Sadie sipped her Martini and thought about the paper mill now nearing completion. She was scheduled to fly to Montreal the following morning where she had a meeting with a potential client. She began going over in her mind the detail of her sales pitch.

'Sadie?'

She came out of her reverie to find that Erin was standing beside her with a smiling man. Erin had given birth to a little girl sixteen months previously whom she'd called Patricia Ann. Erin was still fighting her weight problem having, to her disgust, put on just as much weight as she had having twins.

'I'd like you to meet Rusty Fisher who's a surgeon at the hospital. Rusty, this is Sadie. Sadie, Rusty.'

The two of them shook hands.

'Can I freshen your drink?' Erin asked Sadie. The

Sunday afternoon drinks party was at her house, and there were about three dozen people present, including Courcy with yet another girl-friend.

'Not for me thanks,' Sadie replied, placing a palm over the top of her glass.

'I'm fine also,' Rusty said.

'Must circulate,' Erin smiled, and moved away.

'A surgeon, eh?' Sadie said, judging Rusty to be in his late thirties, possibly early forties. A rather bland face, she thought, but seemed pleasant.

'An anaesthetist actually.'

'Really! That sounds interesting.'

'It can be.'

'I hope you always make sure your patients are well under before the slicing starts?' she said as a joke.

He laughed. 'That reminds me of a story. Didn't happen to me I'm happy to say, but to a colleague of mine.'

As he spoke Sadie found her mind wandering back to the meeting she had the next day, a very important meeting as far as she was concerned. Then she thought of the integrated mill she'd visited in Oregon the previous month, and how fascinating she'd found it. She'd picked up some excellent tips there.

She became aware that Rusty was looking at her expectantly, so she nodded, hoping that was the right thing to do. He frowned slightly, then began to tell another story.

Her mind was still on the paper mill, whose construction was on schedule, when Rusty said, 'If you'll excuse me.'

'Oh! Of course.'

He went off and joined a group of three people, one of whom was Philip Mandela who was there with his wife Diane.

'Well?' Erin demanded eagerly, reappearing at Sadie's side.

'Well what?'

'Did you like him?'

'He was OK, I suppose.'

Erin sighed. 'He's divorced and very available. I was hoping you two might . . .' She waggled her fingers before Sadie.

So that was it! Erin was trying to matchmake again. 'No, we didn't . . .' And she waggled her fingers back at Erin.

'He's an excellent conversationalist.'

'Is he? I'm afraid I was only half-listening.'

Erin pulled a face. 'You're impossible, Sadie. Quite impossible.'

'Sorry,' said Sadie, smiling apologetically.

'Now there's someone else I'd like you to meet. And this time try and pay attention.'

'I suppose he's available too?'

'Why do you think I invited him!'

Sadie groaned.

George collected stamps for a hobby and had a faint whiff of halitosis about him.

Erin shot Sadie a disapproving look when a few minutes later she beat a hasty retreat from the amateur philatelist.

Sadie stared at the red button, knowing that once it was depressed the machinery would start. She lifted a finger and laid it on the button, and as she did so, she caught sight of Courcy out of the corner of her eye.

Turning to him she beckoned him over. 'You do it,' she said.

'Me! But it's your paper mill.'

'And you've done a lot of the hard work bringing it into existence. You do it.'

Courcy flushed with pleasure. 'Are you sure about this?'

'Positive. On you go.'

Courcy took her place in front of the button and seconds later the machinery roared into life.

'I enjoyed that,' he said to her.

'Thought you might. Now where's the champagne?'

Sadie gazed at Courcy's back as he went to get it. She was pleased with him, under her guidance he'd learnt a lot since she'd taken over. He'd developed into a first-class manager.

His problems with the staff had long since disappeared. He treated them firmly, but with compassion and respect, and luckily he'd won their respect in return.

He appeared with two glasses and handed her one. 'You toast,' he said.

She raised her glass. 'To the mill, and its success!'

He was only too pleased to drink to that.

The Moth droned on towards Clare. She was returning from up-country where she'd been making a routine visit.

She began to think of the paper mill and how well it was doing – in fact it was performing far better than she'd dared hope. The time had come to start the manufacturing side of things, she decided. She'd set the wheels rolling in that respect first thing the next day.

Her thoughts turned to little Edward, which made her smile. Donna had taken him to the twins' birthday party earlier that afternoon where she had no doubt he'd had a whale of a time. When she got home she'd hear every last detail about it from him.

She was looking forward to that.

'I have to say the whole operation is working like clockwork. And it's all thanks to you and your vision. I had my misgivings I must admit, but I was wrong and you were right,' Courcy said to Sadie. It was mid-July 1951, and they were in Cindy's where they'd brought Mr Peterson, their bank manager, for lunch, something they'd been meaning to do for some while.

Mr Peterson had just excused himself to go to the toilet.

'Thank you,' Sadie smiled.

'I'll tell you this, you're the best Fitzgerald of all. Better even than Jack. And I mean that, it isn't bullshit. The best Fitzgerald of all!'

His praise made her glow inside with pleasure. 'You're due a lot of credit yourself, Courcy. You've worked like a Trojan, to great effect. Your father and Edward would have been proud of you.'

Courcy dropped his gaze. She couldn't have said anything that could have touched him more.

'Very proud,' she added. 'As indeed am I.'

'Funny how things turn out, isn't it?' he mused. 'Who would have imagined you running the company with me as your number two, or the changes that you have implemented?'

'Yes, it is funny how things turn out,' Sadie agreed.

'But are you happy?'

She thought of little Edward whom she loved and adored to distraction. 'Happy enough. And you?'

He smiled thinly, but didn't reply.

The manufacturing and sales side of their fully integrated mill had been in operation for four months, and had proved a winner right from the start. Mr Peterson had declared himself most impressed with their new profit margins. The collateral Sadie had put up for her programme of expansion, which had not included Clare, was totally safe and secure.

'I've just been thinking,' Courcy said. 'Know what you've done? Created an empire.'

Sadie laughed. 'Hardly that!'

'Well, I'd call it an empire. The Fitzgerald empire.'

The phrase had a beguiling ring about it, Sadie thought. But it would take more than an integrated mill to be called an empire as far as she was concerned.

She glanced at her watch, checking the time. As it was the school holiday she'd arranged for Donna to bring

Edward into town so she could buy him some clothes he was badly needing. They were all to meet up shortly outside Cindy's.

A beaming Mr Peterson reappeared to sit beside them. 'I must thank you for lunch, but unfortunately I have to be going. Business calls!'

'And we want to thank you yet again for all your help, understanding and assistance,' Sadie said.

He held up a hand. 'Think nothing of it! That's what banks are for, after all.'

They rose to leave, Courcy paying the bill *en route* to the door. They said their goodbyes outside to Mr Peterson who strolled off.

'I'll wait with you till Donna shows,' Courcy said.

'There's no need for that.'

'Manners maketh the man, as the English say,' Courcy replied, and winked at her.

Sadie laughed, thinking he must be tighter than she'd thought. They'd all drunk quite a bit of wine during lunch, she herself drinking more than she would have normally done.

'There's Donna now!' Courcy said, pointing to Donna's De Soto. Sadie looked and saw the car with Donna at the wheel. The bouncing shape in the rear would be Edward.

The De Soto was only half a block away when another car came shooting out of an alley to smash straight into it, knocking the car over on to its side.

Sadie stood rooted in horror, not believing she'd witnessed such a scene. Petrol from a shattered tank leaked on to the street a split second before the De Soto caught alight.

She opened her mouth and shrieked, at the same time shaking all over. Beside her Courcy galvanized himself into action.

Fire! Edward! She stared into the roaring flames in the middle of which her son was being burnt just as his father had been before him.

She was still shrieking when Courcy reached the car. He grabbed the handle of the top rear door, jerked the door open and stretched inside. Catching hold of the wailing Edward he pulled Edward from the inferno and staggered backwards.

'Take him!' Courcy gasped, thrusting the boy into a bystander's arms, and returned to the car for Donna.

Sadie flew across the street to pluck Edward from the man's grasp and cuddle him to her. His clothes were scorched, and there was a burn on his cheek, but apart from that he appeared all right.

Sadie found herself crying as she clutched her beloved son tightly to her bosom. 'Oh my darling boy!' she repeated continuously.

Courcy was yanking at the front door, but it wouldn't budge. 'Climb into the back!' he screamed at Donna who was burning before his very eyes.

'Foot trapped,' she replied, and fell sideways.

Strong hands took hold of Courcy and forced him away from the car. 'You can't do any more, buddy,' a voice said.

He turned on the speaker, a middle-aged cop. 'I couldn't . . . she said her foot was trapped.'

'You did all you could. And you got the boy out.'

Courcy gazed at the car which now exploded sending flames and debris flying in all directions. The crowd that had gathered hastily moved away.

The cop left Courcy and strode over to where the driver of the other car, who'd been thrown free in the crash, was sitting on the ground shaking his head. He bent and smelled the man's breath which stank of alcohol. 'Bastard!' the cop hissed.

Courcy went to Sadie. 'How is he?' he asked, reaching up to stroke Edward's hair. He noticed then that his hand was badly burnt, and wondered why it didn't hurt.

'He's OK. Shaken but OK,' Sadie replied, tears streaming down her face.

Courcy glanced at his right hand to discover it was even worse than his left.

'How's my face?' he asked Sadie.

'You've lost your eyebrows and the front of your hair,' she informed him.

'But the face itself?'

'Redder than usual, with a couple of spot burns.'

He grunted in relief.

The De Soto continued to blaze, as they watched the other car driver being handcuffed and then bundled into the rear of a squad car.

Sadie thought Courcy was asleep when she entered his hospital room, but he opened his eyes and smiled at her.

'How are the hands?' she said.

He held them up, wrapped in bandages. 'I'm told they're going to be as good as new. Well, almost!'

As there wasn't a chair available she perched on the edge of his bed. 'They must be sore?'

'I have some pills to take if they become too uncomfortable,' he replied.

'Courcy, I can't begin to thank you for what you did today. It was a total nightmare.'

'How's little Edward?'

'At home where everyone is making a great fuss of him. When I left he was still crying over Donna.'

Courcy's face contorted. 'I can still see her in there. A human torch from head to toe. It's a vision that's going to haunt me till my dying day.'

Sadie looked positively haggard. 'That could so easily have happened to little Edward. If you hadn't done what you did . . .' She trailed off, and shuddered.

'I'm only thankful that I was able to save him,' Courcy said quietly. 'I wish I could have done the same for Donna.'

'It would have been too much to bear if little Edward had gone the same way as his father. It's such a horrible, cruel death,' Sadie said.

Courcy nodded.

'Oh God!' gasped Sadie, and rammed a fist into her mouth. Just thinking how close she'd come to losing little Edward made her want to retch. After the day's events it had taken enormous will-power on her part to leave him behind at home, but she'd felt she had to visit Courcy to whom she and little Edward owed so much.

Courcy thought of his brother Edward burning the way Donna had, and suddenly found he had tears in his eyes.

Sadie removed her fist from her mouth. 'Little Edward and I will be forever in your debt, Courcy. Neither of us will ever be able to repay you. You were exceptionally brave.'

He shrugged that off. 'What about Donna?'

'Her body's in the morgue. I'm going to visit her parents after I leave you. They're quite beside themselves apparently.'

'Understandable,' Courcy muttered.

They talked for a few minutes more, then Sadie got up to go. 'With all my heart, Courcy, thank you again,' she said, and kissed him on the cheek.

When she'd gone he raised a bandaged hand to touch the spot that she'd kissed.

Sadie was embroidering a tablecloth, which was one of her favourite pastimes. She glanced up when Courcy came into the drawing-room. It was three weeks since Donna's death and ten days since he'd been discharged from the hospital. He still hadn't returned to work nor would Sadie allow him to do so until his hands were fully healed.

'Like a drink?' he asked.

'Maybe later,' she replied.

'Do you think you could pour me a whisky and soda?'

She instantly laid her embroidery aside. 'Large one?'

'Sure! Why not?'

'Going out tonight?' she enquired as she crossed to the drinks cabinet.

'Naw.'

'Is Janey coming over then?' Janey was his current girl-friend.

'It's finished between us. It simply fizzled out.'

'I'm sorry to hear that,' Sadie said, placing his drink on a coffee table.

'Are you?'

She glanced at him, wondering why he'd said that in such a peculiar way. It was the angle of course, but for a moment it was as though she were staring at Edward. Then he moved and the illusion was broken.

'She seemed a nice girl,' Sadie replied.

He made a dismissive gesture. 'Aren't they all?'

'You're too fussy, Courcy,' she admonished. 'If you're not careful you're going to end up an old bachelor roué.'

He waggled his partially regrown eyebrows at her, making her laugh. 'There are worse fates than that!'

'Idiot!' she replied.

'I'll have some of that drink now, please,' he requested.

Sadie lifted the glass and placed it against his lips. She also had to help him at mealtimes, Lois substituting for her if she was out.

'As we're both staying in tonight what shall we do?' he queried as she replaced the glass on the coffee table.

'I don't know. Television?'

He pulled a face. 'What's on?'

Sadie consulted the evening paper. 'Nothing exciting, I'm afraid.'

'I have it!' he exclaimed. 'What about a game of little Edward's snakes and ladders?'

She was astonished. 'Snakes and ladders! You want to play that?'

516

'Well, I can't play cards with my hands bound up as they are. But I could manage a board game.'

The idea appealed to Sadie. 'OK then, I'll go and get the box from his room.'

'Another sip before you go?'

'Nice perfume,' he commented when he'd had his sip. 'New?'

'Hmmh,' she confirmed. 'I came across it in Yaeger's.'

'It suits you. Makes you smell like wild roses.'

'I'll get that box,' Sadie said, and left the room. For some reason she was highly delighted that he'd complimented her.

It turned out to be one of the funniest evenings Sadie had had in a long time. Courcy was brilliant company.

When she finally went up to bed Sadie was humming jauntily. Snakes and ladders would never be the same again.

Sadie totted up the column of figures again, checking her calculation. She nodded to herself when she confirmed that the sum was correct.

Reaching for the telephone she made a call. In the middle of this, she realized she was being stared at.

She glanced quickly round, and there was Courcy, who'd returned to work earlier that week, gazing intently at her. As soon as their eyes met he looked away.

Sadie blushed, but not with embarrassment, so with what?

'Yes, yes, that's right,' she said into the telephone.

Later that day Sadie found herself watching him, thinking how totally different he was to the Courcy she'd first known. In some ways he'd become quite startlingly like Edward.

She very much approved of this new Courcy. And he was such fun to be with! When he chose to he could make her laugh at the drop of a hat.

She realized then she was seeing Courcy in a completely new light.

That caused her to blush again.

She should replace the Moth, Sadie thought as she tinkered with its engine, and buy a newer, more comfortable, machine. But she knew she wouldn't. Because it had been Edward's plane she would keep it as long as it could fly.

There again, she thought, there was no reason why she couldn't buy a second machine. An Auster perhaps. There was enough space in the hangar for two planes.

She started when a shadow fell over her.

'Sorry,' Courcy apologized. 'I didn't mean to frighten you.'

She smiled at him. 'I didn't hear a car.'

'I rode over,' he explained. 'What are you doing?'

She told him. 'And to what do I owe this pleasure? I can't remember you ever having been out to the hangar before.'

'I have once, years ago. And the reason I'm here is to ask if you'll take me up.'

She wiped her oily hands with a cloth. 'I must say I'm surprised. Why the sudden interest?'

'I've been thinking recently that it's something I should at least have one go at, and so here I am. Will you take me?'

'Of course! I'd be delighted to. When did you have in mind?'

He shrugged. 'Whenever it's convenient to you.'

She thought about that. 'Then why not now! Edward's old gear is at the back, you can wear that.'

Edward's suit and jacket were large for Courcy, but Sadie assured him that didn't matter. They would keep him warm which was the main thing.

Courcy helped her manoeuvre the plane outside where she placed the chocks in front of its wheels. She then instructed him to climb into the front cockpit where she plugged in his head-set, explaining that they would be able to talk during the flight by means of the Gosport tube connecting both cockpits.

Satisfied that Courcy was settled, Sadie scrambled into the rear cockpit where she busied herself with the instruments and controls. Then she leapt to the ground and went forward to the propeller.

The engine caught and roared into life on the second swing, and a smiling Sadie gave Courcy the thumbs-up which he returned.

Once more in the rear cockpit, with head set plugged in, Sadie pulled the chocks free, hauled them into the cockpit and stowed them away.

'OK?' she asked Courcy. 'Let's go.'

How wonderful to be flying for the first time ever, Sadie thought, remembering her own first flight with Edward. She envied Courcy.

The Moth left the ground and began to steadily climb. Sadie took her up to five thousand feet where she levelled off.

'How are you?' she enquired a few minutes later.

'Fine. Never realized it was so cold up here though.'

'You get used to it.'

'You're not going to turn upside down or anything like that?' he queried anxiously.

'No, I promise you.'

'This must be quite different to flying a Spitfire or a Hurricane?' he said.

She laughed. 'It's the difference between riding a gentle horse and a pure bred racer.'

'I understand,' he replied.

'I can see Cindy's!' he exclaimed excitedly as they flew over town. 'And there's Yaeger's, and . . .'

Sadie smiled to herself as he rattled on. He was now clearly over his initial nerves and was thoroughly enjoying the flight.

She stayed aloft for twenty minutes, then brought the Moth in to land, making as smooth a landing as she'd ever made. She then taxied to the front of the hangar and killed the engine.

'Unplug your head-set before you get out,' she reminded him.

'That was exhilarating,' he enthused, joining her on the ground.

'Would you go up again?'

He furrowed his brow, then nodded. 'Yes, I would. Though I wouldn't want to know about any of that stunt stuff. I doubt I've got either the head or stomach for such antics.'

Sadie admired his honesty. 'Then we'll do it again sometime.'

'Agreed,' he smiled.

There were several moments' silence between them during which neither spoke, simply remained looking at one another, then he said, 'I'd better get this gear off.'

She waved to him as he rode away, after which she went to where he'd hung Edward's suit and stared at it thoughtfully.

Sadie stood at her bedroom window watching Courcy play catch with little Edward; they were both thoroughly enjoying themselves.

She smiled when she saw Courcy reach for a slightly wide ball, and miss it, although he should easily have caught it. The fact was that Courcy wasn't a natural athlete as his brother had been. Courcy himself admitted to being uncoordinated and awkward at times.

Little Edward shouted something, and threw a high ball which Courcy, to his obvious delight, successfully caught. He clapped when little Edward caught the high ball he threw back.

The two of them got on well together, Sadie thought,

which pleased her enormously. For some time now the pair of them had been fast friends.

She was just turning away from the window when, with a yell, Courcy went sprawling to end up on his backside.

Little Edward laughed uproariously, and after a few seconds so too did Courcy.

'A barn dance?' Sadie said.

'Yeah, this Saturday night. I wondered if you'd care to go with me? You're not doing anything else, are you?'

'No,' she admitted.

'And there's no problem with Edward.'

That was true. Hilary, Donna's replacement, was on hand to look after Edward.

'So what do you say?'

Sadie was tongue-tied. She'd gone out with Courcy before, but it had always been business or family related. This was different. This was strictly social.

'Of course if you don't want . . .'

'It's not that at all!' she interrupted.

'Then would you care to go? Or not?'

She made up her mind. 'I'd be delighted to go, Courcy. Thank you very much for asking me.'

'Then it's a date,' he smiled, and strode quickly from the room.

'I have had a terrific time. Couldn't have enjoyed myself more,' Sadie said as they came in through the door.

'It was good, wasn't it?'

'Fabulous!'

Courcy followed her through to the kitchen where Sadie went to see if Hilary had left her a note. There wasn't one, so there couldn't have been any problems with Edward.

'Coffee?' Sadie asked.

He shook his head. 'Drink?'

'Not for me.'

'Then I won't have one either.'

She glanced at her watch. 'It's later than I thought.'

'Tired?'

'Hmmh. That sort of dancing is fairly energetic.'

'I know what you mean.'

He glanced down at his feet, then up again at her. 'Are you making coffee for yourself then?'

She thought about that. 'I don't think I'll bother. I shouldn't drink it directly before going to bed anyway.'

He agreed, and looked down at his feet again.

He was nervous she thought. And then realized why. 'I'll say good night to you here. There are a few things I want to do before going up.'

'OK then. Good night.'

'Good night.'

He hesitated, then started to move away.

'Courcy!'

He stopped, and turned again to her.

'Thank you,' she said quietly, and kissed him on the cheek.

He was smiling broadly as he left the kitchen.

Courcy breezed into Sadie's office. 'Friday again, and almost knocking-off time. How about I take you for a drink to celebrate?'

'Celebrate what?' she queried.

'Whatever you like! It isn't your birthday, is it?'

He was in one of his playful moods, she realized, shaking her head.

'Nor is it mine.' He crossed to a calendar hanging on a wall, and stared at it. 'Nor is it a special day of any sort. Damn!'

'But it *is* Friday,' she said, playing along with him.

'That's it!' he exclaimed, jabbing a finger at her. 'We'll celebrate the fact that it's the end of the week.'

Mad, she thought. Totally mad. 'I think that's a lovely idea. I'll call Miss Ramirez and tell her we're going to be home late for dinner. I only hope it's something Miss Dobson can put on hold.'

'OK, that's arranged then,' he declared, and bunny-hopped from the office.

Sadie closed her eyes and listened to Frank Sinatra crooning in the background. She adored Sinatra.

'Penny for them?' Courcy asked.

She opened her eyes again. 'Just listening to that song.'

Courcy twisted his glass first one way, then the other. 'I've been thinking . . .' He paused, then continued, 'I reckon I owe you an apology for the way I treated you before the war. I was pretty shitty, wasn't I?'

She nodded.

'There were one or two incidents . . .' He trailed off. 'Well, I'm sorry. I apologize unreservedly.'

'Apology accepted,' Sadie smiled.

'A lot of my attitude in those days was because I was jealous of Edward, you see. As I'm sure I've mentioned to you before, I felt completely overshadowed by him.'

'I know.'

Courcy, staring at his glass, now began rotating it. 'Which makes the next thing extremely difficult.'

'Go on,' she prompted when he fell silent.

'I'm spelling this out because I wouldn't want you to get the wrong idea. In other words I want you to know that my motives are entirely honourable.'

'I'm sure they are,' she said.

He drained his glass, then continued twisting it. 'Would you think it wrong for a guy to regularly date his brother's widow?'

'That depends,' she replied quietly.

'On what?'

'Why he wants to regularly date her.'

Courcy took a deep breath. 'Sadie, I've always been attracted to you. Right from the first day you came to Clare. But I never made the running with you, which was entirely my own fault. Then you fell for Edward, and he for you.'

'To be honest, Courcy, I thought you rank poison in those days.'

'I can't argue with that, Sadie, for it's true. I treated women appallingly then, including you.'

Despite the seriousness of their conversation she couldn't resist a little tease. 'And, in my opinion, particularly Heather.'

'Yeah, I suppose so,' he admitted.

She smiled at him. 'Do you think us going out together on a regular basis would be a good idea? You've never stuck with one woman in the past, why should you change now?'

'You're different, Sadie. Always have been.'

She hesitated, then said. 'Are you a hundred per cent certain it's got nothing to do with me being Edward's widow?'

'I swear to you it hasn't. That's why I said I wanted you to know my motives are entirely honourable.'

She stared into his eyes, and believed him. 'What happens if it is short lived like all your other relationships? Don't forget we work together, and live in the same house. A break-up would make things extremely uncomfortable all round, if not downright impossible. Do you want to run that risk?'

'I've already considered that, Sadie, and the answer is yes. That was another reason why it was so difficult to broach this with you. Also the fact you might consider dating your husband's brother distasteful. I would fully understand it if you did.'

Was it distasteful, Sadie asked herself? Some might think it so. But did she? It seemed to her it depended entirely on the circumstances.

'I don't,' she replied.

Courcy sighed with relief.

'And why am I different?' she probed.

He shook his head. 'That's a question I've asked myself a thousand times, and have never come up with an answer. For me, you simply are.'

She was flattered by that.

'So what do you say?' he asked.

'To us going out regularly?'

'Yeah.'

'Let's give it a try,' she smiled. 'And hope neither of us regrets this decision.'

They stared at one another while in the background Frank Sinatra sang on.

With a groan Courcy pulled himself away from Sadie and jumped to his feet. 'I need a drink,' he said, and hurriedly crossed to the drinks cabinet.

Sadie exhaled slowly. 'You certainly know how to raise a girl's temperature.'

'You're not so bad at raising temperatures yourself,' he replied, slopping whisky into a glass.

'Why did you stop?'

'Why? Christ, I was about to explode!'

She regarded him quizzically. 'That doesn't answer my question.'

He returned to stand in front of her. 'I couldn't take any more of that without . . . well going further.'

'Oh, I see! You're thinking of the staff. That they're still up and about.'

'I wasn't thinking of the staff at all!' he retorted.

Sadie was puzzled. 'So why didn't you go further? Don't you want to make love to me?'

'Of course I do! There's nothing I want more.'

525

'Well then?'

'I told you once before you're different. What's going on in my head is all tied up with my feelings for you, and Edward.'

She went very still.

He went on. 'I want to marry you, Sadie. And I don't want to make love to you until we are married. I feel, rightly or wrongly, that because of my history sleeping with you before marriage would somehow demean our relationship, put it on the same level as the others. And I don't want that. As I said, you're different. And that's how I want to treat you, with respect.'

'And Edward?' she asked quietly.

'Again respect, for him and his memory. I've been a rat for most of my life, this is one thing I want to do properly.'

She was deeply touched by what he'd said, and he rose even higher in her estimation.

'Can you understand that?' he asked.

'Yes,' she nodded.

'So there it is, I'm proposing. The first time I've ever done so.'

'Marriage is a big step,' she said.

'I know that. But I love you, Sadie, very much. You've come to mean everything to me.'

She didn't love him, but had become extremely fond of him. Particularly during the five months they'd been seeing each other regularly.

He threw the whisky down his throat and went back to the drinks cabinet where he poured himself another stiff one.

'You're being very quiet,' he admonished.

'I'm thinking.'

'You're going to turn me down, aren't you?'

'I said I'm thinking,' she smiled.

'Well, don't think too goddamn long, this is killing me!' He was instantly contrite. 'No, I don't mean that.

You take as long as you like to think about it. As long as you like.'

It was high time she got married again, she thought. For little Edward's sake as well as her own. And although she didn't love Courcy, she knew that she respected him enormously these days. She liked the idea that he felt differently about her to the previous women in his life. But to treat her, and Edward, with respect, she liked that very much indeed.

'Courcy,' she said. 'I will agree to marry you, but it is only fair to tell you that I can never love you as I loved Edward. I respect you and know that our marriage will be a good one, but it will be based on trust, not on love.'

He stared at her, his expression one of incredulity. 'You *will* marry me?'

'Yes,' she stated simply.

Courcy sighed, and seemed to grow in stature. 'I can't tell you . . . begin to tell you, how happy that has made me. It's as if my whole life has suddenly come together, made sense at long, long last. And I understand entirely your feelings towards Edward.'

He laid his drink aside, took her by the hand and raised her to her feet. 'Thank you,' he said, and kissed her passionately.

They kissed until both were breathless.

'Engaged! You and Courcy!' Erin exclaimed.

'We've been going out for a while now,' Sadie explained.

'That's news to me!'

'We didn't exactly keep it a secret, but we didn't advertise it either. It's going to be a quiet wedding with only relatives and a few friends present.'

'Well, I'll be . . .' Erin shook her head. 'Just wait till I tell Marty!'

'It will work, Erin, I know it will. I would never have accepted him otherwise.'

'You certainly need to get married again. It must have been lonely for you all these years.'

Sadie smiled ruefully. 'I have had little Edward who is a great comfort. As for being lonely, I suppose I was. But I wasn't ready for anyone else until now.'

'I understand. At least I think I do,' Erin said.

Erin didn't though, Sadie thought. Only someone who'd been through what she had would have understood.

'So what have you decided on, where and when?' Erin asked.

'We've still to make the arrangements.'

'Honeymoon?'

'Not a long one because it's difficult for us both to go away at the same time. An extended weekend I thought. Possibly at Cape Cod, taking in Nantucket Island and Martha's Vineyard.'

'I have heard it's very beautiful there,' Erin said.

Sadie smiled. 'Cape Cod it will be then. In the meantime Courcy has gone apartment hunting. He says it would be most improper for him to remain on at Clare now that we're engaged.'

'Good God!' Erin exclaimed. 'Courcy said that?'

Sadie nodded.

'This is a new side to Courcy. One I haven't seen before.'

'That's why it's going to work, Erin.'

Erin's reply to that was to hug Sadie tightly.

Sadie hurried through the falling snow, *en route* to her office. She squealed when she was suddenly seized round the waist and dragged behind a brick wall.

'What are you doing?' she gasped to Courcy who held her fast.

'Me Tarzan, you Jane,' he said, and kissed her.

She wriggled under his kiss.

'What if someone should see us?' she panted when the kiss was over. 'Who cares! You're the boss.' He nibbled first one side of her neck, then the other.

'Courcy, this is ridiculous!'

'I don't think so. I don't think so at all.'

He kissed her repeatedly on the lips, short sharp pecks.

She smiled. 'Your hair is totally covered in snow. You're beginning to look like a snowman.'

'And you look gorgeous. But then you always do.'

She tried to pull free, but he wouldn't let her go. 'I must get back. I have work to do.'

'So have I.'

'Courcy!'

He licked the end of her nose, his tongue hot against the coldness of her skin.

'That's nice,' she murmured.

He repeated the action.

'Save it for later,' she said.

'Oh I am! I am!' he smiled.

His expression, and the glint in his eyes, told her what he meant by that. She shivered at the prospect.

'Now I really must go,' she insisted.

'One more kiss?' he pleaded.

'Just the one then.'

This time she didn't wriggle, but melted against him, kissing him as eagerly as he kissed her.

Sadie emerged from the beauty parlour having just had her hair cut. She decided that she'd go to the restaurant in Yaeger's for morning coffee and apple strudel.

Inside the store she stopped to look at a few of the counters, then crossed to the elevator where she waited for it to arrive. A man came up to stand beside her, whom she took no notice of, being preoccupied with her thoughts.

The elevator arrived, she went in, followed by the man, who closed the gate behind them.

With a slight jerk the elevator began to ascend. And as it did the man inched forward till he was standing directly beside her.

When she turned and caught him staring at her, he immediately glanced away.

She mentally shrugged, and went back to her thoughts.

There he was again, staring at her out of the corner of his eyes. The elevator came to a halt to allow another customer to enter.

Sadie was relieved about that. She was becoming uneasy about this man she'd started out sharing the lift with. Why only the other day she'd read in the *Toronto Star* about a female who'd . . . She dismissed that from her mind, the story had been too gruesome.

They stopped at another floor and two more people got in.

He was at it again! she realized. When she looked at him he glanced away more swiftly.

She had a sudden thought. She hoped he wasn't going to follow her into the restaurant. This time she glared at him, her expression withering. If he was thinking of trying to pick her up he could think again.

They arrived at her floor and they all got out. She had only taken a few steps in the direction of the restaurant when a male voice behind her said: 'Sadie?'

She halted and turned to face the man who'd been in the lift with her.

'You are Sadie, aren't you? Sadie Smith?'

She frowned. How did he know her name?

'Don't you recognize me? Surely I haven't changed that much?'

He did seem familiar now she had a chance to study him.

'It's me, Robbie,' the man smiled. 'Robbie Hendry.'

Chapter Ten

Sadie stared at Robbie in amazement, unable to believe that it was actually him.

'Robbie!' she croaked.

'I saw you out in the street, thought it was you and followed you trying to decide. It wasn't until you got out of the elevator and started to walk away that I was certain.'

'Robbie,' she repeated, tears oozing from her eyes. With a muffled sob she threw herself into his embrace.

'Twenty years,' he stated, eyes moist. 'Twenty long years.'

'But . . .' There were a thousand questions she wanted to ask, but where to begin?

'I work not far from Bald Rock Falls,' he said.

'You do!'

'Moved there three months ago.'

He lived locally! Better still. 'I was on my way to the restaurant. Why don't we go there and . . .' She broke off and shook her head. 'I still can't believe that it's really you!'

They chose a table, sat and ordered coffee from the waitress who instantly appeared beside them.

'Now where . . . ?'

They both began at once, breaking off and laughing.

'You first,' Sadie said. 'You tell your story first.'

Robbie took a deep breath. 'I went to Toronto where I found employment in a drugstore as a stock boy. I studied throughout those two years as well and then decided to try and go to university. I applied, won a scholarship, and read physics. I subsequently became a research physicist, married a girl called Helen who later divorced me after things completely broke down between us. We had one child, whom I'm sad to say was stillborn. At one point I did go back to Peterawa to look for you but Anna didn't have any idea where you'd gone. All she could tell me was that you'd run off with some guy who'd stopped by the house directly after the twister that killed Julius. I came here three months ago to take up a post with the Moose River Atomic Plant which I'm sure you know was built during the war. I can't tell you what I do there as it's classified, I'm afraid.'

He spread his hands. 'And that's me in a nutshell. Now you.'

Sadie stopped halfway through her story when the coffee arrived, then started up again when the waitress had moved off. Robbie listened intently, nodding every so often.

'So there we are,' she said having brought him up to date on her life.

'I'm sorry to hear about your husband,' he sympathized.

'Yes. That was a terrible loss which I felt dreadfully.'

'And now you're marrying again, his brother.'

'In a couple of months' time. What about yourself, is there a girl-friend?'

'Not at present. There have been a few since Helen, but nothing serious.'

They fell silent, their minds filled with memories. 'Is it really twenty years,' Sadie mused after a while.

'Yes. It was the summer of 1932 when I ran away. Twenty and a half years ago to be precise.'

'All that time ago,' Sadie said, and bit her lip. 'Do you remember Mischief?'

'Of course. And the Miller brothers?'

Sadie's face darkened at that memory. 'They were awful, spiteful, nasty creatures. I hope they grew into better men than they were boys.'

'I doubt it,' Robbie said. 'Types like that don't change.'

'A physicist,' Sadie said, and shook her head in wonder. 'But then you always were incredibly bright.'

'And fancy you owning a mini empire.'

'But you must come and meet Edward and the rest of the family. How often do you get to town?'

He shrugged. 'It varies. It's only thirty miles each way, so it's hardly a trek. I suppose I come in whenever I need to. And occasionally when I'm bored.'

'Do you get bored often?'

'Not really. There's always my work which could keep me occupied twenty-four hours a day if I let it.'

'You enjoy your work then?'

'Oh yeah! Though I . . .' He trailed off, then said, 'We won't go into that. We'll save it for another day.'

She suddenly laughed. 'Back there in the elevator I thought you were going to try and pick me up. I was furious.'

He laughed also. 'I guessed it was something like that. But I didn't want to speak until I was certain it was you.'

'And you recognized me out in the street?'

'Yeah. I walked past you thinking how much you looked like Sadie Smith. And then I thought, what if it is her? And it was!'

'You've changed and yet you haven't,' she told him. 'You're really still the same Robbie, just older that's all.' Sadie continued. 'And what do you have out at the plant? Your own house, apartment?'

'Two bedroom home which the plant provide. I have a woman who comes in and keeps me in order.'

Sadie couldn't wait to show him Clare. 'And how many of you are out there?'

'Twenty-eight at the last count, mainly men who are for the most part married with kids. There are only several who are divorced like myself.'

'Sounds a lonely life?'

'It can be, I suppose, but that doesn't bother me particularly.'

'And what about your ex-wife Helen, has she re-married?'

Robbie nodded. 'Happily she tells me. His name is Don and he's in advertising. A high-powered executive type. I like him.'

'Was it an acrimonious divorce?' Sadie was curious about that.

'Are there any that aren't? Yeah, it was pretty horrendous at the time. But the dust has long since settled. We're actually better friends now than we were when we were together.'

Sadie finished her coffee, and noticed that Robbie had done the same. 'Would you like some more?'

'No, thank you.' He glanced at his watch. 'I'm afraid I must make tracks. I have an appointment I can't break, much as I'd love to.'

Disappointment filled Sadie. Now that she'd found Robbie again she didn't want to let him go. He was that precious to her.

'Listen, what are you doing on Saturday night?' she asked him.

'Nothing.'

'Will you come to dinner?'

'I'd be delighted.'

'Good.' She'd see that Miss Dobson laid on something extra special.

They arranged the details, then rose to leave. Robbie insisted on paying for the coffee, after which they rode down on the elevator together, the pair of them laughing again at what had happened on the way up.

Out in the street he took her by the hand. 'Sadie, this means the world to me. I want you to know that.'

'Same for me, Robbie. I still can't believe it's happened. I quite expect to wake up and find myself in bed, and that it's all been a wonderful dream!'

He kissed her on the forehead. 'No dream, Sadie. This really is me. In the flesh.'

Saturday was the day after tomorrow. She was already counting the hours.

'I'll get it!' Sadie cried when the bell rang. She ran past a bemused Lois and threw open the front door.

'Welcome,' she smiled at Robbie. 'Come in! Come in!'

She drew him into the house, and closed the door behind her. 'You found the place OK?'

'Your directions were perfect. What a house!'

'I'll show you round later, but first I want you to meet the family.'

'These are for you,' he said, and handed her a bunch of red roses.

Sadie was impressed. Roses in February. 'Thank you very much.'

Robbie took off his coat which he gave to Lois who'd been hovering.

'Put these in water right away,' Sadie instructed Lois, who then went off with the coat and the flowers.

When they entered the drawing-room everyone rose to their feet.

'This is Robbie Hendry,' Sadie announced proudly.

'Hi!' Robbie said.

Sadie crooked a finger and Edward came shyly forward. 'Robbie, this is my son, Edward.'

'How are you?' Robbie enquired, shaking hands with Edward.

'Fine thank you, sir.'

'And how old are you?'

'Nine, sir.'

'About the same age as your mom when she came to Canada. Right, Sadie?'

She nodded.

'Yes, indeed,' muttered Robbie, thinking of the difference between Clare and the Trikhardt's farmhouse where he and Sadie had gone to live.

535

'He's a handsome young man,' Robbie smiled to Sadie. 'Looks a lot like his father.'

'Oh, I can see you in him as well. Your eyes, I'd say.'

That pleased Sadie who then introduced him to Erin, Marty and Courcy.

'Sadie's fiancé, I understand,' Robbie said as he shook hands with Courcy.

'I have that honour.'

Sadie smoothed down the gown she was wearing, which was her favourite.

'My congratulations,' Robbie replied.

'Will you have a drink?' Sadie asked him.

'Please.'

Marty glanced round and said, 'I'll play barman. What's it to be, Robbie?'

'A Tom Collins if that's OK.'

'Same for me,' Sadie said, as she hadn't yet had a drink.

'Can I have another coke?' Edward asked his mother.

'Of course you can. Tonight, because it's a special night, you can have as many as you wish.'

'Great!' Edward enthused, and hurried after Marty.

'A nuclear physicist, I understand?' Courcy said to Robbie, whom he'd been doing his best to size up since Robbie had come into the room. What he saw was a reasonably good-looking man who exuded a quiet confidence.

'That's right. I'm currently based at the Moose River Atomic Plant.'

'And what exactly do you do there?' Erin enquired.

'I'm afraid I'm not allowed to say. The work is classified.'

'Don't they manufacture heavy water out at Moose River?' Courcy queried casually.

Robbie turned and gazed at Courcy who was suddenly discomfited by a pair of piercing eyes. It was like being on the business end of a microscope, Courcy thought.

'Do you know much about heavy water?' Robbie asked quietly.

'Only that it's needed to make the A-bomb. I read that somewhere.'

'Well, you're quite right,' Robbie acknowledged. 'It is tied up in that process.'

'We mustn't talk about the plant and Robbie's work there if he doesn't want to,' Sadie said.

'I don't mind. As long as we talk in generalities and not specifics,' Robbie informed her.

'Thank you,' he nodded when Marty handed him his drink.

'Everyone must sit down,' Sadie said. 'This isn't formal, you know!'

Robbie chose a settee where Sadie joined him. She raised her glass to him in a toast. 'To old times.'

'Old times,' Robbie repeated, and they both drank.

'As I recall, there weren't many Tom Collinses at the Trikhardts,' he joked.

'Not many,' Sadie smiled.

'And where were you before you came to Bald Rock Falls?' Erin asked Robbie.

'Various places, here and the States . . .'

'The States!' Erin exclaimed. 'So you worked for the Americans?'

'On several different occasions. A certain amount of interchange goes on between their people, the Canadians and UK personnel.'

'You must be very high up?' Marty probed.

Robbie didn't reply to that.

'Sadie told us how very clever you are,' Erin said.

'The only student ever to get an A-plus at the school we briefly attended,' Sadie declared.

'Fair's fair. It wasn't all that much of a school,' Robbie stated modestly.

'He's mainly self-taught. Aren't you, Robbie?'

'There was quite a bit of that up until I went to university,' Robbie admitted.

'What about the war, did you take part in it?' Courcy asked.

Robbie stared into his drink, considering his reply. 'I wasn't on active service if that's what you mean.'

'But you were involved?'

'I played a part, yes.'

Courcy had a sudden thought. 'By God, were you a member of the Manhattan Project team?'

Robbie shifted uncomfortably in his seat. 'I did make something of a contribution,' he confirmed.

'Manhattan Project?' Erin queried.

'The project which developed the atom bomb,' Courcy informed his sister. 'And blew hell out of the Japs. Wiped Hiroshima and Nagasaki off the face of the earth.'

'We mustn't keep on this topic if Robbie doesn't want to speak about it,' said an anxious Sadie.

Robbie looked up, a strange expression on his face. 'I went to Hiroshima after the war, to see it at first hand for myself. It was simply awful, mind shattering. A whole city and its inhabitants just . . .' He waved a hand. 'More or less gone.'

'Are you saying you don't approve of what was done?' Courcy asked.

Robbie thought about that. 'I understand why it was done, but the results filled me with foreboding for the future. As the saying goes, it's not the gun that kills, but the person who pulls the trigger. And now mankind has his finger on the ultimate trigger.'

'The trouble is you can't disinvent what's already been invented,' Marty said.

Robbie looked at him. 'Precisely. And there are some like me who in this instance wish with all their hearts that wasn't so.'

'I'm going to change the subject and it's going to stay changed,' Sadie stated firmly. 'This is all getting far too gloomy.'

'My fault, sorry,' Robbie said.

'It's not your fault at all. It's ours for pressing you on what you did.'

'Blame me,' smiled Courcy. 'And Sadie's right, let's change the subject.'

Robbie glanced over to where Edward was sitting solemn faced, having been absorbing all that had been said.

The conversation brightened after that and a very pleasant and entertaining evening followed.

When Robbie left he was able to declare truthfully that he'd thoroughly enjoyed himself.

Sadie didn't let him go without making arrangements for them to meet again shortly.

'Some noise!' Robbie grinned at Sadie standing beside him. She was giving him the grand tour and they were currently in what had been the old saw mill.

'You get used to it after a while,' Sadie replied in a loud voice.

After that they went to the pulping section where Sadie explained all the various processes and machinery employed there. Robbie was intrigued and asked a number of in-depth questions, all of which Sadie was able to answer.

From there she took him to manufacturing and sales which she informed him were the results of her expansion plan to turn what had already existed on-site into a fully integrated mill.

'I get the distinct impression that it's all been very successful?' Robbie commented.

'Extremely so, as our continually up-spiralling profit margins show.'

'I never saw you as a capitalist,' he teased.

She frowned. 'Do you disapprove?'

'No. Just as long as you remember there's a lot more to life than making money.'

'I couldn't agree more. But don't forget in this instance the creation of personal wealth also creates jobs for other folks. No bad thing, surely?'

'Not at all. All I'm saying is that capitalism is fine, as long as it's viewed in perspective and doesn't become the be-all and end-all. A great high God worshipped to the exclusion of all else.'

'I take it from this that you don't care much for money?'

He laughed. 'Oh I do! It comes in very handy at times. But, to repeat myself, the key word is perspective.'

'Do nuclear physicists get paid well?' she asked, genuinely curious.

'Ample for our needs. As a race I shouldn't think many of us concern ourselves over much with money. We're not really financially orientated.'

'Except from the philosophical point of view?'

He stopped and stared at her, eyes twinkling with amusement. 'Are you having a little dig at me, Sadie? Sending me up?'

She pretended innocence. 'Me? Would I do such a thing?'

His mouth curled into a smile. 'Was I being pompous?'

'Not at all. There's nothing pompous about you. You get very serious on occasion, but not pompous.'

She reached out and touched his cheek. 'It really is marvellous to have you about again. Twenty long years, but in some ways it's as though we've never been parted.'

'I feel exactly the same.' He removed her hand from his cheek and kissed the back of it.

They fell into step once more, she hooking an arm round his. 'I believe I have my values right, Robbie. Though I must confess it is lovely being rich and successful after the start we had in life.'

'I can well understand that,' he replied softly.

'Three bucks a month, remember?'

'Only too well!' he sighed.

'And worked like a slave into the bargain.' She shuddered. 'How I loathed the Trikhardts.'

'Was it worse after I went?'

She nodded. 'I got by, I had to. But it was a lot worse without your support.'

'I'm sorry, but I just had to go when I did.'

'I know that.'

'You never held it against me that I . . .'

'No, of course not!' she interjected. 'My only regret was that I hadn't been old enough to go with you.'

They left the building and went outside where the winter sun was shining brightly casting pools of shadow everywhere.

'I was thinking about your wartime exploits on my drive over here this morning,' Robbie said, 'and wondering if you still flew?'

'Regularly. I have my own plane. A Gipsy Moth that was Edward's.'

'Really!' Robbie exclaimed. 'Is it a single seater?'

'No, it has two cockpits. Why?'

'I'd love a flight sometime. I've always wanted to go up in a small aircraft.'

'You have! Well, that's easily arranged. What about now?'

He stopped and gaped at her. 'You mean this morning?'

'Sure. All we have to do is go to the hangar and within minutes I'll have you airborne.'

He laughed with delight. 'You're on!'

'OK then. I'll just tell Courcy what we're doing, and then we'll be off. We'll go in your car.'

Robbie waited patiently in his oldish Ford while Sadie spoke to Courcy, smiling at her when she joined him. 'No problems?'

'None.'

He engaged gear and they were off.

They drove to Clare and then on to the hangar where they both suited up.

'I feel like a kid who's just woken up on Christmas Day and knows something fabulous is lying ahead,' Robbie said.

'I hope it lives up to expectations,' Sadie replied, struggling into her flying jacket after which she slipped on her helmet.

They manoeuvred the Moth out of the hangar and Sadie went through the usual explanatory procedures. When the engine had caught she clambered aboard and pulled the chocks in with her.

'How do you feel?' she asked Robbie.

'Very alive.'

She smiled, understanding exactly what he meant. He couldn't have given her a better answer.

'Let's go then,' she said, and began to taxi forward.

Robbie exhaled as the plane left the ground. 'This is fantastic!'

'Where do you want to go?'

'I don't know. Anywhere. Everywhere!'

The usual she thought. Lake Baldy, the town, then . . . She had a thought, and changed her mind. She knew where she'd take him.

They climbed to three thousand feet where she set a course for the Moose River Atomic Plant.

'I hope you can recognize your house from the air,' she said.

'I'll recognize it all right. Don't you worry about that.'

'You cold?'

'Yeah. But I'll survive.'

Robbie stared down at the scenery passing below him, loving every second of it. He'd been in commercial planes

542

many times, but they were nothing like this. This was real flying!

'I like the scarlet colour of the plane,' he said. 'It reminds me of the scarlet ribbons you used to have. Real prized possessions they were.'

'I lost them in the twister,' she replied.

'I'm sorry to hear that.'

'But Edward gave me replacements which I now prize even more than the originals.'

The atomic plant came into sight, and the cluster of houses surrounding it. Sadie brought the Moth down and swooped over them.

'That's mine, the one with the three trees in the front lawn!' Robbie exclaimed, pointing.

A wooden construction of no particular style, Sadie noted as they zoomed directly over it. Someone looked up and Robbie waved.

'Fred Zerchenski, plays a great game of chess,' Robbie explained, continuing to wave.

Sadie circled and brought the Moth over the houses again, then began climbing away from the plant and houses.

'Wait till I tell Fred it was me waving at him,' an excited Robbie said.

Sadie flew along the Moose River for a bit, its blue water sparkling in the sunlight, heading west away from Clare. After a while she turned the Moth and headed for home, taking a slightly different, and longer, route to the one they'd come.

The Moth's wheels kissed grass, and the plane immediately began to slow. Sadie taxied to the front of the hangar, and killed the engine.

'How was that?' she queried.

'Incredible.'

'I'll take you up again sometime. Whenever you like.'

'Will you?'

She laughed. 'It will be my pleasure.'

They jumped to the ground where both removed goggles and helmet. 'I can't thank you enough, Sadie. Really I can't.'

'I know how you feel. I remember only too well how I felt after my first flight.'

'Like being a bird.'

The sun caught her hair, highlighting it and throwing her face into relief. He stared at her, thinking how beautiful she was.

'Will you help me get the Moth back into the hangar?' she requested.

And with that the spell of the last few moments was broken.

'Can you cover for me for the rest of the day? I'm off to town,' Sadie said to Courcy.

'Sure.'

'Robbie has just called me telling me he's already there and wondering if I could join him for coffee.'

Courcy frowned, this was most unlike Sadie. Taking time off work to go and have coffee! He'd never known her do anything like it.

'Enjoy yourself then,' he said a trifle caustically. 'I take it I'm still coming over tonight?'

'Of course. Why should that change?'

Courcy shrugged. 'I don't know. Just asking that's all.'

She kissed him lightly on the mouth. 'See you later.'

Jealousy stabbed through him as he watched her walk away. Things had changed since Robbie had appeared on the scene, the two of them becoming as thick as thieves. Robbie was like a brother to her, he reminded himself. There was nothing for him to feel jealous about. Except, of course, that some of the time she was now spending with Robbie would have been time spent with him.

Another six weeks to the wedding. As far as he was concerned it couldn't come quickly enough.

His thoughts were interrupted when his telephone rang.

★ ★ ★

Courcy pulled up in front of Robbie's house, as he and Sadie had been invited for dinner. It was their first visit there.

'Larger than it looks from the air,' Sadie commented.

Courcy wasn't impressed. Nothing more than a glorified box was his view and very uninspiring.

'Don't forget to bring the wine,' Sadie reminded him, getting out.

Robbie opened his front door and smiled at them. 'Heard you arrive.'

Sadie went to him and kissed him on the cheek. Robbie then shook hands with Courcy after which he ushered them inside.

'For you,' Courcy said, handing Robbie the wine.

'St Julien! That will go down well.'

'You mentioned the other day that you were partial to St Julien. I remembered,' Sadie said.

'I'll go through to the kitchen and open it right away so that it can breathe and warm before dinner. In the meantime please take a seat.'

Courcy sat, but Sadie remained standing. She gazed round Robbie's sitting-room, immediately liking its ambience. The floor was highly polished hardwood over which several Indian coverings had been scattered. The coffee table dominating the centre of the room was again of hardwood, and hand carved. The chairs and settee were beige, the settee having an Indian blanket draped over its back. One wall was chocolate brown, the others a stronger beige than the furniture. Hanging on these walls were several pictures depicting Indian scenes, one a magnificent-looking chief astride a pony. Also hanging on the walls were a number of Indian weapons, a lance decorated with feathers, crossed tomahawks, a war bow and a quiver full of arrows.

'I'm disappointed,' Sadie announced to Robbie when he returned.

'In what way?'

'I expected shelves of books and there isn't even a single book to be seen.'

He grinned at her. 'That's easily explained. Come with me.'

He led her, and Courcy who accompanied them, to a door that he threw open. 'The spare bedroom which I use as a study and library.'

Sadie laughed in delight, there must have been thousands of books in the room, the walls one gigantic bookcase that rose from floor to ceiling.

'Impressive,' Courcy muttered.

Robbie waved a hand about him. 'I've been gathering this collection for years. Every time I move I take it with me, which can be expensive, I assure you. I had these particular shelves built shortly after I arrived here.'

'You always loved books,' Sadie said.

'And why the interest in Indians?' Courcy asked.

'I just like them and their culture,' Robbie replied.

'Me too,' Sadie enthused.

For some reason her saying that irritated Courcy. He had the suspicion that if Robbie had said he enjoyed ice-cold showers or riding bucking broncos she'd have said she did also.

'Have you read every single one?' Sadie queried, crossing to the books nearest her.

Robbie nodded. 'Some many times.'

'Trollope, Balzac, Dickens, Mann, Faulkner, Camus, Sartre . . .' Sadie read out. 'You really do go in for the heavy stuff, don't you!'

'I have a confession to make. I absolutely adore Agatha Christie and Dorothy L. Sayers, but don't keep their books after I've read them.'

'So that people don't find out you read that sort of thing?' Sadie teased.

'I'm not a snob!' Robbie protested. 'It's simply that to keep everything would take up too much space.'

'I'll believe you,' Sadie smiled.

'From the looks of them a lot of the others are textbooks,' Courcy said.

'That's right, at least fifty per cent.'

'Any of those by you?' Sadie asked.

'No. Although it is in my mind to write a book at some point, perhaps a few years from now.'

Robbie took them back to the sitting-room where he poured drinks. 'Dinner will be ready in about twenty minutes,' he said.

'What have you cooked for us?' Sadie enquired.

'Goulash and rice. Hope that's OK?'

Sadie murmured enthusiastically.

'Do you do all your own cooking?' Courcy asked.

'Yes. I find it relaxing to potter in the kitchen. Some of my most productive thinking goes on there.'

'I'm afraid I would find it a chore,' Courcy declared.

'That's one word I hate. It reminds me of the Trikhardts,' Sadie stated.

Robbie's brow furrowed. 'Yeesss,' he exhaled slowly.

'What became of Anna after the twister?' Sadie queried.

That began an evening of reminiscing during which Courcy felt more and more left out.

Sadie and Robbie did try to draw him in occasionally, but before long they were back discussing the Trikhardts again, and their days spent together on the farm.

Sadie had told Courcy how close she and Robbie had been. He was beginning to realize now just how close that was.

'Enough!' Sadie exclaimed, and pushed Courcy away.

He stared at her, perplexed. 'What's wrong?'

'Nothing's wrong. I simply don't want to kiss at the moment.'

She'd felt resistant in his arms, stiff and somehow cold. It was the first time she'd experienced this since they'd started up together.

'Is it me? Have I done something?' he queried.

'You haven't done anything!' she replied in exasperation. 'As I said, I simply don't feel like kissing, or being romantic in any way. What I really want to do is just sit back, relax, and watch television.'

'Is there a particular programme you want to see?'

'Nope.'

Courcy puffed up his chest, then let out a long sigh. 'OK then, TV it is!'

He pushed himself abruptly from the settee, crossed to the television and switched it on. 'Do you want me to sit elsewhere?' he asked.

'Don't be silly.' She patted the place beside her. 'Come back here.'

Later, relenting a little, she reached out and took his hand in hers.

On his leaving Clare she did kiss him good night, but a kiss that was more perfunctory than passionate.

'Sorry,' she whispered.

'Don't worry about it. I understand.'

She doubted that. For she didn't herself.

Courcy picked up his telephone. 'Yeah?'

'Courcy, it's Sadie. I'm not coming in today.'

He frowned. 'Something the matter?'

'I don't really know. I'm totally lacking in energy, and have a bit of a headache. I thought it might be best if I stayed at home. I'm going to have a hot bath and then return to bed.'

'Want me to call the doc?'

'I don't think that's necessary,' she replied.

'Is there anything I can get for you?'

'No, the staff will get anything I might need. But thank you for offering.'

'I'll come and visit you tonight. After work.'

'I'll look forward to that.'

'Bye then.'

'Bye, Courcy.'

'Love you.'

She blew a kiss into the receiver, and hung up.

Several hours later, having had a long wallow, Sadie was sitting up in bed reading when she suddenly remembered that Robbie was going into town that afternoon to pick up a new sports coat he'd bought which had had to be altered.

The thought of a rendezvous instantly cheered her up, and put some pep back into her. And her headache had gone, she realized, thanks to the hot bath and taking it easy no doubt.

Yes, she definitely did feel a lot better. Quite her old self again. Reaching for her bedside telephone she called Robbie at the plant who said he'd be delighted to meet up with her, and so they arranged the time and place.

She got out of bed and started to dress, and as she dressed she sang.

Doctor Erb studied the sheet of paper he was holding, while on the other side of his desk Sadie watched him intently.

'These tests are all negative, Sadie. We can't find a darn thing wrong with you,' he announced.

'I see.'

He looked at her, a stout red-faced man with white hair and a bushy white moustache. 'All I can suggest therefore is a strong tonic and a course of vitamin pills.'

Sadie sighed. This recurring lack of energy and headaches were getting her down. Today was one of her good days whereas the previous day had been dreadful.

'Is there anything worrying you? Problems at the mill perhaps?'

She shook her head. 'Everything there is fine. We're going from strength to strength.'

'Anything else then?'

'Nothing's worrying me that I can think of.'

'Is everything OK between you and Courcy?'

Now what had made him ask that? she wondered. 'I hope so, we're getting married in two weeks' time.'

'No apprehensions in that direction then?'

'None at all,' she assured the good doctor.

He picked up the X-ray he'd had taken of Sadie's head. The possibility of a tumour had crossed his mind, but there was no indication on the X-ray of anything like that.

'Maybe you should have a few days away by yourself?' he suggested. 'A sort of pre-wedding vacation.'

'I'll consider it,' Sadie replied, thinking the last thing she wanted was a few days away by herself. She'd be bored to tears. No, if she needed to get away from everything all she had to do was take to the air in the Moth. Up there she was gloriously alone, and in an environment she adored.

On leaving the doctor's she went to the nearest drugstore for the tonic and vitamin pills he'd recommended.

'Sadie, can I have a word?' The speaker was Arlene Ramsay whose marriage had ended the previous year.

'Sure, what is it?'

Arlene took Sadie by the arm, and steered her into a corner. 'Swell party, huh?'

'Well, I'm certainly enjoying myself.' There were about a hundred guests at the party which had been thrown by the Delaneys, he a large land and livestock owner.

'So who's the guy with you?' Arlene enquired.

'A friend of mine from years ago who's recently come to live near Bald Rock.'

'Hmmh!' Arlene mused. 'He's kind of cute. Where's Courcy by the way?'

'Off on company business. That's why Robbie is acting as my escort tonight.'

'Is he married?'

'Divorced,' Sadie found herself replying somewhat coldly.

Arlene raised an eyebrow. 'Does he belong to anyone now?'

'No.'

'He's free then?'

Voluptuous, Sadie thought. She'd never before realized just how voluptuous Arlene was. She positively oozed sex. The idea of Arlene getting her claws into Robbie made her seethe. Arlene wasn't at all Robbie's type.

'I suppose so,' Sadie answered reluctantly.

'I'd like to meet him.'

'I shouldn't have thought he was your type.'

'Why not?'

'He's an academic.'

Arlene's eyes opened wide. 'Terrific! I like a man with brains. Which was something I could never accuse my ex-husband Bob of. All he had between his ears was air.' She paused, then smiled. Lowering her voice she added. 'Mind you he did have talent in another department.'

Sadie flushed to hear that, which annoyed her, because she didn't consider herself a prude. It was because Arlene had said it, she decided, she wouldn't have flushed if it had been said by anyone else.

'Yes,' Arlene enthused, glancing over to where Robbie was standing in conversation with a couple. 'I do like intellect.'

Sadie's lips thinned in self-restraint as she experienced a violent urge to scratch the bitch's eyes out.

'Will you introduce me then?' Arlene requested.

Sadie didn't see that she could refuse. 'If you wish.'

'I noticed him when you first arrived. Now there's an interesting man I thought. What does he actually do?'

'Nuclear physicist.'

'He does have brains if he's that!' Arlene exclaimed in awe.

They reached the threesome, the couple Robbie was talking to being the Falks whom Sadie knew slightly.

'Wonderful party, isn't it?' Arlene gushed to the Falks.

551

'Wonderful,' John Falk agreed.

'Robbie, I'd like you to meet Arlene Ramsay. Arlene, Robbie Hendry.'

'Delighted,' Robbie said, shaking Arlene's hand.

'Sadie has just been telling me all about you,' Arlene replied.

'Really!'

'Do you dance?'

Robbie blinked, taken aback by her directness. 'Yes, of course.'

'Then why don't we do so, I'm absolutely dying to hear about being a nuclear physicist.'

Arlene hooked an arm round Robbie's, and smiled at him.

'Excuse us, won't you?' she said to Sadie and the Falks, still smiling at Robbie.

Sadie watched Robbie and Arlene walk away. That had been done smoothly, she thought. No pussy footing around there, straight in for the kill.

It was with profound shock that she realized she was jealous.

'Postpone the wedding!' a distraught Courcy exclaimed.

'Only for a while I hope,' Sadie said.

'But . . . but . . .' For once he was lost for words.

She took his hand and squeezed it. 'I don't want to get married while I'm like this, Courcy. I'm worried there's something seriously wrong with me. You must understand that.'

'The doctors can't find anything. Neither Erb nor the one you saw at the hospital.'

'Nonetheless, I still have this continuing terrible lethargy, and headaches.'

Courcy stuck a finger in his mouth, and worried a nail. 'Everything's been organized, booked, arranged,' he said.

'I know.'

'And you want to postpone?'

'I think it best.'

'Shit!' he swore.

'Don't be angry with me, please. Try and understand.'

'All I understand is that I love you, and want to be married to you.'

Sadie sucked in a deep breath. 'You're making this extremely difficult.'

'I'm sorry about that,' he answered sarcastically.

She put a hand to her forehead, and gently massaged. Another headache was starting, before long it would be pounding away inside her skull. God, she was tired! When Courcy had gone she'd go straight to bed and sleep.

What was wrong with her! she wondered for the umpteenth time. The hospital doctor had put her through even more tests, a whole battery of them, and again drawn a blank.

'I'm going to look a right fool,' Courcy muttered.

'Is that all that's bothering you?'

He immediately softened. 'No, of course it isn't. If you want to postpone, then that's what we'll do.'

'Thank you,' she said quietly, feeling as though a great burden had suddenly been lifted from her shoulders. This was the second time a wedding of hers had been postponed, she thought ironically.

'Is it anything to do with me?' Courcy asked, grim faced.

'I swear to you it isn't. It's got nothing to do with you, or us. I just don't want to get married while I'm like this. I want to get it sorted out before I do. I mean, it would be absolutely awful for us to get married only to later discover I had a terminal illness, wouldn't it?'

'Sadie, don't say such a thing!' he admonished. 'Don't even think it.'

'But it would be awful, wouldn't it?'

He didn't reply to that.

'Thank you for agreeing to a postponement, Courcy. I appreciate it,' she said.

553

There wasn't really much else he could have done, he thought bitterly. And the wedding only eight days off!

'I'm sorry. I really am,' Sadie said, tears glinting in her eyes.

He went to her and gathered her into his arms. 'I love you very much. You do know that, don't you?'

'Yes,' she whispered in reply.

They remained like that, in silence, for a full minute, then she said. 'Do you think you could go now? I'm desperate for bed.'

'OK. Do I get a kiss?'

He found her lips ice cold. And as they kissed she trembled.

'A call for you from Mr Hendry,' Miss Ramirez informed Sadie.

'Thank you.'

Sadie hurried to the telephone. Robbie was coming to dinner that evening, and was due to arrive shortly. He must have been held up, she told herself.

'Hi!' she said into the phone.

'Sadie, it's bad news. I'm going to have to take a rain check on tonight.'

'Oh!' Intense disappointment flooded through her. She'd been so looking forward to seeing him.

'It's the job I'm afraid. I've run into a snag that I'll have to sort out before I leave, which could take hours.'

'That's OK,' she said, smiling weakly.

'If I could leave this till the morning I would. But I simply can't.'

'I said that's OK. Another time.'

'How are you feeling?' The last occasion they'd been together she'd appeared pale and wan, and had definitely lost weight.

'Not so bad today,' she replied.

'Did you go into the mill?'

'No. Courcy's coping fine without me. And to be truthful, for some reason I've lost all interest in the mill.'

He didn't like the sound of that. 'It won't be long till summer. Lots of fresh air and sunshine should help,' he said.

She laughed. 'Yeah. And maybe a picnic or two, eh?'

'Terrific! As long as I'm not playing gooseberry between you and Courcy, that is.'

'No gooseberry,' she said softly. Thinking, never that. 'Will you call me again tomorrow?'

'If you'd like.'

'I'd like.'

'OK then, I'll call. Bye!'

'Bye!' she said, and hung up.

She stared at the cradled phone, and bit her lip. What had promised to be a marvellous evening had now turned sour. Oh well, it couldn't be helped! His work had to come first, of course. But why couldn't it have happened another night when he hadn't been due for dinner.

Her disappointment hung over her like a cloud for the rest of the evening.

Robbie answered the doorbell to find Sadie standing there. 'Sadie!' he exclaimed in surprise. 'This is an unexpected pleasure.'

'I know it's lateish and . . .'

'Come in!' he said. 'I was only reading.'

'For work or pleasure?'

'A little of both,' he said, helping her off with her wrap.

'I was at home, and restless, and decided to take a drive. This is where I ended up,' she explained.

'I'm glad you dropped by. Can I get you anything?'

'A cup of coffee would be nice.'

'Coffee it is then.'

He took her through to the sitting-room. 'If you wait here I'll put the pot on. Something to eat?'

'Not for me thanks.'

'OK.' And with that he disappeared out of the room.

The book he was reading was lying open, face down. The title on its spine was *The Bomb, What Next?*

'Are you sure I'm not intruding?' she asked when he returned.

'Not a bit. The company is most welcome. Or let me rephrase that, your company is.'

She smiled at him, thinking that sweet.

'Restless you say?'

She shrugged. 'One of those times when I just didn't know what to do with myself. So I decided on a drive. If it had been during the day I'd have gone up in the Moth.'

'And you ended up here?'

'Suddenly thought, I'll go and see Robbie. Take a chance that he's home. And you were.'

'I don't go out all that much,' he confessed. 'Though I have done a lot more so since meeting up with you again.'

'So what is next?' she queried.

He frowned. 'Beg your pardon?'

She gestured at the book. *'The Bomb, What Next?'*

'Oh, I see!' he exclaimed. 'You might indeed ask. The nuclear possibility is a tremendous one of course, for peace and war. It's the peace side that interests me most. And the war side that worries me sick.'

'Do you think man is going to blow up the world?' A shiver ran through her at the thought of that.

'He's certainly fast developing the potential. There are projects in the pipeline that would make your hair stand on end. At least they do mine. Among them bombs which make those dropped on Hiroshima and Nagasaki look like mere firecrackers.'

'And are you . . . ?' She broke off, then said apologetically, 'Sorry, I shouldn't ask.'

'Connected with these bombs and other projects?' he said softly.

She nodded.

'Yeah. Which is getting harder and harder for me to live with.' He paused, and looked thoughtful.

'Are you saying you might leave your work here?' she queried in sudden alarm.

'I could do.'

'Oh!' she murmured.

'Excuse me, I'll get that coffee,' he said, and strode from the room.

Robbie leave Bald Rock Falls! Go out of her life again. She felt wretched and desolated at the thought.

He returned with two steaming mugs which he placed on the coffee table.

'If you left here where would you go?' she enquired.

'The Chair of Physics is about to become vacant at my old university. It's in my mind to apply for that.'

'Toronto,' she recalled.

'I would be able to do the type of research there I want to. It would also free me to instigate something that is dear to my heart.'

'Which is?'

'To try and get the world's leading scientists, American, British and Soviet in particular, to issue a unified appeal for the renunciation of war.'

She stared at him, intrigued. 'Do you think you could do that?'

'Perhaps not me personally. But other colleagues of mine, more influential and renowned, might be able to. If we are to safeguard the future of this planet, politicians must be told, and made to believe, that war, in the light of weapons we now have and those currently being developed, is no longer an option.'

'American and British perhaps, but Soviet scientists?' she queried.

'Those are the ones we need most of all to join any appeal,' Robbie stated, eyes glowing with self-conviction and purpose, indicative of a man with a mission in life.

The renunciation of war. Idealistic maybe, but surely worth the attempt considering what Robbie had just told her, Sadie thought.

'What do you think?' he asked.

'Nothing ventured, nothing gained,' she replied.

'Exactly! Think of a snowball rolling down a mountainside. It's possible that what had started out as a snowball can end up as a thousand, or ten thousand times, its original size.'

'Or as an avalanche,' Sadie stated quietly.

Coffee, she thought, and rose to get her mug. *En route* her heel somehow became tangled in one of the Indian floor coverings pitching her, with a startled cry, forward.

'Are you all right?' Robbie asked anxiously, kneeling beside her.

She came into a sitting position. 'Twisted my ankle, I think,' she replied, rubbing it.

'Here, let me do that for you.'

She was suddenly aware of how close his face was, only inches from her own. All else was forgotten as his eyes bored into hers.

Time seemed to stop as they remained with eyes locked. Dimly she was aware of her heart thumping madly.

'Sadie?' he whispered.

'Yes?'

'I . . .' He trailed off. Then, with a gentle sigh, he placed his lips against hers.

She brought a hand up to rest on his body, a body she was now aware of in a way she'd never been before.

They simultaneously broke off kissing, both alarmed at what had happened, and confused.

'I'll get rid of these coverings. They're a danger I now realize,' Robbie muttered, voice quavering.

'Is that the hour?' Sadie exclaimed, glancing at her watch.

'Your ankle . . .'

'Seems better now,' she said, pulling herself upright. She couldn't meet his gaze, nor he hers.

'If you sit down I'll . . .'

'No,' she interrupted. 'Must get home.'

'There's the coffee . . .'

'I don't feel like it any more.' She tried her leg to find her ankle still sore, but at least she could walk. If she had twisted it, it was only a minor sprain.

'I'll get rid of these coverings,' Robbie repeated.

'My coat?'

'Of course.' He hurried away.

'Christ!' she whispered, and ran a shaking hand over her face. What had they done? What had possessed them? Robbie was like a brother to her.

'Here you are,' he said, returning with her coat into which she quickly shrugged herself.

'I hope that ankle's going to be OK,' he went on, attempting a smile that seemed strained.

'I'm sure it will,' she replied, stumbling towards the front door.

He went after her, and opened the door.

'See you soon,' she said.

'Yeah. Soon.'

'Don't bother coming out to the car with me. There's no need.'

He hesitated, not knowing whether he should or not. In the event he didn't.

Sadie climbed into the Cord, switched on her lights and waved as she drove off.

'Of all the stupid . . .' she muttered to herself. Nor was the blame entirely his, she'd been just as much at fault.

Later, lying in bed, going over and over the incident in her mind she was suddenly startled to realize she'd not only allowed it to happen, but had wanted it to.

Sadie slept in late the next morning. She'd had a troubled sleep filled with strange disturbing dreams concerning her late husband, Courcy and Robbie. When she finally woke it was to discover her forehead bathed in cold, clammy sweat.

She had a long soak in the bath, then slowly dressed, after which she ate breakfast. During all this she thought about the previous evening and what had occurred.

Just before midday the telephone rang and she answered it thinking it would be Robbie. But it was Courcy, enquiring how she was and asking her advice about something at the mill.

'I'll come and see you later,' he said.

'No, don't. I'd rather you didn't,' she replied quickly.

There was a lengthy pause, then he said, 'What about if I drop by tomorrow?'

'Tell you what, I'll call you tomorrow morning. We'll discuss it then.'

'You sure you're OK, Sadie?'

'I told you, just tired that's all. I'd simply rather be alone.'

'All right then. I'll look forward to hearing from you.'

'Bye,' she said as he blew a kiss from his end.

She stared at the recradled phone, willing it to ring again and the caller to be Robbie. She had just about given up hope when it rang.

'Hello?' she said eagerly.

'It's Erin. How are you today?'

Her heart sank. She'd been sure that this time it would be Robbie. 'Not too bad,' she replied.

She and Erin chatted for about ten minutes, mainly talking about the children, and finally arranged to go shopping together later in the week.

It was a little after four that afternoon when Miss Ramirez sought out Sadie to say that Mr Hendry was here, and waiting in the drawing-room.

Sadie halted outside the drawing-room and took a deep breath before entering, closing the door behind her.

'I was concerned about your ankle,' he explained.

'The ankle's fine. Right as rain this morning.'

'Good.'

She could see how nervous he was, as she was herself.

'I'm sorry about last night,' he blurted out.

'I'm not.'

He stared at her.

'I said I'm not,' she repeated. 'Drink?'

'Please. Scotch.'

She'd have a Scotch also, she decided. 'Soda?' she queried from the cabinet.

He shook his head.

'I've been giving the matter of last night a great deal of thought,' she declared, handing him his drink.

Robbie took a gulp of Scotch, and remained silent.

'Shall I go on?' she asked softly.

He nodded.

'You and I have been mistaken in thinking that we're still the same as we were when we were at the Trikhardts. Only that's not so. We were children then, whereas we're adults now, who've met up again after a long separation during which we've both been married and through all sorts of experiences.

'Last night was a revelation to me. I felt like a blind person who for the first time saw what up until then had been a familiar object.'

She paused, then went on. 'We're not brother and sister, Robbie. We were like that once, but not any more. At least, not from my point of view.'

She had a sip of her Scotch which burnt its way down her throat. Her nerves had given way to a complete calm. 'I think you should say something now,' she prompted.

'I, too, have done a lot of thinking about last night, and agree with everything you've just said. Time has changed us. Last night I was . . . shaken to my very core. If that's not being over-melodramatic.'

'Same here.'

'You weren't the old Sadie any more, there was a new dimension to you.'

'Same with you,' she said.

'I . . . wanted you. Physically. But there was more to it than that. Much more.'

'Do you think we're in love, Robbie, and have only just realized?'

'What about Courcy?' he queried. 'After all, you two are supposed to be getting married.'

'I'm not in love with Courcy, which he knows. Fond of him, yes. But not in love with him.'

'And you'd marry him on that basis?'

She smiled thinly. 'I agreed to it before you reappeared on the scene, and everything changed. I do know this, whatever happens between you and I, I won't marry him now. We're finished.'

Robbie digested that.

'I've been so bewildered of late. Not knowing whether I was coming or going. Bewildered, confused, lost even.'

Robbie went to her and took her into his arms. 'Let's do it properly this time, shall we?'

She nodded.

He kissed her. A kiss that made her melt inside, and go light in the head. It seemed to her that there was a rightness about them that couldn't be denied.

'Well?' he asked when the kiss was over.

'I think we've both been idiots not to have realized before now.'

He kissed her again, this time strongly, and passionately, his body hard against hers.

'Can I make a suggestion?' she said when they finally parted.

'What's that?'

'Let's go to bed.'

'Are you certain, Sadie?'

'That's precisely what I want to be. But we can't go here, because of the staff.'

'My house?'

'Let me speak to Hilary about Edward, then I'll be right with you.'

As she left the drawing-room she felt as though she was walking on air.

Robbie glanced sideways at Sadie who was staring fixedly ahead through his windscreen. 'OK?'

She turned her head to him and smiled. 'OK,' she confirmed.

'You looked thoughtful.'

'It was just . . . Well, I was just wondering if this wasn't a bit cold blooded.'

'Does that mean you've changed your mind?' When she didn't reply right away, he said, 'I can easily turn back?'

'Do you want to?'

'Not for myself. But I will if you do?'

'Nerves, I guess,' she said, and rubbed his thigh.

'Me too.'

They drove a little way in silence, then Sadie said, 'I want you to know something. Courcy and I have never been to bed.'

He wasn't sure whether that surprised him or not.

'Courcy has always been the most awful rake, and tried to seduce me when I first arrived at Clare. Seduce! Hell, one day in the basement it was almost rape.'

'But you managed to stop him?'

'Edward did. Edward appeared from nowhere and knocked him flying, much to Courcy's resentment and dismay. Courcy envied his elder brother dreadfully.'

'And yet you were going to marry him?'

'He has changed considerably since Edward's death. He's a nice man now, and fun to be with. I like him.'

'But don't love him.'

'No.'

Robbie neither answered nor commented on that.

'I just wanted you to know,' Sadie said.

A short while later they arrived at Robbie's house and went inside, and there Sadie's earlier calm returned.

'I'd like to use the bathroom,' she requested.

'Sure. You know where it is. Go ahead.'

She closed the bathroom door and leant against it. Then she went to the mirror above the handbasin and gazed at her reflection. Was she doing the right thing? A tiny voice in her mind told her she was. But if the voice was wrong? Right or wrong it should answer the question about her and Robbie.

She freshened her lipstick, and applied a few dabs of her favourite perfume which she was carrying in her purse. She then ran a comb through her hair.

She gazed round the bathroom, taking in all Robbie's bits and pieces, thinking of him washing, shaving and bathing there. She left the bathroom and returned to the sitting-room to find it empty. 'Robbie?' she called out.

He appeared carrying a bottle of champagne and two glasses. 'This was given to me when I arrived here, and now seems a good time to drink it. What do you say?'

She nodded her agreement.

He laid the glasses on the coffee table, then proceeded to struggle with the cork.

'There's a way of doing that,' she said. 'Here let me, I'll show you.'

'I don't open many bottles of champagne,' he apologized.

'You hold the bottom like this see, twist the neck the opposite way and . . .' With a loud pop! the cork went shooting across the room.

They both laughed, Robbie taking the bottle from her and filling the glasses.

'What shall we toast to?' he asked when they were both holding a frothing glass.

Sadie thought about that. 'Happiness?' she suggested.

'Happiness it is!'

They drank, she giggling when some bubbles got up her nose. She became serious again when he took her by the hand and led her into the bedroom where the bed had been already turned down and the drapes drawn.

'Sadie?'

She drifted into that state of being half-asleep and half-awake. She breathed out a sigh of sheer contentment.

He kissed her tenderly on the cheek, then on the mouth. 'Sadie?'

She opened first one eye, then the other.

'We fell asleep.'

'I'm not surprised. I know I was exhausted.'

'I've been lying here, propped up on one elbow, looking at you. I'm now absolutely certain about my feelings, I am in love with you.'

'And I love you, Robbie. There's no doubt in my mind either.'

'Will you marry me?'

She threw her arms round him and drew him down to her bosom. 'As soon as I can get matters sorted out with Courcy.'

'Is that going to be difficult?'

'It certainly isn't going to be easy. Don't forget he loves me too.'

They fell to making plans. And after a while, they made love again.

'Tell me something, what do you think of Robbie?' Sadie asked Edward with whom she was sitting watching a comedy show on television.

'He's OK.'

'Just OK?'

Edward shrugged.

'I mean, you do like him, don't you?'

'I just said that, Mom.'

She smiled. 'It's important to me, Edward, that I know how you feel about him.'

Edward turned to look at her. 'Why?'

'It just is.'

Edward thought about that. 'He's a nice enough guy. We get on.'

'You don't mind his company?'

Edward shook his head. 'He's neat at chess. Showed me a couple of real good moves last time we played.'

'He thinks highly of you. He told me. Tell me something else, how would you like to live in a big city?' she asked.

'You mean Bald Rock Falls?'

'No, a big city. Toronto say.'

'Yeah,' Edward nodded enthusiastically. 'Neat.'

'The idea appeals?'

'Sure.'

She let it go at that as he once more became absorbed in the comedy show. She'd tell him about her and Robbie tomorrow evening, after she'd spoken to Courcy.

She was dreading that.

Sadie woke with Robbie's name on her lips having been dreaming of him. She smiled, wishing he was there beside her so that she could reach out and touch him, kiss him, breathe in his scent.

She ran her hands down her thighs, thinking how well she felt. She was absolutely bursting with energy. She glanced at the bedside clock and saw that it was still early. She decided to take Edward to school herself that morning, give Hilary a break.

Throwing the covers back she leapt from bed and stretched. Then she did a dozen rapid toe touches.

She drew in a deep breath, then another, after which she raised her arms in the air and whirled round and round.

She laughed at her stupidity and continued to laugh when she stopped moving. She'd toasted happiness the previous evening at Robbie's, and that was what she was now – filled to overflowing with happiness, joy, and best of all, love.

A shower and a hair wash, she thought, then she'd ring Robbie. Robbie! Robbie! she felt like shouting, the man she loved and who loved her.

She flung her arms round her upper torso and hugged herself tight, wishing he was there. She couldn't wait to be in his arms again, and his bed. The memory of their love-making brought a flush to her cheeks, and a dryness to her throat.

'Robbie,' she whispered. 'I do love you.'

She changed her mind, she'd call him before the shower and hair wash. She couldn't wait that long to speak to him.

Courcy's face suffused with anger and for a few moments Sadie feared that he was going to hit her. Then the anger drained away.

'You bitch,' he muttered. 'You fucking bitch.'

'I'm sorry,' she said.

'You and Hendry? I thought . . . you said . . .' He barked out a laugh. 'And I believed you! What a fool I've been!'

'We only realized yesterday. I swear to you that's true.'

'My ass!'

'It's true, Courcy. And we both agreed that the best thing, the decent thing, was to tell you straight away.'

'You've just discovered you're in love with one another? You expect me to swallow that?'

'I repeat, it's true.'

Courcy went over to a cupboard from which he took a glass, then found himself a bottle of Scotch and poured himself a huge measure. He didn't offer Sadie one.

'I knew something had gone wrong when you postponed the wedding. I just knew it,' he said quietly, his voice tight and cracking.

'I think my subconscious must have been at work there,' she replied.

Courcy downed the Scotch in one then poured another just as huge.

Sadie thought of Robbie waiting for her in the Cord outside Courcy's apartment block. He'd offered to come up so that they could face Courcy together, but she'd felt it was better that she did this alone.

Courcy gave Sadie a stricken look over his shoulder, tears dribbling from his eyes. 'I love you,' he said.

She walked over to him and placed a tentative hand on his shoulder. 'I know that. But I don't love you. I never once said that I did.'

He swallowed. 'Is there any way I can make you change your mind?'

She shook her head.

'You've just fallen in love since you met up with him again?'

'I can't really answer that. Perhaps we fell in love as children, more likely that was the foundation for the love that suddenly burst upon us as adults. But one thing is certain, I love him and he loves me. We're a match, a pair.'

Courcy turned his head away from Sadie, and dropped it on to his chest. He smiled wryly. This was him being paid back for all the rotten lousy things he'd done to women in the past.

'I am sorry. Truly I am,' Sadie said quietly.

'And to think I never . . .! That I wanted to treat you with respect!' He shook his head. 'Christ, that's rich, it really is.'

He clicked his fingers. 'That's how close you and I were to getting married. As near as that. Now mister nuclear physicist has got you and I'm left with piss all.'

'There are still other women . . .'

'Hah!' he exclaimed contemptuously. 'I've had other women. Legions of them. It's not other women I want, it's you. Understand? You!'

568

She didn't know what to reply to that, so said nothing.

'And what about the mill? How am I supposed to work with you after this?'

'I haven't thought things through properly yet, Courcy. We'll come to some arrangement. I do understand and appreciate the situation.'

He squeezed his glass till his knuckles shone white. If he'd squeezed any harder the glass might well have shattered. 'That's twice I've lost Clare. Once when you turned up as Edward's widow, and again now.'

'But you weren't marrying me simply for that, were you?'

'No,' he croaked. 'Clare was a bonus. I'd have married you if all you had were the clothes you stood up in.'

'I'm sorry,' she said again.

He sipped his drink, then used the back of his hand to wipe away his tears.

There was nothing more to be said, Sadie thought. At least not for now. It was time for her to go.

'We'll speak again, soon,' she told him, and headed for the door.

'Sadie!'

She stopped and turned to face him.

He shook his head. 'Nothing.'

As she left the apartment the only sound to be heard from within was the splash of more Scotch being poured.

Sadie arrived home from Bald Rock Falls where she'd been shopping to find Robbie's car parked outside. She hurried in to find him in the drawing-room staring out of a window.

'Darling!' she exclaimed, and threw herself into his arms.

They kissed, after which he announced, 'I've got news!'

'Which is?'

'All I have to do is apply for the Chair of Physics at Toronto University and the post is mine. So I'll be starting in September.'

'That's marvellous!' Sadie said, clapping her hands.

'I spoke to Dale Weidelmann who's a close friend of mine, and he tells me there's a rather nice three-bedroom duplex for sale in his street which might just suit us.'

Sadie smiled. A duplex after Clare! It wasn't exactly going from the sublime to the ridiculous, but was certainly getting on that way. But all that mattered was that she'd be sharing it with Robbie.

'Sounds OK,' she nodded.

'We'll have to go and look at it. I mean, we can't buy sight unseen, can we?'

'I'll fly us to Toronto this Saturday. We'll stay overnight, and then fly back the next day.'

'Overnight in a hotel together? I like that idea.'

So did she. She liked it very much indeed. 'If you're starting in September, then so too will Edward at whichever new school we send him to. We can move anytime after he's begun summer vacation.'

'What are you going to do about Clare?' Robbie asked.

Sadie explained her intentions and the decision she'd made regarding the mill.

'Sorry if I'm late,' Sadie said to Courcy, sitting beside him at the table in Cindy's where he'd been waiting for her.

'You're not late, I was early,' he replied. 'What do you want to drink?'

'Coffee for me.'

He beckoned with a finger and a waitress came over. 'Coffee for the lady and another Scotch and dry for me,' he said.

'So, what's this all about?' he queried after the waitress had left them.

'Robbie is taking up a post at the University of Toronto,' she informed him.

Courcy raised an eyebrow.

'Which means we'll be living there. Now I don't want to sell Clare, or leave it lying empty. Clare will become Edward's when he's twenty-one and it will be up to him to decide then what he wants to do with it. In the meantime I'm offering it to you to live in.'

Courcy's expression was a combination of surprise and delight. 'Me?'

'You love the house, so why shouldn't you stay in it? On the strict understanding that you'll vacate when the time comes. What do you say?'

'OK,' he nodded. 'Do I pay rent?'

'Your side of the bargain is to maintain the house. Keep it up to scratch.'

'Agreed,' he said.

'The next item is the mill. Obviously if I'm in Toronto I can't be running it. I want you to take complete charge, be number one.'

They stopped talking when the waitress returned with their order. When she'd left Sadie continued, 'With regards to the mill, I feel I owe you something so I'm going to make you a proposition. I'll sign over forty-nine per cent of it to you, retaining a controlling fifty-one per cent which will also go to Edward when he reaches twenty-one. All profits will be split the same way, forty-nine per cent to you, fifty-one to me, and later Edward.'

Part owner of the mill! Elation drove out recent despair. Sadie couldn't have given him anything that would have pleased him more, except herself that is.

'Forty-nine per cent,' Courcy mused. 'You're very generous.'

Sadie's eyes twinkled. 'I have to confess I'm not being entirely altruistic. You'll work harder, and have more commitment, if you're personally reaping the rewards of that hard work.'

Courcy laughed. 'Shrewd. I have to admit, Sadie, you've always been that.'

'So do we have a deal?' she asked, offering him her hand.

'We have a deal,' he agreed, shaking with her.

'First thing tomorrow morning I'll instruct my lawyer to begin drawing up the necessary papers.'

There were sixty-four people at the reception Sadie and Robbie were holding at Clare. Their marriage, by civil ceremony, had taken place earlier that day.

Sadie glanced over to where Courcy was talking to Heather, who'd once worked at Clare. Miss Ramirez had said she needed outside help for the reception and had hired two women from an agency, one of whom, it had transpired, was Heather.

On speaking with Heather, Sadie had been saddened to hear that Heather's husband had died tragically the previous year of cancer.

She and Robbie had thought Courcy would refuse to attend their wedding, but he had confounded them by not only agreeing to come, but also volunteering to be a witness. He explained to them that his attendance, and being a witness, was to show the world he wasn't a bad loser.

Heather laughed, and clapped a hand over her mouth. Her eyes shone when Courcy touched her arm, then whispered something in her ear.

As Heather was now free could Courcy be contemplating starting up with her again, Sadie wondered? He could certainly do a lot worse. She'd always thought and said that Heather would make him a fine wife. Perhaps . . . Well who knew how things turned out? Life dealt the strangest cards. Courcy had sworn she was the only woman for him, but that could soon change.

Staring at Courcy and Heather she lifted a hand and crossed two fingers.

'What have you done that for?' Robbie asked.

She smiled. 'I'll tell you later.'

'Happy?'

'You know I am.'

'Me too. Ecstatically so.'

He reached up and lightly touched her hair. 'I'm glad you wore your scarlet ribbons. They're perfect for today.'

'That's what I thought,' she smiled.

Their conversation was interrupted at that point by one of Robbie's colleagues from the plant. 'Wonderful reception! Absolutely wonderful reception, Mrs Hendry!' the colleague enthused.

A thrill ran through Sadie as she heard that, the very first time she'd been called Mrs Hendry, Robbie's wife.

'Ready?' Robbie asked quietly.

Sadie gazed through the car window at Clare. Not *adieu* but *au revoir*, she told herself. For they'd return from time to time.

They were driving to Toronto in Robbie's car, as Sadie had given Courcy the Cord. Somehow the Cord belonged at Clare, as did the Moth which she was also leaving behind.

Not that she was giving up flying. Once established in Toronto she intended buying an Auster which she would keep at a little aerodrome she knew on the outskirts of the city.

'How about you, Edward?' Robbie asked over his shoulder.

'I'm ready and raring to go!'

Robbie laughed at that. Raring to go was precisely how he felt.

'Goodbye for now,' Sadie whispered. Then, in a strong, firm voice. 'Ready!'

As they drove away she didn't look back, only straight ahead.

THE END

MAGGIE JORDAN
by Emma Blair

When most of Maggie Jordan's family are killed in a freak flood in the small coastal village of Heymouth, she is forced to find work in one of Glasgow's carpet mills. She becomes engaged to Nevil Sanderson, who suddenly decides he must go to Spain and join the Republicans in their fight against Franco.

Although she struggles on without him, Maggie eventually realizes her place is by his side and journeys to Spain to join him. But the newly promoted Nevil has become distant and ruthless, and is fiercely jealous of her new friendship with American journalist Howard Taft.

Years later, married and with an eight-year-old daughter, Maggie has returned to Glasgow. Astonished when Howard reappears, bringing light and laughter back into her life, she is forced to take decisions — decisions which threaten to destroy even the vibrant and courageous Maggie Jordan.

A Bantam Paperback
0 553 40072 X

THE WATER MEADOWS
by Emma Blair

It is May 1926. Glasgow is crippled by the General Strike and the future looks bleak for John Forsyth. Made redundant from his factory job and with no prospect of employment, he and his family only hold together through the determination of his ambitious wife, Madge. Even though this means a dramatic move to the farthest reaches of England – to Devon.

As the family begin a new life in the village of Atherton, their fortunes change. John works in the copper mine, but unused to the appalling conditions finds solace in the Church and in his secret supply of scrumpy; long-suffering Madge ultimately attains love and happiness where she least expects it; and Graham, their eldest child, soon discovers how thrilling – and lucrative – a smuggler's life can be. However, it is Jennie, the Forsyth's wilful daughter, who faces the greatest challenge of them all. Her dreams take her far beyond Devon's green fields and golden sands, and will bring her both devastating loss and passionate love.

'Another cracking read' *Sunday Post*

A Bantam Paperback
0 553 40372 9

A SELECTION OF FINE NOVELS
AVAILABLE FROM BANTAM BOOKS

☐	17632 3	DARK ANGEL	Sally Beauman	£4.99
☐	17352 9	DESTINY	Sally Beauman	£4.99
☐	40429 6	AT HOME	Charlotte Bingham	£3.99
☐	40427 X	BELGRAVIA	Charlotte Bingham	£3.99
☐	40163 7	THE BUSINESS	Charlotte Bingham	£3.99
☐	40428 8	COUNTRY LIFE	Charlotte Bingham	£4.99
☐	40296 X	IN SUNSHINE OR IN SHADOW	Charlotte Bingham	£4.99
☐	40496 2	NANNY	Charlotte Bingham	£4.99
☐	40171 8	STARDUST	Charlotte Bingham	£4.99
☐	17635 8	TO HEAR A NIGHTINGALE	Charlotte Bingham	£4.99
☐	40072 X	MAGGIE JORDAN	Emma Blair	£4.99
☐	40372 9	THE WATER MEADOWS	Emma Blair	£4.99
☐	40373 7	THE SWEETEST THING	Emma Blair	£4.99
☐	40298 6	SCARLET RIBBONS	Emma Blair	£4.99
☐	40321 4	AN INCONVENIENT WOMAN	Dominick Dunne	£4.99
☐	17676 5	PEOPLE LIKE US	Dominick Dunne	£3.99
☐	17189 5	THE TWO MRS GRENVILLES	Dominick Dunne	£3.50
☐	40400 8	A SEASON IN PURGATORY	Dominick Dunne	£4.99
☐	49364 8	A SPARROW DOESN'T FALL	June Francis	£3.99
☐	40407 5	THE GREEN OF THE SPRING	Jane Gurney	£4.99
☐	17207 7	FACES	Johanna Kingsley	£4.99
☐	17539 4	TREASURES	Johanna Kingsley	£4.99
☐	17504 1	DAZZLE	Judith Krantz	£4.99
☐	17242 5	I'LL TAKE MANHATTAN	Judith Krantz	£4.99
☐	17174 7	MISTRAL'S DAUGHTER	Judith Krantz	£2.95
☐	17389 8	PRINCESS DAISY	Judith Krantz	£4.99
☐	17505 X	SCRUPLES TWO	Judith Krantz	£4.99
☐	17503 3	TILL WE MEET AGAIN	Judith Krantz	£4.99
☐	40206 4	FAST FRIENDS	Jill Mansell	£3.99
☐	40361 3	KISS	Jill Mansell	£4.99
☐	40360 5	SOLO	Jill Mansell	£3.99
☐	40363 X	RICH MAN'S FLOWERS	Madeleine Polland	£4.99
☐	17209 3	THE CLASS	Erich Segal	£2.95
☐	17630 7	DOCTORS	Erich Segal	£3.99
☐	40262 5	FAMILY FORTUNES	Sarah Shears	£3.99
☐	40261 7	THE VILLAGE	Sarah Shears	£3.99
☐	40263 3	THE YOUNG GENERATION	Sarah Shears	£3.99
☐	40264 1	RETURN TO RUSSETS	Sarah Shears	£3.99
☐	40583 7	THOMAS	Sarah Shears	£3.99
☐	40582 9	THE SISTERS	Sarah Shears	£4.99
☐	40450 4	BLOOMING	Audrey Slaughter	£4.99
☐	40066 5	PRIVATE VIEW	Audrey Slaughter	£3.99